# Lapis Lazuli for Hope

Ella Wren

*Lapis Lazuli for Hope*

ISBN 10: 1976367190
ISBN 13: 978-1976367199



Scripture quotations taken from the King James Bible.

**Dedication**

To my family with love.

**Acknowledgements**

Grateful thanks to my family, friends and editor for all your encouragement and help.

Ella Wren is an artist and author, based in England, who tells stories in pictures and words in the midst of the beautiful ordinary of her everyday life.

# Clare's Work

# Clare's World

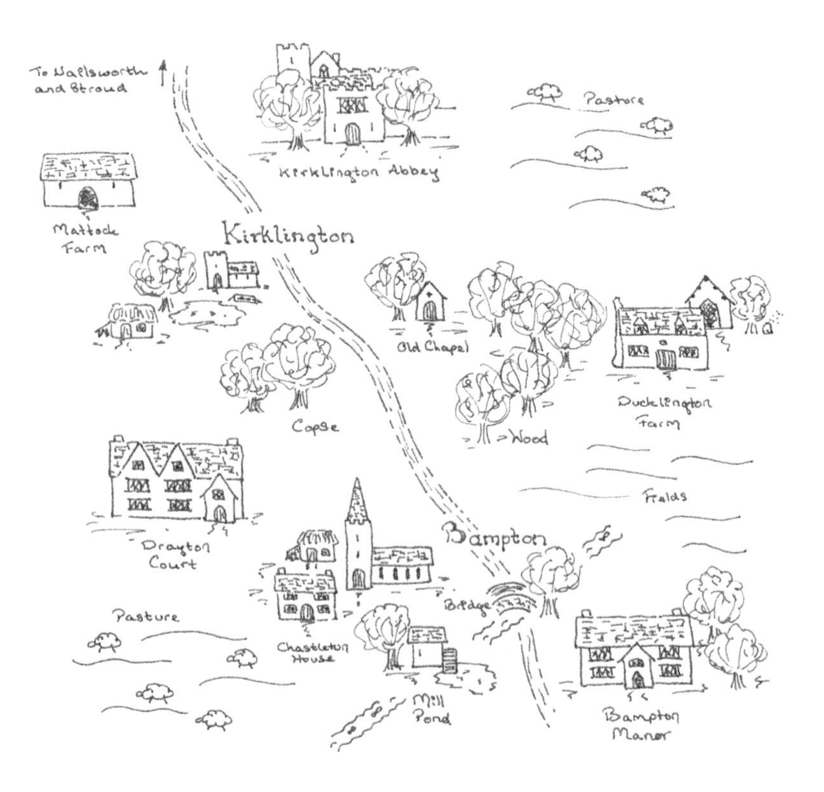

# Clare's Family and Friends

Clare

Bess

Lettice

Mother Abbess

Sister Rosemary

Roger

Jake and Edie

Walter and Mary Rose

Sir Anthony Bampton

Master Beckley

Matthew

Geoffrey and Frances

# Michaelmas

The hardest thing about being a nun was getting up in the middle of the night for prayers. Of course, I was not really a nun, just a novice – a girl learning to be a nun – but I got up every night for prayers just the same. Waking in the bitter cold of a winter night or trying to sleep again in the golden light of a summer dawn was not easy, and remembering it was for God was hard at those times. But I could not imagine any other way of living … at least not until a month before apple picking time in the Year of Grace 1536 when everything changed forever.

I was fifteen years old and ought to have been a nun by then. I had lived for twelve years among the nuns at Kirklington Abbey in Gloucestershire. I became a postulent at eleven and a novice at thirteen. But in 1533 King Henry the VIII of England had divorced his first queen, Catherine of Aragon, and declared himself the head of the church in England. Master Thomas Cromwell and the king's men had inspected all the monasteries and convents in England. At Kirklington Abbey they peered into every corner of the convent and made notes of what they did and did not like. The Mother Abbess visited the bishop and a lawyer. Now, three years later, the king had executed his second queen, Anne Boleyn, and married his third queen, Jane Seymour. Everyone hoped she would bear a baby boy, a prince, the future king of England. Meanwhile the Act of Suppression was being enforced and monasteries and convents were being closed.

In the cloisters of Kirklington Abbey the nuns whispered and worried as soft summer shadows gave way to crisp autumn winds. The leaves of the beech tree that guarded the gatehouse turned from yellow to orange, the colour of a burning torch, as they did every year. But my heart pounded and my stomach clenched whenever I thought of Kirklington Abbey's uncertain future. *What will happen to me if the convent is closed?* Like a dog, the question worried at my heart, especially at night. For once I was glad about getting up for prayers in the company of the nuns.

One night after prayers, as I stumbled along the narrow dormitory back to my bed, a wooden shutter banged and the flickering light of my taper blew out in a draft from the window. I stumbled and stubbed my toes against my mother's old dower chest at the foot of my bed. With a gasp of pain I tumbled under the blankets to rub my aching toes.

"Clare?"

My friend, Bess Drayton, sobbed in her narrow bed beside mine.

"Aye?" My whisper sounded loud in the stillness of the dormitory. Sister Rosemary and Sister Theresa, the lay sisters who worked hard in the kitchen and garden, still slept. So did Lettice Bampton who was being educated at the convent. I lowered my voice even further and breathed, "Have a care not to wake Lettice or she will be in a fearful temper! What ails you, Bess?"

"I want to go h-h-home," Bess sobbed. Her voice was muffled as if her face was buried in the thickness of her blankets. "I pray Our Lord and His Mother will forgive me, but I d-d-do not want to be a nun."

I pulled my blanket up to my chin and nestled into the scratchy wool. "But you will be a good nun!"

"Nay, *you* will be a good nun," Bess argued. "You have lived here almost all your life. I have lived in the world all my life! My father has only sent me here because I am a daughter too many," Bess mourned. "My sisters are fairer than I and my father cannot afford good dowries for all of us."

I stared into the darkness and imagined Bess' sweet face with the dark eyes and the smoky cloud of dark hair. I thought my friend was pretty and I secretly wished I was dark and romantic rather than red-haired and blue-eyed. But apparently even Bess was not pretty enough to be a bride rather than a nun!

Consolingly I said, "Your father knows you are safe and well here and will lead a useful life."

"I do not want to lead a useful life," Bess choked. "I want to marry a good man and be the mistress of a home and the mother of a family. Do you not want a household of your own to manage? Or a husband and a nursery full of babies?"

"The Mistress of Novices says there is no joy to be found in wishing for what I cannot have," I said. I reached for my memories of the world, but they were so vague, they told me nothing: a sunny garden, a motherly embrace that smelled of plain soap and fresh bread, a song that ended in a laugh of delight … that was all. My heart went out to Bess in compassion, because she knew what she was missing, but I did not know how to comfort her. Instead I said, "And, besides, I do not know very much about husbands and babies – only what I have seen in the village."

Bess stifled a giggle and a snort. "If I thought my future husband was going to be a peasant and my future home a hovel, I might be resigned to being a nun too!" But another sob escaped in a squeak. "Imagine never having having a sweet babe of your own. Does it not b-b-break your heart too?"

"I have no more choice in the matter," I said. My heart ached with a deep, sweet longing, but I did not know how to put it into words, so I shrugged it away and confessed, "I cannot remember the world."

"'Tis *beautiful*," Bess said. She hiccuped. "Our Lord and His Mother lived in the world. W-w-why must *we* live in a convent?"

"Hush, Bess!" I exclaimed. "'Tis wicked to talk so!"

"Why?" Bess demanded. "You have read the Gospels too!"

"Aye." I rolled over onto my back and stared into the darkness above my head. I smoothed my long hair and breathed a secret prayer of gratitude that Kirklington Abbey was not a strict convent and had not made me cut my hair when I became a postulent or a novice. "'Tis true Our Lord and His Mother lived in the world, but …"

"Doctor Luther writes that all of us can love and serve Our Lord just as well in the world as in a monastery or a convent," Bess blurted.

"Doctor Luther?" I gasped. "Oh, Bess, I wish you would not read his books! Not here in the convent!"

"I adore his confession of faith!" Bess confided, as if she had not heard my protest. Her bed creaked, and I turned my head in time to see the shadowy form of her figure as she sat up in bed and hugged her knees. Passionately she quoted, "'I believe Jesus Christ, true God and also true man, born of the Virgin Mary, is my own Lord and He has redeemed me, purchased and won me from all my sins, from death and from the devil with His holy, precious blood and with His innocent suffering and death that I may be His own.' 'Tis magnificent!"

"Very," I said. I sat up too and tossed my hair back from my face. Earnestly I addressed the shadowy form of my friend in a whisper: "But 'tis dangerous to read books by Doctor Luther! You are a novice in a convent. You are going to be a *nun*!"

"Aye." Bess flopped back in her bed. "But you have read some of his books too."

"Only because you asked me to!"

"Reading his books is no sin if the convent is suppressed and neither of us is a nun."

In her bed on my other side, Lettice Bampton stirred in her sleep. Bess and I held our breath, but our companion did not rouse.

Bess lowered her voice and hissed, "What do you want with all your heart?"

"I want to belong somewhere and I want to be loved," I confessed after a heartbeat. "I belong here with the nuns and they love me." I stifled a yawn. "I cannot imagine anything better than illuminating religious manuscripts with beautiful pictures."

"Mayhap you can do that in the world as well as in the convent." Bess's next words drifted through the dark, and I strained to catch them: "Doctor Luther writes that the vows of monks and nuns are not binding in all cases. And we are only novices! Mayhap we can live in the world after all."

"Mayhap." I twisted the end of my hair around my fingers. "If the convent is closed, you will return to your home. I do not have a home!"

"You can come with me," Bess said. "We are as good as sisters!"

I choked on a giggle and said, "Your father, I fear, would take it amiss if he sent one daughter to the convent and got two girls back!" I snuggled down and pulled my blanket up to my chin again. "I do not want to leave Kirklington Abbey. I want to be a nun."

Illuminating religious manuscripts was my special gift and work in the convent, so next day I tried to work, but the nuns were whispering. It was against the rules for them to talk, but I could hear their voices, scurrying and scratching like the dead leaves driven by the playful gusts of wind that danced and flirted along the passages and round the corners of the cloisters.

*"Good Queen Catherine ..."*

*"The Queen influences the King!"*

*"Naughty Nan Bullen ..."*

I was sitting at a desk in the cloisters – the square of passages, with flagged floors, carved windows and arching ceilings, that surrounded a grassy lawn – wearing my dark habit and pale wimple with a woollen shawl around my shoulders and knitted mittens on my hands. The parchment page on the top of the desk was covered with rows of even, elegant words written by Sister Joanna. I was working with a paintbrush – made from a quill feather with a tip of squirrel hair stuck in the hollow sheath – and an oyster shell of paint. *Lapis lazuli for hope.* The blue paint was made from precious lapis lazuli stone and white of egg. *Blue for hope.*

*"Queen Jane is like Queen Catherine ... or so they say."*

*"Shh ... 'tis surely gossip!"*

*"If Master Cromwell comes again with reports and orders ..."*

*"Mind you do not speak treason!"*

*"Suppression threatens everything ..."*

The nuns kept whispering, and I tried not to hear. I hunched my shoulders and forced my eyes to focus on a tiny picture at the beginning of the final prayer in the Book of Hours I was illuminating for Sir Philip Drayton and his wife. I could imagine Bess's parents offering the daily prayers, similar to those prayed by monks and nuns, inspired by the life of Our Lady the Virgin Mary. I hoped they would feel inspired by the illuminated pictures and borders of flowers too. I had finished all the borders and wanted this last picture to be perfect.

I had already used a quill pen and sticky black ink to draw the pictures. I had also glued delicate gold leaf to the parchment to highlight the initial letters at the beginning of the prayers and the halos of the saints in the pictures. Now I licked the end of my paintbrush and dipped it gently into the blue paint. The tip of the paintbrush turned blue. *Blue for hope.* I held my breath and painted the sky behind the golden halo of Our Lady the Virgin Mary. *Gold for heaven.*

Next I painted Our Lady's robe and cloak blue like the sky. I reached for the dark red paint – *dark red for love* – to add a slight blush to the Maiden Mother's parchment-white lips and cheeks. With the bright red paint – *bright red for laughter* – and the green paint – *green for courage* – I painted a border of roses. The green stems twined back and forth and the red roses were dotted like stars against the leaves. With the yellow paint – *yellow for kindness* – I added shadows behind the painted plants against the parchment. I squinted at my work and added a scattering of blue flowers, forget-me-nots, among the roses. *Blue for hope.*

I sat back with a happy sigh and smiled at my work. A daddy-long-legs with a long thin body, gangly legs and lacy wings landed on the parchment. I was fond of the ungainly insects but I waved this one away before it smudged my work. It flitted off and I watched it go wistfully. It was free to go where it wished. *Where would I go if I were free?*

The beating of my heart drowned the whispers but my cheeks burned. *What will happen to me if the convent is suppressed and I am turned, alone and penniless, into the world?* Breathlessly I jumped up and hurried to tidy the parchment, paint and tools away into the scriptorium.

The stone room, unusually deserted and hushed, had a vaulted ceiling and an arched window. A manuscript was spread out and weighted down to dry. Beside it egg shells and oyster shells stained with paint lay scattered on the table in the middle of the room. Sister Joanna was the nun in charge of the scriptorium and the library, but her big desk, scattered with pages of manuscripts, stood deserted in the light from the window.

I was happy to have the scriptorium to myself, so I hummed a tune as I tidied the room and imagined I was the Mistress of the Scriptorium and Library, like Sister Joanna.

I found my favourite spoon, the one I always used to mix my paints, flecked with blue lapis lazuli paint. It was a maidenhead spoon so it had a tiny figure of Our Lady, in an old-fashioned headdress from a hundred years ago, at the end of the handle. One edge of the spoon was worn thin and ragged where it had, for more years than anyone could remember, rubbed against a mixing bowl while mixing paints.

Carefully I cleaned the paint off the spoon and put it away.

The wooden shelves held tools: pestles and mortars, knives, bowls and an odd collection of spoons. Beside the spoons was an old tankard that held quills for pens. Another held brushes. Metal weights on chains, for holding books open and pages flat, hung from nails. In a cupboard, behind a curtain, rows of little earthenware pots were arranged on shelves. Inside the pots, I knew, were the ingredients for the paint: herbs and roots and, most precious of all, lapis lazuli and gold leaf.

Sheets of parchment were kept in an old and battered coffer. Nearby, in a stone recess, was a collection of manuscripts, some bound with plain leather covers and some unbound, which the nuns copied when writing and illuminating new books. Among them was a completed manuscript ready to be sent to the bookbinder. The words were even and the illuminations were bright and lovely. Someday, I hoped, I would be able to make a book that perfect.

Somehow the sight of the manuscript calmed my fears. The nuns were still whispering in the cloisters. *But surely God will ensure the beautiful and important work we do at the convent will endure forever.*

I hurried out of the scriptorium and almost bumped into Sister Laura. I blushed and exclaimed, “Pray pardon!”

“Clare!” Sister Laura said. “I am glad I have found you. May God keep you!”

“And you too!” I said. I was still thinking of oyster shells fill with parsley-green, saffron-yellow and madder-red paint. "Were you seeking me?"

"Aye." Sister Laura took a deep breath. "The Mother Abbess wants to see you in her parlour."

Fear clutched at my heart. I could not speak because of a lump in my throat, so I raised my eyebrows in an urgent, silent question.

Sister Laura's face was pale but she shook her head and said, "I beg your pardon but I cannot tell you why. Pray go at once."

I thought of the picture of Our Lady which I had just painted. *Blue for hope.* I swallowed the lump in my throat and nodded.

I whispered a prayer for grace and strength as I walked through the cloister to the Mother Abbess' private living quarters: a tiny parlour and a tinier bedroom, joined by a little door, at the top of a narrow stone stairway. At the top of the stairway I paused and rested my forehead against the cool stone of the wall. The door into the parlour was open and I could see the Mother Abbess writing at a desk.

She was a tiny woman dressed in a black habit, white wimple and black veil, with a rosary hanging from her waist. She was not young, and just now she looked tired. Her eyes, usually bright and twinkling, were dull and sombre. Her habit was strangely dusty and bits of straw clung to the rough wool of her habit.

"Clare!" The Mother Abbess stopped writing and stood up. "I did not see you there, my daughter, but come in."

I emerged from the shelter of the door and curtsied reverently with my head lowered. The Mother Abbess drew me into the room and raised my chin with a cold and trembling hand.

"May our dear Lord bless you and keep you always, Clare, watching over all your ways. Sister Laura asked you to come?"

"Aye, Mother," I said, grateful for the thousandth time for the privilege of having a woman to call "mother". I smiled into the woman's eyes and ventured, "I have, just now, finished illuminating the Book of Hours for Sir Philip Drayton."

"Indeed?" The Mother Abbess smiled for the first time. "God be praised, that is good news! Sister Joanna finished the Psalter for the Stow-in-the-Wold merchant this week too. I will ask Old Peter to carry the pages to our usual bookbinder, and he will finish the work and see both the books safely delivered to their new owners." She closed her eyes for a long moment. "The last book is finished."

"The last book?" I echoed, under my breath, mindful of not seeming curious.

"Yes. The last book. It is finished."

The Mother Abbess walked to the window of her parlour, which looked out over her herb walk and the kitchen garden and apple orchard. My heart felt as if it was beating in my mouth. Finally the Mother Abbess turned and smiled again. Her face was peaceful, but in the clear light from the window I could see fresh lines of worry around her eyes and mouth.

"Come, my daughter, sit here."

The Mother Abbess drew me close to the fire with a gesture. I sat on a stool, and the Mother Abbess sat in a carved wooden chair opposite.

"Master Cromwell, the king's secretary, has been to Kirklington Abbey. You know this to be true. He inspected the ways of the convent and took a great number of notes." The Mother Abbess took a deep breath and continued, "I consulted the bishop and a lawyer who agree that we cannot fight the Act of Suppression and must submit to Kirklington Abbey being closed." She closed her eyes. "We must, I fear, do as these good men advise and prepare for the king's men to come and suppress the convent."

My heart was beating so hard and fast that I wondered why the Mother Abbess could not hear the wild rhythm. I gulped, but did not speak for fear of crying with dismay and fear. Finally, when a log shifted in the grate, I strained every nerve in my body to keep my voice steady and gentle and asked, "What, dear Mother, have we done to deserve suppression? We are not corrupt or idle. We are not indifferent to the things of God!"

"Nay." The older woman sounded weary. "We are not indifferent to the things of God but that is not enough to save us."

"The convent is our home and our mission!" I could hear the tears in my own voice. "Surely Our Lord and the king will grant us favour and security and ..."

"We must prepare ourselves for suppression," the Mother Abbess said. "If we resist ... we may be suppressed with the convent. If we submit, however, we may be allowed to leave this place in peace and establish the spirit of the abbey – continue our works of prayer, charity and industry – elsewhere."

Eagerly I asked, "Do you think we may?"

Quietly the Mother Abbess said, "I pray I may find other religious houses for some of the sisters in England or lead them to France where there are convents of our own order." She sighed. "I am helping some of the sisters return to their homes and take their places in their families again."

I gazed into the gentle face of the Mother Abbess, the only mother I remembered. My heart swelled with love and respect. I stood and said, "I am a novice but may I crave your blessing, Mother, to take my vows and become a nun before Master Cromwell and the king's men arrive?" I whispered, "I long with all my heart to be one of the nuns. I want to go with you to France!"

"I know you do, my daughter, I know …" The Mother Abbess' voice was gentle. She rose, and I was embraced and clasped against the older woman's humble habit and beating heart. "I love you as my own daughter."

I hugged her tightly and shed a few happy tears. My heart was singing with gladness at the thought of taking my vows and staying with the dear nuns.

"Clare …" the Mother Abbess said brokenly, "I am more grieved than I can say, my daughter, but for reasons you will understand someday, I cannot allow you to take your vows and become a nun." Gently she pushed me away and clasped my hands. She gazed into my eyes. Gently – sadly – but authoritatively she said, "I am releasing you, Clare, in the presence of Our Lord and His Blessed Mother and all the saints from the vows you made as a postulant and as a novice."

"But *why*?" The word was wrenched from my heart. Tears overflowed from my eyes, and I could feel them trickling down my cheeks and off the end of my chin. "Am I not worthy to serve Our Lord in this way?"

The Mother Abbess' eyes flashed, and she said, "I could ask for no greater joy than for the convent to be spared and for you, my dear Clare, to become one of the sisters here! You would, I know well and doubt not, serve Our Lord faithfully and worthily as a nun. But …"

The fire in the older woman's eyes died, and her shoulders sagged under an invisible but immense burden.

"We cannot fight what is coming," the Mother Abbess said. "We can only grieve it and do what we can to live holy lives come what may."

"But I want to live a holy life in the abbey!" I cried. "I am scared! I … I know nothing about the world beyond the walls of the convent. I do not know how to follow Christ in the world! How can I live a holy life in a world I do not know anything about?" Fear clutched at my heart. "Please let me be a nun!"

"Clare, my dear, Clare!" The Mother Abbess brushed a tiny hand across her eyes. "I want more than anything to protect the sisters – and you – from the changes that are sweeping through England. But I cannot! I can only give you into the care of Our Lord. I know His work in your heart and life is good. He can be trusted with your dear soul." She sighed. "I am sending you home. You must return to your family. Lettice Bampton and Bess Drayton are going, and you must go too. I do not want you here when the king's men come. Pray pack your things and be ready to return to the world."

"I … I cannot," I said. I had never defied anyone before that I could remember. But now the words flew from my heart to my lips: "I cannot leave. I cannot live in the world!"

The Mother Abbess' eyes were wise with the secrets of a thousand years. "In the grace and strength of Our Lord, dear daughter, you can. Moreover, Clare, you must. You must go into the world and live." Briskly she said, "You have been trained as an illuminator and you do fine work already, but you will do still finer work someday. It is a gift. I want you to take a Book of Hours manuscript. Take a supply of paints and tools. Sister Joanna will give you what you need. You know how to mix more paints?"

"Aye, but it does not matter, because I will never illuminate again," I said sadly.

"Nay!" The Mother Abbess held up a hand. "Pray do not argue! 'Tis foolishness. You must not neglect the gift which Our Lord Himself has given you."

Slowly I left the Mother Abbess and made my way through the cloister and the kitchen garden towards the dormitory. The birds trilled their end-of-summer songs and the air was spiced with the sweet, sad smell of damp earth, dead leaves and ripening apples. All

I could think of was whether I could find a way to stay at the convent. Mayhap I could change the Mother Abbess' mind or appeal to the Mistress of Novices or hide myself away in a secret place?

At the back of the garden, near the barn, I saw the convent reeve. John Hobb managed the business of the convent estate: interviewing and organising the farmers who rented and farmed the land and collecting their rents and tithes. He was talking to a boy, dressed like a yeoman in a rough jerkin and a pair of leather breeches, with red hair. It was the boy, who looked about my age, who made me pause and gaze.

I knew I should not – nuns did not stop and stare at boys – but I was curious. His hair, like mine, was red. His eyes, also like mine, were blue. His face wore a cheerful, honest, settled expression. It was passing strange but I blushed as the boy returned my gaze in a confused and unmannerly way. He looked away and tugged his forelock respectfully when John Hobb spoke, but over the reeve's shoulder, the boy glanced at me again and this time he smiled before he turned away.

*What would it be like to have a family, to belong in a home with brothers and sisters who looked like me?* I had never met anyone who looked more like me than the boy with red hair. *And he looks like a nice boy!* For a wistful but forbidden moment I wondered what it would be like to know boys as well as girls. But a heartbeat later, out of the corner of my eye, I caught sight of a tiny flash of red and black.

It was a ladybird on the catch of the garden gate. I watched it crawl across the metal catch and imagined how I could paint a rambling honeysuckle, as a border round a prayer, with ladybirds peeping between its flowers and leaves. I would use bright red paint for the ladybirds and yellow paint for their shadows. *Bright red for laughter and yellow for kindness.* But then I remembered I was leaving the convent and would never illuminate again.

I ran the rest of the way to the dormitory and sank onto my bed breathlessly. I buried my face in the cover. It smelt of clean wool and fresh air and damp stone. I lay perfectly quiet and still and then, urgently, I whispered, "Sweet Jesus, please help me in my new life!"

"Clare! Is there aught I can do to help?"

I sat up and saw Bess in the doorway, so I brushed my tears away and tried to smile. Bess ran forward and pulled me into a hug. Her eyes were sparkling and her feet were dancing, but her embrace was strong and warm.

"The Mother Abbess is … is sending me away," I gulped.

"Aye," Bess said. "Me too!"

"But you want to leave," I whispered. "I do not have a home to go to or a family to love me."

"Never mind!" Bess soothed. "I love you. I will help you somehow." She laughed giddily. "I am so happy, Clare, I cannot say how happy!" She pulled her pale wimple off her hair and hitched the skirt of her dark habit up to display her embroidered petticoat. She looked like a young girl again. She laughed and pulled a book out of her coffer: Doctor Luther's *Small Catechism.* "I do not need to hide this anymore! I am going to pack my coffer now. Will you pack yours too?"

I noticed now that the dormitory was untidy. Lettice Bampton, who had been educated at the convent but was not going to be a nun, had spread three gowns and various kirtles, smocks and stockings all over her bed. Now, wearing a glorious blue wool dress, Lettice strolled into the dormitory and surveyed her things with her hands on her hips. Bess knelt before Lettice's coffer and tried to help her pack.

"I hope I have not forgotten anything," Lettice said. "I have my prayer book and my rosary beads here." She gazed around the simple dormitory. "Is there aught else?"

I glanced around too and asked, "Where is your embroidery?"

"In the parlour!" Lettice swirled out of the room as if the king's men were on their way and her things were in imminent danger of being confiscated.

She was not gone long.

"Here 'tis!" Lettice exclaimed. She burst into the dormitory with her embroidery and box of sewing things and silk threads. "Is there room in my coffer for my embroidery?"

Bess laughed as she tucked the tapestry cushion and sewing box into Lettice's coffer. "Now you are ready for all that lies beyond the convent walls!"

"Aye!" Lettice said. "I have been a cloister girl for long enough." She sat on the top of her coffer in a billow of skirts. "I have a mind to be a queen's lady now."

Bess and I exchanged a startled glance. Tentatively Bess said, "You do not speak French."

"I sing and play the lute and dance," Lettice argued. "I speak a little Latin. 'Tis said the new queen, Mistress Jane Seymour, does not like the French ways. Anything would be possible if I were a queen's lady." She clasped her hands. "Oh! If only there was a Tudor prince, young and fair as well as noble, waiting to …"

"To sweep you off your feet and make you a princess?" Bess teased. "I fear such a prince does not exist and if he did, he would wed some foreign princess."

"King Henry was a comely prince at one time," Lettice retorted. "And Anne Bullen was no foreign princess, yet *she* married King Henry and became Queen of England. And our new Queen Jane was plain Jane Seymour and served Queen Catherine *and* Queen Anne."

"Hush!" Bess begged. "'Tis not becoming to talk so! Besides, Lettice, to be a Tudor queen is not a fate I would wish for you or any of my friends."

"Treason, Bess, treason!" Lettice cried. "If King Henry heard you now, he would …"

Bess paled and gulped.

I pressed Bess's hand comfortingly and asked, "What of Sir John Alanby, Lettice, who has a mind to make you a knight's lady some one of these days? You will be his lady even if you are not his queen."

"Oh … *him*." Lettice shrugged her shoulders and rose from her coffer with a flounce. "Our betrothal was never a settled thing, and I had word this week that he is to wed an earl's daughter instead." She raised her chin at a proud angle that forbade sympathy. "My honoured father says he hopes to find me a husband yet – and no plain gentleman or mere knight this time! So, you see, if there *was* a Tudor prince …"

Bess laughed and I asked, "And do you regret Sir John Alanby's change of heart?"

"Not I!" Lettice's eyes shone bright with tears, but she spoke carelessly. "We met only once. He was a plain gentleman elevated to a mere knight for a favour he did the king. He was not very handsome or gallant, so waste no tears on me, I beg! My honoured father found me one good match and he will find me another yet." She frowned. "That, I might add, is more than your people, whoever they may be, have done or – I fear me – will do for you, Clare, you must grant." Bess uttered a little exclamation of disapproval, but Lettice persisted. "Do your people intend to find you a husband before you are an old lady?"

I bit my tongue so hard it hurt and looked down at my hands, clasped in my lap, dotted with spots and smears of paint. "I am going to be a nun."

"Well, dear, do not forget to pray for my soul when I am gone from this earth," Lettice said lightly. She laughed. "*I* would not be a nun for anything!" Her eyes narrowed. "Not if I was a daughter too many like Bess or *even* if I was the daughter of God only knew who! You do not even know your parents' names, Clare, but they were probably heretics – and unwed too. You are lucky to be a nun and atone for their sin with your goodness!"

"I do not know they sinned," I said hotly. "Neither do you! I know I come from a local family. Mayhap my father is as respectable and fine as yours and has placed me here for some good reason of his own."

"With your red hair?" Lettice sneered. "I fear not, dear. There is plenty of red hair in this part of the world, to be sure, but it does not run in the noble families hereabouts. 'Tis mostly to be seen in the farmers' and merchants' families. In one family, especially, *all* the children have red hair. I assure you that you do not wish to be one of them however! You had better be a nun after all. Farewell!" She smiled pityingly at us, and her gaze lingered on me. "I will be a queen's lady someday, as you will see, but you, dear, will be a cloister girl forever."

Lettice swirled out of the dormitory, and Sister Rosemary and Sister Theresa helped Old Peter manhandle her coffer down the steps to where a cart was waiting to take Lettice home. I pushed out of my face a few strands of hair that had escaped from my wimple while I watched Bess admire a pair of embroidered stockings then toss them onto her bed with Doctor Luther's *Small Catechism.*

The latch at the door rattled, and Sister Rosemary entered the dormitory. She was a cheerful, devout nun, but a lay sister not a choir sister, because she was a peasant's daughter from a poor family in the village. The choir sisters were from families with more status in the world. Sister Rosemary cared for the abbey animals and garden and worked in the kitchen with Sister Theresa. She had rosy cheeks and bright eyes but always looked hungry. As a lay sister, she was allowed to go home to visit her family, so I knew she still worked hard to help her mother with the house and the younger children.

"God keep you," Sister Rosemary said.

"And you too," I replied. "Are you sent to hurry Bess in packing?"

Simply Sister Rosemary said, "I am sent to hurry both of you in packing."

Bess bundled the stockings with the book into her coffer, and together we pulled our coffers away from the ends of our beds. The nuns renounced their personal possessions when they took their vows, but we were novices and the convent was not strict, so we were allowed to keep a few possessions discreetly and tidily in coffers or baskets. *Does Bess have any other secrets hidden in her coffer with Doctor Luther's books?* I did not have anything hidden in my coffer or much to pack, but I lifted the lid and peered inside at my spare habit and wimple, clean and folded, ready to wear. I had some spare smocks, petticoats and stockings of my very own too. On top of my clothes lay my Psalter. At the bottom of my coffer, in a leather pouch, was my mother's necklace: a jewelled cross on a chain. My dearest possessions, two tiny books, were tucked into a corner.

Neither book was any larger than the palm of my hand. The older one, with a silver case and two loops for hanging from a girdle, had belonged to my mother. I had made a careful copy while Sister Joanna was teaching me how to illuminate. The tiny book was made out of odd, leftover scraps of parchment. On each page was a prayer written in mousy letters and an illumination – a flower, an insect or a decorated letter – no larger than my fingernail. The pages were bound with lengths of dark red silk – *dark red for love* – and encased in front and back covers made of soft brown leather.

"'Tis beautiful," Bess said as she leaned over my shoulder. "The art of illumination is a gift from Christ."

"So the Mother Abbess said," I admitted.

"'Tis something of great value to offer the world and 'twill be an adventure finding a way!" Bess said with conviction.

"I do not have anything of value to offer the world!" I wailed. I thought vaguely of legends I had heard concerning outlaws and heroes. "And I do *not* want an adventure!"

"You notice beauty and illuminate it for others to see and understand," Bess insisted. "And all of life is an adventure!" Her eyes, usually mild and serious, sparkled. "Books and dreams are well enough but *life* is out there somewhere – beyond the walls of the convent – and 'tis the greatest and grandest adventure of all!"

I tried to smile and bit my lip to stop myself from crying. Bess smiled and whisked out of the dormitory. I blinked and rubbed away a runaway tear.

"Dear one!" Sister Rosemary said sympathetically. "Do you

grieve the loss of the nunnery too?"

"Aye." Tears filled my eyes again. "More than I can say."

Sister Rosemary nodded. She sighed gustily. And then, lowering her voice, she said, "I love our patron saint. Sweet Mother Mary will grieve the loss of the nunnery too. I fear what may become of her statues and hangings and …" She glanced around the empty dormitory and dropped her voice all the way to a whisper: "What may become of the relic of her robe?"

"I do not know," I confessed. The church of Kirklington Abbey was dedicated to Our Lady the Virgin Mary, and a precious piece of cloth, believed to be from her robe, was kept in a jewelled casket behind the altar. "'Tis a precious treasure. Mayhap the Mother Abbess will take it into her care."

"I fear the king's men will take it and desecrate it," Sister Rosemary said, her face fretted with concern. "Mayhap you can help. I've a plan but …"

The latch rattled, and the door opened with a bang. Bess, flushed and sparkling, burst into the room and said, "My father has sent a servant to take me home." Her voice shimmered with delight. "I am going home!"

Sister Rosemary, flushed and fretful, slipped out of the dormitory to fetch Sister Theresa and Old Peter to help with another coffer. My heart ached as I helped Bess close the lid. All too soon, Bess and her coffer trundled away in a cart, through the gatehouse and along the road out of sight. And then the choir sisters, the nuns who prayed and sang in church as well as working in the scriptorium and library, gathered in the dormitory.

Sister Veronica gave me a Book of Hours so I could pray the simplified prayers of the daily services. Sister Joanna gave me a manuscript for another Book of Hours with all the paints and tools I needed to illuminate the book.

Carefully Sister Laura placed the little earthenware pots in the bottom of my coffer, with the pots containing the precious lapis lazuli and gold leaf nestled in the middle of the collection for protection. Around the pots she packed oyster shells for holding paints, quill feathers for making pens and paintbrushes, and a little packet of squirrel hair for the tips of the brushes.

Plump, laughing Sister Bridget wrapped a pestle and mortar, a knife, an inkhorn, a silver bowl and spoon and a weight on a chain separately in tufts of lambswool to keep them safe. I winced a little at the sight of them. *I will never use them to illuminate again.* I was relieved when Sister Joanna tenderly covered the tools of the scriptorium with a sheepskin.

We bundled the rest of my belongings on top and then, at the very top of my coffer, Sister Grace, who had a sharp tongue but a generous heart, placed a leaf-brown gown, rescued from the poor box, for me to wear in the world.

"'Tis your dower chest for your new life," Sister Veronica, who was so old she had forgotten the number of her years, said with a cackle of laughter.

"Dower?" Sister Laura looked a little bit shocked.

"I suppose it is," I laughed, as I thought of the money a father gave a bride when she got married, and the coffer in which an unmarried girl collected household items for her future home. "'Twas my mother's dower chest too!"

"Never mind that now," Sister Laura said. "Sister Rosemary and Sister Theresa can help Old Peter with your coffer and then …"

"Hark!" Sister Bridget held up a hand for silence and listened.

The sound of the abbey bells drifted into the dormitory.

I tried to smile and said, "'Tis nearly time for prayers. May I pray with you one last time?"

"Aye," Sister Veronica said. "For Sweet Mother Mary's sake you may. I care not if you be a novice now or nay, my lamb, you be one of us."

Later, praying with the nuns during the night for the last time, I thought of Our Lady and the life she had lived for God. No messenger had come for me yet, so I was safe and sound at the convent for another night. I knelt again for prayers with the nuns in the tiny abbey church while the old priest led the prayers.

My attention wandered away from the words of the service as my eyes looked round the dim church for my favourite image of Our Lady. The church was beautiful with an intricately-carved wooden ceiling supported by two rows of tall and slender honey-coloured stone pillars. Above the altar was a rose window, made with glass all the colours of the rainbow, celebrating the nativity. Beyond the bowed heads of the nuns, I found the stone statue set in a shadowy niche above a flickering candle.

Our Lady looked young and pretty. She sat with a book in one hand and her little boy, Jesus Christ, stood on her knee and smiled into her face. She had an arm around His waist and smiled – almost laughed – at Him in delight. The image reminded me of the song in my childhood that ended in laughter. Something about Our Lady was so sweet and motherly that it made my eyes prick with tears. *What would it be like to have a mother ... and to be a wife and mother myself someday?*

Bess was right. *Our Lord and His Mother did live in the world.* And yet my whole heart longed to stay in the convent. I cried myself to sleep in the dormitory, between Bess and Lettice's empty beds, with Sister Rosemary and Sister Theresa sleeping nearby. Sometime around dawn I woke in time for the first of the morning prayers – sung by the choir sisters with the morning sun streaming through the windows of the church and falling like a blessing on the heads of the worshippers – followed by breakfast of bread and ale, in the refectory, prepared by the lay sisters.

Talking over the meals in the refectory was not allowed so I watched a daddy-long-legs flit to and fro while I silently begged Our Lord, "I prithee, if it pleases You and Your Blessed Mother, let me stay at the convent. *Please*!"

All that morning I thought my prayer might be answered. The sun was shining and there was a nip in the air that whispered of Michaelmas and change. However the nuns glided here and there as usual and I worked with them as quietly and unobtrusively as possible.

In the afternoon, however, I took my sewing box to the dormitory and discovered that my coffer had disappeared and a mustard-yellow kirtle from the poor box was waiting on my bed. I looked at it for a heartbeat and shook my head in dumb denial of the truth.

"Clare?" The Mother Abbess entered the dormitory and put her hands on my shoulders.

"Mother?" I whispered.

"Dear one." The Mother Abbess was pale, with dark shadows under her eyes, but unyielding: "Today, my daughter, you must go into the world." Tears glimmered in her eyes. "Your family has not sent for you yet, so I am sending you home with Old Peter. He and the lay sisters have got your coffer, and he is preparing the horse and cart. Here is a gown to wear instead of your habit. All will soon be in readiness."

"All but me," I blurted. "I will never be in readiness to go into the world! Please," I begged, "let me stay! The convent is my home, Mother, my *only* home. The nuns are my family." I knelt before her on the wooden floor. The wood darkened wherever a tear fell. Through my tears I begged, "Please let me stay!"

"I wish I could, my daughter, I wish ..." The Mother Abbess caught her breath in a sob. "Come." She helped me rise, then framed my face with her hands. "Sometimes, my sweet daughter, Our Lord leads us by strange and twisting paths through life which we choose not. We can but follow Him step by step. You must follow Him! He will show you how to follow Him in the world."

I buried my face in my hands and sobbed quietly.

"My dear!" The Mother Abbess drew me close again and whispered, "May He lead you in the paths of righteousness and may goodness and mercy follow you, as You follow Him, all the days of your life."

I recognised the words of the blessing from Psalm 23: "The Lord is my Shepherd." I had a fleeting idea of Our Lord leading me as the shepherds led their sheep over the hills surrounding the convent. *'Tisn't a bad thing to be a sheep and be led by a wise and compassionate shepherd.*

"Take this," the Mother Abbess said. She gave me a thickly-folded and elaborately-addressed letter. It was sealed with the heavy seal of the convent: a tiny image of Our Lady was imprinted in the red wax. "Old Peter will take you to Bampton Manor and this letter is for the master of the house: Sir Anthony Bampton. He will tell you what to do next."

"Sir Anthony Bampton," I repeated. I ran the tips of my fingers over the hard, shiny wax of the seal. "You are sure, Mother, he will know what I am to do next?"

"Perfectly sure," the Mother Abbess said. She gave me another letter, as fine and heavy as the other, but I caught sight of my name in swirling letters on the front. "'Tis for you, my daughter, to read when your arrive in your new life. With the letter I want you to take this …"

The Mother Abbess reached for the rosary of prayer beads that hung at her waist. I used to be fascinated by the rosary when I was a little girl. Now the pearl and silver beads poured into my hands like drops of pure and sparkling water. I knew, from using my own rosary, that each of the pearl beads reminded me to say an *Ave Maria* prayer and each of the silver beads reminded me to say a *Pater Noster* prayer. The rosary was simple but beautiful – and all the more beautiful because it was a gift from the Mother Abbess.

"For me?" I whispered.

"Aye, for you, my daughter." The Mother Abbess smiled and a flicker of laugher danced through her eyes. "Keep the beads safe – they are my farewell gift to you – but pray do not open the letter yet. Keep it safe, *very* safe, until the time is right. You will know when to read it."

I opened the carved lid of my sewing box and slipped the rosary into the bottom under silks and buttons and the embroidered needlebook Sister Laura had made for me. I laid the letters on top and closed the lid of the wooden box, then fastened the silver catch.

"Good." The Mother Abbess gathered me into a motherly embrace, and we clung to each other and wept the farewell of mother and daughter. "Now, my dear daughter, you must go." She stood back and wiped the tears first from her cheeks and then from mine. "Remember – you must go into the world and live. Do not merely survive – live to the full every moment of the life Christ gives you … with Him."

A sudden babble of sound broke the stillness of the cloister. From the courtyard at the front of the convent came the sound of many hoofbeats followed by shouts. A woman screamed and a bird squawked in alarm.

"Our Lord have mercy," the Mother Abbess said. She crossed herself. "I fear they are here and our end is near." Her gaze fell on me, and she exclaimed in anguish, "I wanted you gone before the first stone fell!" She hurried towards the door. "Change into the gown. I do not know what is best to be done but mayhap you should wait here for now. We may yet be spared!"

I watched the Mother Abbess leave the dormitory with her head high and her step firm, looking more like a queen than a nun, wearing a calm dignity more impressive than a royal robe.

Reluctantly, with my fingers clumsy in a breathless hurry, I slipped out of the habit and veil of the convent and into the sleeveless kirtle. The bodice was a little tight, but I could still breathe when the laces were tied. I wriggled the long sleeves of my smock down to my wrists. My feet were only just visible at the hem of my skirt. My hair hung around my face and shoulders and I braided it into two long plaits.

The colour of the kirtle and the colour of my hair clashed horribly but that did not hurt as much as the realisation that I must look like any other girl now, rather than a novice. *I am never going to be a nun.* A sob caught in my throat, but I swallowed it with a gulp that hurt.

I kissed my habit and veil and left them folded and tidy on my bed, then crossed myself and ran to the window. I could not see what was happening in the courtyard, but I had an irresistible desire to see the abbey books one last time.

For an instant, I hesitated – then, clasping my sewing box in my arms and flitting from shadow to shadow, I hurried from the dormitory to the library. It was a stone room, very like the scriptorium with a vaulted ceiling and an arched window, but it smelt of leather rather than parchment, ink and paint.

Shelves full of precious books about Christ lined with room. The titles of the books read like a poem: *Gospels*, *Psalter*, *De Doctrina Christiana*, *Summa Theologica*, *Adagia*, *A Playne and Godly Exposition or Declaration of the Commune Crede*, *Advice to Anchoresses*. And there were others too. Each of the books was a work of art with precious words and beautiful illuminations bound in fine leather and decorated with embroidery and jewels.

However, as I looked around the room, I realised some of the books were missing. The great *Gospels* was missing and so was the great *Psalter*. Some smaller books were missing, too, but the rest of the books were pushed together in the shelves so there were no obvious gaps between the volumes. I ran my fingers along the books and allowed my gaze to follow. It was odd, but gone were many of the convent books I knew and loved, with their neat writing, glowing illuminations and jewelled covers.

"Hmm." I frowned and fingered a poorly-bound copy of *De Doctrina Christiana*. "'Tis passing strange. I wonder what it means? Mayhap ..."

Suddenly there was a scream. I ran from the library to the parlour which overlooked the courtyard. The convent was oddly deserted and quiet for the time of day. Overturned stools and church hangings the nuns were embroidering had been abandoned in the parlour. I rushed to the window and peeped out into the courtyard.

The courtyard was swarming with horses and men. Two men, astride horses in the shade of the beech tree that sheltered the gatehouse, seemed to be in charge. The tall man was still and silent, but the short man was pointing and shouting, while men ran here and there. The nuns were gathered in a frightened bunch. The old abbey priest stood between the nuns and the men. The Mother Abbess seemed to be arguing with the short man.

My stomach churned as the short man leaned down and shouted at the Mother Abbess. I could hear his words in the shelter of the parlour: "We have heard of the many treasures of Kirklington Abbey and if anything is missing, you will pay for it dearly!"

I did not stop to think but picked up my skirts and stumbled out of the parlour, along the passage and through the front door. I paused on the doorstep with the hollow in the middle where thousands – nuns, guests and pilgrims, poor and needy souls in search of charity or sanctuary – had stepped before me.

"… peacefully," the tall man said. I paused and listened with all my ears. He looked dignified and gentlemanly, and he spoke calmly. "I am more sorry than I can say about this errand, but I must do the bidding of the king."

"I understand," the Mother Abbess said. I thought her voice trembled. But then, firmly – and even graciously – she said, "I assure you that we shall cooperate, Sir Hilary, but it will be pleasanter for all of us if you and your colleagues are courteous."

"As you say," Sir Hilary said. He looked at the short man and said, "Have a mind to courtesy, Master Tolbert." His eyes swept over a small cluster of men who might have been soldiers or ruffians. "You *and* your men, Tolbert."

"As you say, sir," Master Tolbert muttered. "But if we have any trouble, Adam is ready."

A huge man with a barrel of a chest and a patch over one eye stepped forward with a smirk and a leer. He carried an iron bar and looked eager to start breaking and smashing. My heart lurched into my mouth, and I feared I might be sick.

Crisply Sir Hilary said, "Adam will have nothing to do with the sisters. His business is the … er … the buildings." He looked at the Mother Abbess. "Inform me directly if any of the sisters are troubled by my men."

I gulped and blinked back tears. *The buildings? What are the men going to do to the buildings?* Again I feared I might be sick, but I hurried to join the nuns and help them however I could.

"Thank you for your protection," the Mother Abbess said. "I fear the sisters are a little discomposed at present but we will all do our best to …" Suddenly she looked at me. "Ah … Clare!"

I blushed, for I had not stayed in the dormitory, as she had recommended, and she did not need my help, as I had thought.

But the Mother Abbess did not rebuke me, she merely held out a hand for me to kiss, then clasped my fingers fleetingly. Very kindly but stiffly she said, "You are ready to go? Excellent. 'Tis better so. Sir Hilary will ensure you a safe passage through the gatehouse."

"A convent pupil?" Sir Hilary drawled.

"And a pretty one," Master Tolbert growled. He had a florid face and a shifty gaze. "Too pretty, surely, for a convent." He scowled suspiciously. "What is the wench doing here?"

Simply the Mother Abbess said, "Clare is going home." She nodded to my sewing box. "You have got your sewing box. Good girl."

I wanted to correct the men and tell them I was a novice, not a pupil, but something in the Mother Abbess' eyes warned me to keep my peace, so I did nothing but nod.

Sir Hilary grunted and inclined his head towards the gatehouse but said nothing else.

"Old Peter is waiting outside with the rest of your things," the Mother Abbess said. "May God go with you. Farewell."

I looked stupidly from the Mother Abbess to the gatehouse and back again. I had often walked in and out of the gatehouse with the lay sisters – who fetched water from the well, milked the cows and fed the chickens in the fields and orchards close to the abbey walls –

but I had never walked away without coming back.

Suddenly Sister Veronica, who looked old and frail as never before, croaked, “Do not forgot to pray the hours from the Book of Hours.” She smiled, and her eyes were weary but faithful. “Our Lord and Our Lady will hear you in the world as well as in the cloister.”

Through my tears, I stared at the dear faces of the nuns: Sister Anne, Sister Joanna, Sister Laura, Sister Bridget, Sister Grace and Sister Veronica. The Mother Abbess’ face was beloved but blurred by tears. Sister Theresa looked as hearty as ever, but Sister Rosemary was flushed and tearful too. And then I stumbled through the gatehouse and away from my whole life.

“Mistress Clare!” Old Peter called. He was hunched over in the front of the cart the lay sisters used at harvest. My coffer was in the back of it. The old man’s leathery voice was mellow and warm with relief. “Ah, wench, there you be.” He held out a wrinkled hand. “Up you come.” He pulled me into the cart. “Ready?”

I was not – I never would be – but I slipped my sewing box into my coffer and Old Peter clicked to the horse, then we trundled away from the convent. I looked back at the gatehouse and the low, mossy stone-tiled roof and spire of the abbey church rising high above it, with a rush of tears that threatened to choke me.

"Be you alright, mistress?" Old Peter asked. "Do you need me to stop the cart so you can be sick?"

I laughed through my tears and said, "Nay, I thank you, I am well enough." I remembered a prayer Bess loved. Mayhap it was by Doctor Luther but that did not seem to matter now: "I thank You, Lord God and Heavenly Father, for all of Your gifts, through Jesus Christ Our Lord, who lives and reigns with You and the Holy Spirit forever and ever. Amen." Perhaps it was odd to whisper a prayer of thanks at such a time, but the words held and steadied my heart.

The cart rumbled past another cart, pulled by slow, steady oxen, going in the same direction. A local farmer, Farmer Mattocks, was driving away from the convent with a great heap of straw in his cart, although harvest was long over. He raised his whip in silent greeting, and Old Peter touched his forelock.

We rounded a bend in the road, under an overhang of trees, so I could no longer see Kirklington Abbey. I could only see forward into a future in which there was nothing certain.

I bit my lip. *Why am I going to Bampton Manor? Why does the master – mayhap Lettice Bampton's grandfather – care if I live or die? Who were my parents and who am I?* The questions went round and round in my head until it ached. I rubbed my eyes with the sleeve of my smock. I gulped back another sob and raised my chin. *Bess said 'twil be an adventure.* I looked forward as the cart trundled along the road into the village of Kirklington.

"'Tis a hot day for the time of year," Old Peter grunted as he drove into the village. "Begging your pardon, but I'll water the horse before we go on to Bampton Manor."

Old Peter stopped the cart and led the horse to drink from the pond in the middle of the village green, then lingered with it in the shade of the trees with leaves burnished gold and brown. I think he dozed as he leaned against the horse with his hat pulled over his eyes. I smiled a little and looked at the honey-coloured houses and rough hovels and sheds for animals that surrounded the green. *I wonder what sort of house Bampton Manor is.*

But then I shaded my eyes and squinted in the sunshine at a crowd of children and dogs on the edge of the green. They were gathered in a rough circle, and I could not tell what they were pointing at and why they were jeering and laughing. I frowned uneasily. Something about the tone of their voices boded ill for someone.

Suddenly, one of the children screamed and the rest of the children fell about sniggering. I almost tumbled out of the cart and ran across the green. The crowd of children did not part respectfully for me as it had when I had been out with the nuns on visits of charity. I pushed my way through the ranks of small, squirming bodies and stopped, breathless with mingled triumph and horror, when I reached the centre of the group.

A woman was half-sitting, half-lying on the ground, as if she had fallen, then fallen again when she tried to rise. She was mired in the dust of the road. Standing over her protectively was a small boy with ragged clothes and flashing eyes.

The rest of the children finally fell back as I reached the woman and demanded, "What is the meaning of this? Are you tormenting this poor woman and a helpless child?"

I helped the woman up and the small boy, watching me warily, let me shake her ragged skirts and pick her crumpled coif from the dust of the road. The woman seemed dazed and unable to help herself at all.

"Well?" I turned back to the children and insisted, "Tell me what you were doing!"

The children on the edge of the crowd were slipping away, but a few hesitated and one said belligerently, "Blind Dame Mary fell an' 'er runt couldn't 'elp 'er up."

"What 'elp can 'e give 'er?" another cried with a mocking laugh. "A poor son 'e is! Like 'is dad who couldn't stand the sight of 'im an' fled when 'e were born!"

I held the woman's arm and glanced at the tearful face of the small boy. Firmly I said, "You ought to be ashamed of yourselves for teasing a blind woman and her little boy." I took a step and staggered as the blind woman stumbled against me hard. The children laughed mockingly. I stamped my foot and cried, "Are you heartless loons? Will no one help me with this woman? You see she is injured!"

Some of the bigger boys jeered and a stone flicked through the air and thudded against the skirt of my kirtle. It did not hurt, but my cheeks burned with anger and I demanded, "Do you threaten a novice of Kirklington Abbey?"

"You ain't no nun!" one of the boys shrilled.

"Nor no novice neither!" another yelled.

I glanced down at myself in surprise and saw the homespun dress of a peasant girl rather than the habit of a novice. My hair, free from a veil, hung to my waist in two plaits. The boys, who looked bigger and stronger than me, jostled closer. One tugged my skirt. Another tugged my hair. I dug my elbow into the ribs of a lad who put his arm around my waist. He fell back, surprised, but approached again and grabbed my shoulder.

"Eh, my pretty!" he leered. "Shy?"

I shoved him back and exclaimed, "Go away, you horrible boy!" I leaned my strength towards the blind woman to keep her standing and allowed the small boy to cling to my skirts. Urgently, I whispered, "Sweet Jesus and Mother Mary – help!" And then I stood on the tips of my toes in a flash of inspiration. "Peter! Peter!" I caught sight of his bent figure straightening as he looked around. Eagerly I cried again, "Peter! Help!"

The last of the children, grumbling, started to slip away. Old Peter started running, his gait halting but unhesitating, across the green. A horse and rider stopped beside the green and a finely-dressed gentleman strode into what was left of the crowd.

The stranger seemed to grasp the situation instantly. He supported the blind woman on her other side without hesitation.

Authoritatively, he said, "Be gone, children, you ought to be ashamed of yourselves for tormenting the helpless – a woman and child! - and a lady too!" He waved one gloved hand to scatter them. "Be gone, I say, before I summon the village constable." He barely glanced at me but said with a twinkle in his eyes. "What, Mary Rose, causing a fuss again? And away from home! Where is Walter? Never mind. I think you are right this time. The constable of Kirklington is an old friend of mine and will bestir himself on your behalf if I so request!"

I did not know what to make of the stranger's words and whether to smile or not. Instead I said, "I fear this woman is hurt. Her arm is bleeding. If you will lead her to the pond on the green, I can bathe and dress her wound."

The stranger gave me a long, startled look, then he and Old Peter led the woman to the pond. I took the small boy's hand in mine and followed. The woman sat on a fallen tree trunk and seemed to understand she had nothing to fear, because she pulled her son to her side and murmured her thanks. She was not old, as I had thought at first, but quite young and almost pretty beneath the dust and tears on her face. With a pang, I recognised well-meaning Dame Mary who did her best with her lot in life but relied on the charity of the convent.

I tore a strip off the bottom of my petticoat. Part of it I used to wash the mud and blood off the blind woman's arm. The wound was not deep, but it was long, so I bandaged it with the rest of the cloth from my petticoat.

"I wish I had some of Sister Grace's healing salve. I fear infection may follow here." I gave a jagged sigh and tucked the last end of the bandage in neatly. "This will have to suffice." I took the blind woman's hands and gazed into her dull and unseeing eyes. "Rest your arm if you can, and do not take the bandage off for a few days so as to keep the wound from infection." I smiled at the small boy. "I dare say your son will help you to rest your arm." I squeezed the woman's hands and stood up. "God be with you, my good dame."

The blind woman clasped my hands and asked, "Why do you do this for a poor blind woman?" She nodded in her son's direction as if she sensed his presence without the need for sight. "Wat's a fine lad but I am useless."

I glanced at the small boy. He was swelling with pride at his mother's words. Gently I said, "No one is useless. You are a good woman, and your son is a good boy." Honestly I added, "And I could not leave you at the mercy of those children even if you had not been good."

"I know your voice," the blind woman persisted. "And your way. You've 'elped me an' my lad before now."

"Aye," I admitted reluctantly.

"At the convent."

"Mayhap." I avoided the curious gaze of the stranger. "I have been at the convent but I am going … er … home." The word felt strange on my tongue, but it appeared to satisfy Dame Mary and she muttered a blessing in farewell, so I said, "And Christ and His Angels bless you too."

The blind woman dropped a clumsy curtsy and walked slowly away, her hand on Wat's shoulder, as his piping voice told her which way to go. With a little sigh, I washed my hands in the spring that bubbled into the pond, then rubbed them dry on my skirt. And then, with a blush, I realised the stranger was watching me earnestly.

The stranger was a very young man, I realised, a lad rather than a man and dressed finely but not richly. He was tall and thin and reminded me of an amiable daddy-long-legs. His hair was brown with a lock that hung over his forehead and got into his eyes, which were also brown, as well as big and dancing. He had a crooked grin and peaked eyebrows that were raised, now, like a pair of question marks. I smiled tentatively.

The lad smiled and swept his hat off his head as he bowed. "I have been remiss, mistress," he said. "I should have introduced myself heretofore. My name is Roger Chastleton. I am a wool merchant's apprentice from the region of Nailsworth, near Stroud, in Gloucestershire. Who, pray, are you?"

I blushed and frowned because I did not know what was proper. Finally, slowly, said, "My name is Clare. I am … *was* … a novice at Kirklington Abbey." The sound of the words, the meaning of the sentence, struck my ear and my heart like a blow and tears rushed to my eyes. I blinked and gazed at Roger Chastleton's dusty leather boots. Quietly I said again, "I am going home now."

"Where is home?" Roger asked curiously.

"Bampton Manor."

"Oh." Roger raised his expressive eyebrows again. "I thought you might come from this part of the world but …" He paused and studied me from head to toe. His gaze was honest and respectful. Abruptly he said, "I thought, when I saw you first, you were a girl I know."

"Mary Rose?"

"Aye." He looked surprised. "Do you know her?"

"Nay!" I laughed. "You called me by that name when you arrived and scattered the children."

"Did I?" He smiled ruefully and bowed again. "My pardon, mistress. I see now that you are not Mary Rose. You look like her, though!" Thoughtfully he mused, "You are going to Bampton Manor. Mayhap you are Sir Anthony Bampton's granddaughter?"

"Oh, no!" I laughed. "No, indeed, you are thinking of Lettice Bampton. I am Clare."

"Clare Ducklington mayhap?"

"I am just Clare."

"Yet Bampton Manor is 'home'?"

"I do not know …" I hesitated. I did not know how much I should tell this stranger with the kind heart and laughing eyes who had come to my rescue. "Aye. The Mother Abbess sent me – and a letter too. My thanks for your help, but she told us to make haste. Is that not so, Peter?"

The old man jumped and said, "Oh, aye, we ought to be going."

I dropped a curtsy and took a step backwards. As I turned, I tripped over the fallen tree trunk and tumbled ignominiously to the ground, but Roger jumped forward and helped me up. I smiled and dropped another curtsy, then hurried after Old Peter. I scrambled onto the seat at the front of the cart and glanced back at Roger as the cart rumbled into motion.

"Farewell!" He raised his hand and called, "I will not forget you or your kindness to Dame Mary, Mistress Clare."

I smiled and realised, with a happy beat of my heart, I already had three friends in the world: Dame Mary, her son Wat and Roger Chastleton. *But who is Mary Rose? Perchance she is Roger Chastleston's sweetheart. Why else would he have come to my rescue without hesitating?*

Bampton Manor was on the far side of the village of Bampton. Old Peter drove around a village green – with a pond and a pair of stocks beneath the trees – and through a tangle of muddy lanes lined with stone houses and rough hovels and sheds. The church was set back from the green on rising ground. Surrounding the village were fields full of sheep. In the midst of the fields, along a road and over a bridge, was Bampton Manor.

"Here 'tis," Old Peter grunted. He gestured with a grimy thumb. "I've brought you here like the Mother Abbess told me."

The manor house was built of honey-coloured stone and roofed with stone tiles. It was long and low with a front door and a window over it in a central gable. Two rows of windows, with glass that sparkled in the light of the afternoon sun, were set into the walls on either side of the gable. The house was set back from the road beyond a gatehouse. A low stone wall surrounded the stretch of grass, dotted with trees, that stood between the road and the house. Something about the lawn stirred a memory of grass and sunshine and laughter, but I looked at it uncertainly. The manor house was not imposing, but it had an air of belonging and enduring that made me feel a stranger.

"You'd best knock," Old Peter suggested. "There be a knocker on that there gate."

"I suppose so." I blushed. "Are you sure this is Bampton Manor?"

"Oh, aye." Old Peter leaned back on the seat and crossed his arms. He did not look as if he was going anywhere in a hurry. "The Mother Abbess told me to wait until you were taken in here."

I blessed the Mother Abbess in my heart for her thoughtfulness as I stepped down from the cart. And then I took a deep and trembling breath and knocked on the tough, weathered wood of the gate. I felt, as well as heard, the impact of my knock. My heart beat wildly, and then the gate was swung open by a little, wizened man wearing an old-fashioned doublet, and saggy hose on bandy legs. He had a wrinkled face and a pair of piercing but kindly blue eyes.

"Good day." I dropped a curtsy. I was surprised and embarrassed by the intensity of the little man's gaze. "My name is Clare and …"

"Little Clare," the man croaked. His gaze was full of wonder. "Aye … 'tis you, indeed, Little Clare!"

"If it please you," I said. I did not know what else to say, so I dropped another curtsy and held out the letter the Mother Abbess had given me for the master of Bampton Manor. "I have a letter for your master. 'Tis from the Mother Abbess of Kirkington Abbey. And so …" I gulped. "So am I."

"Oh, aye." The little man seemed to pull himself together. He nodded his head up and down and down and up. His blue eyes were watery and his Adam's Apple was as constantly in motion as his head. Finally he spoke and his voice was raspy: "Aye. I warrant you are, mistress, I warrant you are." He took the letter and glanced at Old Peter. "Do you have baggage?"

"A coffer."

"I'll bring it now." The little man went to the cart and spoke a few words to Old Peter. He went to the back of the cart and looked at the coffer, then crossed himself.

Together the men heaved the coffer out of the cart and carried it into the gatehouse.

"I must take you to my wife," the little man said. He sounded breathless. "Come, mistress."

"Oh … then I am to stay here for now?" I asked.

The little man looked at me as if I was crazed. "Aye," he said, as if he was speaking to a small child. "Your mother's daughter won't be turned away from any gate I guard. You're to stay, bless you, for as long as you like."

"Oh," I said again. "Did you know my mother?"

"Aye." He crossed himself again. "I knew her, God rest her soul, all her life. Come. You must meet my wife without delay."

"I must bid Peter farewell first." I ran to the cart as the old man pulled himself up. "Thank you, Peter, for … for everything." He had been very kind to me over the years. I reached up and dropped a kiss on his leathery cheek. Chokingly I said, "Goodbye and God keep you always."

"And you too, mistress." He patted my shoulder. "We'll miss you and your kind ways at the nunnery, but you'll be safe and well here, with your mother's folk, and so I shall tell the Mother Abbess."

I felt as if I was losing a precious part of myself, along with my last link to Kirklington Abbey, as Old Peter drove away. I saw everything through a mist of tears as the little man led me through the gate and up the dusty path to the house. He led me round to the back of the house and through a courtyard then disappeared inside the house.

Left alone, I closed my eyes to stop the tears falling, then took long, deep breaths to stop myself feeling sick. The autumn air was mellow and heavy with the sweet scent of damp earth, ripe fruit and, close at hand, the tang of woodsmoke. I thought of Our Lord and His Mother. *Mayhap they knew and loved this smell too … when they lived in the world.* Slowly but surely my heart and stomach settled.

"Mistress Clare!"

I opened my eyes and blinked. A homely woman with a kind face was standing in the doorway where the little man had disappeared. Her white hair was covered by a coif, and the sleeves of her smock were rolled up to her elbows. Her dark kirtle was covered with a floury apron. She had a smudge of flour on her face and looked as shocked as if she had seen her own ghost. I dropped a curtsy and waited to see what happened next.

"Oh my lamb … my dear, precious lamb!" The woman rushed across the courtyard and clasped my hands. "My baby!" She wrapped me in a motherly embrace that smelled of plain soap and fresh bread. "You've come home!"

I tried to smile but I was bewildered and embarrassed by the embrace of a strange woman.

"Mistress Clare?" The woman raised a roughened but gentle hand to my cheek. Her pale blue eyes were soft and understanding. Her voice was tender: "You don't remember me, do you, my dear?"

Slowly I shook my head although, even as I did so, I realised that something about the woman was familiar. I recalled my memory of an embrace … plain soap … fresh bread.

"I was your nurse," the woman said. "You were the best-behaved baby I ever nursed. And now, look at you, you're the image of your blessed mother but for that red hair!"

"Am I?" I blushed with surprise and delight. "I look like my mother? You knew my parents too … both of them?" A question seemed to leap from my heart to my lips without asking for permission to be heard. "What were their names?"

"Your mother's name was Clare, my lamb. She gave you her own name with her last breath, God rest her soul." The woman crossed herself and swept me across the courtyard and into the house. "Come in and sit down in the kitchen, my lamb, then I'll tell you everything you want to know about your blessed mother."

The kitchen was a dim room, the sun flickering through two small windows, with a long table – cluttered with foodstuffs and utensils – and a couple of benches in the middle of the stone-flagged floor. Bunches of dried herbs hung from the white-washed ceiling and scented the air. Beside the open fireplace, which took up one whole side of the room, was a wooden settle.

The woman gently pushed me into one corner of the settle and pressed a tankard of milk into my hands. She produced a manchet spread with honey and then she and her husband, the little man from the gatehouse, hovered over me and watched me drink and eat until I was full.

Finally, trying to be polite and find a constant in the midst of the variables, I asked, "What are your names?"

"I am Jake Binsey, Mistress Clare," the little man said. "And this is Edie, my wife and your nurse."

"Edie," I whispered. The name felt familiar on my lips. "Edie. Edie and Jake." I forced a little smile and said, "You were my nurse. You say you were and I think … mayhap … I remember you a little bit. But my mother … what was she like?"

"The image of you," Jake said. "Except for that red hair." Edie cleared her throat, but Jake smiled an unworried smile. "Looking at you, Mistress Clare, it's as if your mother lived again."

"She always had a kind word for others," Edie said. "And she was always singing and laughing."

"I reckon she had a will of her own, though," Jake said. "Begging your pardon, but she went her own way."

"She had a lot of courage," Edie said grimly.

"Ah, well, one person's courage is another person's recklessness," Jake said tolerantly.

I laughed and dared to ask the question that was uppermost in my mind: "Was she … wed … to my father?"

"Certainly she was!" Edie said indignantly. "She and your father were wed in church like any decent folk. They …"

Jake cleared his throat and Edie folded her lips together. They both looked disapproving and – oddly, I thought, after all these years – bereaved.

Trying to understand, hoping I was not asking another awkward question, I guessed: "Their families did not approve of their marriage?"

Jake and Edie looked at each other and seemed to relent. Grimly Jake said, "Indeed they did *not*, Mistress Clare. Your mother had never crossed her father in anything before, so it came as all the more of a shock when she upped and married to please herself." Reflectively, almost as an afterthought, he added, "Sir Anthony was never so angry in his life."

"Sir Anthony Bampton? Why did he care?" I glanced from one of the Binsleys to the other. They looked confused and I explained, "I suppose my mother was a maidservant here. Did he demand that he give his consent for all his household to wed?" Vaguely I thought of the Mother Abbess and her absolute authority at the convent. "Will he mind me being here now?"

The Binseys looked at each other again, then Edie sat down beside me and patted my hand. Gently she said, "You were three when you were sent to Kirklington Abbey, my lamb, so I dare say you don't remember a lot about your life before you entered the nunnery."

I shook my head.

Edie took a deep breath and said, "Sir Anthony Bampton was your mother's father. He's your grandsire."

"My … grandfather?" I considered this. And then, saying the first words that popped into my head, I gasped, "If I am his granddaughter then Lettice Bampton and I are some kind of cousins!"

"Aye." Jake grinned. "Cousins – and more like sisters in the early days when you were both little girls."

"I fear I do not remember her," I said. "I mean to say, of course, I remember her from the abbey. But I do not remember her from … before." I blushed. "I do not think she likes me."

"Ah, well, Mistress Lettice has her airs and graces," Jake said. "And speaking of her ladyship, Edie, she'll be wanting her supper soon."

"Aye … and complaining about something," Edie grumbled. She

went to the table and started banging here and there with earthenware bowls and wooden spoons. Over her shoulder she said, "I suppose *you* didn't waste your time at the nunnery, Mistress Clare, coming home with no notion of cooking?"

Cautiously I said, "I did not do a lot of cooking. The lay sisters worked in the kitchen and cared for the animals. I spent most of my time with the choir sisters and the nuns taught me, not cooking, but other things."

"What other things?" Edie looked aghast.

"I'll be going," Jake said, before I could speak. He gave me a nod and a wink. "I'm more pleased than I can say to have you lodging under this roof again, Mistress Clare, of that you may be sure."

He ducked out of the kitchen and Edie exclaimed, "You will never be a notable housewife if you cannot cook and supervise servants and all their kitchen work! What did you learn at the nunnery if you didn't learn cooking?"

Promptly I said, "The nuns taught me reading and writing … and Latin … and how to embroider and sing." I recalled our lessons with the Mistress of Novices. "We all learned those things – Lettice too. I learned to chant the prayers when I became a postulant and how to sing in church when I became a novice."

I thought of parchment and quills and the tiny book I had made. More than anything I had learned how to notice beauty – I had learned the art of the illuminator. Mine was the art of illuminating beauty for others. Or it had been anyway. *I am never going to illuminate again.* But I did not know how to explain all that to Edie, so I said nothing.

"Hmm." Edie looked at me sharply. "What you want, my girl, is plenty of fresh air and good food. You're too thin and pale. You'll have new milk every day to bring the roses to your cheeks. And I'll teach you how to cook." She shook her head and tutted her tongue against her teeth. "The idea of you not knowing how to cook!"

She swept a white cloth out of a coffer and handed it to me, then she seized three pewter plates and three pewter tankards in her strong hands. "You come with me into the great hall and greet Mistress Lettice. You'll eat with her and her mother's gentlewoman, Dame Sybil, today."

I followed Edie out of the kitchen and along a stone-flagged passage, with doors opening on either side into storerooms, then into the great hall. It was a long, low room with a stone-flagged, rush-strewn floor and white-washed walls below a ceiling with wooden beams criss-crossing the plaster. A fire flickered in a deep, generous fireplace set into the fourth wall of the hall. The evening sun cast long shadows through three glass-paned windows onto a window seat. Silently I helped Edie lay a long table with the cloth and pewterware.

"And now, my lamb, come and meet your cousin," Edie said. "Nay, wait!"

Quickly Edie smoothed my hair and straightened my skirt, then ushered me through a door into a smaller room: the parlour. Lounging on a stool by a window, toying with her embroidery, was Lettice. An older woman, sitting primly on the edge of a window seat, was reading aloud from a book.

Edie bustled forward and Lettice looked up. Her eyes widened. She raised her eyebrows. "You!"

Matter-of-factly Edie said, "Mistress Lettice, this is your cousin, Mistress Clare."

Lettice stood up, and her embroidery tumbled down the skirt of her beautiful blue gown and into the rushes at her feet. Blankly she said, "I do not understand. Clare is a novice at Kirklington Abbey. What is she doing here?"

I felt very small and very weary. My mustard-yellow kirtle was faded and tight, my hair was tangled and my hands and face were grimy. I did not feel like a worthy cousin for elegant, fashionable Lettice Bampton.

Firmly Lettice said, "She is a cloister girl!"

"The Mother Abbess sent me here," I said. "She will not let me become a nun and has released me from my vows as a postulant and novice. The bishop says the abbey is going to be suppressed. Today … men came to the convent." I struggled to understand the meaning of my own words. "I did not know I was coming here until today and I did not know I was … I mean, I *am* … your cousin until Jake and Edie told me so."

"My *cousin*?" Lettice sat down again. "A cloister girl. *You* are *my* cousin?"

Briskly Edie said, "Your grandsire, Sir Anthony Bampton, had four children who survived babyhood: Master Harry, Master Thomas, Master Matthew and Mistress Clare. Master Harry married Mistress Joanna and their children are Geoffrey, Catherine and Frances. Sadly Master Harry and Mistress Joanna are dead of the plague, God rest their souls, with Catherine too."

Edie crossed herself, and I did too.

"You're sure to meet your grandsire and the boys – Geoffrey and Frances – soon, Mistress Clare," Edie continued. "Master Thomas married Mistress Maud and their daughter is Lettice. Master Matthew entered a monastery and became a monk. Mistress Clare married to please herself and died in childbed, but her daughter is Clare." She smiled at me, then nodded at Lettice. "Mistress Clare entered a nunnery when she was three years old, but now she's come home. She's the image of her mother and we're very glad to have her here."

"Aye, I dare say, to be sure," Lettice said dully. Finally she shrugged her shoulders and said, "Well, I will take your word for it, Edie." She glanced at me from under her eyelashes. "I must say Clare, with your red hair, I am not surprised to hear your mother married to please herself."

"'Tis said the Lady Elizabeth has red hair too," Edie said quickly.

"Aye," said Lettice. "The Lady Elizabeth and Clare have many things in common."

The Lady Elizabeth had been declared illegitimate by her father after her mother's execution for treason, so I knew Lettice was not being kind, but I clenched my hands so hard it hurt and said nothing.

Edie, looking relieved, curtsied to Dame Sybil and said, "I thought Clare could sleep in the truckle bed in the chamber you and Mistress Lettice share."

"To be sure," Dame Sybil said agreeably. She smiled kindly at me. "You are welcome at Bampton Manor, my dear. Lettice and I shall be glad of your company." She paused, but Lettice said nothing. Quickly Dame Sybil said, "You can share the large bed – which has curtains and a feather mattress – with Lettice. I can sleep in the truckle bed."

I glanced at my cousin's face. It was puckered with disapproval. Quickly I said, "I am not used to sleeping in a bed with curtains and a feather mattress. I will be very comfortable in the truckle bed."

"'Tis true," Lettice said. "Clare and I slept in a dormitory with another girl and two lay sisters – and one of them snored – and our beds were not as comfortable as the truckle bed." She glanced at me from under her eyelashes again. "I think a cloister girl like Clare will be perfectly content in the truckle bed … or maybe she would be more comfortable on a pallet in the porch chamber so she can pray whenever she likes."

"The porch chamber!" Edie exclaimed. "Do you not want your cousin to share your chamber?"

"Clare *likes* praying," Lettice said. "If she can pray without disturbing Dame Sybil …" She shrugged her shoulders. "I do not care."

Dame Sybil blinked but said nothing.

"I think I would be more comfortable in the porch chamber if that is convenient for everyone," I blurted. "That way I can … can *pray* without disturbing Lettice!" Spontaneously I added, "And *Lettice* can practice the lute without disturbing *me*!"

"Very well," Edie huffed. Stiffly she said, "I'll tell Jake to take your coffer to the porch chamber and I'll make a bed up for you there, Mistress Clare, if that's what you want."

"I think it is," I said. I dropped the woman a curtsy. "I thank you for your trouble – you and Jake too."

"It's no trouble, my lamb," Edie exclaimed, melting into her old mood of affection and approval again. "You stay here with your cousin until supper is ready and then, when you've eaten, you can go straight to bed."

Edie bustled away, and I sank onto a stool beside the fire. I was grateful that Dame Sybil read her book and Lettice sulked until supper. I propped my chin in my hand and my elbow on my knee and gazed out of the window at the sun sinking in the sky above the autumnal landscape burnished gold and brown. The parlour was cosy with wood-panelled and tapestry-hung walls and embroidered cushions on the settle and in the chairs. A piece of silk was draped over a table, and a pewter jug full of yellow flowers – the ones Sister Theresa called My Lady's Bedstraw – stood on the silk. Dreamily I looked at the flowers and thought how I would paint them as a border around a prayer on parchment. *Green, for the stems and leaves, for courage. Yellow, for the flowers, for kindness.*

"Maybe she is not hungry," Lettice said loudly. "Clare?"

I started to my feet and followed Dame Sybil into the great hall. Wearily I ate what was set before me without noticing what it was. I was relieved when the meal was over and Edie beckoned me through a door and up the stairs to a room over the porch at the front of the house.

"Come, my lamb, you need your bed," Edie said. "Here is the porch chamber." She sheltered the flame of the candle in her hand and looked around the small space dubiously. "Are you sure you'll be comfortable? I've put a wool mattress on top of a straw pallet and found a feather pillow and there are blankets in plenty. Your coffer is here, and there's a tinder box and a candle on top of this stool which Jake found in the dairy and thought you might like."

I glanced around the room and nodded. It was a small, stone chamber with jars of preserves and boxes of candles under the casement window opposite the door. Somehow the room reminded me of the convent. And it, too, smelt of clean wool and fresh air and damp stone.

"I shall be comfortable here." I leaned forward and pressed a kiss on Edie's motherly cheek. "I thank you for your kindness."

"'Tis no kindness," Edie said simply. "'Tis only what I've longed to do all these many years. Now, Mistress Clare, you sleep well and thank Our Lord and His saints you've come home."

I did not bother to light a candle when Edie had gone. I hung the Mother Abbess' rosary on a nail but left her letter in my sewing box.

And then I almost crawled out of my clothes and into my bed, in my smock, with my eyes closed. My body sank into the wool mattress and feather pillow that were softer than anything at the convent. I pulled the blankets up to my chin and opened my eyes to focus on the moon and the stars that I could see through the uneven window glass. They looked the same from Bampton Manor as they had from the cloisters of Kirklington Abbey.

But everything was different here. Lettice was playing the lute and singing about a lover and his lass. The only thing that was not different was me … but then my eyes closed and I did not try to open them again. *Will I belong here?* I yawned. *And will anyone love me?*

I fluttered my eyelids and sneezed. And then, in a panic, I sat up and squeaked, "Bess! Hurry. We will be late for prayers if we do not make haste!"

Bess did not reply, and I blinked. For a heartbeat, wondering where the other girls and the lay sisters were, I was not sure where I was, but then I remembered: I was in the porch chamber at Bampton Manor.

Sleepily I stared at my coffer on one side of my bed and the jars of preserves and boxes of tallow candles on the other. *I am in my mother's home! She knew and loved this place as well as I know and love the convent. Jake and Edie – my old nurse – remember my mother and remember me as a little girl too.* I flopped back in bed and stared at the casement window. A daddy-long-legs butted against the thick, wavy glass. The insect was familiar but everything else was new.

All day, as I followed Edie through her household chores with my hair twisted into two long plaits and an apron tied over my kirtle, I thought of the nuns. *What did the men do to the convent and the sisters?*

I walked with Jake and Edie across a field and through a copse to the church to attend Mass before breakfast. The words of the prayers were the same as they had always been. *But does the Mother Abbess miss my voice in the choir?* Later I whispered *Ave Maria* as I collected the eggs and *Pater Noster* as I stirred a cauldron full of soup. *Does Sister Joanna miss my help in the scriptorium and library?* I longed for the company of the nuns and the rhythm of the convent, but my heart stirred with a fresh and throbbing interest in my new life, almost in spite of my longing for my old one.

Lettice spent the day in the parlour with Dame Sybil, but I spent the day in the kitchen near Edie. The kitchen wenches, Nancy and Molly, were curious but kind. The kitchen and garden boy, Young Hal, grinned and tugged his forelock. The gardener, Old Hal, smiled and nodded and said I looked like my mother. My heart skipped a beat at the thought of meeting my grandfather and my other cousins, but I beat some eggs for a custard at the kitchen table and dreamed of people who looked like me, as a wooden spoon swirled the whites and yolks round and round in an earthenware bowl. I was still thinking about cousins and brothers and sisters with red hair when the custard was baked and Edie sent me outside.

"Go and explore the garden and get some roses in your cheeks, my lamb! But don't be late for supper," Edie called, "and don't get lost!"

I smiled and waved on my way out of the kitchen courtyard. Being alone and free to go wherever I wanted was strange, but I took a deep breath and ventured into the formal garden with paved paths, box hedges and roses trained over wooden trellises. The roses had bloomed and faded, of course, but I fancied their scent lingered in the chill air. I inspected the plants and imagined the soft, blooming shape and colour of the flowers. *Dark red for love and bright red for laughter.*

Slowly, imagining the roses as a border around a prayer written on parchment, I hugged a knitted shawl around my shoulders and wandered along a path, through a gate and into a kitchen garden. I walked up and down the muddy paths between the beds – bursting with straggling, overgrown greenery – identifying many of the same vegetables that grew in the kitchen garden at the convent: rocket, beans and peas, marrows, carrots and beetroot.

A few bees, tempted by the watery sunshine, buzzed here and there. One led the way through a calm, fragrant herb garden and into an orchard where the air was heavy and sweet with ripening apples. The trees were gnarled and twisted with age and heavy with fruit. I wandered between the trees and foraged some ripe apples from the long grass before I found the bee skips at the end of the orchard and watched the bees buzzing to and fro without a care in the world but that of making the last of the year's honey before winter came.

Beyond the orchard lay a farmer's field, but I kept walking. My leather shoes swished through the overgrown grass, and my thick stockings and long skirt got wetter and heavier. I wondered what it would be like to keep walking forever. *Would I reach London? The English Channel? France where the Mother Abbess and the nuns are going?*

My wet skirts flapped against my legs with every step so I turned and looked back at the manor house. Smoke drifted from the chimneys. The stone-tiled roof was visible over the trees in the orchard, and the sun gleamed on a pane of glass in an upper window. The sound of the chickens clucking and a maidservant singing came drifting together on the breeze. The scene tugged at my heart with a little thrill of gladness.

"Mary Rose!"

The cry startled me with its suddenness. I turned and saw a boy with red hair waving from the gate at the other side of the field.

"Mary Rose!" he called again, his voice soft and heavy with a country burr, in spite of its volume. "Hurry up, will you?" The boy cupped his hand to his mouth and called louder than ever, "I need your help with milking!"

I laughed out loud and wondered what to do for a heartbeat, then I picked up my skirts and ran through the wet grass. I reached the gate and the boy out of breath, but smiling.

"Mistress!" The boy looked at me and flushed to the roots of his hair. He ducked his head and said, "I beg your pardon, mistress, I thought you were Mary Rose."

"And so did another lad … yesterday," I said. "Do I look a great deal like Mary Rose?"

"Aye." The boy dropped down from the top of the gate and bobbed his head in a clumsy bow. "You look just like Mary Rose. I ain't never seen anything like this before but … but have I seen *you* before?"

I looked at him doubtfully. He looked as if he was about my age. He was dressed like a yeoman in a rough jerkin and a pair of leather breeches, and he had red hair. And suddenly I knew he was the boy with red hair and blue eyes I had seen at the convent. Now as then his face wore a cheerful, honest, quiet expression. And now I stared at him as I had not dared to stare at him among the nuns.

The boy returned my stare and said very slowly, "I *have* seen you before."

"Mayhap at Kirkington Abbey?" I suggested.

"I rent some of my land from the nunnery."

"And I saw you there, a few days back, talking to John Hobb."

"We were talking about the rent I owed."

"Oh, aye, John Hobb takes care of all the manor business for the nuns," I explained.

The boy scratched his head and said, "A girl like you walked by. I remember 'cause she put me in mind of Mary Rose. But she was a nun. And then I wondered if …" He stopped and flushed. "Aye, well, you look like Mary Rose is all I can say."

"'Twas a novice you saw, not a nun," I corrected. "And she was me … or I was her … but I have left the abbey now." I did not want to talk about convents and kings and suppression so I looked at the soggy tips of my shoes and said, "I fear I am not Mary Rose and I do not know how to milk cows."

"No need to fret about that, mistress." The boy grinned. "I thank you kindly for the thought but I can manage the milking. Mary Rose should be here soon. You're more than welcome to come and see the farm, though, if you like."

The boy pointed over the fields towards a cluster of ancient farm buildings set against a little copse. A trickle of smoke rose from a chimney against trees whose leaves were brown, red and yellow. Dreamily I imagined how such a scene would look in a book. I would draw the fold of the hills and the rise of the trees, with the farm nestled among, in ink. I would mix some extra colours. And I would add gold – *gold for heaven* – here and there like the light of the setting sun.

"'Tis a fair prospect," the boy said sturdily.

"Aye." Spontaneously I said, "Oh … God made a beautiful world!"

The boy's gaze swung back to me, and I saw his love for the place in his eyes. I wondered what he saw in my eyes.

Abruptly he said, "Come, mistress." He stood back and opened the gate.

I smiled my thanks as I passed through, then I held out one of the apples I had foraged from among the overgrown grass and fallen leaves in the orchard. "Here."

The boy blinked, smiled and took it shyly. "Thank you, mistress."

"Walter!" a voice called from the direction of the manor house, with the same soft and heavy country burr as the boy. "Wait, I say, Walter!"

The boy stopped and turned back towards the gate. A young girl, who looked not much younger than myself, ran across the field. She had long red curls, escaped from a prim coif, that framed her face and tumbled round her shoulders.

I bit my lip and asked, "Is *she* Mary Rose?"

"Aye." The boy grinned. "You're the image of her!" Quickly he added, "Begging your pardon, mistress."

The girl's face was flushed, and her eyes were laughing. She was out of breath. Before she caught it again, however, she saw me and her eyes grew wide with wonder.

The boy jerked his head at me and said, "I shouted at her and called her Mary Rose. I came to find you 'cause I'm short of men to help with milking."

The girl's eyes grew even wider. She dropped a curtsy and tried to stuff her curls under her coif. Breathlessly she said, "I pray pardon for Walter shouting at you, Mistress Clare." Under her breath she hissed, "Walter, how could you?"

"I thought she was you!" Walter growled. And then he stared at me as if he was seeing me for the first time. "Mistress Clare? So you *are* Clare!"

I frowned and tried to laugh, then looked away and said, “Aye.” I dropped a curtsey. “I do not know how you know my name but I am, indeed, Clare. I beg your pardon, I will go now, if ‘tis best. Pray excuse me.”

I made to leave, but Mary Rose caught my hand and exclaimed, “Don’t go! And you’ve no need to beg our pardon, Mistress Clare!”

Walter, flashing the girl who was obviously his sister a warning look, said, “Don’t fret, Mistress Clare, there’s no need for you leave. Are you …” He cleared his throat. “Are you still of a mind to come and see the farm?”

“Oh, aye!” I exclaimed. “What animals do you have?”

“Thirteen cows,” Mary Rose said. “And eighty-six sheep, three pigs and two horses as well as the chickens, ducks and bees besides. And we grow wheat and barley. *And* we have a garden and an orchard and trap rabbits to sell at market.”

“Hush, Mary Rose,” Walter said. “Come along, do!”

Walter started walking with long strides towards the farm, and we followed. Mary Rose kept looking at me from under her eyelashes with a secret-keeping look in her eyes. Like me, she was slight and willowy, with long red hair, but her face was rounder, her nose was snubber and her eyes were brown not blue. But I could see why people called me Mary Rose. I glanced at Walter too. *Does everyone around Bampton Manor have red hair?*

I handed Mary Rose an apple. The girl took it with a blush, a smile and a hint of a curtsy. We walked on together in munching silence.

Walter led the way into a muddy farmyard and said, "So this be the farm." He looked round with a contented gaze. Simply he said, "It's not bad and we're grateful to Our Lord for what He's given us." He jerked his head towards a byre. "Come and see the cows, then, Mistress Clare."

Brother and sister disappeared into the cow byre, but I hesitated in the doorway and gazed around the farmyard at the rambling house of honey-coloured stone, the barn and the outbuildings. Chickens scratched here and there in the mud, cows called in the byre and pigs grunted and squealed somewhere nearby. It felt, as Water and Mary Rose did, like an old friend somehow. I plunged unhesitatingly into the byre, then paused while my eyes accustomed to the sudden dimness.

Walter looked up from the cow he was milking. He grinned and asked, "Do you like the farm?"

"I do," I said seriously.

"'Tis odd for Sir Anthony Bampton's granddaughter," Walter said tersely. He concentrated on the milk streaming into the bucket. "Mistress Lettice ..."

"But I am not Mistress Lettice," I said. "The lay sisters at the convent looked after the garden and animals, and I used to help with some of their work – like planting seeds and harvesting vegetables. I loved the feel of the soil and the shapes and colours in the garden." Ruefully I said, "I had my own work to do and I was not much interested in the kitchen, so I fear Edie is shocked because I do not know how to cook!"

"She says she's teaching you already," Mary Rose said, emerging from the shadow of another cow with a bucket of milk in each hand.

"I believe she is trying," I admitted. "Did Edie tell you my name?" I laughed. "I think gardens are a vast deal more interesting than kitchens!"

"You sound like our dad," Walter said. His face was red and his voice was thick. "He was besotted with the land and the animals."

"Your father?" I asked.

Shortly Walter said, "He and our mam died, with some of the little ones, of the sweating sickness before harvest time."

I crossed myself and murmured, "Oh, how sad, God rest their souls."

Sturdily Mary Rose said, "Our dad and mam trusted Jesus Christ for the salvation of their souls and didn't hold with superstitions."

Mildly I said, "I trust Jesus Christ too." I murmured a few words from Doctor Luther's *Small Catechism*: "I believe Jesus Christ, true God and also true man, born of the Virgin Mary, is my own Lord and He has redeemed me, purchased and won me from all my sins, from death and from the devil with His holy, precious blood and with His innocent suffering and death that I may be His own."

Mary Rose looked doubtful and said, "But you're a nun – or you were going to be a nun – and you crossed yourself. Dad didn't hold with that sort of thing." Her voice was full of loyal pride. "He was a reformer."

"Oh … did he read books by Doctor Luther too?" I asked a little warily, thinking of Bess.

"He wasn't one for reading much," Walter said. "His faith in Christ was all in all to him. But Mary Rose is right – he *was* a reformer."

"Oh." I thought about that. "Lettice does not like reformers. I do not know why. What do you think …"

"If you've finished your share of the milking, Mary Rose, we'd best be taking this milk to the dairy," Walter said abruptly.

"May I help?" I asked. Mary Rose nodded and Walter grinned, so I took a bucket of frothy, warm milk in each hand.

Mary Rose scuttled out of the byre. Walter followed her across the farmyard and into the dairy. I was a little slower, and as I reached the dairy door with the buckets of milk, Walter popped out with a rough pottery mug of milk.

"Here." He grinned. "'Tis still warm."

"I thank you," I said and sipped the milk. "'Tis delicious."

Walter grinned and stroked his upper lip. I did not understand, then I wiped my mouth on my sleeve and removed a milk moustache with a gasp and a blush at doing something so childish. Walter and Mary Rose laughed, and for a fleeting moment it was like having a brother and sister.

Reluctantly I said, "I had best be going now but I thank you for everything."

Mary Rose had a secret-keeping look in her eyes again. She dropped a curtsy and said, "'Tis nice to meet you, Mistress Clare, although 'tis not what we expected!"

"Nay," Walter said. "You're welcome to come at any time, Mistress Clare. I'll take you back, lest you lose your way."

I walked beside Walter across the fields towards Bampton Manor. The sun was setting in the west and casting long shadows as dusk cloaked the world in a purple-grey mist studded with the twinkling lights of the manor house ahead. I shivered as I hugged my shawl around my shoulders and skipped a few steps to keep up with Walter.

At the edge of the orchard, I asked, "Do you know a young gentleman called Roger Chastleton?"

"Aye." Walter gave me a quick, surprised glance. "Do you too?"

"He called me Mary Rose yesterday," I said, ducking between the shadowy branches of the fruit trees. "I did not know why." I smiled at Walter. "I do now!"

I caught the sound of Walter's laugh as we hurried through the darkness, then Edie opened the kitchen door with a thankful sigh and flooded the kitchen courtyard with golden light and good smells of roasting meat and boiling puddings.

"Mistress Clare!" Edie dropped a curtsy. "How glad I am to see you safe! Come in, my lamb, come in." She nodded at Walter. "You're a good lad, Walter. You won't get lost in the dark, going home?"

"Not I!" Walter laughed. "I've known these fields all my life. Farewell, Mistress Clare. And Mistress Binsley too." He nodded and disappeared into the darkness singing, "Who shall have my lady fair, when the leaves are green? Who but I should win my lady fair, when the leaves are green?"

Edie shut the kitchen door and said, "So you've met Walter Ducklington, then, Mistress Clare." Her words were careless but her eyes were concerned. "How did you like him?"

"Very much!" I sank onto the settle and held my wet feet out to the fire. "I met his sister, Mary Rose, too. She did not talk over much."

"Oh?" Edie smiled. "That's a rare thing. She's a chatterbox, is Mary Rose, most of the time. She was here while you were out. I told her that you were around here somewhere."

"She knew my name when she met me," I said absently. "I wondered why." I gazed into the crackling, dancing heart of the fire. "Walter – Ducklington, did you say? - called me Mary Rose today as Roger Chastleton did yesterday. She *does* look like me. Is not it odd?"

"Odd?" Edie's voice was sharp. "Not at all. Red hair is common enough. That's all people have in mind when they mistake you for Mary Rose Ducklington." She shook her head and tutted her tongue against her teeth. "Although how they can make the mistake, my lamb, I don't know." She looked at my feet as if she was seeing them for the first time. "God save us, Mistress Clare, your feet are wet! Go and change your stockings this instant or you'll catch a shocking chill, and I don't want you ill as soon as you've arrived. You always used to catch chills easier than most children. Bring those wet things back down here and we'll dry them by the fire, then ..."

Edie's voice followed me up the stairs to the porch chamber. As I went, I thought of the song Walter had sung. I felt as if I remembered it, although I did not recall hearing it before. *My lady fair ... leaves are green ... green for courage.* Without intending to do so, I found myself humming the tune as I removed my shoes and changed my stockings.

"Who shall have my lady fair, when the leaves are green?" I sang as I entered the kitchen.

Edie looked up with a bright smile and said, "You loved that song when you were a little bit of a baby."

"Did I?" I smiled dreamily. Suddenly, with a little jolt, I realised I did remember it: it was the song that ended in laughter and had nestled in my heart all this time. I did not know how to say so, however, so I murmured, "I suppose that, like red hair, 'tis common enough."

"And you'll see I'm right about *that* being common enough hereabouts," Edie snorted. "Just you wait and see!"

"But I *like* red hair!" I laughed. None of the nuns had red hair. *I wonder ... do I ever look as pretty as Mary Rose?*

I dreamed of my new friends that night and woke up, breathless and hot, as their red heads and cheerful smiles faded into the horrible conviction I was late for the night prayers.

Anxiously I struggled to sit up and wrestle my blankets, which had tangled around my knees with my shift, into order. The room was dark and quiet. For a baffled heartbeat I wondered where the lay sisters and Bess were and why none of them had lit a taper to light the way down the stairs and through the cloisters to the church. But then the moon lit the room and cast a cross-shaped shadow across the foot of my bed. I flopped back against my pillow and pulled my blankets up to my chin while I tried to calm my racing heart with deep breaths.

I was not late for the night prayers. *But I wish I was.* Panic eddied and surged around my heart like a rising pool of water. *Everything is new and strange.*

I took another deep breath and imagined I was illuminating a manuscript. I thought of adding gold leaf for the golden halo of Our Lady. *Gold for heaven.* I thought of drawing a border of flowers. I added bees, ladybirds and snails among the flowers and leaves. *I feel like a snail without a shell.* Almost as if my imaginary work of illuminating was real, I took my squirrel-hair paintbrush and dipped into an oyster shell of blue paint and gave the snail a blue shell. *Blue for hope.* My eyelids were heavy and my pillow was soft. *Hope. All will be well in Our Lord. Lapis lazuli for hope.*

But when I entered the kitchen next morning Edie frowned and said, "Such bruises as you have under your eyes, Mistress Clare!"

She kneaded bread, pushing and pulling it ceaselessly on the floury table, while she talked. "Didn't you sleep well?"

Vaguely I said, "I woke for prayers."

"Prayers?" Edie frowned, then eased her face into an anxious smile. "You're not at the convent now, my lamb. You don't need to wake for prayers."

"I know," I said, "but I forgot in my dreams."

"Hmm." Edie thumped the bread onto the table. "Come and help me knead the bread."

Obediently I joined Edie in pushing and pulling the dough. I tried not to mind that it was oozy and sticky between my fingers while the tips of my fingers were dry with flour.

A knock sounded on the back door. Nancy and Molly were singing in the dairy, so Edie cleaned her hands on her apron and opened the door.

"Mistress Clare?" Edie called. "Here's Mary Rose Ducklington to see you."

I left the bread on the table and hurried to the door with a smile.

"Good day to you, Mistress Clare!" Mary Rose had a small child in her arms, but she dropped a curtsy. Then she smiled and offered me a tiny posy of dried lavender tied together with a piece of twine. Shyly she said, "I thought you might like this."

"I do," I said. Tears sprang into my eyes. "I shall hang this by my bed, to sweeten my chamber."

"Aye." Mary Rose smiled. "I'm glad." She jiggled the child in her arms and said, "This is Aggie."

"God keep you, Aggie," I said.

Aggie smiled shyly and buried her small face in Mary Rose's shoulder.

"She's shy, is Aggie," Mary Rose explained with an apologetic smile. "She wanted to see you, though."

"I am happy to meet her," I said and buried my face in the tiny bouquet. "I wish I had brothers and sisters for you to meet too."

Mary Rose's eyes grew wide and full to brimming with the secret-keeping look again. Spontaneously she reached out and squeezed my fingers with her own, slightly grubby, ones. "You can share mine," she said. "I've got lots!"

"Oh … I thank you, 'tis vastly kind!" I blushed at her generosity. "I have always wanted brothers and sisters." I smiled and twisted the end of one plait around my floury fingers. "And we look like sisters!"

"We do!" Mary Rose laughed and promised, "You'll meet all of us in time – Walter and me and John Henry and Rich and Aggie."

The endings and beginnings of my life were woven together like the threads of wool I broke and mended while learning to spin. I still woke for the night prayers but I grew used to the feel of bread dough and new wool against my skin. I helped Jake and Old Hal pick the apples – reaching between the branches for the fruit as it hung ready to drop into my hand and slipping each one into a basket – or helped Edie and Young Hal sort and store the apples for the rest of the year. And every day I knelt in the porch chamber – with my prayer books on my stool and the Mother Abbess' rosary hanging from a nail on the wall with the lavender posy from Mary Rose – to pray for grace and wisdom to follow Christ in the world.

In my imagination I saw the dark wimples and kind faces of the nuns at prayer. My gaze strayed from the rosary to the sacks and boxes under the window and a sparrow hopping and chirping beyond the glass.

*How can Our Lord be the same in the convent with prayers and manuscripts and in the world with bread and apples and sparrows and cousins?* I sighed. *Everything else has changed – what if He has changed too?*

I crossed myself and blinked back tears I could not explain, then, my kirtle laced and my hair plaited, I hurried downstairs with my shoes in my hand.

Lettice was idling at the table in the great hall. "Good morrow, cloister girl." Lazily she asked, "Where, pray, are you going in such haste?"

I paused in the middle of pulling my shoes onto my feet. I blinked and said, "I am going to find Edie in the kitchen."

"Really?" Lettice murmured. "*My* honoured mother would not like *me* spending my time with servants every day."

"Edie was my mother's nurse and my nurse," I protested. "My

mother loved her and I do not think she would mind me spending my time with Edie. My mother would want me to learn how to be a notable housewife from Edie!"

"Hmm." Lettice looked out of the window while drumming her fingers on the tabletop.

I bit my lip and hurried along the kitchen passage. Outside the kitchen door, I paused and stamped my foot to relieve my feelings, before entering the kitchen. Jake was standing, breathless and panting, beside the fireplace and Edie was wiping her eyes on her apron.

"Why!" I put my hand on Edie's arm. "What ails you?"

"Foxes," Jake muttered.

Edie straightened her apron and patted my hand. "Don't you worry, my lamb. A couple of foxes have been and got into the hen loft, 'tis all."

"And eaten the hens?"

"Not all of them," Edie said. She started banging around at the table with a bunch of herbs, a knife and a chopping block. "We've lost a lot of pullets as should have raised chicks next spring."

"Feathers everywhere, there are," Jake said. He hitched one shoulder and poked the fire viciously. "Lost a lot of good brooders, we have, as well as cocks as would have made good meat for eating this winter."

I thought of the dark, shadowy hen loft and imagined how the hens must have felt when a couple of foxes disturbed their safe hideaway with flashing eyes and snapping teeth. I swallowed a sob.

Nancy and Molly were working in the dairy, but their cheerful, laughing voices sounded a long way away. I dived back into the passage that led to the hall and slipped into a storeroom.

I was shaking and sweating and my heart and head were pounding. *I know how the hens felt.* In my imagination I saw the convent with the nuns as placid as the hens and Thomas Cromwell and the king's men – Sir Hilary Cavendish and Master Tolbert – like the snarling foxes.

"Mother Abbess?" I sobbed. I whispered the names of the nuns: "Sister Anne, Sister Joanna, Sister Laura, Sister Bridget, Sister Grace and Sister Veronica?" I choked as I thought of the kitchen and the garden. "Sister Theresa and Sister Rosemary?" Brokenly I asked, "What became of you when the foxes came?"

A storm of sobs stole my breath and bent me double. Tears made dark spots on the bodice of my mustard-yellow kirtle and soaked the sleeves of my smock as I wiped my face and told myself to stop crying. I could not … but then a rustle betrayed a mouse, and I looked up in time to see a tiny nose quivering and a pair of dark eyes watching me beadily. I smiled through my tears. The mouse disappeared, and I swallowed one last sob.

Gently, like a prayer, I whispered the names of the nuns again, then I crossed myself and whispered, "God keep you all."

I slipped into the kitchen again and hoped Edie would not see my red and swollen face, but of course she did.

"What's wrong, my lamb?" She gathered me into a motherly embrace and rocked me to and fro. "Tell me, my dear."

I did not know how to put my grief into words, but I smiled through my lingering tearfulness.

"Would you like to make some gingerbread?" Edie asked. "'Twas your favourite thing to do when you were a little girl and there's some old bread just right for making sweetmeats."

"I fear I do not remember how to make gingerbread," I confessed. I reached for the little basket where Edie kept the precious ginger. "Pray tell me how!"

"Wait before you do anything with the ginger!" Edie cried. "'Tis an expensive spice! You need bread, butter and honey first." She shook her head. "'Tis still a puzzle to me that the saintly nuns taught you to read and write like a boy but didn't teach you how to make bread or sweetmeats."

Defensively I said, "The nuns taught me how to embroider and sing."

Edie dropped a motherly kiss on my cheek and said, "Well, my lamb, we love you as you are." She shook her head again. "But every girl should know how to make bread and sweetmeats, and I'll see to it you learn!"

I smiled a little bit sadly as I crumbled the dry bread into crumbs and added butter and honey to make a paste with ginger and pepper, but I knew Edie was serious – and wise. *Mayhap, after all, I shall be a notable housewife someday.* But it did not seem to matter when the abbey was ruined and the nuns had gone.

Next day I walked across the fields with some gingerbread wrapped in a clean cloth for Mary Rose. As I walked I worried about kneading bread and spinning wool and the doing of those domestic tasks that seemed to come so easily to Edie.

The hedgerows were full of brown leaves, and the muddy path underfoot was thick with leaves that had died and fallen. As I walked I caught sight of forsaken nests and foraging mice. Attics and barns were full of plenty, but the world seemed to be dying and decaying. I looked over the ridges and furrows of the fields that held nothing but stubble. *What if spring forgets to come again?*

The Ducklington farmyard was muddy and hazy with smoke from the kitchen chimney which the wind was blowing the wrong way. I nodded to the younger boys – John Henry and Rich. John Henry, his face red with effort, was chopping wood with an axe. Rich was stacking logs of all shapes and sizes into a wobbly pile. John Henry nodded seriously. Rich grinned and waved. I walked around the corner of the house and saw Walter staggering across the farmyard with a full bucket in each hand.

I dropped a curtsy and called, "Good day to you!"

"Good day, Mistress Clare," Walter called. "Are you well this day?"

"Very well," I said. "I am looking for Mary Rose."

"You'll find her in the garden," Walter said. "It's over yonder." He jerked his head. "I'll come and join you when I've fed the pigs." He grinned. "It's almost pig killing time and they're getting nice and fat, but every little helps!"

I followed the direction of Walter's nod away from the thwack of the axe splitting the logs and the squealing and grunting of the pigs as they saw their food. I rounded a tangled rose bush and found Mary Rose. The garden was green and overgrown and in the middle of the rocket and marrows, crouching in an earthern bed with her red hair tumbling over her shoulders, was Mary Rose. She was burrowing in the soil with one hand. In the other hand she held a tiny, spindly green plant which she had taken from an overflowing basket. Aggie, her gaze intent, crouched beside Mary Rose and watched her every move.

"... so we'll put the earth in here." Mary Rose scooped a handful into a rough wooden box with low sides and patted it down. "Can you do that too?"

Carefully Aggie took a tiny handful of soil from the ground and scattered it into the box. She looked at Mary Rose expectantly.

"Well done, sweeting!" Mary Rose said. "Let's do it again. We'll make the box nice and cosy for the plants and then ..." She looked over and scrambled up with a blush and a laugh. "Mistress Clare!"

I blushed and blurted, "I ... brought you a gift." I held out the cloth-wrapped gingerbread. "You gave me a gift and I wanted to give you one too."

"You didn't have to do that," Mary Rose said softly, but her face was alight with gladness. She approached with her hands covered in earth – still holding a plant – and her little sister clasping the skirt of her gown. "What is it?"

"Gingerbread," I said. I tried not to sound pleased with myself. "I made it myself … with Edie's help."

"Edie makes the best gingerbread in Gloucestershire!" Mary Rose said. "I'll enjoy it … and aye, sweeting, you shall enjoy it too." Aggie tugged at her big sister's skirts and peeped out, one muddy finger in her mouth, to smile at me. "Thank you, Mistress Clare, you're so kind!"

"Not really!" I laughed, thinking of *yellow for kindness*. And then, to change the subject, I asked, "What are you doing?"

"Planting strawberry runners," Mary Rose said. She thrust the plant at me. "Strawberry plants create long shoots with little plants at the end: they're called runners. If we plant and water the runners then they'll grow into bigger plants and we'll have more strawberries next summer." She grinned. "'Tis a good thing, indeed, because we like strawberries!"

"Like st'w'arberries," echoed Aggie.

"I like strawberries too!" I thought of the tiny, sweet red fruits, and my mouth watered. "I like them *very* much."

"Ve'w'y much," echoed Aggie again. And then, shyly, she ducked behind Mary Rose.

Mary Rose laughed and asked, "Would you like to help?"

I nestled the gingerbread carefully into the end of the basket holding the runners. Aggie slipped a tiny hand into one of mine and tugged me into the middle of the earthen bed. We filled the wooden box with soil and patted it down while Mary Rose untangled all the runners. And then, together, we planted the runners in the box.

Mary Rose sat back on the muddy hem of her skirt and said, "And that's a good job." She smiled at me. "I'll give you some of the new plants next year."

"I would like that above anything!" I said. I was cold but content. I rubbed the bridge of my nose and wriggled my cold toes while imagining my own strawberry patch at Bampton Manor. A small hand tugged at mine, and I looked down at Aggie. "Pray what it is, Aggie?"

The little girl pointed. "Look! Beetle."

"Ladybird," I said. I crouched down and we watched a ladybird cross a leaf. I drew a sad, shuddery breath as I thought of the last ladybird I had watched, at Kirklington Manor, the day the Mother Abbess had said I must leave the convent. But Aggie looked at me expectantly, so I smiled through a shimmer of tears and said, "'Tis beautiful."

"Boootiful," the little girl said.

A voice ringing with part-amusement and part-sternness said, "I'm not sure Edie will agree!"

I started guiltily.

Walter stood at the edge of the earthen bed and said, "I declare, Mistress Clare, you're as muddy as Aggie!"

I giggled but grimaced at the hem of my kirtle, wet and muddy, clinging to my ankles.

Seriously Walter said, “Mary Rose shouldn’t have made you work in the garden.”

“But I *wanted* to help,” I said. “And Mary Rose is going to give me some strawberry plants.”

I walked home through the fields and paused to fill my apron with ripe apples that had fallen from the trees into the long grass of the orchard. My feet were almost numb with cold when I crept into the fire-lit kitchen of Bampton Manor. Edie was not there, and I sank onto the settle beside the fire. I took my shoes and stockings off and held my feet up to the fire. Dreamily I remembered the living green things I had planted in the rich soil, the muddy hand Aggie had slipped into mine, the ladybird the child had spotted.

“Well!” Edie sounded shocked. “And what have *you* been doing?”

I started and said, “I was helping Mary Rose in the garden.”

“By all the saints!” Edie stared. “You’ve got mud on your nose. And look at your feet! You’ll catch your death of cold!” She produced a blanket from a coffer and wrapped it around my shoulders. “I’ll make you a hot posset.”

“But I am not cold,” I protested. I shivered and said, “Not *very* cold anyway. Truly … I *wanted* to help! Mary Rose is going to give me some strawberry plants. Mayhap I could have a strawberry garden and …”

“Well, that’s as may be, but what would your grandsire think of you gardening with Mary Rose Ducklington?” Edie clucked as she measured and stirred by the fire. “You can be sure he wants you to be a lady like your blessed mother. Why else did he trouble to send you to the convent? Well, there, I suppose he had plenty of reasons. But Sir Anthony wants you to grow up better than Mary Rose!" She handed me a steaming tankard that smelled of milk and honey and spices. "If you're going to pick up bad habits from the Ducklingtons, Mistress Clare, it's better you don't see them until your grandsire gives you leave."

"Nay!" I exclaimed in alarm and spilled a bit of the posset on my kirtle. "Do not say so!"

"Very well, my lamb, don't fret," Edie said. "Drink that down and then put some clean stockings on. Leave your shoes to dry by the fire." She frowned. "Where did these apples come from?"

"I picked them up in the orchard," I said meekly.

"'Twas good of you to pick them up before they spoiled," Edie said grudgingly. Then, softening, she said, "Thank you, my lamb, I'll make some stuffed apples for supper." She gathered spices, honey and prunes. "Hurry up with that posset now."

I finished the drink and stood up to go to the porch chamber. In the doorway, shivering in spite of the blanket wrapped around my shoulders, I paused and looked back at Edie who was busy coring the apples and chopping the prunes.

"I thought I was going to be all alone in the world when I left the convent," I said, "but now I have Jake and you and all of the Ducklingtons too. I am sorry if you do not like them but 'tis a very happy thing for me to have them."

"And you have your family here," Edie said, with an apple in one hand and a knife in the other.

"Aye," I said doubtfully, thinking of Lettice. "My family here."

Later, when I was sitting in the parlour with Dame Sybil and Lettice, Edie said, "Mistress Clare needs some new clothes to wear when she meets her grandsire and her other cousins."

"Oh!" I exclaimed in delight. "Do you think so indeed?"

"Indeed I do!" Edie said roundly. She looked me up and down with a critical eye. "And why I didn't think so before now is more than I can rightly say. Tut! Look at you, wearing an old gown and kirtle which Mary Rose Ducklington would be ashamed to wear, they're so plain and old." She narrowed her gaze. "And is that a rip?"

I blushed and said, "I was picking apples with Jake."

"Tut!" Edie said. "I'll mend it tonight."

I glanced down at my leaf-brown gown and mustard-yellow kirtle, and my heart gave a little skip of gladness at the thought of wearing some new clothes. *I cannot remember wearing anything but a habit and veil, and these old clothes!*

Lettice looked me up and down too. She raised her eyebrows and drawled, "I cannot say I am surprised. Clare never dressed with any sense of style at the convent."

I blinked in surprise and said slowly, "I was a novice. I was not there to dress with style!"

"And 'tis just as well, dear," Lettice murmured. "Really, cloister girl, that habit … and this dress!" She rolled her eyes. "I think Edie is right. Pray, make some new clothes as soon as possible!"

"*This dress*, whatever you may say, is modest and warm!" I countered. "'Twas good enough for the nuns! They loved me and I always had good food and good clothes to wear. When I left them, they gave me the best they could and 'tis a good enough dress!"

"Not for Sir Anthony," Edie said grimly, then her eyes softened. "I dare say the nuns did their best for you, my lamb, but that gown and kirtle are a far cry from what Sir Anthony Bampton's granddaughter ought to wear." She chucked me under the chin. "I'll make you something proper and pretty for a young lady like yourself, never you fear." She curtsied to Dame Sybil. "I beg your pardon for disturbing you, good dame, I came but to ask for leave to go through the cloth in the old oak coffer and choose some lengths for Mistress Clare."

"By all means," Dame Sybil said. She smiled at me. "I pray pardon for not thinking of it myself."

Eagerly I said, "I can help with the sewing."

"That's as may be," Edie said. "You wait until I find some cloth, then you can talk of helping with the sewing."

Pleasantly Dame Sybil said, "If we all help with the sewing, we can manage the seams and tucks in no time at all, I dare say. Lettice will be delighted to help her cousin make a new gown and kirtle."

Lettice started and dropped her embroidery, but said, "Why, to be sure, Dame Sybil."

"I thought so," Dame Sybil said. She picked up Lettice's embroidery and gave it back to her. "You need never be ashamed of your skill with the needle or of being kind to others."

I blinked with surprise to hear Lettice being rebuked by the placid gentlewoman. Edie chuckled and bustled out of the parlour. Lettice, in a huff, left the room too. Edie returned with several lengths of cloth and piled them on the table where they formed a glorious waterfall of colour that cascaded onto the rush-covered floor.

"What do you think, my lamb?"

I gazed at the fabric in awe and rubbed it between my fingertips almost reverently. It was fine wool, soft and thick, dyed the bright, intense blue of lapis lazuli, the deep, dusky red of the rosehip and the cool, restful green of hidden moss. *Blue for hope, dark red for love and green for courage.* It was the sort of cloth other girls – girls with homes, families and surnames – wore.

Breathlessly I said, "Do you mean for *me* to wear these colours?"

"Aye." Edie gave a short laugh. "You've not often seen such fine stuff, I warrant."

"Oh, aye, I have *seen* it," I said. "I have not worn it." I smiled at Edie. "I *want* to help with the sewing if you please!"

"And so do I," Dame Sybil said. She smiled at me. "You will rival your cousin in your new finery."

"Oh." I hesitated. "The nuns were very severe about vanity. And I do not wish *at all* to upset Lettice."

"Nonsense," Edie said briskly. "'Tis not vanity, at your age, to dress like a young girl rather than an old hag. As for Mistress Lettice, well, she needs to learn she's not the only pretty young lady in the world."

Later, as I watched Edie cut the fabric on the kitchen table by candlelight, I asked, "Are you sure 'tis proper for me to have such fine gowns?"

"I'll not let you wear anything fancy or immodest, my lamb," Edie said grimly as she used a pair of shears to cut the fabric. "'Tis perfectly proper for you to have kirtles and gowns of good wool and in fine colours. You'll have to wait until Sir Anthony takes you to court to wear silks and velvets."

I laughed. "I can wait!" I tried to thread a needle in the uncertain light of the kitchen fire and the spluttering mutton-fat tapers. "Ouch!" I sucked a bead of blood off my finger. "I do not think my … Sir Anthony will take me to court."

"He's going to take his other granddaughter," Jake said from his seat on the settle beside the fire. The maidservants tittered and whispered. Easily Jake said, "Oh, aye, you'll see: he's bound to take Mistress Lettice."

"Oh, well, 'tis different." I finally succeeded in threading my needle. "*I* have no desire in the world to go to court."

"Like your blessed mother," Edie murmured, her mouth full of pins. "*She* had no worldly ambition, like other members of her family, who could think of nothing but courtiers and fashion. She was too good to live."

"But now we've got Mistress Clare," Jake said. He smiled at me and his eyes were twinkly. "I think you'll be seeing Sir Anthony – and mayhap the rest of your family too – before long. I sent the letter from the Mother Abbess to Sir Anthony at court as soon as you arrived."

"Although not a word have we received in answer," Edie muttered. "As if 'tis not the matter of the greatest import in the world!"

"Aye, but give Sir Anthony time," Jake said tolerantly. "It may be he doesn't have time to write a letter at once."

With dignity, Edie said, "I would have found time to write, if it was my long-lost granddaughter come home, and me with nothing to do but dance attendance on a king who has hundreds of courtiers at his beck and call." She handed me two pieces of cloth, pinned and ready to sew. "There you go, my lamb."

I sewed until bedtime, but next day, of course, I still had nothing to wear but my leaf-brown gown and mustard-yellow kirtle. I scattered stalks of lavender in the great hall to sweeten the air while Lettice walked with Dame Sybil to the village to light a candle before one of the saints in the village church. She would not say what she wanted or which saint she was going to petition, but I did not mind. I scattered the lavender among the rushes on the floor as evenly as possible, and thought of dresses the colour of lapis lazuli, rosehips and moss.

I was startled by the sound of a horse's hooves clattering to a stop before the front door of the house. Curiously, I looked out of the nearest window and caught my breath as an elderly gentleman with imposing features and rich clothes swung himself off his horse. He seemed supremely confident and very much at home.

I stepped back from the window with a beating heart and burning, throbbing cheeks. *Who can it be but Sir Anthony Bampton?*

Just then the gentleman strode into the great hall and tossed his velvet cap onto the settle by the fire.

"Edie!" the gentleman roared. "Edie!" He looked around and his gaze fell on me. I dropped a curtsy, and he said, "Go and get Edie this instant. I am faint and weary from the journey, wench, I tell you straight. Bring bread and ale!"

I blinked but obeyed with a sinking heart. I did not need Lettice to tell me who it was and what he thought of me. *'Tis my grandfather ... and he takes me for a kitchen wench!*

With a shrinking feeling of disappointment and dismay, I called Edie, then hid myself in the kitchen where I poured a tankard of ale and arranged a platter of bread, cheese and a ripe apple for the traveller. Nancy and Molly fluttered and giggled about the master's unexpected return. Silently, wondering what was going to happen next, I carried my offering into the great hall.

"Here she is, Sir Anthony!" cried Edie rapturously. "Mistress Clare, my lamb, put that down and come! This is your grandsire."

I put the tankard and platter on the table with trembling hands and approached my grandfather.

Proudly Edie said, "This is Clare."

I met the old man's gaze honestly but meekly – and thought I saw him wince with pain. He certainly stifled an exclamation. I dropped a curtsy and waited with my head bent.

"Get up, girl," Sir Anthony said gruffly.

I rose and looked up at him again.

He cleared his throat and exclaimed, "By heaven, girl, you are the image of your mother … but for that red hair. God rest her soul. I miss her still." He stifled a sigh, crossed himself and bent to press a fleeting kiss on my forehead. "Welcome home, my dear." He frowned. "Why are you dressed so poorly and working as if you are a maidservant? This must not be." He smiled ruefully. "I suppose you shall be wanting a husband now!" He sighed and drew his gloved hand across his forehead. "I am weary. Do we have ale to slake my thirst?"

"Mistress Clare has ale and some bread and cheese ready for you, Sir Anthony," Edie said quickly. "Sit you down, sir." She nodded at me. "You stay and talk to your grandsire."

I passed my grandfather a tankard of ale.

"My thanks." Sir Anthony slurped from the top of the golden ale and wiped his mouth with the back of his hand. "Bampton ale is the best in England."

I watched as the old man settled himself in the carved wooden chair beside the great stone fireplace. A small fire flickered in its depths. Edie poked it into life and slipped out of the room. I was not sure what else to do so I handed my grandfather the platter of food. He accepted it with a nod. I stood back, my hands clasped behind my back, watching the old man eat.

It was passing strange meeting my grandfather for the first time that I could remember. He was tall and broad with an out-of-doors air in spite of his advanced years and fine clothes. His hair was grey and so was his neatly-trimmed beard below deep, watchful eyes. His mouth, a straight line that neither turned up in laughter nor down in sorrow, looked stern and uncompromising.

"Well, Clare!" Sir Anthony surprised me by catching my gaze and asking, "What do you think of me, eh?"

"Oh!" I blushed and dropped a curtsy. Finally I said, "I do not remember seeing one of my grandparents before, sir."

"Oh, sorry about that, are you?"

"Yes." I spoke the truth boldly.

"Humph." Sir Anthony spat an apple pip into the fireplace. "Well, you saw us all often enough when you were a baby, if that is of any consolation." His face softened. "You used to smile and clap your little hands together when you saw me."

"Did I, sir?" I asked. Wistfully I said, "I wish I remembered."

"Some people are better pleased to forget their relatives," Sir Anthony observed dryly. "I arranged for you to go to Kirklington Abbey so you would live a holy and blameless life. *And* not be argued over by your mother's family and your father's family," he added as if it was an afterthought. "We never dreamed the convent would be suppressed by order of the king some fine day and you cast penniless upon us again."

He sounded so annoyed that I wanted to cry, which was humiliating. I raised my chin and said, "Perhaps my father's family would take me in if 'tis too much trouble for you to do so."

"Hoity-toity!" Sir Anthony looked at me with his eyebrows raised. "You sound like your mother too! Always thinking for herself, she was, which is most unbecoming in a woman." He looked severe. "Remember that, young lady!"

"Yes, sir," I said, looking down so Sir Anthony would not see that I was trying not to laugh in spite of the tears that threatened to overflow. It was not really funny, but I had never heard the Mother Abbess say it was unbecoming for a woman to think for herself. "But who are my father's people, sir?"

"'Tis no concern of yours," Sir Anthony snapped. I blinked in surprise, and he added more gently, "They are respectable people. No noble connections, but no bad blood either. Good, honest, yeoman stock." He raised a finger in warning. "'Tis all you will hear from me about your father's family." And then, relenting a little, he said, "Your mother married against my wishes. 'Tis what happens when a female thinks for herself – she makes irrational decisions based on emotional and religious fervour which is out of all proportion to what is becoming or healthy! I am glad to say I was reconciled to your mother before her death, but I must confess I have never become reconciled to her convictions or her marriage." He glared at me. "And I want you to understand here and now that it is *I* who will choose your husband!"

"My … my husband?" I blinked again. "But … but what if I do not wish to marry at all, sir?"

"Not wish to marry?" Sir Anthony looked as me as if I was crazy. "What else would a woman want to do?"

Again I tried not to laugh, although I knew the matter was serious and my grandfather was not to be trifled with. Meekly I said, "I have been raised in the cloister, sir. I have not thought of marriage until now."

"The Mother Abbess said you did not take the veil."

"Nay." I glanced at him, wondering how he would respond to my next words. "But it is what I have grown up expecting to do. I have not grown up expecting to marry." I smiled. *What would Sister Laura say about such a thing?* Meekly I said, "I have not grown up thinking about my … er … husband!"

"Humph." Sir Anthony stood up and laid a hand not unkindly on my shoulder. "All that – the life of the cloister – is over now. I do not think we in England shall send our sons and daughters to be monks and nuns again for many a long year. Count yourself fortunate, Clare, that you have not taken the veil and are therefore free to marry. I chose a religious life for your Uncle Matthew too and he, poor fellow, will be in a quandary if his monastery is suppressed because he has already vowed himself to a life of poverty, chastity and obedience."

"Will he come here, sir?" I asked eagerly.

"If all the dependants I sent to religious houses return home when their vocations are suppressed, aye, your Uncle Matthew will come here," Sir Anthony said dryly. Abruptly changing the subject, he asked, "Do you have any mind to come to court?"

"No," I said decidedly. But then, because I thought I sounded a little too much as if I was thinking for myself, I added, "That is, sir, I thank you for the honour of asking me if I want to go to court, but I have no mind to do so at present." Simply I said, "'Tis a great change, living in the world after living at the abbey for almost as long as I can remember. I want to live a quiet life, sir."

"'Tis well enough," Sir Anthony grunted and turned on his heel. "It pleases me to think one of my family, at least, will not be ruining me with dressmaker's bills and chasing after rich young men! Very well. I am taking Lettice to join her parents – your Uncle Thomas and Aunt Maud – at court, but you shall stay at Bampton Manor for now. I must return to court before too long but I shall return home at Christmastide and bring the rest of the family with me." He gave me a thin smile. "I shall find you a dowry – only a modest one, mind you – and a husband." His eyes gleamed with sudden, unexpected kindness. "You need a good, respectable man. Do not live in dread lest I find you an ogre. 'Tis no danger of that." He stretched and yawned. "Where, by the by, is Lettice?"

"Praying and lighting a candle at church," I said promptly.

"Eh?" Sir Anthony raised his eyebrows. "Of her own free will?"

"Yes, sir."

"And is this the result of your influence?"

I laughed at the thought of having any influence over Lettice, but said, "Nay, sir, I think not."

"Hmm." Sir Anthony frowned. "I know Lettice. She is not over-given to praying and petitioning the saints! The minx wants something. I wonder what?"

The old man stumped out of the great hall, and I collapsed onto a stool and tried to decide how I felt about my grandfather.

Edie crept into the room and asked, "What do you think of him, my lamb?"

"Sir Anthony?" Putting my jumble of thoughts and feelings into words was impossible. I laughed at the memory of his words about his choice of a husband for me – I thought, after all, he meant to be comforting. Briefly, I said, "He is no ogre."

I left my grandfather in the care of Jake and Edie while I slipped out of the manor house – with a shawl wrapped around my shoulders to ward off the chill – and hurried over the fields to the Ducklington farm. Walter and Mary Rose were always kind and warm. *Mayhap someday my own family will look on me with as much kindness.*

I ducked and dived around the low branches of the fruit trees in the orchard behind the Ducklington farmyard. In the shelter of the house, Mary Rose was hovering around the bee hives. The bees were buzzing sleepily in and out of the hives, gathering as much nectar as they could before winter, from the few flowers which were still blooming. I hesitated, suddenly shy, by the last of the trees. Mary Rose was wearing a blue shawl. *Blue for hope.*

"Mistress Bees!" Mary Rose exclaimed, her breath a white cloud. "Oh, Mistress Bees, you will never believe such news as I have now! I beg your pardon for not telling you before, but I have a new sister. And 'tis the happiest of secrets that …"

Merrily, so as not to hear her secret, I called, "How now, Mary Rose?"

Mary Rose jumped as if one of the bees had stung her and swung around, her face bright red, her eyes overflowing with the secret-keeping look.

"Why are you talking to the bees?" I asked as I joined Mary Rose by the humming hives. "Do you tell them everything?"

Mary Rose nodded but said nothing.

"Why?"

Slowly, almost reluctantly, Mary Rose said, "The bees are lucky. We tell them all our secrets so they know how important they are to us. We don't want them to feel overlooked for fear they get offended and fly away to some other hives."

I had never heard of such a thing before but, wanting Mary Rose to look less embarrassed, I asked, "Have you only just told them about your sister Aggie being born? I think the bees may very well get offended about not being told sooner! Have you told them about me too? But pray pardon for interrupting you when you were telling the bees secrets. I shall go now."

Quickly Mary Rose said, "There's no need!" She caught my hand and pulled me towards the hives. "You tell the bees a secret."

"But I do not have a secret!"

"Nay?" Mary Rose looked serious. "It need not be a secret that you tell. The bees love any gossip!"

I laughed and bent towards the hives. Shyly I said, "Mistress Bees, my name is Clare. I am come from Kirklington Abbey, where I was a novice. I live at Bampton Manor now." I glanced around for inspiration and caught sight of the chimneys of Bampton Manor across the field. "Sir Anthony Bampton, my grandsire, is come from the royal court."

"Is he indeed?" Mary Rose gasped. "And you are come here … to our farm?"

"Why not?" I asked. "Sir Anthony is tending to business or resting or somesuch. I do not think he cares overmuch where I am."

"Mayhap not?" Mary Rose sounded doubtful. "Surely …" She stopped, seeming to bite her tongue, then smiled and said sturdily, "Would you like to see the kittens? Walter found them in the hayloft. The mother won't mind you playing with them if she sees you have a care of her babies."

Eagerly I followed Mary Rose across the farmyard and up a rough wooden ladder into the hayloft above the stable. In the dim light I saw a nest, hollowed out of the straw, holding six kittens. They were playing and rolling, pretending to fight, batting each other with their paws and hissing.

"Oh … they are poppets!" I exclaimed.

I crawled into the hayloft after Mary Rose and accepted a grey kitten to cuddle. It was a tiny beast that was trying to look like a good mouser by fluffing up its fur, straightening its tail and hissing. I was mindful of sharp claws as I cuddled the kitten, but it mewed into my ear in a friendly way.

"What are you going to do with them?" I asked. I smiled into the little creature's big green eyes. "I hope you are not going to drown them."

Simply Mary Rose said, "Their mam is a good mouser. I think their dad is, too, though 'tis hard to be sure. We'll find homes for the kittens."

Wistfully I said, "I wonder if Edie would like one for the kitchen."

"Ask her," a voice said from the void of the cow byre.

I dropped the kitten and gasped as its tiny claws like needles scratched my hands. "Ow!" Quickly I caught the little creature and held it reassuringly. I smoothed its fur and felt it trust me again. Ruefully I looked at my hands and said, "I shall ask Edie for some salve."

"I'm right sorry," Walter said as his head appeared over the edge of the hayloft. "Did it scratch you?" He looked at the grey kitten in my arms. "That one's not spoken for, Mistress Clare, so you can have it – a girl, I think – if Edie's minded to give it a home." He grinned. "I'll answer for it that it'll be a good mouser."

"I *hope* Edie will have it," I said wistfully. I set the little creature down and watched it prance a few steps and pause to mew. "I always wanted a pet but the Mother Abbess was strict about the rule against dogs and cats. We had a kitchen cat, of course, but he was quite fierce – not little and gentle like this one."

Amusedly Walter said, "You'll find this one doesn't stay little and cuddlesome."

"I know," I said. "She shall work for her keep, catching mice, but she shall be my cat and I shall call her Madam Eglentyne."

"What an odd name," Mary Rose said with a laugh.

"'Tis the name of the nun in *The Canterbury Tales*," I said. "Sister Theresa had a copy of the book at the convent although I do not think the Mistress of Novices would have approved!" I reached out to stroke the kitten again. "I cannot call you *Madam* Eglentyne, poppet, for you are too little. I shall called you *Mistress* Eglentyne." The kitten mewed. Happily I said, "Lettice shall go to court and *I* shall stay at home and play with Mistress Eglentyne."

Lettice was in ecstasies about going to court.

"You see!" she exclaimed. She pushed her pewter plate of supper away with her eyes bright and luminous in the light of the candles on the table. "I always knew I would go to court!" She turned to me triumphantly. "Did I not tell you so?"

"Aye," I admitted. "I hope you find it agreeable."

"I will!" Lettice spoke without hesitation. "I will wear silk and velvet and dresses of the latest fashion. I will wear a thousand pins and it will not matter if I lose any, so I shall not waste any more time looking for those I drop! I will see the queen and …"

"You will be a very lowly courtier indeed," Sir Anthony said heavily. He cut a chunk of meat from a chicken leg and speared it on the tip of his knife. "You will still need to have a care for your pins. And a girl from a country family with no title and a middling-sized dowry cannot expect to conquer the court of King Henry."

"King Henry!" Lettice gasped. "I shall see King Henry!"

"From a distance," Sir Anthony said quellingly, with his mouth full. "The king is not likely to notice you, miss, I can assure you of that!" Severely, taking a gulp of wine from a glass, he said, "You will be very decorous and modest, stay with your mother and speak only when you are spoken to, Lettice. If there is any nonsense, you will come home to the country, I tell you straight."

Lettice blinked at him but did not seem disturbed by the threat.

Sir Anthony grunted and said, "The court is full of dangers to a young lady – a *very* young and *quite* unsophisticated lady – and those who love you best will protect your honour, but you must help by being a sensible girl rather than a heedless flibbertigibbet."

Dame Sybil fluttered with concern at the notion.

Unexpectedly Lettice said, "I was praying today that I might go to court."

"Praying, eh?" Sir Anthony rolled his eyes. "I might have known you went to church for something important."

Pertly Lettice said, "My prayer has been answered so I am content, and I promise I will do my best at court."

"Well … 'tis as much as anyone can ask," Sir Anthony said. He spoke grudgingly but heaved a sigh of relief. He turned to me and asked, "What of you, miss? How will you occupy yourself while your family are at court?" He did not wait for an answer but nodded at Dame Sybil. "You will see to it my granddaughter leads a comfortable life at Bampton Manor."

"Yes, sir," Dame Sybil said. She smiled at me. "Clare will be as safe and happy here as I can contrive."

"I suppose the girl can sew and embroider," Sir Anthony mused, as if I was not there. "Edie says she is teaching my granddaughter how to cook. Pray teach her to sing and play an instrument."

"As you wish, sir," Dame Sybil said.

Quickly I said, "The nuns taught me to sing … and sew. I am making some new clothes."

"Oh, aye," Sir Anthony said. "And none too soon, I say." He looked disapprovingly at the garments I was wearing. "I shall bring you some silk and velvet at Christmastide."

I was not sure whether I should be happy at the thought of having a fine dress or not: it was wicked to be vain, but surely a gift from my grandfather could not be wrong. And I felt happy, not vain. I was still puzzling over the difference between happiness and vanity, straining my eyes to sew by candlelight after supper, when a visitor was ushered into the parlour.

Sir Anthony stood and exclaimed, "Master Bekley! How do you

do, Reverend Father?"

I recognised the elderly man as the village priest I had seen at a distance in church. He was spare but sprightly with tufty white hair and eyebrows and a nose like an eagle's beak. He brought the smell of old books and a gust of fresh air into the room.

"Have a glass of wine," Sir Anthony urged. "How can I help you?"

"I heard you had come home," Master Bekley said simply. "I came but to wish you well." His eyes twinkled. "I would not have come at such a late hour if we were not such old friends."

"We are old friends indeed," Sir Anthony said. He poured a glass of wine and handed it to the priest. "I am glad you have come. Ah!" He wheeled round and gestured to me. "Have you met my granddaughter?"

"Mistress Clare?" The priest smiled kindly. "I have seen her at mass and heard her story. You are welcome in the village and the church, my child. May Christ and His angels bless your new life in the world."

I stood and curtsied with a blush of gratitude at his kindness. I had heard he was a kind father to the parish. *I am glad someone will have the care of my soul now I am away from the Mother Abbess.*

As if he had guessed my thoughts, the priest nodded and said, "If you ever feel in need of advice – especially when your grandfather is away at court – you may come to me for help. I am almost always to be found in the church or the priest's house." His eyes had a far-away look in them. "I remember your mother. She used to come and find me in my garden, tending my roses or my bees, to ask me what I thought of some new book or other she was reading."

"She read too many books," Sir Anthony snapped. He looked at me with suddenly beetling eyes. "Do you read?"

"A little, that is to say, not a lot," I stammered. "I have my Psalter and my Book of Hours. We had the *Gospels* at the convent. The nuns read *De Doctrina Christiana* by St Augustine and *Summa Theologica* by Thomas Aquinus. I read *Advice to Anchoresses* with the Mistress of Novices."

I blushed and took a deep breath to confess I had read Erasmus's *Adagia* – a collection of proverbs – and More's *Utopia* too. I thought it would be wiser not to mention Doctor Luther's books and catechisms. I had, after all, only read a few passages here and there when Bess asked me to.

"Oh … is that all?" Sir Anthony sighed with relief and did not give me a chance to say anything else. "You cannot go wrong with books like those." He placed an arm around the stooped shoulders of the priest. "Shall we leave the ladies to their embroidery, my friend? I have much I wish to discuss and there is a fire in the great hall."

Lettice wrinkled her nose when the men had left. Coolly she said, "My honoured mother said Aunt Clare was a reformer who read books by Doctor Luther. I did not know *then* that Aunt Clare was your mother, cloister girl." She gazed at her embroidery as if it was the most important thing in the world. "I would not read anything by Doctor Luther, if I were you, even if *she* did and even if she was my mother, if I wanted to please my honoured grandfather."

I wanted to say it was Bess, not me, who read books by Doctor Luther, but I ignored the point of Lettice's words and asked, "Did not the king write a book against Doctor Luther?"

"He did and he was granted the title *Defender of the Faith* for his work," Dame Sybil said. "Queen Catherine was granted the title too."

I nodded absently, but my heart was glowing. Anything about my mother was precious – especially the fact that she had read some of the same books I had read … even if she had read them of her own free will and I had read them only to please my friend. *My mother was a reformer like the Ducklington's father.* But I said nothing and Lettice, too, was silent. *Did my mother ever thank God for all of His gifts through Jesus Christ Our Lord as I do?*

I was on my way up the stairs with a taper in my hand when my grandfather called, "Clare?"

"Aye?" I turned back and the light shone down into the old man's face. He was smiling. Respectfully I asked, "How may I serve you, sir?"

Unexpectedly the old man said, "By being up betimes in the morning and ready to ride."

"But I do not want to go to court!" I blurted.

"You are not going to court," Sir Anthony said impatiently. "When I return at Christmastide, I expect to find you happy, for which you need friends. Master Beckley agrees with me. There is no danger of *you* becoming a flibbertigibbet!"

In search of friends for me, therefore, Sir Anthony ordered a groom to saddle his horse early next morning. He mounted the animal and pulled me up to ride pillion behind him. I held onto his belt while the horse ambled from Bampton Manor to Drayton Court, where Bess and her sister lived. The stone house was a little larger and grander than Bampton Manor, but very pretty, nestled among a formal garden, with box hedges and paved walks, which I guessed would be lovely in summer. We dismounted and a serving man ushered us into a wood-panelled parlour where a crowd of girls were sitting with embroidery and books.

"Clare!" Bess cried. She flew across the room to hug me. "I cannot tell you how glad I am to see you again!"

"Bess!" I exclaimed. "And I am happy to see you too!" I remembered my grandfather and said, "Sir Anthony, this is Bess, who was also a novice."

Bess blushed and dropped a deep, respectful curtsy. "Sir Anthony, I beg your pardon, I did not see you there." She smiled. "Clare and I are the best of friends!"

"So I see," Sir Anthony said. "I am glad of it." He looked round the room and bowed to the other girls, who stood up and curtsied. "With your permission – Mistress Katy and Mistress Mary – I would like to introduce my granddaughter Clare."

The taller girl came forward. She was quiet and womanly, but she had bright, luminous eyes like Bess and a pretty laugh.

"'Tis an honour to know you," she said. "I am Katy Drayton. I have heard of you from my sister Bess. And this is my sister Mary." A younger girl with blue eyes and golden curls smiled with a shy blush. Katy continued, "I wish my mother was here, but she and her gentlewoman are busy in the still room this morning. Will you come and sit by the fire?"

Sir Anthony bowed and said, "With your permission, young ladies, I shall seek your father in order to pay my respects." We curtsied and the old man left the room.

Bess drew me further into the room. It was homely and cluttered with embroidery in hoops, a half-sewn dress and an open receipt book scattered across the table with a quill pen and bottle of ink beside a bunch of dried lavender. A lute and a pile of music resided in the corner of the settle. Someone had arranged a rainbow of silk embroidery threads over the carved back of a wooden chair. I felt comfortably at home and sat on the cushioned seat of the settle between Katy and Bess with Mary on a stool nearby. Shyly we looked at each other, then Bess and I caught each other's eyes and giggled.

Katy asked, "Is it very strange, Mistress Clare, living in the world after living in a convent?"

"Bess says she finds it a little strange, but she is glad to be home and we are gladder than glad she is here again!" Mary exclaimed.

The three sisters shared a smile, and I longed again for brothers and sisters of my own.

Sweetly Bess said, "Clare was like a sister to me at the convent, and I am glad we are together in the world now."

I smiled at her and said, "The world is passing strange. I find I have a great deal to learn about … well … most everything it seems!" I grimaced a little at the recollection of my failures with baking bread and spinning wool. I glanced at Bess and said, "You were right, though, it *is* beautiful!"

Bess smiled and blinked away tears.

"And it seems full of kind people," I added. "Some of my neighbours are Walter and Mary Rose Ducklington, and I have met Roger Chastleton too."

"He is here today," Mary said.

Katy explained, "He and his father are consulting our honoured father at present on some matter of business, but mayhap you will see him before you go." She smiled. "I am acquainted with most of the gentle folks and yeoman farmers in the parish and I know the Ducklingtons are good, honest farming folk and …"

The parlour door opened with a bang, and a head of ruffled hair looked around it while a voice asked, "May I come in? I have been exiled from your father's presence as a callow youth!"

We all stood up and Katy said, "Mistress Clare, I think you know Roger Chastleton." She frowned in pretended severity at the newcomer. "Pray come in, sir, and make your bow to Mistress Clare. Roger, she says she knows you already."

Roger Chastleton burst into the room. He was dressed less finely than before, wearing a simple wool doublet and hose and a leather belt, with a black blot of something on his nose. He had a quill pen in his hand and I guessed the blot was ink. I smiled, as our eyes met, because I could not help it.

"Mistress Clare!" He came forward with a bound and a grin, reminding me all over again of an amiable daddy-long-legs. Enthusiastically he said, "We meet again!"

"How?" Bess asked curiously. Everyone looked at her and she blushed. "Pray pardon. I mean … how comes it that you know each other? We grew up with Roger but you grew up in the convent and he was never there as far as I know!"

Enthusiastically, Roger said, "We met in Kirklington. Mistress Clare helped a blind dame when the village children were cruel to her and her little boy."

"Truly?" Bess asked. "I suppose 'twas Blind Dame Mary you helped. But when?"

"'Twas when Old Peter took me home," I said. "But Roger Chastleton helped me *and* Dame Mary, so he deserves the most praise."

"I was riding through Kirklington and heard Mistress Clare call for help." Roger grinned at me. "I thought at first you were Mary

Rose Ducklington, but now I know you are not."

"No, indeed," Katy said, sounding a little bit shocked.

But Mary giggled. "You *do* look like Mary Rose."

Roger shrugged and said, "'Tis an odd thing, but I am glad to know Mistress Clare too." He bowed as if he was a court gallant and I was a fair lady. Bess giggled and I blushed. Changing the subject, Roger said, "Sir Anthony Bampton says you come from Kirklington Abbey like Mistress Bess. It is famous hereabouts for its library and scriptorium. Did you ever see the nuns writing and illuminating books?"

I blushed and hesitated but Bess said, "Of a certainty!"

"My parents say 'tis a marvellous thing to watch someone who is trained in the art of writing or illuminating," Roger said. "They would envy you the privilege of watching books being made." He grinned and rubbed his nose. "I must confess I am all for printing because …" His hand came away from his nose smeared with ink. For a heartbeat he looked at it in dismay. "By all the saints, I beg your pardon, but what is amiss?" He rubbed his nose and the blot grew larger. "Is that a little better?" he asked anxiously.

Bess and her sisters were giggling, and I wanted to laugh too, but I did not want to hurt Roger's feelings. Gently I said, "I fear it is a little worse, sir. I think 'tis … ink?"

"Oh." Roger looked at the ink on his fingers and at the quill pen in his other hand. "I am not old or grand enough to be 'sir', but I fear you are right about it being ink."

He looked so crestfallen – so little like the exuberant, joyous daddy-long-legs who had burst into the room – that I wanted to cheer and comfort him somehow. Impulsively I said, "Pray do not worry on my account. I often do the same when I am painting. I get a little lapis lazuli on my fingers, then I touch my face and *then* I go to prayers adorned like an illuminated manuscript. 'Tis very lowering!"

"Very!" Roger said cordially, but he looked less embarrassed. Curiously he asked, "When do you paint? And what, pray, do you paint?"

"Oh!" I blushed and mumbled, "'Tis something I did at the abbey because I … I was trained in the art of illumination." The last words were almost a whisper and Roger had to duck his head to hear.

"I think that sounds very interesting," he said. He looked sincere and as if he had a lot more questions hovering on the end of his tongue. His arched eyebrows were peaked enquiringly, but all he said was, "Mayhap you will tell me more about your painting another time … perhaps when I do *not* have an ink blot on my nose!" In a whisper he confided, "I fear I blot everything I write so, of course, I have a great deal of sympathy for those who say print is cleaner and easier to read. I think I would like to be a printer if I was not to be a wool merchant. But …"

The door opened, and three gentlemen entered. One was Sir Anthony and the others, I guessed, were Roger's father, Master Chastleton and Bess's father, Sir Philip Drayton. Roger looked around and caught sight of Sir Anthony. Instantly his demeanour changed. He looked as quiet and respectful as a young man should as he bowed. *Like a daddy-long-legs on his best behaviour.*

"How do you do, sir?" Roger said. "We are enjoying good weather this autumn."

"Very," Sir Anthony said dryly. He nodded at me. "Come, Clare, we must be going."

The gentlemen, however, began to bid each other a long and elaborate farewell, so Bess pinched my arm and whispered, "Are you well?"

"Well enough," I said. And then I whispered, "Oh, Bess, *everything* is different in the world!"

"'Tis harder for you than for me," Bess admitted. "I still verily believe, Clare, your gift for noticing beauty and illuminating it for others to see and understand is a gift of great value to offer the world. 'Twill be an adventure finding a way!" Tentatively she asked, "Are you enjoying the adventure of living in the world a *little* bit?"

I started to shake my head but I could not help smiling as I thought of all the lovely things about my new life. I hugged Bess and spoke around the lump in my throat: "Mayhap a *very* little bit." I stood back and confessed, "I feel all wrong, somehow, in the world. 'Tis all very well to … to notice beauty and illuminate it, but I cannot make bread or spin wool."

Bess looked sympathetic.

"I believe Edie despairs of me being a notable housewife someday," I confided. "Even the hens would not eat my bread yesterday, and I spun only a handsbreadth of wool!"

The gentleman were still bowing and paying each other compliments – although I thought I heard them talk of crops and prices too – and Bess pulled me behind the settle. Earnestly she said, "Pray remember how long it took for you to learn how to sing … and embroider … and illuminate. But now you do all those things as finely as any of the nuns. I swear you will be a notable housewife someday." Tears shone in her eyes. "Your skill in illuminating *is* a gift – and mayhap 'tis less about drawing pictures and mixing paints and more about seeing the world a certain way. You see beauty everywhere. And you always live with courage, with kindness and most of all with hope."

"Do I?" I asked.

"Always."

Sir Anthony called my name, and Bess pushed me gently out from behind the settle and back into the world again.

I thought about what Bess had said as Sir Anthony's horse jogged back towards Bampton Manor. I thanked my grandfather for his kindness and slipped away to the porch chamber. Suddenly I wanted to paint flowers and saints in bright, heavenly colours that would be beautiful forever.

*I said I would never illuminate again.* I leaned against the door and looked at my coffer. *But mayhap I could just look at the tools of the scriptorium and the manuscript in my coffer.*

Breathlessly, thinking of the nuns and how carefully they had packed my things, I knelt beside my coffer and lifted the lid. Quickly I lifted my spare smocks, petticoats and stockings out of the coffer. I placed my tiny books on the stool before the rosary. And then, taking a deep breath, I lifted the sheepskin that covered the Book of Hours manuscript and the paints and tools in the bottom of my coffer. Instantly, as I saw the little earthenware pots and smelt the ingredients of the paint, I was transported to the scriptorium in my heart.

I laid the manuscript on my bed and smoothed the parchment. One by one, I lifted the pots out of my coffer and raised their lids to peep inside before arranging them carefully on the floor. There was a lumpy package of something or other, which I did not recognise or remember, wrapped in another sheepskin, but I did not need it now, whatever it was, so I left it in my coffer. I found the oyster shells, quill feathers and paintbrushes and arranged them beside the little earthenware pots. Finally I sat back on my heels and sighed happily.

The manuscript of the Book of Hours was written in English: it was a Primer which any literate person could read. I studied the parchment and realised that I, not Sister Joanna, had written the manuscript. I looked at my neat, rounded script and decided it was fair enough but not as fair as Sister Joanna's fine and flowing script. Around the edge of the words on every page there were spaces for illuminations.

A picture of Our Lady was a usual choice for the first page of a Book of Hours. I needed to begin by drawing a picture in ink.

Quickly, with flushed cheeks and trembling fingers, I crept into the kitchen and made thick, sticky ink using sticky gum from Kirklington Abbey and chimney soot from Bampton Manor while Edie was scolding one of the maidservants in the dairy. Carefully I carried it back to the porch chamber and arranged the manuscript and the inkhorn on the flat, smooth top of my coffer. I took a quill pen, dipped it into the ink … and paused.

Illuminating was a craft but it was also a kind of prayer: a way of worshipping Jesus Christ with my imagination and my hands.

*Can I illuminate here, so far from the convent, now I am an ordinary girl not a novice?* I glanced up and caught sight of the Mother Abbess' rosary. I had called her 'mother' for twelve years and she had told me not to neglect the gift of illumination. I bit my lip and whispered, "Help me to do my work well, Sweet Jesus, here in the world."

Carefully, almost reverently, I dipped the quill pen into the ink and started drawing. Slowly, thinking of my favourite image of Our Lady, I drew the Virgin Mary with a book in one hand and her little boy, Jesus Christ, standing on her knee. *Our Lady lived a life which was different from what she had expected.* Mother and Son were smiling, almost laughing, at each other. In the background I drew the tiny abbey church at Kirklington Abbey with the rose window. *If God gave Our Lady grace then mayhap He will give me grace too.* Working slowly but surely now, biting my tongue in concentration, I drew a border of roses in honour of Our Lady. *Mayhap my life can honour Jesus Christ too.*

I remembered the ladybirds I had seen at Kirklington Abbey and in the Ducklington garden, so I added some ladybirds between the flowers and leaves that surrounded Our Lady, then I pushed a long strand of red hair out of my face and gazed at my work critically. And then, slowly, I let out a long breath of satisfaction because my work was good. But my eyes filled with tears I could not explain.

"Sweet Jesus, thank You for this gift in the convent and … and in the world." I sniffed and rubbed the tears away. "Help me to know how to use this gift and use it well."

"Mistress Clare?" Edie's voice called from beyond the door of the porch chamber. "Are you ill, my lamb?"

"Nay." I put the quill pen and inkhorn down and scrambled to my feet as Edie pushed the door open. I realised I must look a strange sight – sitting on the floor, in a cold chamber, wrapped in an old shawl with ink all over my fingers – and I was not sure I wanted anyone to know what I was doing. I stood between the door and my coffer and said, "I am well enough, I thank you, Edie."

Edie poked her head round the edge of the door. She wore an anxious frown. "Do not stay here and get chilled, Mistress Clare, I don't want you ill with a fever." Almost as an afterthought she added, "Mistress Lettice and Dame Sybil are asking after you for help with packing Mistress Lettice's coffer for court."

"I will come directly," I promised.

When Edie left, I cleaned my pen and put the lid on the inkhorn to stop the black liquid from drying out. I left the manuscript on the top of my coffer so the ink could dry. Quickly, rubbing my fingers on my skirt, I hurried to find my cousin.

Lettice was standing in the middle of the chamber she shared with Dame Sybil. Her coffer was empty and her clothes were strewn all over the bed.

"Here you are!" Lettice turned anguished eyes on me and announced, "I have nothing fit to wear to court!"

"Will not you have new things to wear at court?" I asked, perching on the edge of the bed, sitting on my hands to hide the ink. "Sir Anthony spoke of new silk and velvet dresses."

"I am sure he will not buy me more than one," Lettice said tragically. "I will look a dowd!"

"You always look lovely," I said honestly.

"I thank you." Lettice smiled faintly, then frowned. "What have you been doing, cloister girl? You are *covered* in ink! You look as bad as ever you did at the convent!" She turned away with her nose in the air. "I will never be chosen to serve the queen in *this*." She poked the blue dress I had always thought beautiful. "I need dresses like those the queen and her ladies wear!"

*Blue for hope.* I licked a finger and rubbed at the worst of the ink on another knuckle. *Hope for what? Fine dresses? A glittering career at court?* At least Lettice knew what she wanted. I smiled even though I did not know what I wanted. My thoughts wandered along the passage to the porch chamber. *At least I have my own scriptorium.*

# Christmastide

The Drayton girls and I often met and worked on our embroidery together after Sir Anthony and Lettice left for court. I prayed for the nuns every day as mellow autumn tumbled into sharp winter – with increasingly bitter frosts every night – as apple picking time and pig killing time came and went. Dame Sybil said I needed to fill my dower chest with items for my future home so I started embroidering a tapestry cushion. I thought of the Mother Abbess every time I opened my sewing box and saw her letter under the familiar jumble of my sewing things. I longed to open it, but she had said I would know when the time was right, so I waited for that moment.

One wintry afternoon, just before Advent, the Drayton girls came and worked with me under Dame Sybil's watchful eye. The grey kitten, Mistress Eglentyne, purred beside the fire in the great hall at Bampton Manor while I deliberated between two shades of red silk. *Dark red for love or bright red for laughter?*

Pensively Katy said, "I admire your needlework, Clare, 'tis so bright and cheerful!" She looked at her needlework doubtfully. "I fear my work is a little drab by comparison."

I looked at the lady surrounded by a bower of honeysuckle which Katy was stitching in cream, rose and gold. Sincerely I said, "'Tis very beautiful."

"Is the lady anyone special?" Bess asked with a teasing smile.

"Nay," Katy said, but she blushed. "She is but a lady waiting for her gallant."

Bess looked at me expressively and said, "I wonder who her gallant may be."

"Nicholas Ralston, of course," Mary said.

"Mayhap," Katy said. She blushed more deeply than before. "But pray do not suspect me of betraying my heart so lightly!"

Bess giggled and shot me a mischievous glance.

Confidentially Mary said, "Katy is betrothed to marry Nicholas Ralston. He is a wool merchant but he has a manor house in the countryside near Stroud. He is very handsome *and* very kind." Her small face was pensive. "Our honoured father is arranging for me to marry Peter Atkins, and I hope we shall be happy as Nicholas and Katy."

Katy smiled but said, "I am sure you will be, Mary. Our honoured father wants us to be happy, so he has chosen Nicholas and Peter carefully. You know he and Sir James Atkins have spoken about your dowry, so 'twill not be long before you are betrothed now."

"Peter Atkins is *nice*," Mary said thoughtfully. "He is not at all handsome though."

"As if that matters!" Bess exclaimed. She looked at her sister over her needle, which twinkled in the light from the fire, as she held it poised over her needlework. "He is a good lad who will treat you well and make you happy – 'tis *that* which matters!" Her voice was full of yearning, and she blushed and bent over her needlework again.

I often crossed the fields to visit Walter and Mary Rose Ducklington, and I liked to pretend they were my own brother and sister. Bess, however, felt like my sister in every way.

Quickly, hoping to ease her heartache by making her laugh, I said, "I wish I knew how to talk about ladies, knights and hearts too, but I fear I do not, for we did not speak of such things at Kirkington Abbey!" I laughed. "Can you imagine, Bess, what Sister Laura would say?"

Bess shot me a grateful glance and laughed with her sisters. Merrily she said, "No, indeed, I would rather *not* imagine such a thing! Sister Laura was a good nun." Soberly she added, "She was a better nun than I would have been."

"'Twas she who taught me to embroider," I said, determined to be cheerful, as I glanced into my sewing box and saw the letter from the Mother Abbess peeping out from under my needlebook.

"Did she teach you how to choose and match colours?" Katy asked. "You are not afraid to use silks of every imaginable colour."

"I love colours of all kinds," I confessed. "Blues and reds and greens and golds and every other colour … they are all beautiful."

"And yet I imagine colours were frowned upon at the convent."

Bess laughed and said, "Only for the nuns!"

"The nuns wore grey or black and white," I admitted. "But we … they … loved colours! The glass in the rose window of the church was beautiful – all the colours of the rainbow. The saints in the wall paintings in the church were bright. And in the scriptorium we made paints in all sorts of colours for illuminating manuscripts."

Boldly Bess said, "Sister Joanna said Clare had a special gift for illumination that was given to her by Christ. Her work is *truly* beautiful."

With a little blush, I shrugged my shoulders and said, "The nuns taught me the art of the scriptorium, and illuminating a manuscript gives me great pleasure. Even now I cannot see a bright colour or a beautiful flower or an interesting beetle without thinking of how it would look if I painted it on the page of a manuscript."

"'Tis a beautiful gift," Katy said earnestly.

"I wish I could paint," Mary said. "Do you paint here?"

"Well … I *do* have some of my work here," I confessed. I took a deep breath. "Would you *truly* like to see it?" Katy nodded and Mary smiled. I stood up and said, "Pray wait for me here but a *Pater Noster* while."

Upstairs in the cold, dark porch chamber, I gathered the precious manuscript I was illuminating. Downstairs again, my heart beating almost in my mouth, I spread the parchment pages on the table and arranged them in order so the Drayton girls could see the illuminations. The picture of the annunciation of the birth of Our Lord by an angel was finished. So was the picture of the visit of Our Lady to her cousin Elizabeth. The picture of the nativity was drawn in ink.

"Clare?" Bess looked up from the first page of the manuscript and the illumination of the Virgin Mary and the Christ Child surrounded by a border of roses. "Is not this picture of Our Lady like the statue in the church at the convent?"

I nodded and confessed, "'Twas my favourite statue of Our Lady."

"Mine too. And this is Kirklington Abbey behind Our Lady," Bess said. She glanced at the other pictures. "Our Lady is in the cloisters of the convent at the moment of the annunciation and here, visiting her cousin Elizabeth, she is in the village of Bampton." She studied the illumination of the Virgin Mary and the Christ Child again. "This picture is my favourite."

Bess touched the paint and the glimmers of gold – for the halos of mother and child, the gilt page edges of Our Lady's book and the glitter of sunlight upon the abbey – with gentle fingers. With a little start of surprise, I realised there were tears in her eyes, although she was smiling.

"Why, Bess, I prithee pardon," I said. "I did not mean to grieve you in any way."

Quickly Bess said, "You have not grieved me." She wiped her eyes on the cuff of her smock. "'Tis nothing. But …" Her gaze lingered on the picture. "'Tis a beautiful picture of Our Lady and reminds me of much that is close to my heart."

I remembered her crying in the dormitory at the convent and wondered what she meant. We exchanged a little smile and returned to the fireplace and our embroidery with Katy and Mary.

With a little sigh, Mary said, "I wish I could paint."

Katy said, "Your gift for illumination, Clare, is a gift indeed! The pictures are beautiful … works of art. I thank you for letting us see your work." She smiled. "Our honoured father taught all his children to read from a Book of Hours and at Michaelmas he gave my mother a present of a Book of Hours. 'Twas in honour of their wedding anniversary and he said 'twas done by the nuns of Kirklington Abbey. I see from your work that 'twas likely done by you, Clare, for I recognise your drawing and choice of colours."

Quickly I said, "Sister Joanna did the writing. I only did the illuminating."

"'Tis a treasure nonetheless," Katy said. She smiled again. "But come! Since you understand colours, Clare, pray tell me what colour to use next!"

I bent over Katy's embroidery.

"I would use this colour," Bess said, handing her sister a deep, rich rose-coloured thread.

I selected a softer shade and said, "I would use this one, however, because 'tis gentler and more suited to your other colours."

Bess leaned over for a closer look and agreed, "Aye, you are right, Clare."

Happily Katy said, "'Tis settled then!" She squinted to thread her needle in the dull light from the window and the flickering light from the fire. "It grows dark and stormy."

Mary shivered and said, "I wonder when our honoured father will …"

Just then there was a thunderous knock on the front door. We looked at each other and Dame Sybil a little anxiously.

Katy, her needle poised over her embroidery, suggested, "It may be our honoured father or a servant come to take us home."

Jake was coming from the kitchen with a halting step and grumbling words. The candle flames danced and guttered in a sudden draft, the door from the hall into the passage banged open, then the wintry wind almost blew a tall, thin stranger into the hall.

We looked at each other nervously but Jake ushered the man into the hall and helped him remove his cloak. Anxiously he croaked, "Oh, Master Matthew, I fear seeing you here today means there's trouble afoot."

The man was thin, almost gaunt, dressed in the simple habit of a monk. I had not seen anyone committed to a life of prayer since I had left the convent. The dedication in the man's face and the simplicity of his presence gave me a painful lump in my throat.

"You speak more truly than you know," the monk said. His eyes were intelligent, mild and haunted with sadness. "I have lost my home, my brothers and my vocation. Thanks be to Our Lord, I am alive, but I fear 'tis in body more than spirit. Good Jake, my monastery is suppressed, that is the awful truth."

"And I'm sorry to hear it, Master Matthew, I am indeed," Jake said. "Come you in and sit by the fire. Edie shall bring you ale and food. And, look, here is your niece home from the nunnery. She, too, has lost everything at the command of the king."

The monk crossed the room to the fire as I rose and curtsied. He raised me up and shook his head with a little smile on his lips. "Do not curtsy to a humble brother," he said quietly. "I am your uncle: Matthew. I gather you and I are alike, dear niece, fellow pilgrims cast adrift from all we know and love."

"I feel I have lost everything I know and love, but I think I do not suffer as much as you, truly." I lowered my gaze and confessed, "I was only a novice."

Matthew's eyes were kind. "Say not 'only'. But you had not taken the vows of a nun before you left Kirklington Abbey?"

I shook my head. "I wanted to but the Mother Abbess would not let me. She released me from the vows I took as a postulant and a novice." Sadly I said, "The Mother Abbess thought it best to send me home but I … I feel as if I have betrayed the nuns by leaving them in their hour of need." The words spilled out of my mouth, and I blushed. "I beg your pardon. I did not mean to speak so freely!"

"You have no need to beg my pardon," Matthew said gently. "You have done no wrong and spoken no ill of anyone. I share your sorrow that you were not allowed to become a nun. I also understand your feeling that you have betrayed those you love." His gaze grew distant and sorrowful. "I feel I should have done more for my brother monks, and yet I know I did all I could to save our monastery and I … forgive me, Lord, but I failed." He closed his eyes. "I have failed and our monastery has been suppressed. Someday, perhaps, I shall understand what this is about. For now, however, all I can do is grieve for all we have lost." He bowed to Dame Sybil and the girls sitting by the fire and tried to smile. "Good mistresses, pray forgive me if I am not the best of company." He turned back to me. "Where is my father?"

"Sir Anthony?" I asked. "He is at court with the rest of the family."

"Ah, of course." Matthew nodded. "'Tis just as well until I am a little more resigned to my lot. I have much to consider. Pray for me, dear niece, that I may know the will of God for me in the days to come. I must beg you to excuse me now. I have travelled hard and slept little for too long."

When Matthew had left with Jake, I said, "I wonder what my uncle will do now."

Katy said, "Doctor Luther teaches that the vows of monks and nuns are not binding in all cases."

"So I have heard." I glanced at Bess. "I do not know why he says so."

"Doctor Luther used to be a monk but came to feel his vows were wrong," Katy said. "He married a nun who felt the same about her vows."

I opened my eyes wide. Curiously I wondered out loud, "What of the fact that the vows were made before God?"

Firmly Bess said, "I think Doctor Luther is right. How can a wrong vow be right to keep – even if 'twas made before God? Doctor Luther understands such things."

Curiously, because my mother had read books by Doctor Luther, I asked, "What else does he say?" Bess raised her eyebrows and I confessed, "I read bits of his books to please you, but I fear I cannot remember all of what I read."

Bess shook her head but smiled. Eagerly she said, "He believes all Christians are saved by grace through faith in Our Lord and any Christian can live a holy life in the world. 'Tis not necessary to live in a monastery or convent. I *am* glad!" Bess blushed. "I am sorry if 'tis a sin, but I did not want to live in a convent, away from the world and everyone I love." Tears filled her eyes. "I am happy to be living in the world again. I think Doctor Luther is right and 'tis possible to live a holy life in the world and honour Him with needle and thread or pots and pans as well as with prayers and songs. Doctor Luther says the first and highest – indeed the most precious – of good works is faith in Christ."

"Mayhap," I said cautiously. "I mean to say, I think you are right about faith in Christ, but as for living a holy life in the world … everything is changing and I fear me where it will end."

Composedly Bess said, "I do not know that but I know one thing."

"What is that?" I asked doubtfully.

"Our Lord never changes … whatever Doctor Luther says and whatever King Henry does," Bess said very seriously.

Merrily I asked, "And is that all the comfort you have to offer my honoured uncle and I and all our fellow pilgrims cast adrift from our vocations?"

"It is the best comfort I have to give." And then Bess smiled and said, "And do not forget you have a gift from the convent for the world: the way you see the world. You see beauty everywhere." She looked at the greyness beyond the windows of the hall and laughed. "Perhaps 'tis why Our Lord has led you out of the cloister. Perhaps your gift is meant to be shared."

Later, lying in bed before going to sleep, I thought about Bess crying over the picture of Our Lady. I had never made anyone cry with my work. I dreamed of ladies and ladybirds that night and next morning, full of ideas, I burst into the kitchen. Edie looked flustered and hid something bright and soft under her apron with a fleeting frown and a hasty exclamation of surprise.

"I pray pardon." I took a deep breath and blurted, "Where does Sir Anthony keep parchment?"

"Parchment?" Edie echoed. She looked blank. "I do not think your grandsire has parchment, my lamb. What would he want with parchment?"

"Oh." I blinked in surprise. "I thought he might have parchment for writing letters and keeping accounts."

"He uses paper for letters and ledgers for accounts," Edie said briefly.

Jake looked up from the wood he was carving with his knife beside the crackling, flickering fire. Kindly he asked, "What be you wanting with parchment, Mistress Clare?"

"Er …" I hesitated. Carefully, not sure what Jake and Edie would think of illuminating, I said, "I wish to make a gift for a friend."

"Aye … for Christmastide," Jake said. He nodded thoughtfully. "'Tis the season for making and giving gifts, of course, Mistress Clare, but I reckon I don't know where you'll find parchment."

Edie, looking mysterious, said, "There's more than you making gifts, my lamb. 'Tis like your kind heart to think of it, just like your mother."

I glowed with pleasure at the comparison but asked, "Does everyone give gifts at Christmastide?"

"Aye," Edie said. "Most family and friends do."

Simply I said, "We did not at the convent." I decided it was a delightful custom, then returned to the real problem. "But where am I to get some parchment?"

"I'm sure I don't know," Edie said.

"'Tis an old-fashioned thing for a young lady to want," Jake said.

I sighed and retired to the parlour with my embroidery to think. The countryside, beyond the window, was hushed and sparkling under a thick gilding of frost. I looked at the whitened hills and bare trees. *It looks like a scene drawn in ink on parchment and waiting to be painted.* Crossly I jabbed my needle into my embroidery and pricked my finger. *Where on earth am I to get some parchment?* I pouted but dared to beg Our Lord, "I prithee, if 'tis not too much trouble, may I have some parchment?"

I tried to forget about it but later, when the watery sun had risen higher in the sky and melted some of the frost, Dame Sybil glanced out of the window and observed, "Roger Chastleton is here."

"Indeed?" I jumped up and scattered my sewing things and the letter from the Mother Abbess on the floor as I ran to the parlour window for a better look. "I can ask him about parchment!"

Dame Sybil looked startled but I was too busy, picking my sewing things out of the floor rushes, to explain. I looked up with a bright, eager smile when Edie ushered Roger into the parlour. He met my gaze and flushed, then picked up the Mother Abbess' letter and gave me a beaming smile.

"Oh … I thank you," I said. "I would be grieved, indeed, to lose that letter."

Dame Sybil said everything polite and proper and went to find a recipe that Roger's mother wanted to borrow.

I tucked the Mother Abbess' letter into my sewing box. I glanced at Roger uncertainly, then confided, "'Tis from the Mother Abbess."

"My mother always said she was a noble lady," Roger said. "However I hear the treasure of Kirklington Abbey was missing when the king's men arrived."

"The treasure?" I echoed.

"The relic of Our Lady's robe," Roger explained. "'Tis said it was kept in a jewelled casket."

"It was," I said. "It is … I mean … I did not know 'twas missing. 'Tis passing strange. Some of the abbey books were missing when I left too." My stomach clenched, and I bit my lip. "I wonder where the books and the treasure are now." I stared at Roger anxiously. "The casket was precious, but the relic was *more* precious."

"Mayhap the Mother Abbess took the relic into her care," Roger suggested.

"Mayhap," I said. I remembered Sister Rosemary worrying about the relic of Our Lady's robe, and I remembered saying the Mother Abbess might take it into her care. I tried to smile and said, "I swear the Mother Abbess did her best."

"To be sure," Roger said. He smiled again and asked, "But how do you do, Mistress Clare?"

"Very well, but I want some parchment," I blurted.

"I beg your pardon?" Roger blinked and echoed, "Parchment?"

"Aye." Eagerly, my words almost tumbling over each other, I repeated, "I want some parchment."

"I see." Roger blinked. After a heartbeat he smiled and said apologetically, "I am sorry, Mistress Clare, I do not have parchment but …"

"But why not?" I wailed. "We always had parchment at the convent, but it seems Sir Anthony has none and now you have none too!"

"I do not have a great need for parchment," Roger said apologetically. "I daresay my father may have some. Shall I get some for you?"

Relief flooded through me, and I nodded. "If you please, I should like that, if 'tis not too much trouble."

"None at all," Roger said promptly. "I am happy to help you however I can."

Spontaneously I said, "You are kind!"

Roger flushed and said, "I am not kind out of the common way, I assure you, Mistress Clare."

"Nay?" I was doubtful. "'Tis the second time you have been kind to me, and you always smile at me in church and at the Drayton house when we happen to meet."

"'Tis different," Roger said quickly. "By the by, if you do not mind me asking, why do you want parchment?"

I hesitated, and Roger peaked his eyebrows and bent his head. I took a deep breath and said, "Do you recall, sir, that I paint?"

Roger's face brightened. "Of course. What do you paint?"

"Pictures," I said. "I ... that is, the nuns taught me the art of illumination when I was at the convent, so I … er … paint."

Eagerly Roger asked, "Pictures of saints and flowers and things?"

"Aye." I blushed and looked away from his admiring gaze. "I have paints and brushes, but no parchment. However I want to paint a picture for Bess Drayton for Christmastide …"

"… and so you need parchment," Roger said understandingly. "Of course."

"Yes," I sighed with relief because he understood.

"I swear I will find the best I can." Roger frowned, and confessed, "I do not know how much 'twill cost if my father does not have any."

"Cost? I had not thought of that." I bit my lip. "I do not have any money."

Roger considered the problem, then suggested, "I will pay for it and your grandfather can settle the debt when he is here."

"I cannot go into debt for my Christmastide gifts," I said firmly, because I was shocked at the notion. I bit my lip again. Regretfully, feeling tears pricking at the back of my eyes, I said, "I thank you for your offer of help, sir, but do not trouble yourself. I will ask Sir Anthony to buy some parchment when he comes home."

"But that is no good when you need parchment now," Roger said. He smiled and raised his peaked eyebrows. "I shall buy parchment, and it shall be my Christmastide gift to you but you shall have it now."

I clasped my hands and said, "Oh … you *are* kind! But are you sure 'tis no trouble?"

"Nonsense," Roger said. "I *want* to, you goose." He nodded decidedly and the lock of hair that hung over his forehead bounced jauntily. "'Tis settled. I will bring parchment as soon as may be." Hastily he added, "I will bring it, that is, on one condition."

"And what is that?" I asked.

Roger grinned and said, "That you stop calling me 'sir'. I am not *nearly* old or grand enough! And, besides, I had rather we were friends."

Cordially I said, "And so had I!"

Roger Chastleton brought parchment before dark that day and I was happy all through the long weeks of Advent. Sometimes I sewed beside the fire in the parlour or the kitchen. Sometimes, ignoring my fingers which were stiff with cold and minding my candle which spluttered hot fat, I painted in the porch chamber. Carefully I copied the picture of Our Lady and the Christ Child surrounded by roses, the one I had painted in the Book of Hours manuscript I was illuminating, onto a fresh piece of parchment. I added some little details just for Bess. And then I added the gold and paint.

The preparations for Christmastide were less reverent and more boisterous than any at Kirklington Abbey. The cold turned my cheeks and fingers a rosy pink, but I felt as if I smiled all day long at the thought of the celebration to come. I threw myself into the bustle – helping Jake haul a yule log into the great hall and helping Edie weave a kissing bough out of mistletoe. I set a tiny figure of the Christ Child in the midst of the greenery while singing *O Come, O Come, Emmanuel.*

On Christmas Eve Jake brought armfuls of holly, ivy and mistletoe into the house, and I helped Dame Sybil decorate the great hall and the parlour with the greenery. Later Edie taught me how to make mince pies in the kitchen. Wrapped in an apron, to protect my new blue dress, I chopped the thirteen ingredients – including chopped mutton, dried fruit and ground spices – one ingredient each for Our Lord and His twelve disciples.

At about midday, Jake burst into the kitchen and announced, "Your grandsire and the rest of the family are here, Mistress Clare."

"Run along, my lamb," Edie said. "Stay! Take that apron off first. What a mercy your new clothes are finished at last and you look as you should!"

I did as I was told and hurried into the great hall, smoothing the skirt of my new gown and enjoying the warmth of the new kirtle underneath. I peeped out of the window and watched Sir Anthony dismount with his breath like a white cloud in a grey world. A slightly younger gentleman with a similar appearance turned and spoke to a lady, wrapped in furs, who was riding in a litter hung on shafts between two horses. Lettice and two strange boys brought their horses to a standstill behind the litter with a jingle of harness.

Jake and Edie welcomed the travellers, and the maidservants and menservants bustled around seeing everything was in good order. Sir Anthony and the younger man stood talking in the porch to Jake. Edie ushered the tall, languid lady through the great hall and up the stairs to a bed chamber. I gulped as Lettice swept into the great hall with rustling skirts. She looked at me critically across the room with a spark of the old hostility in her eyes.

I smiled.

"The cloister girl!" Lettice tossed her head and spoke contemptuously: "So … you are still here!" She threw her hooded cloak back from her face. "You cannot imagine how fine court is!"

It was not a promising beginning, and my cheeks glowed with mortification as I helped Edie with the last of the preparations for supper. As soon as everything was in readiness, I slipped into the hall, where the family was gathering. Sir Anthony greeted me and introduced me to the rest of my family. The younger gentleman was Uncle Thomas and the lady was Aunt Maud. They were grandly dressed and finely mannered beings from another world: that of king and court and – I vaguely supposed – of gallantry.

Lettice, of course, I knew – and the satisfied way she tossed her head. Our boy cousins, Geoffrey and Frances, were different. They held their heads with the same jaunty confidence as Lettice and were dressed in brightly coloured doublets and hose with short cloaks swinging from their shoulders and short swords hanging from their belts. They looked like court gallants who would easily eclipse Roger Chastleton's country finery. Geoffrey gazed at me with serious eyes, but Frances was a laughing, joking schoolboy who rolled his eyes at Sir Anthony's suggestion that I was, like Lettice, another cousin and almost like a sister.

Geoffrey pretended to cuff his younger brother and said, "Pray do not mind him, Cousin Clare, he does not mean to be rude."

"I do not mind him," I said. And I meant it too. Frances's cheeky but friendly pretence of dismay at the thought of another cousin who was almost like a sister was less hurtful than Lettice's consistent unfriendliness. "I always wanted some brothers and sisters, and I am happy to have you for my cousins now – even, though I am sorry if it pains you, if it means you have another cousin, like Lettice, as part of the bargain!"

"Not *quite* like me," Lettice murmured. She frowned at my gown and fingered the fine wool fabric without asking leave. "I recognise this cloth."

It was the glorious blue I loved … and I blushed at a sudden realisation. Lettice had worn a dress of the same cloth at the convent. She had not been interested in my new clothes before she left for court, and she must not have realised I was to have a gown of the same fabric.

Gently, but with as much dignity as I could muster, I said, "Edie cut it out for me, and I sewed it together myself."

"So I suppose," Lettice said carelessly. "It does not have the appearance of a gown made by a court dressmaker."

"I am not at court," I said, "so it cannot matter."

"Nay," Lettice said readily. "Perhaps 'tis just as well you are not at court."

My cheeks flamed, and I bit my tongue to restrain a retort. Quietly I said, "Sir Anthony saw nothing wrong in this gown, that he spoke of, when he was last here."

"I did not." I had not seen my grandfather approach but now the old man spoke from behind me and frowned at Lettice. "That is enough, young lady, there is no fault to be found in your cousin's gown." Lettice looked not at all abashed. As if it was the end of the matter, Sir Anthony said, "I asked Clare if she wished to come to court when I was last here, but she declined, stating that she preferred a quiet life." He glared at Lettice. "So any modest, sensible girl *would* in these days of trouble and unrest."

Lettice sank into a curtsy, and Sir Anthony walked away.

I was deeply touched by the old man's defence, so said nothing, but looked after him gratefully.

"Even so, cloister girl," Lettice whispered, narrowing her eyes as she arose from the curtsy, "*never* make a gown like mine again."

"Oh, stop being so melodramatic, Lettice," Geoffrey said

impatiently. "I wager you are cross because that blue looks better on Clare, with her red hair, than it does on you and you are jealous."

"I am not!" Lettice said indignantly. "Why should *I* be jealous of *Clare*?" She tossed her pale gold hair with a satisfied flourish. "Flaxen hair is the most ladylike. Pray excuse me. I believe my honoured mother is asking for my attendance."

Lettice floated away, and Geoffrey shook his head. Looking slightly embarrassed, he said, "Pray forgive our cousin, Cousin Clare."

Curiously I asked, "Do you always apologise for your brother and cousin?"

"Aye," Frances said. "'Tis very tiresome!" He spoke with a twinkle in his eye. "Geoff has such high notions of dignity and gallantry that I offend him every moment of the day. Since he takes it upon himself to apologise for me, however, I am saved the trouble."

"Do you mean you are saved the trouble of trying not to offend or of apologising when you do, you young monkey?" enquired Geoffrey.

"Both!" Frances said and pranced away before his older brother could respond.

I laughed, and Geoffrey laughed too.

"I am glad you are here, Cousin Clare," Geoffrey said. "Christmastide is the jolliest time of the year and 'tis pleasant to be gathered here together. Even Uncle Matthew is with us this year!"

I glanced at Matthew's tall, gaunt figure standing by the fireplace talking to Sir Anthony and confided, "He is very kind!"

I meant no reproach to Geoffrey, but he seemed to realise that it was not, perhaps, the most graceful of speeches under the circumstances. Hastily he said, "I mean, of course, it is very sad the religious houses are being suppressed and the monks and nuns are left homeless, but since it has happened, I am glad Uncle Matthew is here." Geoffrey changed the subject abruptly. "Would you like to come skating on the mill pond before supper, Cousin Clare?"

"Yes, indeed I would!" I said delightedly. And then I confessed, "I mean … I have never been skating before, but I would like to learn."

"And so you shall," Geoffrey said reassuringly. "I will teach you in no time at all."

"And will Lettice come too?" I asked.

"No indeed!" Geoffrey grinned. "She thinks herself too much of a lady!"

I wrapped my shawl around my head and pulled an old sheep-skin jerkin of Jake's – which lived on a hook behind the kitchen door, ready for anyone who needed an extra layer in winter – over my old leaf-brown gown and mustard-yellow kirtle, then went outside with Geoffrey and Frances, who carried bone skates slung over their shoulders. Together we tramped through the snowy gardens and a leafless spinney, our breath like clouds, our footsteps crunching with every step. I arrived at the millpond with tingling cheeks and numb lips.

The stationary watermill and the millpond were frozen into stillness by the cold that nipped at my nose and bit through my gloves to my fingers. The spot, so busy at other times with villagers coming and going and the water frothing around the great wheel which turned the stones and ground the flour inside, was deserted today.

"Yahoo!" Frances yelled. "This is better than anything at court!"

A bird in a tree was startled and flew away with a flurry of wings and a loud call of disapproval.

Geoffrey, laughing, exclaimed, "Hush, you young imp!"

"Why?" Frances demanded. He bounced to the edge of millpond and tested the strength of the ice. Over his shoulder he shouted, "'Tis strong enough!"

Eagerly the boys sat on stones at the edge of the millpond and laced the skates onto their feet over their shoes. They skimmed up and down, then Geoffrey slithered to a stop in front of me. Fumbling through his gloves with the straps, he tied a skate over each of my shoes, then stood up and pulled me to my feet. I was surprised by the slipperiness of the ice and the thinness of the bone blades. I wobbled violently and sat down abruptly.

"Oh, dear." Geoffrey looked concerned. "Are you hurt?"

"Not at all," I laughed. The frigid air stung my lungs with each intake of breath, but I could not stop laughing with giddy delight. "I watched the village boys and girls skating on the village pond when I was a novice. It looked like fun!" I smiled at Geoffrey. "And now, here I am, skating!" I laughed again. "I am sitting and laughing on the ice anyway! Pray help me up, Cousin, I fear I am stuck otherwise."

Geoffrey gave me his hand and pulled. And then he tucked my hand in his and started skating with sure, steady strokes. I followed uncertainly with short, jagged ones. I felt free as I never had before but there was a hand holding mine. I glanced sideways at my cousin. He met my gaze and smiled reassuringly. *Is this what having a family is like?* I sighed wistfully. *Will there always be a hand holding mine or will I someday be alone?* I wanted to be free but I was not at all sure I wanted to be alone.

A heartbeat later, something caught my foot and I plunged nose-first onto the ice. It happened so quickly that I was not sure what happened. My hand was wrenched from Geoffrey's, my palms struck the ice and my knees struck it harder but were cushioned by my skirts. I skidded and came to an abrupt stop, with my face full of snow, at the edge of the pond.

"Clare, Clare!" Geoffrey came skimming over the ice. "Are you hurt?"

"I … I do not believe so," I said breathlessly, trying to untangle my legs from my skirts and an odd stick which had come from nowhere, but was wedged between my skates. "W-w-what happened?"

"You tripped," Frances said, arriving as if from nowhere with a shower of ice from his skates, his cheeks and nose the colour of ripe berries. "You fell and skidded over the ice. My pardon for laughing, but it was *too* funny!"

"'Tis not funny!" Geoffrey exclaimed. "Imagine what Grandfather will say if our cousin is hurt!" He looked at me anxiously. "Mayhap we should take you home."

"Nay!" I sat up, then caught his worried gaze and laughed. Brokenly I said, "Truly, I am well, but I have never done anything like this before!" I wondered if this was how people felt when they had drunk too much ale at harvest time, because the air, exercise and laughter were intoxicating. "I want to try again, so pray help me up, Cousin!"

Geoffrey pulled me to my feet again. I staggered against him and my skates slipped on the ice, then I found my balance. Cautiously I let go and stood on my own.

"Well done," Geoffrey said encouragingly. He hovered around me watchfully. "Now try skating."

I took a careful stroke forward and then another. I was wobbly, but I was still standing. I laughed at my cousins in delight and just then there were shouts from the edge of the millpond.

"How now?" I thought I heard Roger Chastleton call. "Well met!"

Geoffrey swung round and started skating in one fluid motion. I looked over my shoulder, but as I did, I lost my balance and my feet slipped from under me without warning. I sat down with a bump that jarred my teeth.

"You *do* like sitting on the ice!" Frances said. He stopped beside me with another shower of ice from his skates. "*I* shall help you this time." Breathlessly, I clambered to my feet with Frances's help and pushed my hair out of my eyes. "You are well enough," he said comfortably. "You will have a bruise though!"

"I dare say I will!" I groaned. I rubbed my behind ruefully. My skirts were sodden and heavy from the dampness of the ice. "Never mind." I set my teeth. "I *want* to skate."

"Well done!" Frances said approvingly. He snorted with sudden, boyish laughter, then skated a few steps, his feet pointing in different directions and his arms waving, his body weaving to and fro. He stopped and looked back at me with a cheeky grin. "You have no notion *how* funny you look!"

"Do I *really* look like that?" I asked doubtfully.

"Aye," Frances said. "But do not fear. Everyone does at first. Try again!" He skated backward a few paces and called, "Skate to me!"

Slowly, I did so, stopping beside my cousin with a rush and a bump but without falling.

"That was much better!" Geoffrey exclaimed. He skated up with a grin. "Roger Chastleton is joining our skating party with Nicholas Ralston and Peter Atkins."

Roger joined us in the middle of the ice with Nicholas, who was betrothed to Katy Drayton and Peter, who was to be betrothed to her sister Mary someday. Peter was short and skinny with big ears and a generous smile while Nicholas looked brave and dashing on skates. Roger, wearing skates and a muffler wound twice around his neck with the ends reaching to his knees, made me think of a daddy-long-legs again.

"I propose a race," Nicholas said. "Let us go three times around the edge of the millpond and see who is fastest."

Frances and Peter jostled forward, with Roger, while Geoffrey and I glanced at each other.

"I shall be judge," I said.

"Aye, 'tis fair, as you are the only lady," Geoffrey said. He skated with me to the edge of the pond and dusted the snow off a stone. "Sit here. You shall skate again presently. Do not get cold!"

He skimmed over the ice to the others and the boys lined up. A moment later, Nicholas shouted a word of command and the five boys started skating in a laughing, jostling bunch.

I tried not to shiver as I watched the boys and declared the winner when they appealed to me. Nicholas had skimmed along at the front of the crowd. Geoffrey and Roger had skated neck and neck. Peter had skated at their heels. Frances, red and puffing for breath, had skated in the rear with his short legs pumping his skates forward in short, determined strokes.

Laughingly I said, "Master Ralston is the winner, but Cousin Geoffrey and Master Chastleton skated well too!"

Roger looked doubtful and said, "I fear, Mistress Clare, I am not 'Master Chastleton' any more than I am 'sir'." He came to meet me and clasped my hands in time to stop me falling again as I stood up and ventured onto the ice. He grinned and said simply, "Master Chastleton is my father and I am just Roger!"

"But you call me 'Mistress Clare'."

"Aye." Roger looked doubtful. "'Tis different." He smiled down at me. "I hazard a guess life in the world is very different from life in the cloister."

"Vastly different," I said.

Tentatively Roger asked, "What do you think of it?"

"I am not sure yet," I said slowly. My heart ached with a sudden, yearning pang for everything I had lost and everything I had gained at the same time. I shivered and laughed as Frances, chased by Peter, rushed past in a whirling ball with arms and legs waving. "I like it very much today!"

"I am glad to hear it," Roger said. He grinned and pointed to the bridge. "I will race you now if you like!" Roger won easily but I skated behind him breathlessly and joined him at the bridge. "Now I will race you to the watermill!" Roger called.

He still won but I caught up with him more quickly.

"And now I will race you to the stone where you sat just now!" Roger shouted as he skated away.

I almost ran into him from behind as he stopped.

"I skated and I did not fall over this time!" I exclaimed as he swung round and caught my elbows.

"You skated excellently well," Roger agreed as we spun together. Cheerfully he said, "I will have to be careful or you will beat me in our next race!"

I laughed … and then stopped as a man on the bridge caught my gaze. He was short with a florid face and shifty gaze. My stomach lurched into my mouth and my legs felt weak as I recognised him from the day I left Kirklington Abbey. It was Master Tolbert. I stopped laughing and grasped Roger's hands.

"What ails you?" Roger asked. He screwed his head round towards the bridge as I ducked to hide behind him. "Have you seen a ghost?"

"I wish I had." I gulped and whispered, "That man, on the bridge, is Master Tolbert. He came to the convent with Sir Hilary Cavendish and a horrible man with an iron bar when they ..." I gulped again. "He came when they suppressed the convent."

Roger frowned and said, "He looks like a toad. And he is staring at us." He gripped my hands and said, "You are safe with us. Do not worry about him!"

"But why is he here?" I asked.

"I do not know," Roger admitted. "It may be for no bad reason, however." He spun both of us round again and said, "He is going now. Come on – I will race you again!"

"Can we join in?" Frances asked plaintively. "Peter and I cannot keep up with Geoff and Nicholas." Roger ruffled Frances's hair and my cousin dodged and gave me one of his cheeky grins. "Young ladies miss a lot of fun, because they are worried about their clothes and their hair, but you see how much fun you can have when you do not care!"

I smiled and decided not to argue. But later, when we said goodbye to the other boys and walked home, I followed my cousins round to the back of the manor house and slipped into the kitchen.

Quietly I hung Jake's old jerkin behind the door and crept past Edie who was bending over a cauldron in the fireplace. Nancy and Molly opened their eyes wide and shook their heads but said nothing. I hoped I would reach the porch chamber without letting Lettice see how bedraggled I was, but I met her on the stairs.

"Look at you!" Lettice said. She turned up her pretty nose and held her skirts out of my way. "You look like a drowned mouse!"

Boldly, still feeling intoxicated by the fun and suddenly not caring what Lettice thought, I tried not to laugh and said, "I do not care. I have had the best of times!"

In the porch chamber, I peeled my old dress off and with it my wet petticoats and stockings, then rubbed my wet and stringy hair dry. With chattering teeth I remembered it was Christmas Eve. I changed into a dry kirtle and my new blue gown – *blue for hope* – with a smile of delight at the square neckline, tight bodice and hanging sleeves and the skirt which was gathered round my waist and full round my feet. I tied my hair tied back in a ribbon to match my dress and hesitated.

I remembered all the warnings from the nuns about vanity but more than anything, tonight, I wanted to wear my mother's necklace. It was so simple – a single jewel on a chain – that wearing it could not, surely, be sinful.

Carefully, so I didn't crease my skirt, I knelt beside my coffer and lifted the lid. Cautiously I rummaged for the leather pouch containing my mother's necklace. It was wedged between the side of the coffer and a lumpy package of something or other wrapped in another sheepskin. I pulled the pouch and the package out of the coffer together.

I held my breath as I shook my mother's necklace out of the pouch and admired it in the light of the setting sun as it shone through the window. A cross hung from a simple gold chain. The cross, turning this way and that in the dim light of the porch chamber, had an amethyst – *amethyst for faith* – in the centre. A flower was engraved on each of the four gold arms and at the end of each arm was a pearl.

With a lump in my throat, as I thought of my mother wearing it before me, I clasped the necklace around my neck and settled the jewel on my chest above the square neckline of my bodice. My heart danced at the thought of wearing my mother's necklace tonight, on Christmas Eve, when I ate supper with my whole family for the first time.

I stood up, and the sheepskin package tumbled off my lap onto the floor. I did not recognise or remember the package, but I pulled one of the sheepskin edges back from the bundle. As I did so, something within the package caught the last light from the sun, glittering gold. With my heart thumping in my mouth, I opened the package, revealing a golden casket studded with sapphires. I swallowed, my mouth dry, my stomach tight. I had seen the casket before but I knew with all my heart I had not put it in my coffer.

Dizzily I prayed, "Sweet Jesus, how is this here?"

Breathlessly I perched on the edge of my coffer and gazed at the casket with wondering eyes. My thoughts scampered and scuttered like frightened rabbits. Kirklington Abbey was dedicated to Our Lady the Virgin Mary, and everyone in this part of the world knew a relic of her robe was kept in a jewelled casket behind the altar. My hands trembled. I had been allowed to see the casket and the relic, as a novice, but I had not touched the casket … and I certainly had never touched the relic!

Surely the relic would not be in my coffer too? Carefully, whispering an Ave Maria, I peeped inside the casket. To my mingled horror and relief, the scrap of blue cloth, worn and thin around the edges, was where it belonged, safely inside the casket. My hands trembled more than ever. I shut the casket and took a deep, trembling breath.

The relic had been here, in the porch chamber, all this time! *I have been sleeping and saying my prayers and illuminating in the company of Our Lady's robe at the bottom of my coffer!* The thought of the bundle at the bottom of my coffer jiggled my memory of my last day at Kirklington Abbey. *Sister Veronica said my coffer was my dower chest for my new life, and Sister Laura looked shocked. Neither of them would put the relic in my coffer!* I bit my lip. *Sister Rosemary was worried about the relic.* I remembered her flushed and tearful face when I left the convent. *But how would she get the casket from the church?* I took a deep breath. *Is it a miracle of Our*

*Lord – meant to honour His Mother?*

Quickly, praying Edie would not choose this instant to call me for supper by knocking and putting her head around the edge of the door, I bundled the sheepskin around the casket and buried it in my coffer.

*Is it another gift from the Mother Abbess? Surely not. But why else is it in my coffer?* I knew I had not stolen the casket, but my hands were damp and sweaty although the porch chamber was chilly, because I was not sure who would believe me if the relic was found in my coffer. *What happens to novices who steal priceless caskets and precious relics?*

Vaguely I thought of being arrested and thrown into prison for treason, my grandfather and cousins being tortured for complicity and the manor house being sacked and taken by the crown for recompense of their crimes. I bit my lip and swallowed a painful wave of anxiety and nausea.

"Mistress Clare?" It was Edie's voice, dulled and thickened by the wooden door of the porch chamber. "Are you dressed and ready to sup? And where are your wet things?"

Quickly, taking a deep breath, I opened the door and tried to smile like normal.

"My lamb!" Edie gazed with her mouth open and her eyes damp. "Look at you now! Never have I seen you look so beautiful. You're the image of your mother indeed!" She leaned closer and touched my necklace with a tender fingertip. "Your mother loved that necklace above any of the other jewels Sir Anthony gave her when she was a girl. I remember she was wearing it when she came back from marrying your father in church." She nodded, suddenly brisk. "'Tis very proper that you should wear it tonight."

I reached for my necklace, and my hand brushed against Edie's hand. For a heartbeat, as I tried to forget the secret of the dower chest, we smiled at each other. *But I wish my mother was here now. I need her. What am I going to do with the casket and the relic of Our Lady's robe?*

Downstairs, in the great hall, Sir Anthony did not say anything about my necklace but I saw his gaze linger upon it and I thought his voice was more gentle than usual as he said, "Come, Clare, 'tis time to sup. We shall go to Midnight Mass anon."

I allowed my grandfather to usher me to the table. Everything was a bit of a blur, and I was grateful I did not have to do anything but sit and eat. Geoffrey sat beside me and offered me all the good food on the table. My heart warmed, and my heartbeat slowed. Sir Anthony was talking of court with his son and daughter-in-law, but I paid little attention until I caught the sound of a familiar name.

"'Tis said by Lady Arbelle Marbury that Master Chastleton is bidding to purchase the ruin of the abbey in Kirkington and the convent manor," Aunt Maud said. She ate a spoonful of pease-pudding and wiped her fingers on a white cloth napkin. "She declares everyone at court is talking about the suppression of the religious houses and the way the lands and ruins are being given to the king's favourites or sold with the proceeds going to the royal coffers."

"It will be well for Master Chastleton if he buys the ruin," Sir Anthony said. He took a slurp of wine and wiped his mouth with the back of his hand. "He has a good head for business and an ambition to leave a goodly inheritance for his heir."

"'Tis said by Lady Arbelle Marbury that he has aspirations to be a gentleman," Aunt Maud said.

Musingly Sir Anthony said, "His grandfather was a yeoman and he only has a merchant's mark, of course, not a coat of arms, but if he acquires a manor then he may do very well for himself and his children too." He chewed thoughtfully on a hunk of bread. "If he gets the ruins – and, more to the point, the manor – he will remain within easy reach of Bampton and Nailsworth but his influence in the county, in Stroud and beyond, will increase. 'Tis an excellent notion of his. Roger will inherit a manor and may marry a gentleman's daughter. But you say the abbey at Kirklington is ruined?"

My heart was thumping hard. Was the abbey nothing but a ruin now? I had seen the king's men with my own eyes. *But I hoped the convent had been spared at last. How is it possible it has been suppressed and the buildings have been ruined?* I thought of the nuns who were my friends and the Mother Abbess who was the only mother I had known before meeting Edie. Kirklington Abbey – with its peaceful cloisters, industrious scriptorium and beautiful church –

was my home. I loved it dearly and cherished it, in my heart, even now.

"Cousin Clare?" Geoffrey's words interrupted my thoughts. "Is something wrong?"

Dully I whispered, "I … I do not feel well. The abbey …"

"I am sorry." Geoffrey looked concerned. "Here, I beg, sip this …" He lifted a glass of wine to my lips. "'Tis very sad. I hope you will soon feel better."

Matthew, his eyes full of sympathy on the other side of Geoffrey, murmured, "You will recover from the shock, dear niece, in time. Try not to think of your home, your vocation, in ruins. Preserve the memory of it, as you knew it, in your heart."

"Who, then, is to marry Roger Chastleton and be the mistress of the abbey ruins?" Lettice hissed. It was not done for young people to talk at the table in the presence of their elders, but Lettice laughed and her voice dripped with scorn. "I dare say one of the local girls will settle for Roger, in spite of his merchant's mark, if he is to be the lord of the manor!"

"Settle for Roger?" I echoed. I stared at my cousin in wonder. "He is the nicest boy I have ever met and …"

"You did not meet many at the convent," Lettice said blandly.

I blushed and said, "I do not think it matters whether he has a merchant's mark or a manor house!"

In a superior voice Lettice said, "Most of the local girls want to marry a *gentleman*." She laughed. "Happy girl, whoever Roger's bride may be!"

"I am surprised you care," Geoffrey said coolly. "Roger – if his father buys the, er, abbey – will still be a merchant and *you* are determined to be a duchess."

"I do not care," Lettice countered without conviction. "I would as soon care if Walter Ducklington married a beggar girl! Roger Chastleton is no concern of mine." She ignored our cousin's crack of laughter. "You cannot think *I* am in danger of succumbing to the charms of a merchant – a mere owner of sheep and dealer of wool!" She tittered. "His bride, whoever she is, will find it a bit inconvenient living in a ruin!"

Idly Geoffrey said, "I suppose Walter Ducklington will be Master Chastleton's tenant. I believe he rents land from Kirklington Abbey: 'twas church land – part of the convent manor property – but I suppose 'tis not now." Respectfully Geoffrey asked Sir Anthony, "Do you suppose Walter Ducklington will pay rent to Master Chastleton, now, sir?"

"I neither know nor care," Sir Anthony grated.

Everyone looked at him in surprise, apart from Uncle Thomas and Aunt Maud, who looked at their plates. Their expressions were disapproving and embarrassed. Geoffrey looked hurt.

More gently Sir Anthony said, "You ask too many questions, Geoffrey, my boy. Count your blessings that this estate, your inheritance, is untouched by this madness. You owe no man for your livelihood."

Geoffrey murmured a reply and grimaced at me. Quietly he said, "I was but trying to take an intelligent interest in business that will one day be mine, but heigh ho, 'tis of no matter." He smiled. "I will contrive to see Roger as soon as may be. He is sure to tell us everything we want to know about this business of his father buying the abbey ruins and convent manor."

At Midnight Mass, led by Master Beckley, the priest, in the village church, the fasting season of Advent changed into the feasting season of Christmas. The candles flickered through the screen before the altar and brought the church to life with golden light and dusky shadows in every corner. Like a secret gift, I cherished the miracle of Christmas in my heart, first as the sacrament was administered and later as I walked home to Bampton Manor with my family.

The night, which was cold and still with a sky full of stars above the white countryside, felt like a dream. *The snow looks like fresh, new parchment waiting to be illumined with colours and a whisper of gold.*

Back at Bampton Manor the great hall was lit by the fire dancing in the fireplace and the bedtime candles were waiting on the table with mince pies baked to look like a crib for the Christ Child. Dreamily, warming my cold toes by the fire, I sipped a tankard full of a warm drink Edie called Lambswool: beer infused with roasted apples, sugar and spices with a frothy top that looked like the creamy fleece of a lamb.

"I wish you a merry Christmastide, Cousin Clare," Geoffrey said, bringing my candle through the dusky shadows. He inclined his head and whispered, "I am glad you and Uncle Matthew are at home for Christmastide. Sleep well."

"I think I am glad too," I whispered. I accepted my candle from Geoffrey and smiled at Frances as he joined us and yawned immensely. "May Christ and His angels guard you both this night."

I went up the stairs, lighting my way with the uncertain light of my candle, which wavered in the draughts that found their way into the old house. *I am at home for Christmastide with my family.* The realisation was a gift which I tucked in my heart along with the miracle of Christmas. Standing in my smock, my shawl wrapped around my shoulders, I lingered at the window of the porch chamber before getting into bed. My heart felt tossed to and fro by the events of the day: meeting my family, finding the treasure in my coffer and hearing the abbey was ruined.

"Anything might happen to me, because of the casket and the relic, even if the abbey is not sacred and has been ruined," I murmured sleepily. "But ... Christmas is here!"

Quickly, shivering, I blew out my candle and jumped into bed. I pulled my blankets up to my nose and warmed my icy feet through my smock. Drowsily the tune and words of *In Dulci Jubilo* wound their way through my heart as I drifted into sleep: "In sweet rejoicing let us our homage show."

*Suddenly there was a crash and a tinkle as stones fell from heaven and glass – all the colour of the rainbow – fell like raindrops. The walls of the abbey church crumbled and I was surrounded by the broken, jagged remains of the rose window.*

*"No!" I screamed. I felt as if my lungs would burst with screaming the word into the wind which whipped around the ruins. My heart overflowed, and so did my eyes.*

*Through my tears I saw the nuns, driven out of the ruins, while rough men swore oaths and waved swords. The nuns staggered under the weight of boxes and bundles. Sister Joanna, her eyes strained from her work in the scriptorium, could not see where she was going. Sister Veronica, bowed and slow with age, stumbled and fell.*

*I shouted, "I want to go with you and be a nun!"*

*The Mother Abbess turned from a great distance and said, "You must go into the world and live."*

*I sank onto my knees and whispered, "I cannot."*

*Suddenly the nuns had gone, and the abbey was crumbling around me.*

*"Why must this be?" I screamed. My voice rose, and my lungs threatened to burst again.*

*One of the men – a huge man with a barrel of a chest and a patch over one eye – turned and towered over me. He brandished a sword and leered, "And where are the casket and the relic?"*

*I tried to stand and run but my legs would not move. I was stuck. My sobs increased until they threatened to break my heart.*

And then I started into wakefulness. Breathlessly, I sat up in bed and pushed my hair out of my face. My cheeks wet with tears, sobs were torn from my chest and my heart seemed about to break. The room was cold, but I burned as if with fever. My head felt as if it was being struck with a hammer. *The abbey is ruined and the nuns have gone!* I flopped back onto my pillow and stuffed the edge of a blanket into my mouth to silence the noise of my crying. *Everything has changed and here I am, with strangers who say they are my family, with a piece of Our Lady's robe in a valuable casket in my coffer.* Wretchedly I sobbed into the blanket. *I cannot even bake good bread or spin strong thread!*

A glimmer of light flickered under the door, and someone scratched on the wood. The door creaked open a crack. I tried to hold my breath in the darkness, but my secret tears escaped in a snort which made me giggle in spite of my grief.

Edie slipped into the room with a shawl wrapped around her head and another draped around her shoulders. She looked like a ghost as she glided across the floor in a long, white shift with a candle held in one hand. She wedged the candle safely and knelt beside my bed.

"What ails you, my lamb?" She placed a cool hand on my forehead. "Are you ill?"

"N-n-nay," I sobbed. Edie gathered me into a soft, warm embrace, and I did not resist. Into her motherly bosom I wept, "The abbey is ruined and the nuns are g-g-gone. I h-h-hate the king!"

"There, there," Edie soothed. She rocked me back and forth,

gently, like a baby in her arms. "You're safe here with us now, and we won't let the king and his men touch a hair on your precious head."

"B-b-but the nuns …" I lost my words in my sobs. Finally I said, "The M-m-mother Abbess said I had to go into the world and live, but I fear I cannot. I am too s-s-scared!"

Gently Edie said, "You've come into the world and done a fair bit of living since you arrived. At Michaelmas that was – and now 'tis Christmastide! You can't live all of life at once. Just live a day … and another day … and another day. We'll help. And Our Lady and Our Lord are watching over you now."

Gradually, gently, I quieted and rested in Edie's arms. A tiny flicker of memory sparked in my heart. I could not remember how or when, but I knew for a certainly I had been held like this by Edie before now. I nestled closer and said nothing.

Edie's voice was like a lullaby now: "You've no need to rush, my lamb. There are good things in store for you in the world: a kind husband and a comfortable home and some babies of your own. The world can be very harsh, but it can also be very beautiful. You'll always see the beauty, my lamb …"

Later, waking up calm and contented in my bed in the light of dawn, I was not sure where the dream ended and the lullaby began. But now someone pounded cheerfully on my door.

I sat up and tossed my hair out of my face. Sleepily I called, "Aye? Is something amiss?"

From the other side of the door came a shout of laughter. In a squashed sort of voice, as if he was pressing his lips against the crack between the door and the door frame, Frances called, "'Tis Christmastide!"

Impetuously I bounced out of bed, dragged a shawl around my shoulders and opened the door with a bang. Frances was standing outside in his shirt. He was holding his hose – the cloth leggings that covered his legs and attached to his jerkin with little strings called points – up with one hand. He gaped at my surprise, then grinned.

"Merry Christmastide to you!" I called. I shut the door in his face. A heartbeat later, I opened it again and giggled at my cousin's surprise. Boldly I said, "I dare say I shall be dressed and ready before you!"

I was waiting for Frances when, still tugging his doublet into place, he walked gloomily into the hall.

"'Tis my beastly points," he said darkly. "They take an age to tie, and I durst not hurry for fear of them failing me and my hose falling about my ankles."

I giggled at the thought of my cousin's points letting go and his hose bagging around his knees and ankles as if he was bandy-legged, but I said consolingly, "Never mind, 'tis the season to be merry, so have some Lambswool to drink."

The Twelve Days of Christmas passed like a dream and every day was full of merriment and laughter. Friends came visiting and bearing gifts. Carollers and mummers came and Walter Ducklington winked at me as, muffled to the eyebrows, he sang carols in the hall with other lads from the village and farms. I went skating with my cousins, Roger Chastleton and the Drayton girls on the millpond. I missed the solemnity of the season at the convent but refused to think about the fact that the abbey was ruined and the nuns had gone.

Only at night did my heart betray me, filling my dreams with visions of the abbey church falling into ruins again and again, while the nuns stumbled into an unknown future. Sometimes I woke crying and Edie came with comfort, but sometimes I slept through the pain and woke to a new day and a new resolution to celebrate the miracle of Christmas with all my heart. I feasted, danced and played blind man's buff until my sides hurt with laughing.

On New Year's Day, in keeping with tradition, everyone exchanged gifts. Jake presented me with a spoon he had carved from cherry wood from the orchard. Edie gave me a grey woollen shawl, soft and warm, knitted with her own hands from Bampton wool. At church, I gave Bess the parchment I had illuminated and rolled into a scroll, tied with a blue ribbon – *blue for hope* – made from the cloth I loved.

I had added some little details, just for Bess, to the picture of Our Lady that she loved. Our Lady still smiled serenely, but there was a hint of kind laughter in her eyes. Kirklington Abbey still stood behind her, but there was a little house nestling in the shelter of its walls. The roses in the border were not all blooming: there were tight buds and opening flowers as well as blooming roses. Between the foliage lurked ladybirds and in opposite corners a lady and a knight peeped out with smiles.

Bess stared at the picture with tears in her eyes, then she hugged me fiercely and whispered, "I shall cherish it forever!"

I felt a little overwhelmed by how much Bess liked her gift, and I left the church in a daydream. *I can give everyone illuminated manuscripts for every Feast Day and Holy Day!*

"Mistress Clare!" Roger Chastleton called breathlessly. He joined me at a run and gave me a little bow. "Merry Christmastide!" He produced a slightly misshapen orange ball. "Pray accept this token of my … er … in remembrance of the season."

"Oh!" I gazed at the ball and glanced at Roger. "Is this for me?"

"Yes." Roger grinned.

In consternation I whispered, "I thought the parchment was your gift."

"The parchment? Oh … *that.*" Roger flushed and looked away over the churchyard. "I got the parchment for you because we are friends. 'Twas nothing." He nodded to the ball. "'Tis my *true* Christmastide gift. The fruit inside the skin is the best you can imagine. My mother candies the skin and uses it in cakes too."

I felt the fruit and sniffed it curiously. It was cool and soft and smelt sharp and sweet at the same time. I did not know what it was but did not want to hurt Roger's feelings by asking.

Carelessly Roger said, "I dare say the nuns did not eat oranges, but I thought you might like it, for 'tis delicious."

I breathed a sigh of relief and exclaimed, “Nay, you are right, the nuns did *not* eat oranges!” I smiled and dropped a little curtsy. “I thank you for your kindness.” For some reason tears filled my eyes, but I blinked them away and felt inside the folds of my cloak and produced my gift for Roger, a scrap of fabric embroidered with his initials and a ladybird. Helpfully I said, “‘Tis for you to use when you write – to wipe your pen, you know, when it blots.”

“So now I must thank you for your kindness too!” Roger said with a laugh. “‘Tis kind of you think of my pen and my, er, nose for I fear I am sadly prone to blots!”

“Aye,” I said saucily. “‘Tis why you are all for printing when written books are beautiful!”

“Well … aye … I suppose ‘tis so,” Roger admitted. “Printed books are clean and easy to read.”

I wrinkled my nose and said, “Printed books are not beautiful!”

Frowning, we looked at each other for a long moment, then broke into laughter. A heartbeat later, I realised my cousins were waiting. I nodded farewell to Roger, joined my cousins and carried the sweet orange home carefully.

I thought the colour – intense and vibrant – was remarkable. *What is orange for?* I was still wondering, later, when there was a knock on the kitchen door while I was helping Edie. I glanced at Edie, but she was arranging the vegetables for a salad to resemble the Bampton coat of arms. I rubbed my hands on my apron and went to open the door.

Outside in the kitchen courtyard, bundled up in jerkins and

scarves, stood Walter and Mary Rose who was holding Aggie's hand. As soon as they saw me, they cried, "Merry Christmastide!"

"Merry Christmastide!" I said in return. "Oh … I am *glad* you are come!"

I was full of questions about their Christmas festivities and how they were enjoying the season, but I did not know where to start. Meanwhile brother and sister glanced at each other with rosy cheeks and sparkling eyes.

"We have Christmastide gifts for you," Walter said with a slow grin.

"We hope you like them," Mary Rose added.

"And I have gifts for you too!" I blurted. "Will you wait but a *Pater Noster* while?"

Without waiting for an answer, I dived into the house, then hurried through the kitchen and up the stairs to the porch chamber. I took some little packages back to the kitchen door where I found Walter leaning against one of the courtyard walls and Mary Rose dancing up and down in the cold.

Quickly I said, "Pray come into the kitchen."

Mary Rose started for the door, but Walter grabbed her arm and said, "Thank you, Mistress Clare, but we'll stay out here." He dug in one pocket and pulled out a tiny object. He gave it to me and said shyly, "I made it."

It was a tiny carving of a kitten – like Mistress Eglentyne who was sleeping by the kitchen fire. Delightedly I stood the kitten on the palm of my hand and looked at it eye to eye. It had the big ears and tufty fur of a real kitten.

"And I made this," Mary Rose said. She pushed something at me and rubbed the bridge of her nose shyly. "I hope you like it."

It was a little purse that could be hung from a girdle. It was made of wool and embroidered with daisies. Tears started into my eyes again, but I blinked them away and thrust the little packages at my friends.

"Baby!" Aggie said seriously. She held out the little doll I had made. "Pretty baby!"

"'Tis for you," I said. I bent down and smiled at Aggie. "Merry Christmastide!"

"Mewwy Ch'w'is-mas," Aggie echoed. "I ta'nk 'ou!"

The little girl hugged the doll and and leaned forward to drop a fairy kiss on my cheek before I straightened up.

"A purse!" Mary Rose exclaimed. Delight tumbled out of her smile as she surged past Walter and gave me a tight hug. "We thought of the same gift!" She stood back and examined the purse I had made from a scrap of the blue cloth and embroidered with roses. "'Tis beautiful!"

Walter nodded and grinned. "And I thank you for this fine hat." He clapped the woollen cap I had knitted on his red head. "I'll wear this to milk the cows." He leaned against the wall again and crossed his arms comfortably. "I think the animals miss you – I know the children do."

"Me too!" Aggie tugged on my skirt.

I blushed with pleasure and said, "I hope to come again soon."

As I closed the kitchen door, my gaze fell on the orange from Roger, glowing in the light of the fire. Suddenly I knew what the colour orange was for. I picked the orange up and nestled it in my hands with Walter's kitten and Mary Rose's purse: *Orange for friendship.*

I ate the orange from Roger – and enjoyed every bite – long before the end of Christmastide, but Twelfth Night, the last day of the celebrations, was the best night of the Christmas season. The Chastletons, Draytons and other friends were invited, and so was Master Beckley. Edie and the maidservants were busy from dawn preparing a lavish feast with a boar's head, roast goose and lark pie with spicy puddings and warm salads. The guests arrived in good time for supper, and Lettice and I helped to serve mince pies and Twelfth Cake: fruit cake with a bean hidden in one of the pieces.

Everyone was in a good mood, so supper was lively with jokes and toasts. I laughed until my sides hurt, while Frances fell off his chair with a bump. Finally our elders retired to the parlour with their glasses of wine, but my cousins and I lingered with our friends at the table in the great hall. The boys cracked nuts and the girls nibbled sweetmeats while the last of the yule log flickered in the heart of the fire that crackled and danced in the fireplace.

"I want to play blind man's buff," Frances announced. "Who will play?"

"I will," Mary said. She slipped off her stool and reached for the blindfold Frances was holding. "If I can be *it*."

With a show of indifference – although I guessed he was disappointed not to be *it* – Frances folded the blindfold and wrapped it around Mary's fair head. She reached out, and Frances jumped back out of her reach.

"I will play too," Bess said. "You cannot have a proper game with two people only."

Geoffrey and Roger exchanged a glance and went to join the others. I supposed Lettice was too fine and Nicholas and Katy were too serious to play, but I joined the others anyway. The hall rang with laughter as we played. Bess, when it was her turn to wear the blindfold, caught me. Laughingly, I submitted to Geoffrey tying the blindfold over my eyes, then reached unseeingly for one of my cousins or friends. I could see nothing but could hear laughter from all sides. I picked up my skirts and made in the direction of Bess' familiar voice. Finally I caught Frances – who squealed like a stuck pig – and pulled the blindfold off. Bess popped up from behind Sir Anthony's carved wooden chair. I grinned at my cousin who stuck his tongue out. To my surprise, Lettice and Katy were playing, laughing as hard as everyone else.

When Frances caught Geoffrey, Geoffrey shook his head and panted, "Nay, I cannot! I think I ate too much for supper. I feel a little sick." He flopped down beside the fire and fanned his face with his hands. "Let us play something quiet now."

"We could sing," Bess suggested. She put her head on one side and considered the matter. "Carols and *The Twelve Days of Christmas*."

Frances and Mary stopped pouting, and everyone gathered around the fire. Lettice fetched her lute and accompanied us while we merrily sang *The Boar's Head Carol* and *The Cherry Tree Carol*. Everyone grew calmer as we sang *In Dulci Jubilo* and then my favourite carols: *Righteous Joseph* and *I Sing of a Maiden.*

I thought of the scrap of blue cloth from Our Lady's robe, hidden in my dower chest, as I gazed into the heart of the fire and sang, "Mother and maiden – there was never, ever one but she; well may such a lady God's mother be."

A thoughtful silence fell and I gave a little smile as my gaze met first Frances's and then Roger's gaze across the circle. Frances grinned cheerfully and seemed eager to be noisy again. Roger looked at me solemnly.

And then Nicholas, sitting quite close to Katy, broke the silence by starting *The Twelve Days of Christmas*. He glanced so lovingly at her as he sang that she blushed and everyone laughed: "On the first day of Christmas, my true love sent to me a partridge in a pear tree."

Katy, the next around the circle, blushed again and continued in the traditional manner: "On the second day of Christmas, my true love sent to me two turtle doves and a partridge in a pear tree." She glanced shyly at Nicholas as she sang and everyone tittered again.

Frances was next and he chose his own gifts before listing the others. Cheerfully he warbled, "On the third day of Christmas, my true love sent to me three thrusting daggers …"

Geoffrey's gaze met mine and we both rolled our eyes. Round the circle went the song. Everyone added a gift of their choice and tried to remember all the gifts that had gone before. Roger added six sheep a-baaing, Geoffrey added seven ducks a-swimming and Bess added eight girls a-sewing. By the time it was my turn there was a long list of gifts to remember.

"We promise to help you remember," Geoffrey said.

"And we promise not to laugh when you get it wrong," Frances said. His face puckered into a grin before he finished speaking. Honestly he said, "At least, we promise not to laugh *too* hard!"

Merrily, after thinking hard but quickly, I sang, "On the twelfth day of Christmas, my true love sent to me twelve sweet oranges, eleven horses trotting, ten apple pies, nine bees a-buzzing, eight girls a-sewing, seven ducks a-swimming, six sheep a-baaing, five gold groats, four fat pigs, three daggers thrusting, two turtle doves …" Triumphantly I concluded with all the others: "And a partridge in a pear tree!"

Christmastide was almost over, and it would soon be Plough Monday: when husbandmen started ploughing in the new year and women started spinning wool into thread again. For now, however, we seemed to agree it was delicious doing nothing in particular. Eventually Frances started murmuring about a game of follow-the-leader and everyone stood in a chattering, laughing group.

Suddenly Geoffrey glanced up and said, "Look! We are standing under the kissing bough."

With a grin he slipped an arm around my waist and drew me close to drop a kiss on my cheek. Bess was on his other side and – with a tiny hesitation and a slight flush – he kissed her too. Behind his back, Bess and I glanced at each other. I felt shy about being kissed by my cousin, but Bess was blushing a rosy red.

Mournfully Frances asked, "Who can I kiss?"

"Me!" I exclaimed.

Quickly I bent down and kissed his rosy cheek. He put his arms around my neck and kissed me back warmly. I tousled his hair and stood upright with a smile.

"What about me?" Roger asked.

I blushed and said, "I cannot kiss *you*!"

"Nay? I thought your true love sent you twelve sweet oranges and I know *I* gave you one sweet orange!" Roger grinned and leaned close to kiss me. "I think everyone has kissed someone now!"

I was thinking about *orange for friendship* and blushing so hard I thought I might burst into flame, but everyone else was laughing.

"Come along," Roger said. He dug Geoffrey in the ribs. "*I* am going to play follow-the-leader. You had better come and play too!"

The boys hustled away to play with Frances. We girls settled themselves by the fire again and watched the boys prance around the hall, leading each other in wilder and wilder movements, until they were hopelessly confused.

Dreamily Bess whispered, "Your cousin Geoffrey *is* nice."

"I know," I said. "I never met a nicer boy!" Honestly I added, "At the convent, of course, there were not a great many boys."

Bess nodded with a blush and a laugh. Leaning her head closer to mine, she asked, "Did Roger Chastleton really give you twelve sweet oranges for Christmastide?"

I blushed again and shook my head. "He gave me one and that, I swear, is *not* what I meant in the song!" I shrugged my shoulders. "I could not think of anything else."

"Roger is a nice boy too," Bess said. She glanced at me with a little smile. "He never gave me or my sisters oranges for Christmastide."

Simply I said, "We are friends."

Bess looked at me thoughtfully, and I wondered what my friend was thinking, but Bess was not telling.

The day after Twelfth Night brought rain and wind and it seemed as if the snowy days of rejoicing were to truly be succeeded by the short days and long nights of the hardest part of the winter. There was a long weekend between Twelfth Night and Plough Monday, the first Monday of the new year after Christmastide, but Uncle Thomas and Aunt Maud were talking about returning to court already. In the dullness of the afternoon, I tucked myself into a shadowy corner of the parlour beside the flickering fire, keeping company with my cousins as they played forfeits.

Geoffrey held out a handful of sticks with even tops and said,

"Pick one, Cousin Clare, to see if you get the short stick. If you do, you must pay a forfeit or tell a secret."

I did so and the stick was short.

Quickly, before anyone else could speak, Frances glanced over his shoulder at the adults – Aunt Maud was watching Uncle Thomas and Sir Anthony playing chess at the parlour table – and asked, "Do you want to go to court?"

"Nay," I said. And then, honestly, I said, "I mean … I do not *think* I do. I suppose it would be a fine thing to see the king and the queen, but …"

"The queen is nothing out of the ordinary," Lettice said with a toss of her head. "A little, drab woman is Mistress Jane Seymour. I cannot think how she caught the eye of the king when he was wed to Mistress Anne Bullen. *She* was beautiful! But, then, 'tis said she enchanted the king into loving her with her beauty. And in the end it did her no good for she was an adulteress."

I knew my eyes grew round at the thought of this beautiful, wicked woman whom the nuns had called *Naughty Nan Bullen*, but I could not help it, even if Lettice *did* think I was a simpleton.

"Nonsense," Geoffrey scoffed. "Queen Anne *was* beautiful, but she was also pious and virtuous. 'Tis said she was a fond mother to the Lady Elizabeth." He glanced at me in the flickering firelight and said, "'Tis also said she was a reformer. I have heard it whispered at court that her enemies plotted her downfall because she was influencing the king about religion."

I smiled a little and, thinking of Sir Anthony, guessed, "I daresay she thought for herself."

"Aye." Geoffrey spoke grimly.

"Sir Anthony says women should not think for themselves," I said.

"It did Queen Anne no good," Geoffrey said seriously. "For myself, however, I do not see why women should not think for themselves if they have good minds and honest hearts."

"*I* would never be so forward!" Lettice said. She tossed her head. "I shall let my husband do the thinking in my household."

"And just as well," Frances jeered.

Dryly – with an echo of Sir Anthony's own tone – Geoffrey said, "And you must hope Uncle Thomas chooses you a husband who can think wisely and well." Lettice flounced away without a word and Geoffrey explained, "Our uncle has not, as yet, had a great deal of luck in the matter of making a marriage for Lettice … and neither, for that matter, has our honoured grandfather had much luck in the making of a marriage for me."

"I know Lettice wants to marry a noble lord," I said. "Do you want to marry a noble lady too?"

"Nay!" Geoffrey grinned at the thought. Then, looking into the heart of the fire as if it was painful to admit, he said, "I was to wed a girl from a noble family, but my honoured parents and dear sister died, God rest their souls, then another young man at court inherited a title and a great deal of money, so her father broke our betrothal and married her to him before the end of a month."

"Oh!" I bit my lip. "How *crushed* you must have felt. I am sorry."

"'Crushed' is right," Geoffrey said with a crack of laughter. Philosophically he added, "Aye, well, 'tis what comes of being no more than the grandson of a knight."

I blinked.

Easily Geoffrey explained, "Uncle Thomas and Aunt Maud want Lettice to make a noble marriage, and they want *me* to make a noble marriage, too, because I am the heir and will be the head of the family someday. 'Twas not something my father and mother ever spoke of, but I suppose Grandfather wishes it too. We spend a vast amount of time at court for that reason, anyway, but we do not have a great deal to offer. Grandfather is a gentleman of coat armour and a knight bachelor besides, but we are from good, honest, farming and merchant stock with just the gilding of a title." He laughed. "I will be plain Master Geoffrey Bampton all my days and that suits me very well."

"How curious," I said. "'Tis almost exactly how Sir Anthony described the Ducklington family." Geoffrey looked at me sharply. Quickly, thinking he might be offended, I said, "He said they are good, honest country stock. Only they, of course, do not have a coat of arms or a title."

"Aye, well, there is truth in that," Geoffrey admitted. "Do not mistake me, our family has held this land for many a generation and we are an honourable family, but ..." He frowned as if he were looking for the right words. "We are respectable rather than noble, and all the noble matches in the world will not make us otherwise." He sighed. "Lettice likes being at court and is all for fine acquaintances and great alliances, but I would rather stay at home to tend the land, then marry a local girl with my old friends to dance at our wedding."

I looked at my cousin with interest and respect. Tentatively I said, "I thought you were like Lettice. Your clothes are so fine, and your manners are so gallant!"

Geoffrey laughed shortly. He glanced at Frances but the younger boy looked as if he were asleep, lying on the hearth, his head pillowed on his arms.

"I do what I must to keep our honoured grandfather happy but ..." Geoffrey hesitated and made an expressive face. In a low voice he confessed, "If I am ever my own man, I will take to farming my land and marry Bess."

"Bess?" I questioned, deeply interested. "Bess Drayton who was at the convent with me?"

"Aye." Geoffrey flushed and gazed into the fire. "I liked her when we were children, but then she was sent away to be a nun and my honoured parents ... well ... I was not here either. Now she has come home, and she has grown into a pretty, quiet girl with no pretensions to grandeur. I happen to know she is, besides, an excellent housekeeper already. She would be a better mistress for this house than any fine lady from court."

"And I like her too," Frances said, sitting up and speaking unexpectedly. "If you marry some fine lady, she will be forever scolding me about my manners or the mud on my shoes. Bess is a nice girl. She will let me be."

Crossly Geoffrey said, "I did not know you were awake and listening, you young imp!" He glanced over his shoulder at their elders. "Pray do not breathe a word of this to Lettice or Grandfather. He will make whatever matches he wishes for all of us. It is none of our business until he chooses to tell us of his decisions."

Frances laughed and said, "Have no fear, brother, I will not babble of this to Lettice." He caught Geoffrey's eye and added, "Or Grandfather."

"Or Bess," Geoffrey said.

"Or Bess." Frances looked disappointed as he gave this last promise. "'Tis such a good idea, though, Geoff."

"I know," Geoffrey said quietly. "But … well … we shall have to wait and see what Grandfather chooses to arrange." He held out the handful of sticks to Frances and said, "Your turn again. Choose that one. Now tell me what *you* want!"

I felt very wise and womanly as I watched the firelight dance over Geoffrey's face. He was older than me, I knew, but he looked very young today. I thought he had paid me the greatest of compliments by confiding his dream of a quiet life and a country wife. *He could not choose a nicer girl to marry than Bess. I wished there was a way I could help his dream come true!* I started with surprise when I thought Frances spoke my name.

Quickly I said, "Aye?"

"Why not?" Frances demanded. "Mayhap I can stay at home from court with Clare."

"Cousin Clare may be coming to court with us," Geoffrey pointed out. "And, besides, Grandfather will wish to find another place for you." He glanced at me and explained, "Frances has been serving as a page in a noble household – learning manners and gallantry – but his master lately died and his mistress has reduced her household. Grandfather will wish to find another noble house where he can finish his education."

"I do not wish to be a page," Frances grumbled. "You speak of wishing to farm the land rather than be a courtier. Well *I* do not want to be a courtier either! You, at least, will inherit the manor and the money from Grandfather someday and be respectable. I will not! I will be the worst kind of poor hanger-on at court." He made a face. "I cannot bear the thought of it! Imagine me wearing fine clothes I cannot afford and dancing attendance on rich and childless dowagers in the hope of inheriting a fortune that is not rightfully mine." He shuddered. "I have no stomach for it. And with the king turning into a tyrant, too, being at court is a risky business."

Geoffrey blinked at what appeared to be a revelation. I hugged another secret in my heart and vowed to pray for both the boys.

Shortly Geoffrey said, "Mayhap you can find a position at court and earn your living that way."

Frances made another face.

With a glance over his shoulder at the adults, Geoffrey assumed a resolute air and said, "If I was deciding what is to be done with you, young Frances, I would apprentice you to a wool merchant without delay. How would that suit you?"

"Very well," Frances said promptly. "I like sheep. And I like

Roger. His father is a wool merchant, and Roger is his apprentice, you know, so I could be his apprentice too."

"An excellent notion!" Geoffrey exclaimed, then he laughed and sighed. "These are all pie crust dreams," he warned. "We are none of us masters of our own fate. We can but pray."

"And have faith our prayers make a difference," I offered shyly. The boys looked at me curiously. I blushed but said, "We can pray and have faith in Our Lord."

A sudden light of hope shone in Geoffrey's eyes. Slowly he said, "'Tis better than doing nothing. I thank you. I shall pray, trusting that … what did you say, prithee?"

"Our prayers make a difference." I smiled into my cousin's hopeful face. "Christ hears our prayers. Mayhap He will be pleased to grant our requests or grant us grace to trust Him in our want. But we must pray with faith in Him."

"Aye, 'tis true."

Geoffrey sat up a little straighter. I smiled and thought of Bess – blushing at Geoffrey's brotherly kiss under the kissing bough – as I caught a glimpse of the strong, kindly, determined man I knew he would be one day.

Plough Monday came and Edie started spinning again. I walked to the Ducklington farm to see if Walter had started ploughing in spite of the rain. He had, but it was hard work because the ground was heavy and wet. I came back with my petticoats ankle-deep in mud, so I was content to spin instead of plough that day.

It was almost dark, and I was standing by Edie's spinning wheel, mending a broken thread for what felt like the hundredth time and trying to ignore the weight of anxiety in my heart about the treasure in my coffer, when Sir Anthony walked into the hall.

"God keep you," I said, as the spinning wheel started spinning and the broken thread was transformed into a thread fit for weaving or knitting. I stopped the wheel and curtsied. "How may I serve you, sir?"

"Carry on with your work."

I started the wheel again and looked at Sir Anthony expectantly as the wheel whirred and the teased lump of wool spun into thread.

"I am returning to court with the rest of my family," Sir Anthony said. He cleared his throat. "I want you to come too."

"Me?" I bumped against the spinning wheel and the thread broke again. "I beg your pardon, sir, but you want *me* to go to court?"

"Aye." Sir Anthony retreated to the doorway as if he did not care to linger and talk. Irritably he said, "Pray do not looked so shocked, Clare, I am not taking you to a den of iniquity! Queen Jane is a sensible women, who does not encourage any fol-de-rol and foolishness at court." He smiled thinly and added very seriously but quite kindly, "Edie says you have nightmares about the suppression of Kirklington Abbey: you need a change." He stumped away, then returned and said, "And I want you to see the king is not a monster."

I dropped a curtsy, then left the spinning wheel and the broken thread and went outside again. I pulled Jake's old jerkin on and was grateful for its warmth. The wind had dropped, but it was bitterly cold and the air was damp and heavy with the rain that had fallen. I hugged myself for warmth and walked down the paved paths between the clipped hedges of the box garden to the very end of the garden. I looked over the countryside beyond and longed, wildly, to walk away from everything I did not like about my new life in the world.

"Clare?"

I was poised for flight to another part of the garden, but I stopped as I turned and saw Matthew approaching in his habit and a cloak. His presence was restful, so I waited for him to join me. I felt my heart grow calm as he smiled down at me with kindness and understanding. Together we stood and watched the dusk gather over the hills and woods.

Finally Matthew said, "My father has told me that he is taking you to court and I see you seek solitude in your distress. I apologise for intruding but I thought we might share comfort." His gaze became distant, then he roused himself and said, "But come! You cannot stay here to catch your death of cold. Will you walk with me for a while?"

Matthew started walking through the purple gloom – *amethyst is for faith, but this is darker, mayhap faith in time of trial?* Silently, gritting my teeth to stop them chattering, I followed him along the paved paths.

"We both know the heavenly peace and simple joy of the cloister," Matthew said. "Now our world is upside down and inside out."

I breathed a sigh. "Aye." My breath hung like a white cloud in the still atmosphere.

"The great question is how to live a holy life in the world when one had been trained for years to do so in the monastery." Matthew turned, and I caught sight of his smile through the dusk. "Or the convent."

"Aye," I said. "I am still learning how to follow Christ in the world."

We walked to and fro in silence, then he said, "I think I shall find another religious house of my order."

"In England?"

Matthew paused, then he said deliberately, "Nay. I think not. I could find one now, of course, but ..."

"But what?" I prompted. "There are many religious houses, large ones with many monks and nuns, which are not being suppressed."

Matthew's words were deliberate: "Only small monasteries and convents are being suppressed at present, Clare, but the suppression of the larger religious houses will follow ... of that I am certain." I skipped to catch up with his long strides as he said, "I consider myself bound by my vows. I need a community, a brotherhood, to help me keep them well." He spoke decisively. "I shall go to France." He smiled down at me. "I believe the Mother Abbess of your convent was wise when she refused to let you become a nun."

I spoke pensively: "I did not understand why at the time, but I wonder now if she …"

"If she *knew* that times were changing beyond imagining and you would need to live in the world not the convent?"

"Yes. Somehow." I took a deep breath. "I confess I thought her unkind."

"Not at all," Matthew said. "What you call unkindness was kindness in truth and in deed. She wanted you to be free."

Softly I said, "She said I must live."

"Yes, *live*," Matthew said. "'Twas kindness indeed: she gave you a new life." He stopped and looked at me seriously. "I believe Christ desires you to live in the world now – and live with all your heart. With you rests the privilege and the responsibility of finding a way to a holy life in this new world of ours. You learned wisdom in the cloister – you must use that wisdom in your new life: now and in the future as a wife and a mother. You must find a way to transform the secular into the sacred by faith."

I gulped and nodded.

"My nephew, your cousin Geoffrey, is my father's heir and needs to marry." Matthew smiled again through the gloom and started walking towards the manor house. "He likes you well enough," he said musingly. "Perhaps …"

"Lettice would not like that," I said demurely.

"Nay!" Matthew laughed. "Nor would my father."

"By your leave, uncle, I do not think my cousin Geoffrey likes me well enough to desire my hand in marriage," I said earnestly. I thought of Bess but chose to keep Geoffrey's secret. "I believe he wants to marry … a different girl."

"Indeed? He is bound to do my father's bidding, but 'twould be good for the lad if his pleasure and my father's decree agreed. I was fortunate I had a mind for the cloister before my father announced he wanted one of his sons to be a churchman. Heigh ho! Geoffrey has time to make up his mind about his future … and so have you."

Matthew relapsed into thought while I blushed and smiled in the dark. Talk of marriage was still so new! *What would the Mother Abbess say?* A heartbeat later I knew she would approve and rejoice. *But I am not so sure about Sister Laura!*

"Come inside, now, you must be chilly," Matthew said. It was only a few steps into the manor house but, chill or no chill, he paused and observed, "Lettice considers Roger Chastleton her personal property. I suppose you have realised that?"

"Indeed?" I was surprised. "How can she think so?"

"Since she wants to be a court lady and he is a country lad, who must earn his living even if he inherits a manor from his father someday, I do not know," Matthew said. "Be careful not to trespass upon her pleasure in your friendship with him." He paused in the doorway and grinned down at me. "Not, at any rate, until Lettice is betrothed to her duke!"

I blushed again and laughed and said, "It is very strange, thinking I would be a nun all my life and now living in the world and being supposed to marry someday."

"How old are you now?" Matthew asked.

"Fifteen, sir."

"Fifteen, hmm? Still young, then, but old enough to be a wife – a housekeeper – a mother," Matthew said. "Go to court as you are bid but pray you may come home again soon. Marry when the time is right and teach your children to love and honour Our Lord. It must be passing strange for you to think of doing all these things, but do not fear them, Clare. The Mother Abbess released you from the convent to live and you *must* live fully and for the glory of Our Lord. I have made vows that must be kept, but you have not, so you are free."

"Free?" I breathed the word gently. "Free."

"Thank Our Lord you are free and ask Him to bless the Mother Abbess for her wisdom." Matthew's gaze and voice were intense. "When you have done that, Clare, you must do as the Mother Abbess said and live. Do not be held back by fear. *You must live*! And live for Jesus Christ's sake: 'tis your holy work in the world."

A moment later the door opened, and I was surrounded by light and chatter.

One of the maidservants dropped a pan and Edie scolded, "Hush, you careless wench, the master is resting!"

"Is Sir Anthony unwell?" I asked.

"He has a sick headache," Edie said. She looked harassed. "Sir

Anthony has not been in the best of tempers all day, and he has now retired to his chamber." She lowered her voice and said, "'Tis my belief that your uncle and aunt are vexing him with worries and are anxious to return to court as soon as may be. Your grandsire is not, to my way of thinking, fit for travelling. And in the depths of winter too!"

Soothingly I said, "I am sorry for your trouble."

"No trouble of yours," Edie said. She smiled at me. "You never give me trouble, my lamb."

"I thank you!" I cried with a merry laugh. "I am sure 'tis only because I have not been here for very long!" Seriously I asked, "Shall I make Sir Anthony a draft of feverfew and see what I can do to ease his discomfort?"

"You may try what you can do," Edie said doubtfully. "Sir Anthony is not usually in the best of tempers when he has a sick headache, so be warned and mind your words."

I smiled in spite of my nervousness. I busied myself preparing a feverfew draft, then carried it to Sir Anthony's chamber. I knocked at the door and a gruff voice bade me enter, so I pushed the door open cautiously. The light from the fireplace was flickering bright and quick upon my grandfather's face, and I winced at the thought of the pain it must be inflicting.

"Who is there?" the old man barked, wincing as he tried to raise his head from his pillow.

I curtsied and said, "Clare, sir. I have brought you a physic for your headache."

"I do not take pills and potions!" he snapped.

"No, sir." I drew closer to the bed with its dark carvings and rich hangings. "I have made you a simple draft of feverfew." I paused, waiting for him to object, but he said nothing. Tentatively I continued, "The Mother Abbess at Kirklington Abbey taught me how to make this draft. She took it when she had a sick headache and it always did her a lot of good."

"Eased the pain, did it?" Sir Anthony barked. He shielded his eyes from the light of the fire and squinted at me again. "What is in this draft, then?"

"'Tis nothing, sir, but clear spring water boiled with the flowers of feverfew and some honey."

"No squashed spiders or boiled mice, eh?"

"No, sir!" I tried to hide a shudder at the thought of such monstrosities in medicines. "'Tis nothing but what I would take myself."

"Hmm," Sir Anthony grunted, "Very well, I will try it, then. The king once wrote me a recipe for a draft to cure a sick headache that worked wonders. My lady wife, God rest her soul, used to make it but now I must suffer the pain as best I may. I will try anything that is medicine, not magic. Hold it here, will you, girl?"

I helped Sir Anthony to drink the draft, then watched as he lay back and closed his eyes. *How can a king find it in his heart to write a healing recipe for a friend yet condemn a wife to death?* I kept my thoughts to myself and made a screen, with two chairs and a woollen blanket, between the fire and the bed to block the dancing light from my grandfather's weary eyes. Finally I took the empty tankard and returned with a soft cloth and a bowl of icy cold water from the well. Sir Anthony flinched when I first laid the cloth on his forehead, but he said nothing, then his tense jaw relaxed. In time the little lines of pain eased from around his eyes. I dipped the cloth in the cold water again, and started when I turned back to my grandfather and discovered him watching me.

Gruffly, as I laid the cloth on his forehead again, Sir Anthony said, "You are a good nurse. So, as I recall, was your mother."

I smiled. I had not known this before but it pleased me. Demurely I said, "Aye, sir."

"Why do you do it, eh?" he snapped.

"Do it?" I echoed blankly. "Do what, sir?"

"Give yourself trouble for me." His eyes gleamed. "I do not think I have been extraordinarily kind to you."

I blinked and scrambled for an answer. Finally I said, "You are my grandfather, sir. I do not wish you to suffer. And, besides, you arranged for me to be raised in the cloister. I have been taught all my life to help others." I rearranged the cold cloth. "'Tis no great trouble to me."

"Trouble enough," Sir Anthony said. He shifted his head on his pillow. "'Tis what your aunt Maud thinks anyway. Your uncle Thomas will not say boo to her, and she is all for a successful career at court and a fine match for Lettice and the boys, your cousins, too." He snorted. "As if they deserved the children of dukes and earls as she fancies!"

My heart beat fast as I thought of Geoffrey and Frances and their secret ambitions. I did not want to tell their secrets or offend my grandfather, but I did want to help. I might never have another opportunity so I breathed a silent prayer for wisdom and took a deep breath.

"Perhaps, sir, your grandsons are not of Aunt Maud's mind." I tried to keep my hands and voice steady as I rearranged the cloth again. "Perhaps they do not wish for a career at court. Perhaps they wish for a simpler life at home."

"Eh?" The old man's eyes were like gimlets. Indignantly, as if it was the first thing his mind had fastened on, he said, "I know the boys are my grandsons. You do not need to remind me of my responsibility." He paused, then said, "Lettice is just like her mother – wanting a noble husband and turning up her nose at the local lads!"

I said nothing and waited.

Slowly Sir Anthony said, "I am trying to find a gentleman's daughter to be Geoffrey's bride. The lad needs a wife of good family. Perhaps …"

I bit my lip, then suggested, "Perhaps one of the Drayton girls, sir?"

"Humph." The old man's eyes were clear and thoughtful now. Almost to himself he said, "A knight's daughter. Katy is too old and Mary is too young – and they are both betrothed or as good as betrothed already. Bess is the right age for wedding Geoffrey. Her father did not expect to have her back at home and will be glad to have her off his hands again. I might propose the match if I thought the boy would stay at home and run the manor – farm the land and manage the tenants. But what of Frances?" He seemed to realise I was still there. Sharply he said, "I suppose you have a suggestion to make for his future too!"

"I think he should be apprenticed to a wool merchant," I said promptly. "Perhaps Master Chastleton …"

"You have thought of everything."

"No, sir," I said earnestly. "Not at all." And then, greatly daring, I said, "Why do you not ask the boys what they want?"

"*Ask* them?" Sir Anthony looked shocked. "But they are boys! They do not know their own minds!"

"I do not know how old Geoffrey is, sir, but I am fifteen and I know he is older," I laughed. "He is no child!"

"Frances is only twelve."

"Then he is about the right age to be apprenticed," I said pertly. I stood up with the bowl and cloth in my hands. "If you are better, sir, I will leave you now."

Sir Anthony made no sign of hearing me, so I left his bedside and opened the door, starting with surprise when he spoke: "Will it distress you very much to come to court?"

I hesitated. I had spoken the truth for my cousins but it was harder to speak the truth for myself. *What will Sir Anthony do if I defy his wishes? Will he ever love me?*

"Well?" he prompted. "Answer me."

"I do not wish to offend you when you are so generous," I said. I gulped and whispered a prayer for the right words. "The truth, sir, is

…" My heart was pounding in my ears and made it hard to think. I squeaked, "The truth is that I do not wish to go to court. I desire a quiet life. I have no wish to mix with kings and nobles."

"Your aunt Maud and cousin are insisting on going and your uncle Thomas will go as a matter of course," Sir Anthony said. "I have matters of business to conclude so I must go – even if I do as you so kindly suggest and abandon worldly ambition for myself and my grandsons. You can keep your cousins company. We shall be home for Easter." He folded his lips into a determined line. "At any rate, *I* shall be home for Easter and I will bring you with me."

Meekly, careful of what I said and mindful of a sudden desire that this abrupt but well meaning grandfather of mine should love me, I asked, "Do I have a choice, sir?"

"Nay."

"Then it is as you decide, sir." I left his chamber in a hurry. I felt my eyes overflow with tears but kept walking down the stairs and – ignoring Geoffrey and Frances who were waiting for me – slipped into the kitchen.

"Whatever is the matter, Clare?" Geoffrey asked, following me into the kitchen. He looked sympathetic. "Was our honoured grandfather unkind?"

"Nay." I put down my burdens and wiped my eyes on the ruffled cuff of my smock. "He has decided I must go with you to court."

"Oh, good!" Frances said. He had followed Geoffrey, and now he grinned at me. Gallantly, in an obvious effort to cheer me up, he said, "I shall like having another cousin – almost a sister – at court."

"I wish I had vows to keep like Uncle Matthew that stopped me going to court," I confessed. *Will the king guess I have the casket and the relic which his men should have taken from the convent to the court?* But I smiled through my tears at the memory of Frances's words: *almost a sister*. My grandfather might or might not love me, but my cousins were my true friends. I wiped my eyes and added, "I shall be very happy to have you, my very own cousins, at court too."

Sir Anthony, true to his promise, summoned a tailor from Stroud who rode through the January snow to measure me for a court dress of the latest fashion: the finest of its kind, Aunt Maud said, with sudden interest. But it was a bitter winter. Poor villagers and homeless beggars knocked at the kitchen door of the manor house every day and asked for old bread or leftover meat to eat. Edie was generous and gave what she could.

One day, when I was hunting for a precious egg to make paint, there was a knock on the kitchen door. Edie was nowhere to be seen, and Nancy and Molly were busy elsewhere.

I started at the sound. *What if the king has sent his men to look for the casket and the relic and they find it in my coffer?* I took a deep breath and tried to calm my fears. *How could the king's men know I have the treasure here?*

Trying not to think of eggs and paint and illuminating, I opened the door. A strange woman stood on the step, wrapped in a shabby cloak.

"God keep you," I greeted the woman.

"And you too," the woman said. "Can you, of your goodness, spare a poor woman and her family some bread?" A heartbeat later she looked up and gasped, "Clare!"

I gazed at the woman curiously. She was pale and thin and her clothes were faded and patched. Everything about her spoke of despair and hunger, but there was something familiar about her too.

Slowly I said, "Why … Sister Rosemary!"

The former lay sister dropped her gaze. She blushed and wrapped her cloak around her body. Finally she whispered, "Aye." And then, pushing her greasy hair out of her eyes with a gaunt, grubby hand, she said, "You oughtn't to call me 'Sister Rosemary' now." She grimaced. "I'm just Rosemary."

Impulsively I stood back, opened the door wide and said, "Pray come in and sit with me beside the fire." Rosemary hesitated, and I urged, "'Tis no trouble, and Edie has been baking so there are manchets and honey to eat. Please. 'Tis so long since I have seen anyone from the abbey!"

At my last words, Rosemary slipped inside, pushing the hood of her cloak back from her head. She seemed to relax in the warmth of the kitchen. Perhaps the sight of the table and the smell of the baking reminded her of her work in the convent kitchen.

I tried not to stare at Rosemary and see all the ways in which she had changed, although it was hard, as I beckoned her to a seat on the settle beside the fire. I busied myself with cutting a manchet and spreading it with honey, and fetching a tankard of the weak ale we ladies of the manor drank. Rosemary ate and drank hungrily, then sat back on the settle with a gusty sigh.

Gently I said, "I heard the news about the abbey being ruined." Tears picked at the back of my eyes. "I have been praying for the nuns."

Shortly Rosemary said, "The nuns, may God bless them, need all our prayers."

"What …" I gulped. "What happened after I left that day?"

"The king's men went through all the accounts and assets and turned us out a few days after you left," Rosemary said quietly. "'Twas too much for Sister Veronica. She died, God rest her soul, in her sleep during our last night at the nunnery." We crossed ourselves, and Rosemary said, "We buried her in the graveyard. 'Twas the last thing we did together before … they left." Tears trickled down the girl's face. "The Mother Abbess said she was going to France, and she offered to take with her as many of the choir sisters as wanted to go too. Sister Anne and Sister Grace went with her. The rest of them and us lay sisters … well … we stayed."

"Stayed at Kirklington Abbey?" I asked.

"Nay, for there was nothing to stay for, even if the king's men had let us stay," Rosemary said bitterly. "Sister Joanna went to London to keep house for her widowed brother and his apprentices. Sister Laura returned home to her family and to look after her nephews and nieces. I don't know about the rest, but for Sister

Theresa, who's living with her parents again. As for me … I couldn't leave my family." Rosemary's voice was expressionless. "Mam needed me to help with the house and the younger children. I don't know what would have become of them if I'd upped and gone to France or some place else. And now I'm expecting a child of my own."

I did not know what to say. It was all too big and sad. More than anything else I wanted to know why Rosemary, a nun, was expecting a baby.

Suddenly, almost fiercely in spite of the tears in her voice, Rosemary said, "I don't want you thinking badly of me. It's true, I've broken my vows, but I didn't know what else to do … and my baby has a father."

My heart ached for how the rosy-cheeked, bright-eyed peasant girl I had known at Kirklington Abbey who had become a hungry, weary woman.

"I've known Rich all my life," Sister Rosemary said. "He's not a bright lad, but he's got a good heart. He was sweet on me before I joined the convent. When I left the convent, well, he offered me a home and his name and we were married in the church porch at Michaelmas."

"I hope you will be happy," I said.

"Happy enough," Rosemary said shortly. "I didn't marry for happiness. I married for food and protection and the hope of having a child because I need someone to care for me when I'm an old woman. I hope and pray Sweet Mother Mary will forgive me for breaking my vows."

Gently I said, "I do not pray to Our Lady, only to Our Lord, but I try to follow the example of Our Lady everyday. And she was a mother too."

Hope flickered in Rosemary's eyes, but it was drowned in tears. Brokenly she said, "Thank you for saying so, Clare, you were always the kindest of the choir sisters."

"I was never a nun," I said softly, "just a novice."

"You were as good as any of them," Rosemary countered. "And you were going to be a nun. Some of the choir sisters didn't understand how hard it was for us lay sisters – not having fine families and good educations, having to work as well as pray, worrying about our families outside the convent – but you were as good and kind and polite to us as you were to them. I haven't forgotten."

I blushed and did not know what to say.

Suddenly, quietly, Rosemary asked, "Have you got it safe?"

"Safe?" I frowned. "Have I got what safe?"

"You *know*," Rosemary said significantly. She lowered her voice even further, and I had to strain my ears to hear: "I was worried about what the king's men would do with the relic of Sweet Mother Mary's robe, so I hid it in your coffer, because I knew you'd keep it safe."

The kitchen seemed to do a little dance in front of my eyes. I closed them for a heartbeat. When I opened them, Rosemary was still there, looking at me hopefully.

Confidentially Rosemary said, "The Mother Abbess thought the king's men had stolen the relic when she discovered it was gone. The short man, Master Tolbert, was vexed because the books in the abbey library weren't as fine as rumour had said, and he shouted and swore terrible about one of us taking the casket and hiding it so it wouldn't go into the royal coffers. I was sore frightened about what was going to happen! In the end the Mother Abbess said our safety was more important than the whereabouts of the relic and the tall man, Sir Hilary Cavendish, said he wouldn't make us give him the casket." Warmly, without any hint of doubt in her voice, she said, "I'm glad I thought of hiding Sweet Mother Mary's robe in your coffer."

I felt sick as I remembered Rosemary's words before I left the convent: "Sweet Mother Mary will grieve the loss of the nunnery … I fear what may become of the relic of her robe … I fear the king's men will take it and desecrate it." *Rosemary must have put the casket, with the relic inside, in my coffer before she and Sister Theresa helped Old Peter carry my coffer to the cart.* And now the weight of anxiety about the coffer was heavy on my heart.

As gently as possible I said, "I found the casket and the relic in my coffer at Christmastide. I did not know why they were there." I swallowed the lump in my throat. "I thought mayhap 'twas by a miracle of Our Lord."

*But 'tis not a miracle.* I had felt sad about the suppression of the convent before, but now I felt angry too. Sister Rosemary had stolen and lied to protect the relic, and then broken her vows in exchange for a way to live in the world. *All because the king has suppressed the convent!*

"I will keep Our Lady's robe safe," I blurted. I stood up. "Will you take some bread and meat home for your family and your husband?"

Rosemary's gratitude hurt my heart as I fetched a wicker basket and lined it with a clean cloth. Carefully I packed bread and cheese, some cold meat and one of Edie's fresh pies, made with dried pears from the manor orchard, into the basket.

On the doorstep, clasping the basket as if it was a treasure, Rosemary said, "If my baby is a girl, I'll call her Clare, so she'll grow up as kind as you."

Tremulously I promised, "I will stand godmother if you like." I smiled sadly. "Christ and His angels watch over you, my friend."

"And you too." Rosemary paused in the doorway of the kitchen courtyard to wave. "May Sweet Mother Mary reward you for your kindness."

*Kindness.*

I closed the kitchen door and leaned against it.

*Yellow for kindness.*

I burst out of the kitchen and headed for the stairs and the porch chamber as if I could run from the fear that was choking me and making my stomach clench and flutter.

"Ah, Clare!" Aunt Maud called from her bedchamber as I passed. "Come here, my dear." She looked up brightly from a mass of fabric. Even in the flickering firelight and the winter light from the windows, I could see the richness of the fabrics. "A messenger has arrived from Stroud and brought your new dress from the tailor," Aunt Maud said. "Would you like to try it on?"

I did not just then, but I nodded dutifully. "Aye." I tried to smile. "I thank you for your kindness."

Almost in spite of myself, the dress took my breath away. Never before had I worn – or dreamed of wearing – anything so fine. Velvets and silks shimmered while Edie and Aunt Maud laced and pinned me into the bodice, skirt and sleeves, pulling this together and that tight until I was dressed. Slowly, very slowly, I turned around in the middle of the room.

With tears in her eyes Edie said, "Your blessed mother would be proud of you, my lamb, that she would."

Coolly Aunt Maud said, "It is certainly worth dressing you finely, Clare, I really had no idea but … well … I must say you look very nice."

The velvet of the bodice and overskirt was not blue – not blue like lapis lazuli anyway – but darker and deeper like the colour of the sky at midnight. *Is this blue for hope too?* The skirt of the kirtle, revealed by a split in the skirt of the blue gown, was embroidered with an intricate pattern of roses and leaves on cream satin. *Bright pink for laughter and green for courage.* So were the linings of the lower sleeves, which were turned back for display between the tight upper sleeves and the lacy cuffs of the fine smock underneath.

Aunt Maud produced a mirror from her coffer, and I glanced at my reflection shyly. In the mirror I caught sight of my red hair and blue eyes, my pale skin and pink lips, then a square neckline, a tight bodice and a skirt that billowed and swirled when I moved.

I smiled as I felt I should, but I did not feel like myself in my new dress with its low neckline, hanging sleeves and wide skirts. I rustled when I walked, and I could not chase Frances through the house when he poked his head into the bedchamber and stole my shoes.

"'Tis just as well you cannot chase your cousin," Edie said severely, pulling me back into the bedchamber. "What an unbecoming thing for a young lady to do indeed!"

Together Edie and Aunt Maud fussed around me, pinning this and that and wondering out loud if something should be tightened or loosened.

"Cousin Clare?" Geoffrey poked his head round the edge of the solar door and waved a pair of shoes. "Are these your shoes? I took them from Frances a moment ago and thrashed him for you."

"He meant no harm," I protested.

"I dare say," Geoffrey said with a grin. "I did not hurt him – do not look so alarmed!" He disappeared but reappeared an instant later. "I must say, Clare, that gown is remarkably fine. Roger Chastleton is here, and I am going to ask him about his father's plans to buy … er … the abbey ruins and convent manor. Dame Sybil is sewing in the great hall so 'tis perfectly proper. Pray join us if you can."

"In *this*?" I asked doubtfully.

"Oh … he will not care," Geoffrey said airily. "Make haste!"

"'Tis just as well to wear your new dress and get used to managing the sleeves and the skirts," Aunt Maud advised. "Do not be too long."

"And don't you be getting it dirty!" Edie added.

Awkwardly I pulled my shoes onto my stockinged feet and curtsied to Aunt Maud before hurrying after Geoffrey as quickly as I could and joining the boys beside the fire in the great hall.

Roger stared at me as if he had not seen me before and it took me a moment to realise it must be because of my new dress. I had heard from the nuns and the girls who were being educated at the convent that fine clothes made a difference in the way a woman was treated in the world, but I had not understood how, until now.

Roger looked like a daddy-long-legs on his best behaviour, as if I was a fine lady, not a friend. He stood and bowed and offered me Sir Anthony's carved wooden chair beside the fire. I blushed and wished the neckline was higher, the sleeves were tighter and the skirts were smaller. My new dress felt like a suit of armour intended to intimidate and distance enemies and friends alike.

Uneasily (and unaccountably) thinking of sweet oranges and kissing boughs, I wondered if Roger was going to talk to me at all in his usual, friendly, cheerful way, as I eased myself onto the edge of the chair – as far back as the bulk of my skirts would allow – and waited for one of the boys to speak.

It was Geoffrey who began: "We have heard your father is bidding for the church land in Kirklington."

"Truly?" Roger's eyebrows peaked questioningly. "My father thought the business was private and not generally known."

"I beg your pardon for mentioning the matter," Geoffrey said. "Aunt Maud had the news in a letter from a friend at court and so, you see, 'tis … well … not a secret."

"So be it," Roger said philosophically. He inclined his head to me and said, "Kirklington Abbey was your home, and I do not wish to distress you by speaking about my father buying the church lands now … er … the abbey has been ruined and the manor put up for sale." He eased the collar of his doublet with his fingers. "I would not for the world have wished for the convent to be suppressed, but since it has, sadly …" He glanced at me and demanded, "Do you care?"

Quickly I said, "I am sorrier than I can say than the convent has been suppressed, but if anyone is to buy the lands, I am glad 'tis you."

"Well … 'tis my father," Roger said. "But thank you, Mistress Clare, you are very good." He sounded relieved and said, "Kirklington Abbey was famous hereabouts for its library and scriptorium and my father is eager to find as many of the books from the library as possible and keep them together in the library of … er … of his new house." Roger looked embarrassed, then laughed. "'Tis an awkward business, talking of my father's plans for the abbey ruins, but cannot be avoided since … well … I am, God willing, to benefit from the arrangement someday."

I smiled, but my heart was caught by Roger's next words. The abbey church, he said, was destroyed … as it was in my dreams. I took a deep breath and blinked back a rush of tears. The boys were still talking. The living quarters were in good condition. If Master Chastleton was successful in his bid to buy the property, he intended to make the place a home and work the land too.

"My father is in a fury because many of the religious houses the king has suppressed have libraries," Roger said seriously. "Some of the king's men steal the precious stones from the bindings and burn the pages. But most of the books are of no value to the king's men who tear down the walls and roofs, so the books are left behind in the ruins to be destroyed by wind and rain and misused by villagers. At present he has me riding about Gloucestershire seeking and preserving all the books I can find."

Amusedly Geoffrey said, "You are a rescuer of unwanted books!"

"I am something of the kind," Roger admitted.

Eagerly I asked, "Will you rescue the books of Kirklington Abbey?"

"If I can," Roger said sturdily.

"They are worth preserving," Geoffrey said. "The abbey books are said to be very fine."

"But my father cannot find them," Roger blurted. "He has been to the ruins of the convent and found the library very nearly empty."

"How can the library be empty?" I asked. Anxiously I looked at Roger, but all I could imagine was the abbey library as I knew it: the stone chamber with the sun slanting through the windows and shining on the leather covers of the parchment books that lined the walls on shelves. Slowly I said, "'Tis hard to believe."

Sadly Roger said, "I fear 'tis so." He ruffled his hair and explained, "A few cheap, poor volumes were in the library, and a few pages were found in the remains of a bonfire but not enough to explain all the missing books." He looked at me and confessed, "'Tis a mystery like the missing treasure."

My cheeks burned like fire as I thought of the casket and relic in my coffer but all I said was, "The books were beautiful."

"No doubt the abbey plate is on its way to the coffers of the crown," Geoffrey said. "I daresay the treasure – a relic in a casket if I remember correctly – is with it. 'Tis only a country story to say 'tis missing."

Absently I said, "The abbey plate was very beautiful and of great value." My stomach clenched and fluttered. "Especially the casket and the relic: they were beautiful and valuable in every way." Finally, thinking about the books, I blurted, "The nuns loved and respected the books. They were the work of many generations and some of them, indeed, were the life work of the nuns. They would wish the books to be preserved."

"Perhaps they took the books with them," Geoffrey suggested.

"What?" I gazed at my cousin in amazement.

"They might have carried the books with their other things,"

Geoffrey explained.

In my imagination, as in my dreams, I saw the nuns – the dear, gentle nuns I loved so well – being driven in a rag-bag band from the convent.

"Mayhap," Roger said. "I had not thought of that."

"Do talk sense!" I snapped and stood up with a flounce of my skirts which I knew was most unbecoming to a fine lady. All the anger I felt about the king and the suppression of the convent flashed out like a sword in hot words: "You are both heartless loons! How could the nuns take the books from library with them when they were driven away by the king's men at the point of a sword? Do you suppose they carried the books upon their backs and left their clothes and other necessities? 'Tis unkind to think of such a thing when there are so many who are suffering in this way!"

Suddenly I realised I was shaking, and the boys were looking at me in consternation.

"I beg your pardon," I gasped. "I am sorry but I am not well. Do you not … can you not imagine how terrible it was?"

I fled to Aunt Maud's bedchamber in a hurry to be free of my unfamiliar finery. Aunt Maud was silent as she helped me out of my new dress, and I found my feelings had calmed and gentled by the time I stepped into my familiar dress of soft rose-coloured wool which felt so comfortable and pretty and right.

Gratefully I slipped into the porch chamber and closed the door. I leaned against it and closed my eyes for a heartbeat. "Sweet Jesus, what now?" I whispered. "I cannot bear it! 'Tis too sad."

The Mother Abbess' rosary was hanging above my prayer books. I touched the beads and thought of Rosemary. I felt sad and angry about the plight of the nuns all over again as the beads slipped between my fingers. *The Mother Abbess would be sad and angry too ... surely she would ... 'tis not her fault the convent was suppressed.*

Suddenly I wanted to read the letter the Mother Abbess had given me. I slipped it out of my sewing box and held it with trembling fingers. I knew, deep down inside, this was the right time to read it, so I took a deep breath and curled up on my bed, tilting the page towards the light from the window, straining my eyes to see and my heart to understand every word the Mother Abbess had written.

The Mother Abbess wrote as she talked, so I could almost hear the dear, kind voice in my imagination as I read. And there it all was: her release of me from the vows I had made as a postulent and a novice, her advice about living a holy life in the world, her encouragement to keep writing and illuminating and thus not neglect my gift of the scriptorium. And there was more:

*I want you, my dear daughter, to have the best of the abbey books. Mayhap they can be your dowry. I do not want them to fall into the hands of ungodly or ignorant men. I have wrapped and hidden them where they cannot be easily found. St Kyneburgh will guard them well. The farmer knows my rosary. When the time is right – when the world is safe for the books – I want you to have this true treasure of Kirklington Abbey.*

I bit my lip and gazed at the uneven square of winter sky I could see through the window. It was strange how the boys had been talking about the missing books and I had decided to read my letter from the Mother Abbess – and she had asked me to find and keep the best of the abbey books – all in one day.

Slowly I tucked the letter into the bodice of my dress and slipped downstairs and into the kitchen. Mistress Eglentyne was sleeping by the fire, and Edie was mixing a pudding. I wrapped myself in an apron and started stirring breadcrumbs and herbs together for dumplings. *What am I to do with the casket and the relic … and now the finding of the abbey books?* I was mixing and whispering Doctor Luther's prayer of thanks – trying to mean every word I uttered – when a voice spoke my name.

"Here you are," Geoffrey said. He joined me at the kitchen table and said, "How now, Cousin Clare?"

I glanced at him from under my eyelashes and dug the wooden spoon into the breadcrumb mixture.

"My pardon for vexing you earlier," Geoffrey said. "I spoke thoughtlessly. What do you think, however, of Roger inviting us to visit the … er … the abbey?"

"To look for the books among the … the ruins?"

"Aye. 'Tis, indeed, the notion."

"I believe I should like nothing better," I said slowly. "But …"

I tipped some milk and eggs into the breadcrumbs. I added more herbs. The mix turned into a heavy, sticky dough. I made up my mind and said, "The Mother Abbess gave me a letter before I left the convent."

"Oh?" Geoffrey sounded only just politely interested.

"She said I would know when the time was right to read the letter so I read it today … just now." I blushed. "I read it after I left you and Roger in the hall." I glanced at Geoffrey as I pushed the bowl of dough towards Edie."'Tis passing strange, when we were just speaking of the abbey books being missing, but the Mother Abbess wrote about the books in the letter."

"Indeed?" Real interest thrilled Geoffrey's voice now. "I shall tell Roger this moment!"

"Is he here still?"

"Aye." Geoffrey paused in the doorway. "He did not think it right to leave without making peace." He grinned. "He also hoped you might be so pleased with the idea of visiting the ruins that you might offer us some honey cakes!"

"How does he know Edie made honey cakes today?" I laughed. I untied my apron and reached for a platter of round honey cakes with the finger hole in the top oozing honey, then slipped my free hand through my cousin's proffered arm. "Come, then, let us go and make peace."

Roger looked up in greeting as we entered the hall.

Quickly, before I could say anything, he bowed and said, "I pray pardon for hurting your feelings." He looked at the plate of honey cakes and asked, "Are those honey cakes for us to eat now?"

"Aye," I said. Roger reached out to take the plate, but I kept my hold on the pewter. With a blush and a curtsy I said softly, "I pray pardon too for not behaving as a gentlewoman should."

"No matter," Roger said airily. He waved one hand in a dismissive way. "Think no more about it. We were all of us thoughtless for a little while." He looked wistfully at the cakes and gave the plate a gentle tug to release it from my grasp. "Shall we sit and eat and be comfortable now?"

I laughed and released the plate. Roger, to my relief, seemed himself again. *Perhaps 'twas the strangeness and unfriendliness of my new dress – my court dress – which put everyone in a bad mood.* Dame Sybil was sewing in the last of the light from the windows so we gathered around the fireplace and the boys started munching as, with our heads close together, we started whispering.

Geoffrey, with his mouth full, said, "Clare told me in the kitchen just now that she has a letter from the Mother Abbess of Kirklington Abbey in which she writes about the books."

Stickily, but to the point, Roger asked, "Does she tell you where the books are?"

I shook my head, and the boys exchanged a disappointed look. Quickly I said, "I have the letter here." I slipped it out of my bodice and handed it to Geoffrey with a little nod. "Pray read this bit aloud …" I pointed.

Clearly Geoffrey read, "'I want you, my dear daughter, to have the best of the abbey books. Mayhap they can be your dowry. I do not want them to fall into the hands of ungodly or ignorant men. I have wrapped and hidden them where they cannot be easily found. St Kyneburgh will guard them well. The farmer knows my rosary. When the time is right – when the world is safe for the books – I want you to have this true treasure of Kirklington Abbey.'"

Thoughtfully Roger nodded, "Aye … 'tis fair enough that you should have the books."

I blushed and said, "Nay, I did not mean that, only …"

"But I *do* mean it," Roger said decidedly. "If the books of Kirklington Abbey are found, I should like you to have them. I am sure my father will agree. They can be your dowry, as the Mother Abbess suggests." A smile lurked in the depths of his dark eyes. "Mayhap a dowry of books is the ideal dowry for you."

"Mayhap," I murmured. "I truly do not mind if you have the abbey books. I would like above anything for them to be safe. It does not much matter where."

Restlessly Roger said, "Aye, you are right, but where *are* the books?"

The rest of us looked at him blankly, and he raised his peaked eyebrows. Using a finger to mark each point, he said, "Most of the books are missing. The Mother Abbess has packed and hidden the best of the books. 'St Kyneburgh will guard them well.' Who by all the saints …" I tittered, and Roger rolled his eyes in good humour. "What I mean, Mistress Clare, is *who* is St Kyneburgh?"

I was a little bit shocked at his ignorance and explained, "St

Kyneburgh was the beautiful daughter of a Saxon king. Some say she married the King of Northumbria, but others say she fled from the prospect of marriage to a pagan prince and vowed herself to a life of celibacy. She worked as a baker's maid before her martyrdom." I hesitated because I felt torn between a smile and a tear as I remembered the nuns and what Rosemary had said about their fate. Quietly I concluded, "Sister Veronica, God rest her soul, was devoted to St Kyneburgh, but I do not know how St Kyneburgh can guard the abbey books."

"Nor I," Roger said briskly. He took a turn about the hall and came back to the fireplace. "'Tis very mysterious indeed." Finally he said, "At least the books are not exposed to the elements among the ruins. I have looked for them in vain. Wherever they are, if they are at the ruins, they are safe."

"But where?" Geoffrey asked.

"St Kyneburgh is guarding them," Roger said. "And, more to the point, the Mother Abbess said she packed and hid them where they cannot be easily found. I do not think, therefore, they can be hurt by wind and rain. But we shall find them," Roger said firmly. "Never you fear." He looked at the almost-empty plate. "Do you mind if I eat the last cake?"

I pushed the plate in his direction.

Roger ate the cake in three large bites and sucked the last of the honey from his fingers. Abruptly he asked, "Why are you going to court?" Quickly he added, "I pray pardon for asking, Mistress Clare, but I am curious."

I smiled slightly and said, "Sir Anthony has bade me go. I wish I could stay at home."

"I wish you could too," Roger said. Mournfully he said, "I shall be alone hereabouts with my family and the Drayton girls."

"The Ducklingtons will be here," I suggested.

"True," Roger agreed.

"And you will have your sheep," Geoffrey said consolingly.

Roger made a face and retorted, "'Tis little consolation when *you* and the rest of my friends are having a fine time at court!" He brightened. "When my father is master of the church lands and you return from court, mayhap you would like to come to Kirklington Abbey and we can look for the books again."

"I should like that!" I exclaimed. And then, remembering the convent was ruined, I caught my breath and said, "That is to say, I think I should, because I should like to find the abbey books." I smiled. "You promise we shall look for the books when I return from court?"

"My word of honour," Roger said promptly.

"You are giving *your* word of honour although 'tis to be your father's property?" Geoffrey queried with a grin.

Roger shrugged his shoulders and raised his peaked eyebrows at a comical angle, then we both laughed.

Idly Geoffrey asked, "By the by, Roger, will not the books belong to the crown – the king – if they are found? Surely all the abbey's goods and chattels were confiscated by the king's men and became the property of the crown."

Doubtfully Roger said, "I am not entirely sure, but I think not if the Mother Abbess hid the books before the king's men arrived and if she wrote a letter giving the books to Mistress Clare. I have heard of the king's men taking the seals and charters and most of the treasures of the religious houses but allowing the abbot or prior to keep a measure of the treasure: perhaps some of the cups and plates used during Mass." More confidently he said, "I believe the rest of the treasure became the property of the crown at the time of dissolution." He nodded in a deciding way. "I do not think the books are the property of the crown."

I suddenly felt as if I could not breathe. I gulped and asked in a small voice, "What of other things … of real treasure?"

The boys looked at me curiously.

Brightly Roger asked, "Do *you* have some of the abbey treasures, Mistress Clare?"

I hesitated. *Should I tell them?* In an even smaller voice than before, I said, "Yes."

The look of surprise and dismay on Roger's face was comical, but I could not laugh. The anxiety about the relic was choking. I gulped.

For a long heartbeat there was silence.

Finally Geoffrey asked, "Do you speak seriously, Clare?"

"Most seriously," I said.

And then, although I knew it was not ladylike, I drew my knees up to my chest and tucked my toes onto the edge of my seat. I hugged my knees and buried my chin in the comforting scratchiness of my skirt where it billowed and bunched over my knees before cascading around my feet. I felt very small and lonesome with the boys looking at me in shocked surprise.

"In faith!" Roger said. "You have stolen all our breath away." One of his hands shot out and grasped my clasped hands. "Never fear! We shall see you safely through this business."

Quickly – and very kindly – Geoffrey said, "Aye, Roger speaks truly. But can you tell us aught of this treasure?"

I glanced around the hall, but Dame Sybil was concentrating on her sewing and singing under her breath. The boys gathered closer.

In a low voice, but quickly as my heart overflowed into words which it was a relief to speak, I said, "I found it in my coffer on Christmas Eve when I looked for my mother's necklace." I touched the necklace that hung around my neck. "I had no notion it was there, but it was, wrapped in a sheepskin and hidden at the bottom of my coffer."

"The treasure?" Roger asked. "I mean … the treasure I told you was missing?"

"Aye." I looked at him seriously. "'Tis a treasure indeed." I took a deep breath. "Our Lady was the patron saint of the convent, and we had a piece of her robe." The boys gasped. I smiled faintly and said, "'Twas kept in a jewelled casket behind the altar. I thought 'twas there still until I found it in my coffer."

"The relic?" Roger asked.

"Or the casket?" Geoffrey suggested.

"Both."

The boys looked at each other, and both of them gave a long, low whistle.

"Aye." I laughed nervously. "I did not know what to think but that 'twas a miracle of Our Lord. But then …" I lowered my gaze. "One of the nuns, who did not go to France and is very poor, came here for charity. She asked me if I had the relic safe. I do not think she cared about the casket! She said she put the treasure in my coffer to save it from the king's men. I promised I would keep it safe, but I know not how."

"By the saints," Geoffrey said. "I had no notion we had any treasure under our roof. I know not what to do with it either. Mayhap Uncle Matthew …"

"I do not think 'tis fair to involve your uncle in this matter when he was a monk in another religious house," Roger said abruptly. "I think we should consult Master Beckley." He stood up and glanced out of the window. "I do not think there is any time to be lost. He will know what to do. We might take him some honey cakes to sweeten his temper if he is inclined to be tetchy."

I stood up and asked, "Do you really think he will know what to do?" I caught my breath in a tiny sob of relief. "'Twould be a mercy to know." Briskly I said, "I shall get the honey cakes."

"I shall come too," Geoffrey said firmly.

Quickly, my heart warmed by the boys' kindness and loyalty, I slipped into the kitchen. I wrapped some honey cakes in a clean napkin – thinking uneasily that Edie would wonder why all the cakes had disappeared so quickly – and tucked them into a basket, then I pulled a cloak around my shoulders and joined the boys in the hall.

Roger, who seemed to consider himself the leader, nodded in greeting and asked, "Do you want to bring the treasure?" I hesitated. Quietly Roger said, "Mayhap 'twill help Master Beckley to see the treasure … and ease your mind if he is willing to keep it safe?"

The casket, wrapped in the sheepskin, fitted neatly in the bottom of the basket. I covered it with the honey cakes and concealed it with a napkin but my heart beat very hard and fast all the way to the church in the village. I was relieved when Geoffrey knocked on the door of the priest's house – a modest building tucked in a small garden behind the church – and Master Beckley opened the door. Quickly I dropped a curtsy and the boys bowed and doffed their caps.

"Why, good morrow to you, my gentle mistress and brave gallants!" The priest seemed to be in a good mood. "Will you be pleased to step inside my humble home?"

The priest ushered us through a passage and into a small hall with a fire crackling in the fireplace and a great litter of books, papers and quills on the table that stood in the middle of the room. Master Beckley found a stool for me while the serving man brought ale and dried apple rings from the kitchen and buttery across the passage.

"And now, my young friends, how may I assist you?"

I glanced around to check the serving man had really gone. The boys were looking at each other and grimacing. Impulsively I lifted the napkin-wrapped cakes onto the table.

"Ah … that is very kind," the priest said. "From Mistress Edie?"

"Nay, not exactly," I confessed. "Master Roger thought you might like them."

"The cakes are excellent," Roger said sincerely. "'Tis not that which we wish to discuss with you, however, sir."

"'Tis this," I said.

Quickly, my fingers trembling, I lifted the casket onto the table and opened the wrapping of sheepskin to reveal the gold and jewels of the treasure.

"In faith!" the priest exclaimed. He looked at us over the top of the spectacles he had perched on the end of his beaky nose. "'Tis the missing treasure of Kirkington Abbey unless I miss my guess!" The priest reached out to touch the casket with reverent fingers but let them fall on the table.

Geoffrey said, "My cousin did not know she had the casket and the relic until Christmastide, sir, when she found them in her coffer."

Quickly, as a dreadful thought occurred to me, I said, "I swear by Our Lady I did not steal her relic from the convent!"

"'Twas another nun who took it from the abbey church and put it in my cousin's coffer," Geoffrey said.

"Indeed, sir, Mistress Clare is innocent of any wrong in this business!" Roger said hotly.

"Pray do not trouble yourselves!" Master Beckley held up a hand in gentle but firm protest. Simply he said, "It did not occur to me that

Mistress Clare had stolen the treasure." He smiled at me. "I knew your mother – her daughter would not steal and lie."

I relaxed.

"We are hoping, sir, you will advise us," Roger said. "What should we do with the treasure now?"

"Aye … 'tis a puzzle indeed," the priest said. He rubbed his chin. "I must think on this for a *Pater Noster* while at least."

I said the *Pater Noster* prayer five times while Master Beckley sat with his eyes closed in thought. The fire spat, and the logs shifted on the hearth. The boys looked at each other and communicated in a wild series of grimaces and gestures.

Finally, without opening his eyes, Master Beckley asked, "Do you know if this is just the casket or if the greater treasure of the relic is still inside?"

Shyly I said, "Our Lady's robe is inside the casket, sir. I did not touch it, but I thought 'twas just the casket – not the relic – in my coffer so I opened the casket. I did not know, then, how it came to be in my coffer. I thought mayhap 'twas a miracle of Our Lord."

"I understand," Master Beckley said. He opened his eyes and clasped his hands before him on the table. "Would you be willing to leave the treasure in my care for now?"

I glanced at the boys and nodded.

"We must think what is best to be done," the priest said. "The casket is but a worldly trifle but the relic? 'Tis a dear token of Our Lady the Virgin Mary who is Our Lord's blessed mother. For myself, I am not concerned with what happens to the casket, as long as the relic is not destroyed or sold for money."

Again I glanced at the boys. Again I read their agreement in their faces and nodded.

"God reward you for bringing this treasure to me." The priest took the casket between his hands and leaned over the table. Seriously, looking at me and the boys one at a time, he asked, "Will you trust me to keep it safe and advise you about what to do with it hereafter?"

Each of the boys nodded soberly.

I felt as if a weight had rolled off my heart and said heartily, "Yes, good sir, with all my heart."

"'Tis well said and 'twill be well done," Master Beckley said. He jumped up from the table and rubbed his hands together. "And now, I beg your pardon for seeming inhospitable, but you must go so I can take care of this business before nightfall. Pray thank Mistress Edie for the cakes."

We were ushered outside. On the muddy path between the front door and the wicker gate into the road, I hesitated, breathing in a clean, sharp smell of rain and woodsmoke. Gratefully I whispered, "Sweet Jesus, thank You for Your mercy in this matter and for the kindness of the boys."

"Mistress Clare?" The priest stopped me with a hand on my elbow. "Your mother – for all her reforming ways – would be proud of you for acting thus." My attention was caught by the mention of my mother and I opened my mouth to ask a question, but the priest nodded in farewell as the winter sun flashed on his spectacles. "May

Christ and His angels bless you."

My heart was overflowing with happiness as I walked back to the manor house behind the boys. *Life could not be better ... if only I did not have to go to court!*

# Candlemas

I began to wonder if the winter would ever end.

Sir Anthony made enquiries and announced that the king and queen were settled at Greenwich Palace, near London, for the rest of the winter. Uncle Thomas assessed the weather and the state of the roads every day, looking for a propitious time to start the journey. Aunt Maud and Lettice were in a flutter about new dresses and court gossip sent by letter from Aunt Maud's friend Lady Arbelle Marbury. But we woke to frost and snow morning after morning. Rosemary did not come again, but I often gave food to Blind Dame Mary and Wat who walked from Kirklington in the hope of receiving charity.

And then one day Sir Anthony announced that it was time.

"Time?" I asked in consternation. *'Tis not Candlemas just yet!*

"Time to go to court!" Lettice exclaimed. She had been drooping over her breakfast of bread, cheese and ale but now she dropped her bread onto the table and jumped up from her stool so suddenly that it tumbled over. "Oh!" She clasped her hands. "Finally!"

I looked at my grandfather. He was watching me with a quizzical look, but his lips were set in a firm and uncompromising line. He dabbed his mouth with his napkin and nodded. I lifted my tankard of ale to my lips and stared into the depths of the pale liquid but could not drink because of the lump in my throat. *I am going to court whether I like it or not.*

I slipped away from the table as soon as I could and found refuge in the kitchen near Edie. Miserably, stirring a cauldron of soup over the fire as I was bid, I listened as Edie talked feverishly.

"We must pack saddle bags with clothes and food for the journey," she said. "And there are baskets and coffers to fill with fine court clothes as well as comfortable bedding and pewter plates, tankards and spoons." She counted a finger for each item. "The baskets and coffers will be sent ahead by ox and cart so they're ready and waiting at court when you arrive." Edie paused and mused, "I'll send a barrel of sweet butter and a jar of honey to sweeten the royal servants. Country butter and Bampton honey cannot be beaten. 'Twill ensure the servants have a care for the things when they arrive." She frowned. "And I must bake an extra batch of bread and some pasties for your journey. I don't want any of you to starve on the road. I don't believe the gentry eat properly at court – 'tis all flummery and sweetmeats – but I can't do anything about that now."

I said nothing, but concentrated on guiding the spoon round and round then back and round the other way in the metal cauldron.

"What think you, then, Mistress Clare?" Edie asked at last.

I said nothing but gulped.

Edie, suddenly still in the midst of her activity, asked, "What's wrong, my lamb?"

Quaveringly, but refusing to cry, I said, "I do not want to go to court. I want to stay here." I glanced around the dim, homey kitchen. I was not sure I belonged here yet but I said, "I have just got used to being here. I am *comfortable* here. I fear I am s-s-scared of going to court."

"Bless you, my lamb." Edie folded me in a motherly embrace, then stood back with tears in her own eyes. She lifted my chin and smiled into my eyes. "You do as your grandsire says and go to court like a good girl. Sir Anthony will see you come to no harm, and you'll have your cousins for company. 'Tis hard for you, I know, but I don't doubt you've got a good heart to see you through. Our Lord will be with you." She chucked me under the chin. "I'll be here – aye, with Jake and all your friends, too – when you come home."

I tucked the words of comfort into my heart and gave Edie a wobbly smile and a hug.

"My thanks, Edie," a gruff voice said from the kitchen doorway.

I swung round – spoon in hand – and curtsied to Sir Anthony.

"Come," the old man said. He gestured for me to accompany him. "I would speak with you."

I left Edie to the maidservants and their preparations for the journey. Wondering what Sir Anthony was going to say, I followed him as he stumped through the biting cold of the frosty morning to the stables, then ushered me into the shelter of the building, sweet with the smell of hay and horses.

"I have something to show you here," Sir Anthony said.

I twisted my hands nervously behind my back but curtsied and waited.

"First, however, I must say I know you do not want to go to court," the old man said. "I do not have to explain myself to a chit of a girl, but I do not want you thinking me unkind from heartlessness. I am taking you to court because you need a change and I want you to know the royal court of England and see for yourself that Bluff King Hal – King Henry to you – is not a monster."

Dully I said, "'Tis as you wish, sir."

"Aye," Sir Anthony said grimly. "And that puts me in mind of another thing. Your uncle and aunt are staying in the courtiers' apartments in Greenwich Palace, with Lettice no doubt, but you and your other cousins are staying with me nearby. Dame Sybil is coming, and we are staying with some old friends of mine: Sir Humphrey and Lady Scott. I believe you will be more comfortable staying at their house than sharing a truckle bed in an attic room with Lettice."

"An attic room, sir?" I was surprised into asking the question. "Is not everything at court – in a royal palace – very fine?"

"For the king and his family, aye, fine enough," Sir Anthony said grimly. "For the crowd of courtiers and hangers-on, nay, court is not about comfort and finery. 'Tis about being close to the king and his nobles in the hope of gaining position and power. Your uncle and aunt attend Lord Crewe who is a member of the privy council. The hope is that some day or other Lord Crewe may recommend your uncle for some task and he will perform the duty so well that he is given a title or some such bauble in reward." He snorted. "Your aunt, of course, hopes by way of her friend Lady Arbelle Marbury to secure a position for Lettice as maid of honour to the queen and thus find her a noble husband. Well … we shall see! But come!"

I felt slightly dazed by all this information, but I followed Sir Anthony into the depths of the stable and stopped when he did before a pretty rowan mare with a star on her forehead and three white socks.

"Well?" Sir Anthony barked. "What do you think?"

"She is a fine animal, sir, with a pretty colouring."

"Pretty?" the old man snorted. "She is a lady's mount with a sweet nature – or so I am told. Well, go on, make friends with her: she is yours now."

"Mine?" I gasped. "You … you are giving *me* a horse?"

"I believe 'tis my intention," Sir Anthony said drily. "You need a mount to carry you to Greenwich Palace and home again." His hand fell heavy and warm, but not unkindly, on my shoulder. "Her name is Meadowsweet."

I stepped forward to stroke the animal's dark, velvety nose. Gently Meadowsweet wickered and nuzzled her nose into my shoulder. I looked at my grandfather delightedly. *Mayhap he loves me a little bit!*

"Pleased?" Sir Anthony was grinning almost boyishly.

"Very pleased, sir!" I exclaimed. I dropped a curtsy and reassured Meadowsweet with a gentle hand on her shoulder. The horse was a fine surprise, but my grandfather's pleasure in giving me the gift was a treasure I tucked into my heart. "My thanks and thanks again!"

We lived in a breathless whirl of packing and preparing for court now. Geoffrey looked grim and Frances was restless and pert, while Lettice rustled her skirts and tossed her hair and spoke of nothing but gowns and gallants. Reluctantly I placed the half-illuminated manuscript for the Book of Hours in my coffer and closed the lid on paint ingredients and gold leaf for the time being. I walked across the fields and bade farewell to the Ducklingtons. And then, one cold morning before it was properly light, I hugged Edie goodbye. Matthew gave me a special blessing. Sadly I mounted Meadowsweet and rode away from Bampton Manor.

Everything about the journey, which took a number of days, was new to me. Lettice complained about the cold, but Sir Anthony said the frost made the mud hard and the roads passable: in wet weather it might be impossible to travel to court through a muddy mire. Lettice bit her lip and said no more about the cold.

I ached all over from riding every day. At night I shared a bed with Aunt Maud and Lettice as well as Dame Sybil in an inn or the house of a gentleman known to the family. Lying there, I closed my eyes, but I still saw the beauties of the countryside in my heart: rolling hills and dense woods; frost lying like a silver gilding across the landscape and encrusted bare branches, long grasses and spiders' webs with tiny drops of frozen dew like jewels; farms and villages, with homes and churches, where the air was redolent with woodsmoke and resounding with the calls of animals, the bustle of work and domesticity and the laughter of children.

The only harshness in the picture was Sir Anthony's dismay on finding a hospitable monastery, where he had intended to spend a night, had been suppressed. The wind prowled through the empty ruins. I bit my lip and turned my gaze away from what felt like the desecration of a friend.

Finally, however, after a night in a noisy inn on the edge of London, we made our way through the narrow, winding streets of the city. I was overwhelmed by the bustle and noise of the crowds on every side and the overhanging eaves of the houses almost blocking the sky from sight overhead. *I might not belong forever at Bampton Manor, the way I thought I belonged at Kirklington Abbey, but I belong at the manor more than in the city!* Then London Bridge carried us over the River Thames and into the suburb of Southwark. Out in the countryside, where I could breathe deeply and easily again, we crested a hill and Sir Anthony called a halt while the horses tossed their heads and jangled their harnesses.

"Look!" Sir Anthony pointed with his riding whip. "Behold what the king calls his sweet manor of Greenwich."

I forgot my cold nose and tingling toes as I looked at the Palace of Greenwich spread out below me like a picture map.

The palace, built of red brick with towers and turrets reaching into the sky, nestled beside the river and a tiny village including monastic buildings. The palace was bigger than I had imagined a building could be – less of a single building and more of a rambling complex of buildings arranged around three quadrangles and surrounded by a mass of outbuildings which looked, to me, like palaces in their own right. I caught sight of a garden and a tiltyard with red brick towers of its own. Flags and penants flew bravely from the towers and smoke drifted lazily from the countless chimneys. And in a deer park on the other side of the road were archery butts at the bottom of the hill and a tower, guarding the palace, at the top.

"Come!" Sir Anthony set his horse in motion again. "We must not delay if we want to be a-bed before nightfall."

Uncle Thomas spurred ahead and Aunt Maud's litter followed with Lettice trotting alongside. Geoffrey and Frances waited with me as I lingered, gazing at the towers and turrets of the palace.

"Do you like what you see?" Geoffrey asked.

"'Tis like nothing I have seen before," I admitted, as I dragged my fascinated gaze away from the palace. "'Tis like an illuminated picture of heaven."

Doubtfully Geoffrey said, "I fear the palace and the court are quite different from heaven."

"It puts me in mind of a marchpane palace," Frances said. "You know the kind, Geoff, made of marchpane molded into the shape of a palace and gilded with *real* gold and served at the end of a banquet?"

"Aye!" Geoffrey laughed. "I have never thought so before but now I see you are right."

Gloomily Frances said, "I would rather have the marchpane kind."

"As you say," Geoffrey agreed quietly. "But, come, we must not fall behind the others." Over his shoulder he said, "Mayhap you will like court better than you think and want to stay, like Lettice, Clare."

"I do not fear so," I said. I urged Meadowsweet forward and smiled at the notion of me being as pretty, bold and ambitious as Lettice! Aloud I said, "I hope to go home soon." *Home ... where I almost belong. If only I can go and still be loved. What will Grandfather say if I go without his leave?*

"Never fear," Geoffrey said. He tightened his lips in a fleeting impression of Sir Anthony. "I do not intend to waste my time here for long. As soon as our honoured grandfather gives me leave, I shall go home. You can come with me if you wish."

"I will come," I promised. I tucked the comfort of my cousin's promise into my heart with Edie's reassurance and my grandfather's pleasure in the gift of the horse. Maybe Geoffrey and Frances would love me like a real sister someday. Quickly I added, "I mean to say I will come the instant Sir Anthony gives me leave."

"Can I come too?" Frances demanded. "If I promise to do everything you say on the road?" Quickly he added, "*And* if I promise to mind you well at home?"

Geoffrey grinned at Frances. "Very well, imp, if you wish and get proper leave. For now, however, come!" Heroically he exclaimed, "Let us hasten to the palace and the service of the king!"

I giggled and Frances sniggered, but we urged our horses forward and followed Geoffrey down the hill with our cloaks billowing behind us in the cold air. Uncle Thomas, Aunt Maud and Lettice trotted along the road between the park and the palace and disappeared into the palace gatehouse. Sir Anthony led the rest of us through the village of Greenwich and along a road to the village of

Lewisham. Here, in a modest and mellow stone house overlooking the water meadows of Ladywell Fields and the Church of St Mary the Virgin, Sir Humphrey and Lady Scott gave us a kind welcome.

Later, lying in Sir Humphrey Scott's third-best four-poster bed beside Dame Sybil, with the curtains drawn against the chill, I heard my cousins bickering on the other side of the bed-chamber wall. I smiled wearily as I shifted my stiff body on the softness of the feather mattress. *Tomorrow I am going to court. I will wear my court dress, and I might see the king.* My thoughts drifted back, along the way I had come that day, to the homeliness of Bampton Manor, to Edie mending by the flickering light of the kitchen fire, to the light of the moon shining through the window of the porch chamber and gleaming upon the silver links and pearl beads of the Mother Abbess' rosary as it hung beside my bed like a benediction.

Next day, laced and pinned into the strange finery of my court dress, I tried to breathe as my senses were overwhelmed by the little kingdom – a princely realm within the realm of England – which was the court of King Henry. The Palace of Greenwich looked nothing like marchpane as I rode Meadowsweet through the palace gatehouse between Sir Anthony and Dame Sybil. A road, from which I caught sight of wintry trees in walled gardens, led to another gatehouse. I had a confused impression of guards in livery – *dark red for love or*

*bright red for laughter?* – and grubby stable boys as my grandfather helped me off my horse and ushered me into the palace.

A young gentleman in a fine suit with a jaunty swagger greeted Sir Anthony. *Mayhap he is a page or one of Lettice's famous gallants!* He led us across courtyards and through galleries into a great hall crowded with men and a few women in the grandest clothes I had ever seen: doublets and gowns made of luminous silks and soft velvets decorated with furs and jewels that caught the light and shone brighter than any illuminated manuscript. The clothes of the courtiers were the finest things in the room, however, which was hung with tapestries rather than cloth of gold as I had vaguely expected in a royal palace. Sir Anthony drew me into a clear space.

Curiously I whispered, "I pray pardon for asking, sir, but what are we to do here?"

"We wait patiently some little while and then we see the king," Sir Anthony said shortly. "Why else do you think we are here?" He frowned and looked me up and down. "Aye, you are becomingly attired, 'tis well. If by some chance the king should acknowledge you or say a few words to you, be gentle and humble." His eyes were beetling. "Remember, Clare, 'tis most unbecoming for a woman to think for herself!"

"Aye, sir, so you say," I murmured, dropping a slight curtsy. Impulsively I confided, "I doubt that I *could* think for myself if the king spoke to me: I would be all a-flutter!"

"Perhaps 'tis just as well," Sir Anthony said drily, but his eyes gleamed with humour. In a hoarse whisper he said, "Forget the shocking tales you have heard of 'that monster Henry Tudor'." Sir Anthony snorted. "A lot of silly people believe any gossip they hear about the king. He can be cruel, there is no doubt about it, but he can also be compassionate. I never met a man with a keener interest in music, medicine and shipbuilding." The old man shrugged. "I do not understand what he is about half the time, but 'tis none of my business. He is the king and he holds the heart of his people: 'tis that which matters."

The room was humming and echoing with voices as men diced at tables and women gossiped and tittered in corners but suddenly, as if someone had given a sign, a hush fell over the room.

"Make your curtsy!" Sir Anthony hissed. "The king is coming!"

A bevy of trumpets blew a fanfare. A wave of murmuring and rustling swept across the hall as courtiers, haughty and humble alike, sank into bows and curtsies. A way was cleared through the crowd of courtiers and servants as a little group of men entered the hall.

I curtsied in the billowing velvet of my court dress and watched the king approach from under my eyelashes. He stopped now and then to speak with courtiers – his voice genial and his laugh contagious – setting people at their ease while retaining his dignity. He wore no crown, only a velvet hat with a curling feather, above ginger hair and a beard. He was a heavy man, with shoulders impossibly broad, wearing a yellow, skirted doublet of some rich, embroidered stuff – slashed and jewelled with a white shirt puffing through the holes between the pearls and rubies – and a red jerkin with a deep, thick collar of brown fur which added to his size and appearance of strength. Below the skirt of the doublet the king wore white hose and white shoes. Busily I tried to remember all the colours.

As the king got closer, my legs ached, still bent in the deepest curtsy of my life. All I could see now were dirty floor rushes and the king's shoes with square toes and slashed tops.

"Ah … Sir Anthony Bampton," a voice said. It was cultured and melodious but held a note of sternness. "'Tis long since we have greeted you thus at our sweet manor of Greenwich. Stand up, man, stand up! And who is this?"

I felt Sir Anthony's hand on my shoulder and stayed where I was with my eyes lowered.

"Is this the granddaughter you told me of – the one fresh from the cloister?"

"Aye, sire, 'tis my granddaughter Clare," Sir Anthony said. And then he grunted, "Pray greet his majesty, Clare."

Shyly I glanced up at the king and smiled. I did not know what to say. All I could think of was the Mother Abbess' greeting I loved: "May our dear Lord bless and keep you always, sire, watching over all your ways."

"Aye." The king crossed himself at the mention of Our Lord. "We thank you, Mistress Clare, for your kind words."

The king smiled, and I caught a fleeting glimpse of the handsome prince he had once been.

"'Twould be a pity to waste so much sweetness in the cloister," the king said. He pinched my cheek. "You put us in mind of our daughters. I suppose you want a dowry and a husband too! I shall send you a wedding gift in thanks for your blessing." He turned to Sir Anthony and asked, "What do I hear about the price of wool from your country of Gloucestershire?"

I was relieved to be ignored as the king talked of taxes and exports with my grandfather. He was pleasant enough, but his eyes were distrustful. I felt both frightened by the monarch and sorry for the man. *What must it be like to be King of England and suspect everyone of liking you only because you are powerful and ruthless?* And then, with a nod and a restless gesture with his big, jewelled hands, the king walked on. With the pressure of my grandfather's hand removed from my shoulder, I rose stiffly, my legs cramped and my skirts crumpled into disarray.

"In faith! You have done well for yourself," Sir Anthony remarked. "For a maid who did not want to come to court, indeed, you have done *very* well!" But not until we were riding back to Sir Humphrey Scott's stone house in Lewisham did the old man ask, "And what did you think of Bluff King Hal, child?"

"'Tis surely of no importance, sir," I said.

"Nay, to be sure, but I am curious," Sir Anthony said amiably. "I wanted you to see, as I have told you before, the king is not a monster. Are you satisfied on that score?"

I blushed and laughed uneasily. Cautiously I said, "As to that, sir, the king seemed courteous and noble. I do not understand how cultured and virtuous a king could find it within himself to suppress Kirklington Abbey."

"He did not know it and love it as you did."

"I suppose not," I admitted grudgingly. "But 'tis a pity any of the religious houses have been suppressed and 'twas done at his order."

"With more orders of a similar kind to come," Sir Anthony said sagely. "I suspect we have not seen the end of the changes this era has wrought in England."

"I see, as you say, King Henry is not a monster," I concluded. I thought of saying he seemed unhappy but thought better of it and said mildly, "He is handsomer than I expected – and kinder to me than I dreamed. I cannot think how it is that he divorced Queen Catherine and condemned Queen Anne to death!"

"The king has been unlucky in love," admitted Sir Anthony. "Queen Catherine, God rest her soul, was a saint but, as I understand it, the king truly believed he sinned when he took her, his dead brother's widow, as his wife. I do not know the particulars, but I am told Queen Anne betrayed the king. Now he has married Queen Jane – a nice, quiet woman who knows her duty – and we all hope he will be happy."

"I hope so too," I said softly.

"Aye," Sir Anthony murmured. His gaze grew distant. "I was never one of the king's close friends, but I remember the early days of his reign. He was the handsomest prince in Christendom and led the court in dances and tournaments. He would be up at dawn to hunt, tend to matters of state, send an order to his shipbuilders and supervise his servants in the still room, then retire to compose a song before winning a tournament and dancing the night away. He and

Queen Catherine were like the king and queen in an old romance." He sighed. "The good old days are gone forever, I fear me, but the king has a new queen and even he cannot be unlucky in love forever."

"Lettice hopes Queen Jane will have a baby."

"Everyone hopes that," Sir Anthony said dryly. "The king loves babies and needs a son and heir: 'tis a thousand pities all those babes he and Queen Catherine had – all but the Lady Mary – died in infancy and Queen Anne had only the Lady Elizabeth who survived." The old man frowned. "The princesses are not enough. 'Twould be easy enough, when King Hal dies, for the nobles to seize power from the princesses and plunge the country into civil war again. When I was young, the nobles fought over who was to be king. We do not want those days to return, so England needs a prince. But look!" He pointed with his riding whip. "Your cousins are come to greet us!"

All that week I dutifully went to court again with Sir Anthony and Dame Sybil. Sometimes Geoffrey and Frances went too. Lettice was a court beauty, and the boys and I were beneath her notice most of the time. She flitted here and there with the younger of the queen's maids and other girls while the boys and I stood with my grandfather in the great hall where I had met the king. Nobles came and went and some of them stopped with a bow and a smile to greet Sir Anthony.

One tall and elegant young gallant with languid eyes, Sir Endymion Morton, greeted my grandfather and gazed at me admiringly, but said nothing. I found this flattering but disconcerting.

A tall man with a dignified and gentlemanly air and a calm manner looked hard at me and asked Sir Anthony, "Was your granddaughter ever a convent pupil?"

I gasped and blushed, but Sir Anthony twinkled and said, "Two of my granddaughters were, in a manner of speaking, convent pupils." Deliberately he said, "A convent education cannot be bettered, sir, for ensuring girls are nice and modest and certain to be notable housewives someday."

I thought a little doubtfully of my baking and spinning which were still far from perfect. *I fear I will only be a notable housewife if heavy bread and lumpy wool become the latest fashion!*

"As you say," the man said. He did not look at all embarrassed. "All my daughters were convent pupils in their time." He nodded at me and said, "I think I saw one of your granddaughters at Kirklington Abbey in Gloucestershire."

"Indeed?" Sir Anthony frowned, then pulled me forward and said, "This is my granddaughter Clare." He paused then said, "She was a pupil for many years, since I intended her to be a nun."

"Ah." The man nodded. "I understand." He turned to me and said, "You were there when I arrived from court with an Edict of Suppression."

My mouth went dry as I recognised Sir Hilary Cavendish, who

had come with Master Tolbert to suppress Kirklington Abbey. I lowered my gaze and dropped into a curtsy.

A little tetchily, I thought, Sir Hilary said, "Do not look so frightened, girl, I meant you no harm that day and you are safe enough now. I did but do the bidding of the king." He lowered his voice and said, "'Tis a sad business – the suppression of religious houses." But then, as if he regretted the confession, he drawled, "I suppose you know a local merchant, one Master Chastleton, who is sueing for the manor and ruins of Kirklington Abbey?"

"Aye, sir," I said, surprised by the question.

"The treasure of Kirklington Abbey was missing when the rest of the paraphernalia and plate were surrendered," Sir Hilary said. "'Twas said to be a jewelled casket containing a relic of Our Lady's robe. We could not find it anywhere."

My heart was thumping almost in my mouth, and my cheeks were burning, but I said again, "Aye, sir."

"The king doesn't begrudge the nuns the relic – 'tis a wondrous thing, indeed, more suited to a convent than the court – but I confess I am disappointed the nuns stole the casket," Sir Hilary mused. "I thought better of the Mother Abbess of Kirklington Abbey – a noble lady if ever there was one. Heigh ho, 'tis the way of things, especially in these days when we are all of us driven to desperate measures." He turned away and spoke to Sir Anthony, then turned back to me and said, "If you ever learn the whereabouts of the casket, young lady, I would be glad to hear of it. I suppose 'tis not likely but …" He shrugged his shoulders and concluded, "The relic is of no use to the king – the nuns may keep it with his good will – but he wants the casket."

I curtsied and murmured, "As you wish, sir, I …" My heart pounded as I thought of the casket and relic in the care of Master Beckley. *Mayhap we can send the casket to the king … but the relic will be safe!* I swallowed the lump in my throat and promised, "If I hear of the treasure again, sir, I will do what I can to send word or …" I was suddenly not sure how to continue so I concluded, "I will do what I can."

"I thank you," Sir Hilary said. He smiled kindly. And then he was gone.

Sir Anthony looked at me curiously. Slowly he said, "I hope you have not had a hand in skulduggery and stealing some riches."

With a clear conscience I said, "No, sir, but I have heard talk of the treasure and I may be able to help Sir Hilary."

"Aye, 'tis true, mayhap you may if you keep your wits about you," my grandfather said. "Look – here comes your cousin."

Lettice said little but grabbed my hand and pulled me along galleries and through courtyards, before ushering Dame Sybil and I up a staircase and through a throng of courtiers, into a room hung with tapestries and lined with guards. A number of courtiers were gathered in gossiping, tittering groups. The windows overlooked a courtyard on one side and the great hall and chapel on the other.

"Where are we?" I asked in an awed whisper.

"The privy lodgings," Lettice said as if that explained everything. "These are the queen's rooms. The king has a set of rooms just like these on the other side of the palace. His windows overlook the river."

Nervously I asked, "Is it not very bold of us to enter the privy lodgings?"

"Nay," Lettice said. She preened herself. "*I* may be here because my honoured mother and her friend Lady Arbelle Marbury know Lady Crewe. She is one of the queen's ladies in waiting and her husband is a member of the privy council." She smiled in a superior way. "And *you*, cloister girl, are here with *me*. Besides … 'tis only the queen's watching chamber we are in now. Beyond, through those doors, is her presence chamber where she receives guests. Beyond that, so they say, is her privy chamber. 'Tis only her ladies in waiting and maids of honour – and some very important guests – who may enter the privy chamber. We wait here."

"Why?" I whispered.

Impatiently Lettice said, "Because the queen will come this way."

I watched a young lady dressed as fashionably as Lettice cross the chamber and pass through the doors into the next room. She was not as pretty as Lettice, but she walked with confidence and even more superiority.

Lettice inclined her head and said, "'Tis Lady Ursella Holford – one of the queen's maids of honour." Lettice sighed. "Someday *I* shall …" She gasped and gripped my arm. "Hush!"

The guards swung the doors open and a bevy of ladies emerged into the watching chamber. The courtiers drew back and curtsied low. I curtsied with Lettice as a small woman, with pale skin and light hair only just visible under her gable hood, acknowledged the courtiers with a dignified glance. A moment later, she and her ladies and maids swept out of the room. The courtiers began to disperse and Lettice ushered Dame Sybil and I out of the room too. Slowly we descended the staircase which Queen Jane and her ladies had just used. Lettice was dreamy and starry-eyed, and I was not sure what to say about my glimpse of the queen that was both polite and true. *Going to court is a lot of fuss about nothing … but I cannot say that to Lettice!*

As we emerged into the courtyard below, Geoffrey, lounging against a wall, stood up.

"Well met!" He grinned. "Sir Endymion Morton was asking after you, but he is gone about some business for the king, so you will not be bothered by his gazing at you from afar again!"

I blushed and ignored my cousin while Lettice frowned and demanded, "What is this about Sir Endymion?"

"Nothing of note," Geoffrey said quickly.

"I am glad he is gone," I said. "I did not know what to say to him anyway."

"Never mind him!" Frances said. "Did you see the queen?" He stood up with a stretch and a yawn. And then, coldly, he said, "Master Toad is coming this way."

"Who?" I asked. I looked around and caught sight of a short gentleman with a florid face and a shifty gaze. I shuddered and said, "Oh … Master Tolbert?"

"I do not know his name but I call him 'Master Toad'. He is one of those men I am determined not to be," Frances said coldly. "He is a hanger-on looking for a fortune."

"A nobody," Geoffrey said dismissively. "He may be nice enough but …" He shrugged his shoulders. And then he seized my elbow and hissed, "Is he not the fellow who stood on the bridge and watched us skate on Christmas Eve?"

I nodded urgently. Just then, before I could say anything, Lady Ursella Holford appeared and beckoned Lettice away, leaving me with the boys and Dame Sybil, as Master Tolbert approached.

"I do not like him," I whispered.

"No indeed," Geoffrey murmured. He looked shocked at the notion.

Frances pretended to be sick.

"Nay," I protested, trying not to laugh. "It is not his fault he is not the sort of man we wish to know."

"It might be his fault," Frances argued in a piercing whisper. "The other day he came and talked to me and asked questions about us and where we live."

"I hope you did not tell him anything," Geoffrey said severely.

"Of course not!" Frances said indignantly. "But he knew we come from Bampton in Gloucestershire and asked me about Kirklington Abbey. He said he had heard it had a fine library and he is very concerned about the books, so he had a mind to ride into Gloucestershire and see for himself if the library is safe."

"Why is it any concern of his?" I asked.

"'Tis not," Frances said. "I told you he was a fortune-hunter."

"Hush, you young imp!" Geoffrey hissed.

Master Tolbert stopped in front of us and bowed. Smugly he said, "Well met, young sirs. How fare you today?"

Frances opened his mouth and looked very much as if he was going to say something rude, but Geoffrey kicked his brother's ankle and said, "Well enough, thank you, sir. I trust you are in good health too?"

"Not bad, not bad," Master Tolbert said. "And who is the lady?" He bowed low to me and narrowed his eyes. "She must be the pretty maiden of the cloisters I have heard so much about! I swear I saw you at Kirklington Abbey. You were a pupil? And she is your … sister?" He looked back and forth between the boys, then spoke to me: "I know your family comes from the region of Kirklington Abbey."

"Oh … indeed?" I said vaguely.

"The convent was famous for a very fine, very valuable library," Master Tolbert said. "I am exceedingly anxious about the welfare of the books." There was an edge of rough urgency in his voice. "Have you seen ought of them?"

"Nay," I said briefly. "Not since the convent was suppressed." Even when talking to Master Tolbert, I could not keep the sadness out of my voice, but the man did not seem to notice. Pertly I added,

"Since you had a part to play in suppressing the convent, sir, I imagine you know more about the whereabouts of the library than I do."

Master Tolbert sneered and inclined his head. I backed away and came to rest against the wall, beside Geoffrey, who stepped a little forward. Harshly Master Tolbert grated, "The library was full of books – cheap and mean editions with plain covers. They were worthless and we threw them on the bonfire!"

I winced at the thought of the books ascending to heaven in a cloud of smoke.

Master Tolbert hissed, "No, wench, the books I speak of are treasures. Where is the great *Gospels* and the great *Psalter*? I have heard tell of the books. Where are they?"

I blinked and said, "I do not know."

My heart fluttered as I remembered the missing books in the library and the way the other books had been pushed together to hide the gaps. *He cannot find the books that were missing from the library that day.* I gulped but returned Master Tolbert's stare. Geoffrey nudged me with his elbow, and I knew he was thinking of the Mother Abbess' letter too. *She wants me to have the best and more beautiful and valuable of the abbey books!*

"If you do not mind me asking, sir, why do you care about the abbey books?" I glanced at him curiously. "Do you like to read?"

"Not I!" Master Tolbert said. "I mean, of course, books are most beautiful and very instructive." He glanced over his shoulder and lowered his voice. "I am, to be honest, more interested in the monetary value of the books than any scholarly or religious merit. A man can make a very desirable amount of money by collecting the discarded books of a religious house and selling them to certain gentlemen and nobles – some will pay for fine words and illuminations and others will pay for costly jewels." He shrugged. "There are those, my dear young lady, who pay handsomely for a fine volume. A fortune may be exchanged for the rarest volumes!"

Horrified, I asked, "Are not such books the property of the crown?"

Master Tolbert chuckled and said, "I consider, my dear young lady, that anything left in the ruins when the king's men have done their work is the prize of he who finds it." He shrugged his round shoulders in his gaudy doublet. "The king's men are not particular about the libraries. If I am there and happen to find some unwanted books then I win the prize! And no one cares except me – and, of course, a few gentlemen at court who are only too pleased to pay me for manuscripts or jewels and not ask questions about where they were found."

I stared at Master Tolbert in disbelief and disgust.

"But, come now, I do not know why I am telling you all this!" Master Tolbert exclaimed. "I meant only to ask what if anything you know about the abbey books in Kirklington. The missing books are supposed to be some of the finest in the country – beautifully written, exquisitely illuminated and dazzlingly bound with the finest leather and precious jewels." He sighed at the thought of such riches. And then, with a sudden change of tone, he said briskly, "I shall have to ride into Gloucestershire and search the ruins again for myself. The books must be somewhere, and I do not give up easily! Excuse me."

Master Tolbert disappeared into a crowd of courtiers, and I was left alone with my cousins.

"You see," Frances said. "I told you he was a fortune-hunter."

I laughed and said, "He seems to have a very odd idea about books!" I tossed my head. "But, of course, he does not *care* about books at all! He just wants to sell the pages or covers to nobles at court – strangers who will not keep them together or care that they came from the abbey!" I looked at Geoffrey with sudden, hot tears in my eyes. "I want to go home."

Reassuringly Geoffrey said, "I do not think Master Toad will find the books, Clare, even if he does go to Kirklington Abbey."

"I do not care about finding the books," I said sturdily. "Of course, I *do* care, but ..." Suddenly my heart filled with homesickness, and my eyes overflowed with tears. "I just want to go home."

"Oh." Geoffrey looked at me solemnly, then pulled me and Frances into a private corner of the courtyard. Quietly he said, "I want to go home too. I have long been sick of court and our life here. I came this time because our honoured grandfather required it, but I want to speak to him again and ask him for leave to go home. If I go now, I should be in time to help with lambing and the spring sowing of crops, which is what I want."

I nodded and wiped my eyes on my velvet sleeve. *I want to belong somewhere and be loved, but I do not belong here and I have to go home even if it means Grandfather does not love me.* In a moment of heart-shaking clarity I realised I *needed* to go home … home to Edie and Matthew and Roger, home to where the air was fresh and honest above the green hills that rolled away to the blue sky, home to where my heart and fingers were free to find beauty and capture it for others in illuminations.

Geoffrey bit his lip and added, "'Tis the life I shared with my honoured parents and Catherine and Frances when we were a family. We have had no reason to be at home since they died, God rest their souls, but now you will be there. 'Tis a good reason for us to be there. And there is the manor and the home farm and the tenants. Being sure the books are safe would be an excuse but I cannot use it if I take you and … and 'tis, besides, better to be honest."

"Yes." I smiled at my cousin. "'Tis best if Sir Anthony knows where your heart lies."

"And there is another matter," Geoffrey said. He looked embarrassed and placed his hands playfully over Frances's ears in spite of his brother's wriggling. "I need to ask Grandfather to stop trying to make a great alliance for me and ask if he would approach Sir Philip Drayton and see if, perchance, I have any hope of winning Bess's hand in marriage."

"Oh!" I gasped with delight and clapped my hands. "I am so

glad!"

"My thanks," Geoffrey said with a lopsided smile. "'Tis far from settled however! There is Grandfather to deal with and Sir Philip Drayton may not like my suit even if Grandfather does. And there is Bess to consider also."

"Oh, never fear, *she* will like your suit!" I said. I felt an odd surge of mingled loneliness and longing which I did not understand. I ignored it and asked, "Think you that I should speak to Grandfather and ask for leave to go home too?"

Before Geoffrey could answer, Frances said, "I have never heard you call him 'Grandfather' before, Clare."

"Did I just do so?" I blushed with pleasure. "Well … 'tis who he *is*!"

"Aye." Frances did not seem to want to argue. He stuck his hands into his belt and pouted. "*I* want to go home too."

"I shall ask Grandfather for leave for *all* of us to go home," Geoffrey said.

"And so shall I," I said decidedly.

Geoffrey hesitated and said, "I do not wish to appear to hide behind a girl when I have something unpleasant to say."

"Well, if you wish, I will leave the talking to you," I said. I smiled at my cousin. "Most of it, anyway, if you please!"

In spite of our determination, however, it was not until the following morning that Geoffrey and I got to speak to Sir Anthony.

I was embroidering, making a purse from my old leaf-brown gown and mustard-yellow kirtle – *yellow for kindness* – to carry my prayer books to church, when I saw Sir Anthony out of the window of Sir Humphrey Scott's great hall. I pricked myself and almost fell off the window seat where I was perched.

"Ouch! Geoffrey!" I called. "Geoffrey! Make haste!"

"What's ado?" Geoffrey looked up from the horse harness he was polishing and asked, "Is Grandfather coming?"

"Aye." I smoothed my hair and straightened my skirts. "Come!"

"Shall I come too, Geoff?" Frances asked.

"You can say a prayer," Geoffrey said. There was a tight look of anxiety about his mouth. "Say a *Pater Noster* for us."

"I shall," Frances said piously. He gave me a sudden hug around the waist and pleaded, "Do not be too long in coming and telling me how things are settled!"

Together Geoffrey and I charged out of the front door of the house and ran down the drive to greet Sir Anthony. He was wearing a leather gauntlet, and a peregrine falcon, with a hood over its eyes, was perched on his wrist. The old man looked more content than he had since arriving at court, and I glanced at Geoffrey hopefully.

"Good morning," Sir Anthony said.

I curtsied, and Geoffrey bowed.

"Aye, aye, you have my blessing," Sir Anthony grunted. He looked from one to another. "Well, what is afoot? I can see you are both bursting with words, so let us hear some of them."

I blushed, and Geoffrey laughed in a strangled sort of way. I glanced at him and saw he wanted to speak, so said nothing. Geoffrey cleared his throat.

"Well?" Sir Anthony glanced back and forth with narrowed eyes and demanded, "You are not asking permission to pay the girl court, are you, boy?"

"Clare? Good heavens, sir!" Geoffrey exclaimed. "As much as I love Clare as a sister, I am not asking for her hand in marriage! But …" He took a deep breath. "I have found a girl to whom I *do* wish to pay court."

"Eh?" Sir Anthony looked surprised. "'Tis not for a young gentleman of your station in life to find a girl and pay her court. I have got the matter of your marriage in hand, boy, never you mind!"

Quietly Geoffrey said, "But, sir, I *do* mind. I am not a child. And I do not wish to make a noble connection with my marriage." He took another deep breath. "My wish is to run the manor, sir, so I want a *comfortable* wife."

"I dare say." Sir Anthony did not explode with anger or give any impression that he was in danger of doing so. He was looking at Geoffrey with an odd light in his eyes. "So who is this girl you consider so comfortable for a helpmate?"

Geoffrey squared his shoulders. "Bess – I mean Elizabeth – Drayton, sir."

"Bess Drayton," Sir Anthony repeated. "Hmm." He stroked his beard thoughtfully. "Have you spoken to her father?"

"Nay indeed, I could not do so properly, sir … and I would not do so without your approval anyway."

I blinked as I saw Sir Anthony hide a smile.

"Hmm." Casually Sir Anthony said, "I suppose you mean my

*permission*?"

"Nay, sir," Geoffrey said steadily. He seemed to grow taller as he spoke. "I said your approval and I meant your *approval*, not your *permission*." He paused and gave Sir Anthony a respectful but warm smile. "I value your judgement but I am almost a man now. You found me a noble bride when I was younger, however that match came to nought. I appreciate you bothering yourself with trying to find me another such bride, but I am old enough to have some say in my life now. I want to farm the manor and marry Bess and live a quiet life in the country rather than live the life of a courtier." He bowed. "I want you to know, and I want your permission and your blessing to leave court now."

"Now?" Sir Anthony frowned. "Is this not rather sudden?"

"Aye, sir, it must seem so but I have thought for some time I want to be home for lambing and the spring planting. I want to take Frances. And ..." Geoffrey caught my eyes and gave me a tiny smile. "Clare wants to go home, so it would be proper for me to escort her back to Bampton Manor."

"I see." Sir Anthony wheeled round on me. "And you? Is that what you want or is there something else?" His eyes narrowed. "I will not let you choose your own husband, my child."

"Nay, indeed," I said, startled. "I am come to ask for your leave to go home." My eyes filled with tears again, but I raised my chin to meet my grandfather's gaze. "I have done as you bid me and come to court but I find I am not myself here. I need to be at home." I lowered my gaze and allowed my tears to fall. *Grandfather will never love me now.* "Please, Grandfather, may I go home?"

For a heartbeat – a long heartbeat – there was silence.

Finally Sir Anthony cleared his throat. I held my breath and waited for him to announce his displeasure. But gruffly he said, "Very well, my child, you may go home. Your mother always said she was not herself at court either." He cleared his throat again and began musing aloud as if to himself: "I suppose Thomas and Maud will stay and Lettice with them. Her betrothal is almost settled, but Thomas can conclude the negotiations about the dowry. I shall leave court too."

I glanced at Geoffrey in amazement and caught his grin of surprise and delight.

"Very well," Sir Anthony said. "We can leave tomorrow and ride together into Gloucestershire. Dame Sybil will be with us for propriety's sake. Young Frances can come with us – it will do him good to help with farming rather than loafing around at court. And then ..." His eye fell on me. "Aye ... that business must be concluded too."

"Sir?" I was confused.

"Never you mind, my child," Sir Anthony said. "All will be revealed in good time, and I believe 'twill be for the best." He smiled and stroked his beard. "Aye ... I verily believe 'twill be for the best. Now, be gone! Inform Dame Sybil of our plans and prepare yourselves and young Frances to ride tomorrow at first light."

"Yes, sir!" Geoffrey said. "I thank you, sir, you have been very kind."

Sir Anthony waved his hand dismissively.

I hesitated before hurrying after my cousin. Mt grandfather was looking at me almost affectionately. *Mayhap ... mayhap he loves me a little bit anyway!* Without giving myself time to think, I stood on tiptoe and pressed a quick kiss onto Sir Anthony's grizzled cheek.

I rode away from Lewisham and past Greenwich Palace with a light heart.

Consolingly Dame Sybil said, "You will soon be comfortable at home again, and when you are at home you will remember your time here at court." She smiled. "King Henry's court is not easily forgot."

"Because of all the finery?" I suggested.

"Aye, there is a great deal of finery, to be sure," Dame Sybil admitted. "I was thinking that some of the cleverest and bravest people in England are at the royal court."

"Aye," I said doubtfully. "I do not think I shall forget this time but, oh, I am glad to be going home!" *Home to Bampton Manor.*

All along the road from Greenwich in Kent to Bampton in Gloucestershire, I saw signs of spring, whispers of beauty to come. All the colours I saw seemed bright and fresh as if I was seeing them for the first time: green grass – *for courage* – and blue sky – *for hope* – and the delicate, drooping petals of snowdrops shining like stars in the undergrowth at the sides of the roads. Finally, as dusk was gathering on a bitter afternoon, I almost fell off Meadowsweet's back and into Edie's embrace.

"I am home!" I said. Mistress Eglentyne purred and twined herself around my ankles. I stooped to stroke my kitten who had grown into a cat, and looked up with a happy smile. "Oh … I am so glad to be home!"

"And we are glad to have you here," Edie said. "Never doubt it, my lamb. Now come you in …"

I did … and settled happily back into the routines of the household.

Geoffrey and Frances spent most of their time out of doors around the manor and at the home farm with Jake and Sir Anthony. Matthew divided his time between prayer, study and work on the farm. The Ducklingtons, Draytons and Chastletons were still nearby. And spring was following Candlemas into the world.

The day after my homecoming, I found a loaf of dry bread in the kitchen, so I made gingerbread. I made it on my own and stood back with sticky hands and an unexpected rush of tears, because I had not known how to make the sweetmeat a year ago. I left half of it for the boys and wrapped half in a clean cloth for the Ducklingtons.

I almost fell over a family of chickens on my way out of the kitchen courtyard. The mother hen, fluffy and proud, was one of the pullets that had survived the fox before Christmas. Now she kept a maternal eye on a brood of cheeping chicks that scuttled here and there around her feet. Wistfully I thought of the nuns. *I hope they are faring as well as this hen. Mayhap their hearts are full of new life too.* One of the chicks pecked at the toe of my shoe. I laughed and whispered, "Sweet Jesus, may it be so for the nuns, if it pleases You."

The hedgerows were covered in a green blush of new growth, and the ploughed fields were ready and waiting for seed. *Spring is here and 'tis beautiful!* I heard birds cheeping and twittering and caught sight of a tiny wren with a long straw and a little feather in its beak. My world was as full of life now, after Candlemas, as it had been of death and decay before Michaelmas.

Just then I heard the unmistakable sound of pigs squealing and serious thoughts vanished as I entered the Ducklington farmyard in time to see Walter wrestle a small orange creature into the dust.

Mary Rose was doubled-over with laughter but straightened and waved when she saw me. "How glad I am to see you again, Mistress Clare." Her eyes were full of the secret-keeping look. "I was worried you might stay at court forever!"

"Not I!" I said as I joined Mary Rose. "I am glad to see you," I added, "but what, pray, is Walter doing?"

"Rich didn't latch the door of the pigsty when he fed the pigs this morning," Mary Rose said. "The piglets escaped and there were piglets *everywhere*. Walter is helping John Henry catch them."

Walter joined us with a squirming piglet in his arms. He grinned and said, "Good day to you, Mistress Clare. I think this is the last of the piglets."

He dropped the creature over the wall of the pigsty, and I watched it burrow into a pile of its brothers and sisters at the side of their large, sleepy mother.

Walter studied the piglets, sighed and said, "'Tis hard to be sure when they wriggle about so, but I think one is missing still."

"I will help you look for it," I said. "Where might it be?"

"The last one was gobbling up the hen's breakfast," Walter said. He pushed his hat back and scratched his head. "I'll check the cow byre."

I watched him leave and wondered where I would explore or hide if I were a baby pig. I heard a squeal from the direction of the barn, so I thrust the gingerbread at Mary Rose and followed the squeal. Aggie appeared in the doorway of the barn and beckoned with her eyes alight. I allowed myself to be tugged into the dark interior of the barn.

Aggie crouched down and peered under the wagon that stood in the middle of the barn. A small animal was snuffling and grunting in its shelter. I crouched down and found myself nose to snout with a baby pig. The creature was tiny with big ears and inquisitive eyes.

"Piglet," Aggie whispered loudly. "I get Walter!" She scampered out of the barn.

I murmured coaxing nothings and stealthily reached for the plump body. "Come here, sweeting, come …"

Bang!

The barn door opened and the piglet fled under the wagon as I fell forward and bumped my head on the wheel.

"Found it?" Walter asked.

"Aye … and I had almost caught it!" I said crossly.

"And I scared it away? Don't fret. I'll catch it," Walter said easily. He made some odd noises, and a twitching snout appeared. A lurch and a roll later, Walter stood up, the piglet in his arms. He grinned at me and said, "I thank you for your help."

"I did nothing," I said with a little toss of my head. "Shall I carry it back to the pigsty?"

"If you like."

I took the wriggling piglet. It quieted in my arms and snuffled under my chin. I laughed and paused by the pigsty wall to stroke the bristly body. Aggie stood on tiptoe to stroke it too.

"Better not get too fond of it," Walter said. "It's good meat for next winter."

Aggie made a face and put her fingers in her ears.

"Oh!" I slipped the creature into the pigsty. "What a horrid thing to think about!"

"'Tis life." Walter shrugged. "Our Lord provides food for us. Some of it we grow and some of it we fatten and kill for meat." He grinned. "The baby animals are sweet, though, so I have to remind the girls that they're good food too." As we walked away from the pigsty he rubbed his muddy hands on his tunic and said, "You must have missed your friends when you were at court."

"Aye," I confessed. "I missed all of you."

"All of us?" Walter grinned. "Now that's kind of you, Mistress Clare."

I smiled and said, "You and Mary Rose are as much my friends as Roger or Bess."

I talked and laughed with Walter and Mary Rose, but I could not forget the king and what Sir Hilary Canvendish had said about the casket and the relic. Next morning, while the boys were bothering Edie for an after-breakfast treat in the kitchen, I slipped away to the porch chamber and lifted the lid of my coffer. I sniffed deeply and smiled as I inhaled the familiar scent of the scriptorium: the smell of the parchment and the ingredients for paint: madder roots, saffron flowers and dried parsley. At the same time, with a little shudder, I recalled finding the treasure of Kirklington Abbey in my coffer on Christmas Eve.

Again I remembered what Sir Hilary had said: *The king doesn't begrudge the nuns the relic – 'tis a wondrous thing, indeed, more suited to a convent than the court – but I confess I'm disappointed the nuns stole the casket. I thought better of the Mother Abbess of Kirklington Abbey – a noble lady if ever there was one.*

Impulsively I jumped up and hurried downstairs to the kitchen. Geoffrey was just leaving, cheerfully whistling *Summer is a-Coming In* and pulling on Jake's old jerkin, a piece of my gingerbread held carefully in one hand.

"Stay, if you please!" I called. "I crave a word!"

"Is something amiss?" Geoffrey asked mildly.

"I want to tell you something." I hustled him out of the kitchen door and away from the curious ears of Nancy and Molly. "I was thinking about the relic of Our Lady's robe."

Geoffrey frowned in thought, then his brow cleared and he said, "Aye. What of it?"

I hugged myself against the chill and said, "I have a mind to go and consult Master Beckley again and ..." I took a deep breath. "I want him to send the casket to Sir Hilary Cavendish for the king."

"And the relic?" Geoffrey asked.

I shook my head and hugged myself more tightly. "Sir Hilary said the king wanted the casket but the nuns might keep the relic."

"What do you want Master Beckley to do with the relic?" Geoffrey asked. He frowned again and started to take off the sheep-skin jerkin. "Here, take this, you are chilly."

"Nay, I thank you," I said a little impatiently. "I want to keep you here but a moment. Mayhap Master Beckley will keep the relic in the church. What do you think?"

Geoffrey took a huge bite of gingerbread and chewed it thoughtfully. With his mouth full he said, "Edie makes the best gingerbread in Gloucestershire!" Finally, slowly, he said, "I think 'tis an excellent notion. Do you want me to come with you?"

"I can go alone," I assured him. *I must do this alone for the Mother Abbess and the nuns.* "I will take Dame Sybil and ask for a private word with Master Beckley."

"Very well," Geoffrey said. "Put a cloak on, however, for 'tis none too warm and Edie will eat me if you catch a chill and she thinks 'tis my fault!"

I laughed and retreated, then wrapped myself in my cloak and walked to the church in the village with Dame Sybil. I was nervous but reminded myself that Geoffrey had mistaken my gingerbread for Edie's. *Mayhap, if my gingerbread is as good as Edie's, I will be a notable housewife after all!* Somehow the thought was both comforting and strengthening.

The priest's house was deserted and the priest's servant, busy chopping wood, nodded his grizzled head towards the church. Dame Sybil waited in the porch while I ventured into the dim stillness of the church alone. I thought at first the servant was wrong and Master Beckley was elsewhere. I took a deep breath and allowed my heart to settle among the deep shadows and golden pools of sunlight between the tall stone pillars and stained glass windows of jewel-bright colours. Just then, as if he knew he was wanted, Master Beckley emerged from a small doorway.

"Ah … Mistress Clare." The priest smiled. "And to what do I owe the pleasure of this visit?"

I curtsied and glanced over my shoulder. The church door was open, allowing the morning light to stream into the building, but Dame Sybil was out of sight around the corner of the door.

Quickly the priest asked, "Have you come about the secret matter?"

I nodded.

"Do not be afraid to speak if you do so quietly," the priest said. "You are plotting no treason!"

I laughed quietly and nervously, then blurted, "I want you, kind sir, to send the casket to Sir Hilary Cavendish, at court, to give to the king. I saw him when I was at court with Grandfather. He said he was disappointed with the nuns – and the dear, kind Mother Abbess – for stealing the casket." In a fierce whisper I said, "I do not want Sir Hilary or the king thinking the Mother Abbess stole the casket!"

Steadily Master Beckley asked, "And what of the relic?"

"Sir Hilary said the king wanted the casket but the nuns might keep the relic." I took a deep breath. "I thought, in your goodness, sir, you might keep that here. Sir Hilary said 'tis a wondrous thing but more suited to a convent than a court."

"Wait for me here but a *Pater Noster* while, Mistress Clare," the priest said. "I want to show you something if I may."

The priest disappeared into a dark corner, and I heard a chinking sound as if two stones were rubbing against each other. The priest returned with dusty hands and two boxes. One was the jewelled casket and one was a small, plain wooden coffer.

Simply Master Beckley said, "Here is Our Lady's robe."

With my heart beating hard and fast, I asked, "Where, sir?"

Master Beckley smiled and handed me the casket. "Pray open it and see for yourself: 'tis empty."

The casket was empty as Master Beckley had said. Silently he opened the lid of the coffer and revealed the scrap of blue cloth nestling inside.

I breathed a sigh of relief and asked, "What are you going to do with Our Lady's robe?"

Briskly the priest said, "I am going to do as you suggest and send the casket to Sir Hilary Cavendish. I shall write a letter explaining that the son of the new owner of Kirklington Abbey – Roger Chastleton – brought the casket to me and that I am sending it to the king, for the royal coffers, at your request. I shall say nothing about the relic." He closed the lid of the wooden coffer. "I have a hiding place, quite secret, here in the village church. It shall be safe here."

"Forever?" I breathed. I thought of Master Tolbert and his hunt for riches at the expense of both church and king. "The king's men will not find it and destroy or desecrate it?"

"I pray God they will not," Master Beckley said. He smiled. "I had a long talk with Roger Chastleton while you were at court. What say you, Mistress Clare, about placing the relic in the chapel Master Chastleton is going to build on the site of the abbey church?"

Uncertainly I said, "I have heard the church is ruined."

"'Tis sadly so," Master Beckley said. "Master Chastleton, however, intends to build a chapel in its place. Roger says his father is willing to place the relic in the chapel. I can think of no better place for the relic to rest."

I thought about that and nodded. Slowly I said, "I think the Mother Abbess would like that, and so would Sister Ro … one of the other nuns."

"Just so." Master Beckley smiled. "I shall hide the relic for safety now."

The priest disappeared into the dark corner again, hidden from sight by a stone pillar and the shadows, with the wooden coffer. I heard the sound of two stones chinking together again. *I think Christ will be pleased about this too.* A heartbeat later, the priest reappeared.

I smiled gratefully and said, "By your leave, sir, I shall go now."

"And I shall write a letter to Sir Hilary." Master Beckley held the jewelled casket carefully, but less tenderly than he had held the coffer containing the relic. "'Tis best done as soon as possible." Wisely he said, "I think, Mistress Clare, 'tis a secret well kept between those of us who already know about this business: yourself, your cousin and Roger. 'Tis better not to gossip it around."

"I shall not tell anyone but the boys," I promised. I curtsied. "I thank you for your help." And then, hesitating in the doorway, I remembered what the priest had said the last time he had said goodbye. Curiously I asked, "*Was* my mother a reformer, sir?"

"Your mother? Aye." Master Beckley smiled. "She was a woman of great thoughtfulness who truly desired to be a good Christian. She read a great deal and was influenced by Doctor Luther's books. She loved Our Lord however." He smiled. "'Twas their faith that first united your mother and father in love."

Sadly I said, "I do not know who my father is."

"Mayhap someday you will," Master Beckley said. "I knew him as well as I knew your mother, and I can assure you that he was a good man. You have no need to be ashamed of their union." He made the sign of the cross. "Bless you, my child."

In the days that followed, I felt deliciously comfortable and free, knowing the relic of Our Lady's robe was safe and the casket was going to be sent to Sir Hilary Cavendish who would give it to the king. I still did not know where the abbey books were – and I shivered when I thought of Master Tolbert finding them by some mischance. *But 'tis enough to know the Mother Abbess wanted me to have the books and they are in safe keeping somewhere.* I was happy to be at home, happy about Our Lady's robe, happy to see my friends again.

Walter and Mary Rose Ducklington brought a fresh egg to the kitchen door and Aggie gave it to me with a sweet smile and a little curtsy. I saw Roger Chastleton at church, and he smiled at me. Edie kept me busy with baking and spinning but there was time for illuminating a few more pages of the Book of Hours manuscript. The first primroses – *yellow for kindness* – opened dainty petals to spring rain and sunshine. And I went to see the Drayton girls.

Geoffrey escorted me and Dame Sybil to Drayton Court. My cousin went off on some business of his own while we ladies were ushered into the cluttered, cosy parlour where the three sisters were sitting with their mother's gentlewoman. Katy and Mary were absorbed in their embroidery, and the two older women settled down to gossip.

I smiled at Bess and asked, "How now?"

"A little vexed," Bess said. She was pale, and her eyes were red. She embraced me almost compulsively and whispered, "I must talk to you, at once, if you please."

"Of course," I said. "Is ought amiss?"

Bess drew me through a door into the rose garden. It was bare and cheerless at this time of year, but Bess did not seem to notice. I wrapped my cloak more tightly around me and waited for Bess to speak.

"I am in *such* a scrape," Bess blurted.

"*You*?" I was shocked. Bess was gentle and good and surely above any sort of real trouble.

"Yes." Bess hung her head. "I am *so* ashamed."

"Tell me what is troubling you," I said, bracing myself for a dreadful revelation. "I will do what I can to help."

"You can do nothing," Bess said calmly. There were tears in her eyes but they did not fall. "'Tis my own fault." She took a deep breath and said, "My father told me today that he is …" She gulped. "He is arranging a marriage for me. He said he has received a surprisingly good offer for my hand. He must mean a man of great nobility. You know I want to marry a good man and I adore babies, Clare, but I do not want to marry a noble and spend my days at court!" Brokenly she said, "I have no choice if that is the life my father chooses for me. Convent or court – my destiny is in his hands. And I have done the worst possible thing." Her eyes were wide and anguished. "I do believe, Clare, I have fallen in love with … with your cousin Geoffrey!"

"Oh!" I almost laughed with relief. "Is that all?"

"All?" snapped Bess. "You do not understand! My father, for all I know, has pledged my hand to an unknown suitor. He may be anyone!" Her voice was thick with unshed tears. "And I have fallen in love with Geoffrey. I would marry him tomorrow if he asked and be a country gentleman's wife all the rest of my days. I would be the happiest woman alive and would do my best to be a good wife, besides praying every day for Our Lord and His Blessed Mother to bless our union." Her voice suddenly became emotionless. "Instead I have to marry a stranger. I did not mind the thought until … until I realised I had fallen in love with Geoffrey."

"But Geoffrey …" I blurted, then stopped and folded my lips. I was not at all sure my cousin would forgive me if I told Bess the secret of his affection for her and his dreams of their future together. Vaguely I said, "Geoffrey is very nice."

"I do not think my father will care how nice he is," Bess said. "I am a fool!"

Suddenly Bess's face crumpled and she burst into tears. I pushed her gently towards a bench and we sat down together between the bare stalks of two rose bushes. I did not know what to say, so I stroked Bess's shoulder comfortingly and waited. It was still early and the garden was quiet, but the sun was melting the last of the morning mist into nothing. I caught a whiff of damp earth and let my cloak slip back from my shoulders.

Gently I said, "Perhaps if you speak to your father and tell him how you feel about Geoffrey …"

"He will think it is a youthful passion," Bess said despairingly. "And he may already have pledged his honour with my hand in marriage."

"Is your father determined to marry you to a great man at court? Can you not explain that you would prefer a quiet life in the country?" I faltered. "Your father seems a kind man. If you told him that you like Geoffrey …"

"I do not *like* Geoffrey," Bess said. "I *love* him and my heart will break if we are separated forever, but we will be, as many have been separated from their true loves before now. I must survive … somehow."

"Good morrow, gentle mistresses."

Both of us started, and Bess looked away to hide her red and swollen face.

I gasped and tried not to giggle in surprise as I recognised my cousin. His eyes were sparkling and his hair was ruffled into disarray as he pulled his dark red cap off his head – *dark red for love* – and stuffed it through his belt. He was breathless as if he had been running. Bess gave a gasp of horror and blushed up to the roots of her soft, dark hair. She sat stiff and tall with her head turned resolutely away from Geoffrey.

Trying to pretend everything was normal, I said, "Good day to you, Cousin. Have you finished your business?"

"Not yet, but it is progressing as well as I can hope, so I think I will complete it soon," Geoffrey said. He looked as if he was trying not to laugh. After a moment he stopped trying and gave in. His voice was still rippling with laughter as he said, "I could not help hearing some part of your conversation just now and there is something I wish to say which I think … I hope … will please you."

He looked past me at Bess, and his eyes were suddenly soft and serious. "I do not deserve to be loved by you, Bess, but …" His voice broke but he continued, "I must confess you have long been loved by me. Now you are free from the convent, but I have not spoken before because I did not dare to hope that your father might … we might … that you, so good and gentle as you are, might love me and be content with what I can offer. But now …"

Geoffrey faltered into silence. I felt Bess relax at my side, but she made no sign to Geoffrey. He went to her and took her hands as he knelt on the paved path at her side.

"Bess?"

Stiffly, as if every word hurt her heart and she was holding her tears back with difficultly, Bess said, "My father has received an offer for my hand in marriage. For all I know he has already pledged my hand to some unknown suitor." She turned her head and gazed into Geoffrey's eyes. "I am sorry," she whispered, "so sorry."

Geoffrey did not say anything, but kissed Bess.

With a start and a blush I realised I was probably a great deal in the way. I slipped off the bench and almost tiptoed up the path away from the couple who were gazing into each other's eyes. Once I glanced back.

Geoffrey said something I tried not to hear – something about age, inheritance and permission. Sir Philip Drayton was named. Geoffrey said they must be patient, but spoke of the future. Bess laughed and the sound seemed to dance on the breeze.

I went inside the house and slipped into a curtained alcove where

I plopped onto a carved coffer in a billow of moss green skirts. Breathlessly I thought that never in my life had I witnessed anything as beautiful as that little scene of romance between Bess and Geoffrey. At Kirklington Abbey Bess had asked if I would not rather get married than be a nun.

*I said I did not know very much about the world, but I did not realise how much I did not know!* Bess loved Geoffrey so much that she cried. And Geoffrey loved Bess, too, enough to tell her so. And then he had kissed her and she had melted into his embrace and grown from a girl into a woman in that instant. *Is my heart being ensnared by the world? Nay. For did not God create the love of a man and woman? And other things besides love!*

With a little smile, I thought of the freshly made bread spread with butter and honey. I thought of the Ducklingtons, with red hair like my own, running and laughing in the field behind the manor house. And I thought again of Bess and Geoffrey loving each other enough to want to get married.

"I do not want to be a nun," I said. And suddenly I did not care who heard. *Uncle Matthew was right. I am free and must do as the Mother Abbess said: I must live.* I caught my breath in a little sob of gratitude and whispered, "Sweet Jesus, I thank You with all my heart for this gift I did not know I had until just now."

Next morning, recalling the sweet moment between Geoffrey and Bess and realising all over again that I did not want to be a nun now, I felt excited and restless for no reason. Geoffrey and Frances were out again, and I could not concentrate on baking or spinning with Edie. Finally I begged a few precious eggs from Edie and mixed some paint at the kitchen table.

Carefully I boiled madder roots in water and crushed saffron flowers while the water turned red. I mixed the red water with white of egg and put the saffron flowers into a little bag which I dipped and left in white of egg until the clear sticky liquid turned yellow. Meanwhile, I ground dried parsley in my pestle and mortar, then mixed the green liquid with white of egg. Finally I made the blue paint from lapis lazuli.

With the paint mixed and ready in oyster shells, I was going to retreat to the porch chamber as usual, but the table in the great hall was empty and inviting. Feeling brave and bold, I fetched the half-illuminated Book of Hours manuscript and the rest of my illuminating tools. I settled myself on my stool at the end of the table and immersed myself in the scene I was painting, while Dame Sybil sat and sewed by the fire and Mistress Eglentyne chased the dust motes in the sunlight that shone through the windows.

Busily I worked with my brushes and the paint. I had already drawn the outlines in ink and added the gilding, and now I used paints to add colour. The pictures showing the life of Our Lady, illustrated throughout the prayers, were finished. Next I illuminated the Psalms included in the book: the Psalms of Ascent and

Confession.

Around each psalm I painted a border of flowers, but among the flowers people frolicked, smiling up from the parchment. With a little smile, I painted a picture of a knight kneeling before a lady in a bower of roses. On another page, a lady played the lute under a wreath of daisies. Yet another lady walked with a friend, both of them strolling through a canopy of honeysuckle, followed by a dancing, prancing grey kitten.

Eventually, waiting for the paint to dry, I sat back. My hands were all the colours of the rainbow from the paint, but I pushed my hair back from my face and smiled. Then I heard a foot-fall behind me and swung around.

I expected to see Edie or one of the maidservants but it was Roger Chastleton. He stood before me, looking sheepish, wearing a bright red cap – *bright red for laughter* – and holding Mistress Eglentyne.

"Oh!" I stood up so quickly that I knocked my stool over. "I … er … I did not know you were here."

"I came with a message from my father, and the front door was open," Roger said. He sounded contrite, but his eyes were alight with friendly curiosity. "I could see you through the window, so I came in without knocking." He bowed to me and to Dame Sybil. "I pray pardon for intruding."

Dame Sybil smiled graciously and kept sewing.

"Oh, nay, 'tis no trouble," I said. I blushed and frowned and tried to hide my hands. "I am only … er … surprised."

My daddy-long-legs friend came closer and asked, "What are you doing?"

I looked down at the toes of my shoes as they peeped out from under the hem of my skirt. Quietly I confessed, "Painting … that is, I mean to say, illuminating." I stole a glance at Roger from under my eyelashes. "I think I told you before 'tis something I did at the convent. The nuns taught me the art of illumination."

Roger's eyes lit up and he said, "Aye … I remember now. You told me when I had an ink blot on my nose."

I laughed in uneasy agreement.

"And 'tis why you wanted parchment at Christmastide. Mistress Bess told me something of your work too," Roger said eagerly. "Did you illuminate a Book of Hours for Sir Philip Drayton at Michaelmas?"

I nodded.

Roger peaked his eyebrows and asked, "If it please you, may I see your work?" He smiled coaxingly. "I prithee?"

Torn between embarrassed reluctance and shy delight, I stood back and motioned to the parchment on the table. Eagerly Roger put the cat down and stepped forward. He leaned over the table while I twiddled the paintbrush in my hand and nibbled the end.

"In faith!" Roger looked up with shining eyes. "You truly have a gift for illumination!"

"Nay," I said. I blushed and shook my head. "'Tis kind of you to say so, but my work is not as good as the work of many professional scribes." I joined Roger at the table and explained, "Many books are printed now. 'Tis a hundred years or more since many books were written by monks and nuns. Most manuscripts – books written by hand – are made by scribes. Monks and nuns only make a small number of books for the gentry folk who wish to give their money to the church rather than a business. And not all manuscripts are illuminated." I smiled shyly. "'Tis an old-fashioned art."

"I like it," Roger said decidedly. "Your depictions of Our Lady are beautiful." He pointed to the first picture I had illuminated at Bampton Manor: "Here Our Lady seems to be at Kirklington Abbey." He pointed to a page with a picture of the nativity: "But here the Holy Family seem to be in … well … in Walter Ducklington's cow byre!"

I rubbed the bridge of my nose and smiled.

"Here are the shepherds with the Holy Family in the byre, and here are the kings adoring Our Lord by the fire in Edie's kitchen!" Roger looked at the pictures again. "Here are the shepherds grazing their sheep in the fields where my father and I graze our flocks, and here are the kings coming down the lane from Nailsworth. The psalms are surrounded by all the flowers of the countryside." He grinned. "I wonder who the knight is! But is this you and your kitten?"

I blushed and smiled again but did not say anything. *He understands!*

"And here, in these other pictures, are all the things of the everyday world: bread and brushes and a spinning wheel!" Roger said. "'Tis wondrous!" He bent and looked more closely, before glancing up with a grin. "I like the knight and the lady among the roses in the border!"

"The monks and nuns of old used to put all sorts of devices in the borders of illuminated manuscripts," I said. "'Tis *very* old fashioned, but I saw it in one of the abbey books and decided to put devices in these borders too." I smiled. "When I was at Kirklington Abbey … well … the convent and the art of illumination were all I knew. But now? I know so much more than I knew there was to know …"

Suddenly, without meaning to, I thought of Geoffrey and Bess as my gaze and Roger's gaze met. Quickly, blushing, I started to gather the sheets of parchment together.

"My uncle Matthew spoke of living a holy life in the world," I said, because I could not think of anything else to say, but the thought popped into my head. "Do you think 'tis possible?"

"I do," Roger said earnestly. He sat down at the table and leaned his arms on the top. Tentatively he said, "I have read some books by Doctor Luther."

I smiled. *He reads books by Doctor Luther too – like me and Bess and my mother!*

"He teaches that all Christians – not just monks and nuns – can live a holy life." Roger ran a hand through his hair. "'Tis their vocation to live for Christ in the world. If Doctor Luther is right, all the things of our everyday life can be used to honour Our Lord."

"I can honour Him with my spinning wheel and Walter Ducklington can honour Him with his plough," I said promptly.

"Aye. And I can honour Him with my sheep too." Roger grinned. "I spend a lot of time with sheep, especially at this time of year, when they are lambing. And I also spend a lot of time thinking about sheep and wool and cloth. So I *hope* 'tis possible to honour Our Lord in this work!"

I was curious about something so I sat down, rested my chin in my hands and asked, "Do you like sheep?"

"Aye, well enough," Roger said. "They are silly creatures, but not vicious. And think how well they have served England – and my family too!" Quickly he explained, "The wool trade and the cloth trade have made England wealthy and 'tis with the money my father – and his father and grandfather before him – has made as a wool merchant that he has bought Kirklington Abbey."

I thought about the woolly animals with their funny faces and contrary ways and decided, "I like sheep too." Curiously I asked, "And you going to be a wool merchant someday?"

"In a way," Roger said. He settled himself more comfortably and explained, "I am apprentice to my father and learning the wool trade from him, but I am learning something of the cloth trade from a clothier in Nailsworth too. Sometimes I go with my father and the clothier to do business in Stroud. And I help to tend our flock of sheep, of course, as well as buying wool from other wool growers."

"Other wool growers?" I asked with a laugh. Mistress Eglentyne sprang into my lap and I stroked her gently. "Does wool grow?"

"It grows on the back of sheep," Roger said. "We call the smaller farmers the wool growers."

"You have sheep!" I giggled. "Are you a wool grower too?"

"Well …" Roger grinned. "I am not a wool grower, no, but I do not think I shall ever be a great merchant like my father – *he* is an influential merchant in Gloucestershire *and* England. You have heard of the Wool Staple – the company of merchants who control the wool trade? My father is a member of the company! But I am different. He went to school at St Paul's School in London but I went to the grammar school in Stroud. And now he has bought a manor for our family but I will still have to work the land and manage the business." Roger shrugged his shoulders. "I do not mind. A man needs to work. I shall be content with a good life and an honest trade to earn a living for my family."

Our gazes met again.

Quickly I asked, "It is a hard trade?"

Roger looked thoughtful and said, "I do not think so but I may sing a different song when I have been doing it all my life! 'Tis marvellous, really, how wool grows on sheep. My father buys it in tods and sacks and sells it for making cloth – nearby or in London – in cloves and sacks."

Mystified, I said, "I know what a sack is but what is a tod and a clove?"

"A sack is three-hundred and sixty-four pounds," Roger rattled off. "There are thirteen tods or fifty-two cloves to a sack."

"Oh," I said. "And the sacks – or tods or cloves – are full of wool?"

"Aye."

"I see," I said, without understanding at all.

Helpfully Roger said, "Cloves are called nails sometimes." He looked hard at me hard and asked, "Do you *really* understand?" Without waiting for an answer he added, "Now tell me about your painting." He peered into an oyster shell. "What is this?"

"Lapis lazuli," I said.

"It looks like blue to me," Roger said doubtfully.

"'Tis blue made from tiny bits of lapis lazuli," I said. "Azure blue paint can be made from an azurite stone and violet blue paint can be made from the seeds of turnsole plants but ultramarine blue paint, like this, is made from lapis lazuli."

"I never saw such a *blue* blue before," Roger said. "What, pray, *is* lapis lazuli?"

"'Tis a precious stone from a land of deserts and mountains, far beyond France or the Holy Land, almost as far away as China," I said. "'Tis more precious, even, than spices and silk! Sister Joanna said 'tis a mystery how lapis lazuli comes to England – carried by traders on creatures called camels and in carts and ships."

"And how does it turn from a rock into this paint?" Roger asked.

"'Tis ground into powder, boiled and allowed to settle then mixed with white of egg," I said. Under my breath I said, "Blue – lapis lazuli – for hope."

"For hope?" Roger looked at me brightly. "Do colours make you think of virtues?"

I hung my head and gazed at the blue – the deep, intense blue of lapiz lazuli for hope – in the oyster shell. Apologetically I said, "Grandfather says 'tis not becoming for a female to think for herself. When *I* think for myself, I think of all sorts of odd things, like green for courage, yellow for kindness and lapiz lazuli for hope."

"And why not?" Roger asked. "I do not think 'tis unbecoming for you to think for yourself." He jiggled the oyster shell of paint and said, "I believe you are very courageous in leaving the convent – and I know you are very kind. But mayhap you *do* need one thing more."

"What, pray?" I asked.

"Hope," Roger said, "like this blue paint. Hope in the faithfulness of Jesus Christ and in the good times to come by His grace."

Our eyes met, and we gazed at each other for a long heartbeat.

"Mistress Bess says you truly love Our Lord," Roger said.

"I do," I said. "I mean … I try to love Him as He deserves."

"And so do I." Roger smiled and quoted: "I believe Jesus Christ, true God and also true man, born of the Virgin Mary, is my own Lord …"

"… and He has redeemed me, purchased and won me from all my sins, from death and from the devil with His holy, precious blood and with His innocent suffering and death …" I continued.

Together we concluded, "… that I may be His own."

We smiled at each other.

Simply Roger said, "I try to hope in Him."

"Hope." Tears sprang into my eyes, but I blinked them back. "I shall try to hope in Him too."

Our gazes met and lingered.

"Speaking about the good times to come, Mistress Clare, I almost forgot I am here to tell you about a good time to come very soon!" Roger said abruptly. "My father has given me leave to take some friends to see the abbey ruins, and I promised to invite you when you were home from court. Think you that you and your cousins can come soon?"

I hesitated and glanced at the picture of Our Lady which I had copied, from memory, from my favourite image in the abbey church. *The abbey is ruined.* But I wanted to go and look for clues about the abbey books.

Quickly, before I could change my mind, I said, "If Grandfather gives me leave, I would like to come." I gulped. "My thanks for your kind invitation." I lowered my voice – mindful of Dame Sybil sewing by the fire – and said, "I am glad you are to have the treasure of Kirklington Abbey."

I meant the relic of Our Lady's robe, and I knew Roger understood.

"So am I," he said quietly. "Although the Mother Abbess, in her letter, said the abbey books are the *true* treasure."

I was not sure about that, since the relic was a priceless treasure, but I said nothing.

Roger propped his elbows on the table and his chin up in his hands and said, "I have been puzzling about what the Mother Abbess said in her letter." He quoted more or less correctly, "I want you to have the abbey books so I have wrapped and hidden them. They cannot be easily found. St Kyneburgh will guard them well and the farmer knows my rosary."

Eagerly I asked, "What do you think it means?"

"Well … Farmer Jeffreys farms some of the church land near Kirklington Abbey and he has a bull called Farmer," Roger said. "I do not suppose the Mother Abbess knew *that* however. But there is a copse near Bampton called Farmer's End. I went there and poked around in the bushes but could find nothing." He sighed. "I thought perhaps she might have buried the books in the copse."

I giggled in spite of myself at the thought of the Mother Abbess digging a hole for treasure in the middle of nowhere, perhaps at the dead of night, surrounded by the precious books.

Resignedly Roger said, "You are right. 'Twas an odd fancy I had! And it does not take St Kyneburgh and the rosary into account besides."

Sweetly I said, "'Twas very good of you to go and look for the books in the copse."

"Think nothing of it," Roger said gallantly. He grinned and added, "'Twas the best adventure I have enjoyed for some time!" He frowned thoughtfully and ruffled his hair. "I cannot think how St Kyneburgh can guard the books. As for the rosary … mayhap you should take a step for each bead … but what has that to do with a farmer or a bull?"

"Or a copse. 'Tis a mystery indeed." Shyly I said, "I thank you for your trouble." I was touched by Roger's thoughtfulness. "I will not forget your kindness."

Roger gave me a lopsided grin. I wondered about the dancing twinkle in his eyes when he glanced at my face, but I dismissed my curiosity. Only when he had gone did I discover a streak of blue paint adorning my forehead and one cheek.

"Oh!" I spat on the hem of my apron and rubbed my face. The paint stained my apron. Hopefully I asked Dame Sybil, "Is that better?"

"Truthfully, my dear, it is a little worse," Dame Sybil said. "I think you had better ask Edie for some soap and water."

Mortified, I said, "Roger saw me like this – all covered in paint like a child!"

"I do not believe he minded," Dame Sybil said with a smile. "He is not the sort of lad to mind a little paint on a friend's face."

"Nay, well, I will not mind it either," I decided. *Roger is so nice that it does not really matter. Besides … I am going to see the abbey in ruins. Nothing else matters.*

The strange thing about baking and spinning was that just when I thought I was never going to spin a smooth thread or make a light loaf of bread … I did. It was the day after Roger's visit. All of a sudden I felt being a notable housewife – who spun and baked and brewed and sewed – was a real possibility. But then my thread broke and my bread burned. I was glad when Blind Dame Mary came to the back door for charity with her son.

I found some old (but unburned) bread and broken meats, and carried them to the blind woman and Wat as they waited in the kitchen courtyard. Blind Dame Mary fumbled with her battered basket and dropped a curtsy as she mumbled her thanks.

Gently I said, "'Tis no trouble. You are a good woman and 'tis a pleasure to give what we can from our blessings."

"Christ and His Saints bless you," the blind woman said. Her vacant eyes were pitiful as she squinted and seemed to search and strain for a glimpse of my face. "You're well, Mistress Clare, I trust?"

"Aye!" I laughed at the remembrance that broken threads and burned bread were very small ills. My heart was crowded with visions of the Mother Abbess' rosary, Edie's face, Sir Anthony's gruff voice and affectionate smile, Geoffrey's thoughtfulness, Bess's laughter and Roger's daddy-long-legs self and the smile which, I suddenly realised, made my heart skip a beat. In a burst of contentment and gratitude I said, "Indeed I am, I thank you, my good dame. I hope you and Wat are well too."

"Well enough," Dame Mary said. "'Twas a cold winter, but the worst is over." She raised her face to the warmth of the sun and I wondered if she could hear the birds trilling as sweetly as I could. "We do miss the dear nuns in Kirklington, we do."

"So do I," I said softly.

Reminiscently the blind woman said, "'Tis Sister Veronica I miss most. She always knew 'ow to make a body laugh. An' she were proper devoted to St Kyneburgh."

"Aye, she was," I said. *In the spring, the season of her birth, she took candles and flowers to the old chapel in the woods that was dedicated to St Kyneburgh ... but no more.* I sighed and asked, "Is Sister Rosemary, who married Rich, well?"

"Aye," Dame Mary said. "She's 'nother kind soul, Mistress Clare, who always 'as time for a poor old blind woman an' 'er lad. She'll be a good mam to 'er babe."

I smiled sadly as I thought of Rosemary and her broken vows. *But a baby is a good gift from Christ.* Our Lady, I felt sure, would understand. *And maybe Christ would too.*

"... always asking questions," the blind woman grumbled. She frowned. "I've told Wat, 'ere, not to talk to 'im."

"Who?" I asked, but anxiety was already tiptoeing up and down my spine.

"A gentleman," Dame Mary said. "At least 'e speaks like a gentleman."

"And 'e dresses like a gentleman," Wat said, unexpectedly joining the conversation. "'e's short with a red face an' a dishonest eye. Always coming to Kirklington an' asking questions, 'e is, as if we've got nothing better to do but gossip."

I gulped and asked, "What does he ask questions about?"

"The convent an' the blessed nuns," Wat said promptly. His eyes narrowed and he frowned. "'e's got a thing about books an' secrets, 'e 'as, which is mortal strange. An' asking about you, 'e was, last time 'e came. Not more than a few days ago, that was, but we said nought about where you live. Mam an' me …" He glanced at his mother affectionately. "Mam an' me don't say nothing about you."

"I … I thank you," I said quakingly. "Our Lord and His Blessed Mother be with you."

I was worried about the stranger and his questions all day, but Geoffrey was quite calm when I told him about them after supper.

"Are you not worried too?" I asked, slightly aggrieved. "The man must be Master Tolbert, and he must be looking for the abbey books."

"I dare say," Geoffrey said. "He asked for you because he thinks you know where the books are, but you do not! I do not think he will come here – he must know where you live because he knows you are part of our family, and everyone knows where Sir Anthony Bampton lives – but if he does, Jake will turn him away from the gatehouse. Even if he asked you where the books are, Clare, you do not know!"

"I suppose you are right," I said slowly. "I do not know where the abbey books are. But I like him not at all!"

"Neither do I," Geoffrey said cordially.

I did not feel, however, he cared a great deal about the abbey books just then, and I had a vague idea it was something to do with Bess. I sighed and kept my next thoughts to myself. But later, lying in bed and looking at the Mother Abbess' rosary shimmering in the moonlight from the window, I hugged my cousin's words to my heart: "you are part of our family". I smiled. *I have a real family! And my cousins do not care whether I am a notable housewife.* I rolled over and snuggled down, so the scratchy wool of my blanket tickled my chin. *But I will not forget my first family at Kirklington Abbey. And tomorrow ...*

I lost the end of my thought in sleep, but I remembered as soon as I woke up next morning. I sat up in bed and gazed at nothing through a tangled mass of hair. *I will take flowers to the old chapel in memory of Sister Veronica.*

It was easy enough to fill a basket with primroses – *yellow for kindness* – but nothing else went according to plan. Sir Anthony was stalking around looking torn between satisfaction and severity. Edie was talking about turning me into a notable housewife more than usual – even for her – and looking at me anxiously. Geoffrey was working on the home farm, but Frances had toothache and was being tended to by Dame Sybil. I felt as if I were escaping from the manor house when I crept outside with my basket.

Matthew, walking along the sunny path from the home farm with the breeze stirring his hair and his habit, smiled and asked, "Where are you going, Clare?"

"To the old chapel in the woods," I said.

Matthew frowned. He was looking less gaunt and more settled now, although he still talked of going to France. "'Tis a long way for a pretty maid to go on her own."

"'Tis not so very far," I said. "I will not be long."

"Dame Sybil is tending young Frances," Matthew said with a frown. "What ails the boy?"

"Toothache," I said briefly, with a little shudder. "I hope Dame Sybil can help."

"I pray so," Matthew said. "Frances eats too many sweetmeats." He saw my basket and seemed to understand the primroses. "Mayhap I should accompany you to the old chapel."

"I thank you." I bit my lip. And then, shyly, I said, "'Tis not far and quite safe and … 'tis, besides, something I want to do by myself, if I may, for the nuns."

"Ah." Matthew's face softened with sorrow and sympathy. "I will not bar your way, then, but I will come and find you if you are over long."

"I thank you," I said, then I dropped a curtsy and hurried on my way.

The woods, soft with green buds and spring sunshine, were full of birdsong. At first I sang, too, as I walked. But it was further than I thought – and nearer to Kirklington than I remembered – and I was soon tired.

Finally, I entered a clearing and saw the old chapel. It was a lonely spot. *Perchance I won't stay long at the old chapel, just leave the flowers, in remembrance.* I was thinking about Sister Veronica and Rosemary and perhaps that was why I did not see Master Tolbert coming until he and another fellow – a huge man with a barrel of a chest and a patch over one eye – stepped into the middle of the path. I stopped with a little shriek of surprise – that I instantly regretted –

which silenced the birds.

In the silence Master Tobert stopped looking surprised and smiled – although it was more of a sneer than a smile – then said, "We meet again." He bowed and somehow made a mockery of the gesture. "What an unexpected pleasure."

"Good day," I said with as much dignity as I could. Unfortunately, I could not pretend to mistake the short man with the florid face and shifty eyes. I ignored the other man and said, "Pray let me pass, sir."

"In good time," Master Tolbert said. "First, though, I want to know something."

Warily I said, "What, pray, do you want to know?" I took a step back and frowned. "What, indeed, do *you* want with *me* at all, sir?"

"My dear young lady," Master Tolbert said, "I want the abbey books."

"You said you threw them on the bonfire," I said shortly. I looked away, through the trees, in the direction of the road that ran from Kirklington to Bampton. "I fear they are gone forever."

"Only the cheap and mean editions the nuns left in the library are gone forever." Master Tolbert sneered. "I want the books like treasure – the great Gospels, the great Psalter … and others. And you, wench, know where they are!"

"I do not," I said calmly. I hugged my basket and dug my fingers between the woven branches of willow. I forced myself to look Master Tolbert in the eyes and said, "I speak truly: I do not know where the abbey books are."

For a heartbeat Master Tolbert faltered, then he hissed, "You lie!"

"I do *not*!" I frowned at him. "I do not lie. And I do not know where the abbey books are!"

For a moment, Master Tolbert frowned at me and tapped his foot on the ground.

Impulsively I said, "But I would not tell you if I *did* know."

"No?" Master Tolbert sneered. "We will see about that. Adam? The girl is going to the chapel. Pray help her on her way!"

The huge man, who had held an iron bar at Kirklington Abbey, stepped forward. Master Tolbert jerked his head in the direction of the chapel. Adam seized me, and my basket flew out of my grasp, scattering primroses across the mud of the path, like yellow stars with green auras. I stared at them stupidly, trying to gather my wits, then screamed. A rough hand was clapped over my mouth. I writhed and kicked, but it was no good. Adam jogged across the clearing towards the chapel. Out of the corner of my eye, I saw Master Tolbert open the door, then I was tossed inside, and the door was slammed.

I landed on the earth floor with a bump that jarred every bone in my body and made my head throb. All I could do was grope my way into a dim corner and prop myself up until the world stopped spinning. I buried my head in my hands and wondered why I tasted blood.

For a long time there was silence apart from the drumming of my pulse in my ears and the birdsong outside the old chapel. People said it was built in the days of the saints before the coming of the Norman conquerors. The earth floor was hard and damp and the stone walls were ancient and rough. Light filtered through the cracks between stones and mortar – and so did a draft that made me shiver. It was a long time since a priest had officiated behind the bare and forlorn altar. Now Sister Veronica was dead, I realised, no one came to the old chapel.

Panic surged into my heart. I staggered to the door and kicked it. Outside Master Tolbert laughed unsympathetically and asked, "Well, wench, are you ready to tell me where the abbey books are?"

"I do not know where the abbey books are!" I yelled. I pounded on the door with clenched fists and added, "My cousin calls you 'Master Toad', and he is right to do so!"

Master Tolbert laughed again and I thought I heard Adam laugh too, then the sound of their voices grew distant.

I crept back into the corner and whispered, "Sweet Jesus, please help me!" I leaned my head against the wall and closed my eyes. "I do not know where the abbey books are, but I do not want to die here in the old chapel. I confess I do not want to die at all yet! I want to live in the world – truly live, to the full, as the Mother Abbess said – and live a holy life like you and Our Lady."

"Where are the abbey books?" Master Tolbert roared through the door.

I bit my lip – and tasted blood again – but said nothing.

He retreated.

In the silence I whispered, "I want to get married and have babies, like Your Blessed Mother, as Bess and Edie and Matthew said."

I felt a bit confused as I thought of Geoffrey kissing Bess, of my daddy-long-legs friend Roger Chastleton and of tiny Aggie Ducklington, all together, as if I had drawn them with careful lines and bright colours in an illuminated manuscript.

"I want to be a notable housewife even if I never spin and bake as well as Edie and Mary Rose." Tears escaped from under my eyelashes and I felt them trickle down my cheeks and off the end of my chin. "Sweet Jesus, I want to *live*."

I must have slept, as time passed, because the next thing I knew was someone shaking me awake and a familiar voice saying my name and urging me to make haste.

I blinked and rubbed my stiff neck. Stupidly I gazed into a familiar face. And then, slowly, I said, "Oh … Roger."

"Aye," he said. He left me and poked his head outside the door. "Make haste, I beg, before they come back."

"Come back?" I repeated. I tried to stand up, but my feet had gone to sleep and I stumbled and almost fell into his arms as he turned back into the chapel. "Who?"

"Your persecutors," Roger said. He grasped my elbows and gave me a little shake. "Wake up, sweeting, I prithee!"

Dizzily I wriggled my toes to restore feeling, and recalled, "Master Tolbert and the man he calls Adam …" I stared at Roger, then almost pushed him out of the chapel. "Oh, Roger, hurry up!"

Roger laughed, but grabbed my hand and held me back, then glanced around the clearing and nodded. "'Tis all clear. Let us go quickly now!"

Together we ran for the shelter of the trees. The ground was uneven, but we helped each other along as we plunged through the briars and brambles until the chapel was out of sight. Finally, we collapsed against the gnarled trunk of a friendly oak. Roger was panting and laughing. I was embarrassed to realise I was sobbing.

"Oh, Clare, pray do not cry!" Roger said. He was still panting, but he sounded dismayed. "I prithee!"

I leaned my face into the hard, bumpy wood of the tree and sobbed harder.

"You are safe now," Roger said. He swept the lock of hair out of his eyes and gave me an awkward hug. I wept into the front of his doublet and he said, "I promise Master Tolbert and Adam – whoever they are – will not hurt you now."

"They threw me into the old chapel and locked the door," I wept. "They wanted me to tell them where the abbey books were but I do not know." I gulped and added, "And I would not have told them anyway!"

Roger gave me a squeeze. "I daresay the abbey books are very fine and truly lovely, but you are more important then all the books in Christendom!"

My heart warmed and gave a funny skip, as I sniffled into his shoulder then realised I was hugging my daddy-long-legs friend in the middle of the woods. I blushed and withdrew from his kind embrace with a wobbly laugh.

"Are you well now?" Roger asked. He grinned and said frankly, "You look a sight indeed!"

"I do?" I smoothed my hair and noticed my hands were muddy.

Roger grinned again and said, "You have mud here …" He touched my chin with one finger. "And you have a monstrous bruise here …" He touched my forehead and I winced. He said, "I pray pardon. I think you have also bitten your lip."

Crossly I said, "'Tis not my fault!"

"Of course not," Roger said. "Come, sweetheart, let me help you home."

He held out his hand and I placed mine in it.

We were almost home when I realised he had called me 'sweetheart'. *'Tis nought but kindliness. Mary Rose and I call Aggie sweeting too. But not sweetheart.* And I blushed and smiled at Roger as we hurried through the dusk to the golden pool of light spilling out of the kitchen door.

"Well, Mistress Clare, here you are!" Edie exclaimed. She dropped her rolling pin with a clatter and swung round from the kitchen table with her hands on her hips. "Mistress Clare … and Master Roger too! Where have you been?" She pulled me into a motherly embrace, then rounded on Roger: "You ought to be ashamed of yourself for keeping Mistress Clare away from home for so long!" She looked at me, and her mouth dropped open. "But what has befallen you this day? This mud … that bruise … and why is there this blood on your face, my lamb?"

Quickly Roger said, "She bit her lip – hence the blood." He smiled at Edie and said simply, "Clare went to pray and was attacked in the woods, but all is well. I found her and brought her home."

"Attacked!" Edie gasped. "What, by all the saints, is the world coming to when Sir Anthony Bampton's granddaughter is attacked? But why, my lamb, did you go on your own? All the men are looking for you!"

Wearily I said, "I went to the old chapel in … well … in remembrance for the nuns. I went alone because I wanted to be alone and I have often walked to the Ducklington farm on my own. Matthew knew where I had gone."

"He said you'd gone to the old chapel of St Arilda in the east woods," Edie said. "He went looking for you at noon but found no sight or sound of you in the woods."

"Oh." Everything seemed a long way away. "I went to the old chapel of St Kyneburgh in the west woods."

"But 'tis near Kirklington!" Edie said in consternation. "Matthew would never have let you go that far on your own!"

"I did not know about the old chapel of St Arilda," I said. Tears burned the back of my eyes. "I pray pardon for doing wrong and worrying everyone."

"Do not try to talk more now," Roger said. He guided me to the settle and pushed me gently onto the seat. "You are safe at home now." He grinned. "And Master Tolbert still does not know where the abbey books are!"

I tried to smile. Edie was bustling around making possets and gathering warm water and soft clothes to bathe my face. Wearily I closed my eyes.

Roger settled beside me and whispered, "Master Tolbert – is he the man Frances calls 'Master Toad'? - is no match for us!"

I opened one eye and gave him half a smile, but I did not say anything because just then Matthew hurried into the kitchen and demanded, "Is she here? Jake says she is. Roger?"

"Here I am, sir," Roger said. He stood up and bowed. With a courtly gesture he said, "And here she is too."

"Clare!" Matthew came to my side and gazed down at me anxiously. "My dear niece, what happened?"

Roger and I looked at each other and Roger said bluntly, "She went to the old chapel of St Kyneburgh – not St Arilda – and I fear she was attacked, but …"

"Roger rescued me," I blurted.

"Rescued you?" a voice thundered. "From what, pray?" Sir Anthony stalked into the kitchen. He was wearing riding boots and a cloak. "What is this I hear of attacks and rescues?" He pulled me to my feet and wrapped me in a grandfatherly embrace that took my breath away in surprise. Emotion glimmered in his eyes like tears, but he glared at me. "I thank Our Lord and His Saints you are safe …

but you, girl, have been gadding about without a gentlewoman and getting into trouble! Do you realise all the men of the place have been looking for you since noon?"

I shook my head in dismay.

"We were that worried about you – me and Roger and Sir Anthony Bampton," another voice said, I looked up and there was Walter Ducklington crowding behind Matthew and Sir Anthony. He stared at me hard and demanded, "But what's amiss with your face, Mistress Clare?"

Just then there was a shout outside, and I thought I heard Geoffrey calling, "Have you news of Clare? It grows too dark to seek her now without torches!" He bounded into the room – also wearing riding boots and a cloak – and drew up short when he saw me. "Clare! God be praised, you are safe, but whatever is amiss?"

Suddenly the room was full of people talking and jostling. I sat down again. Edie was trying to bathe my face and Dame Sybil was clucking about my wounds. Frances was staring at me, and I could see he had a thousand questions at the tip of his tongue. It was hard trying to talk to everyone at once.

Quietly Roger said, "Clare had an adventure. She went out alone, to pray at the old chapel of St Kyneburgh in the woods, as she has often walked to the Ducklington farm." Sir Anthony frowned, then shrugged. Roger continued, "I dare say she did not know how far the chapel is from Bampton Manor. Master Tolbert …"

"I *knew* it!" Frances exclaimed with a bounce. His toothache seemed to be better, and he was in the best of spirits. Almost triumphantly he said, “He tried to make you tell him where the abbey books are!”

I nodded reluctantly.

“Oh.” Geoffrey went pale. “Clare, I beg your pardon, I never thought he would stoop to such a thing or I would have …”

“Of course you did not,” I said quickly. “‘Tis not your fault. But Frances is right – Master Tolbert wanted me to tell him where the abbey books were and he locked me in the old chapel when I said I could not.” I smiled. “I said I could not *and* would not!”

“Good girl,” Geoffrey murmured. “Still … I prithee pardon for underestimating the toad.”

Matthew looked miserable, and Sir Anthony looked as if he might explode.

Quickly I said, “Anyway, ‘tis over now, because Roger rescued me.” I gave him a grateful smile. Edie left with the dirty water and damp clothes and began to confer with Dame Sybil. I smiled at my family and said, “The mud is gone and you see I have only a little bruise.”

“A *monstrous* bruise!” Frances said admiringly.

“And a bloody lip,” Roger said.

Crossly I said, “Pray stop reminding me!”

“I prithee pardon,” Roger said with a cheeky smile that was not at all contrite. “But, since you have suffered for them, I confess I want to find the abbey books more than ever now!”

“Aye,” Sir Anthony said grimly. “And I have a mind to know exactly what ‘the abbey books’ are and why there is all this fuss about them – *especially* because there is a letter come for you, young lady, from court."

"For me?" I echoed in amazement.

"Aye, for you, for Mistress Clare Bampton," Sir Anthony said.

Walter, lounging against the wall beside the fire, opened his mouth then shut it again. Roger winked at him. I glanced at the boys curiously.

"But what *is* all this about – treasure and books and letters from court?" Sir Anthony demanded. He crossed his arms. "Sir Hilary Cavendish had special speech with you at court. You consulted Master Beckley on some secret matter. And now you have a bloody lip for refusing to tell a stranger about 'the abbey books'. What are they? I have a mind to hear the whole story. Come into the great hall and tell me everything. You too, Walter, for you have proved true this day."

Walter grinned at me and jostled Roger, but there was no time to talk as we did what we were bid. The boys and I sat around the table in the great hall. Sir Anthony sat beside the fire in his carved chair and listened with occasional huffs and puffs. He read the Mother Abbess' letter and grunted with approval. And then he gave me the letter from court. I broke the seal, with Frances joggling my elbows and Geoffrey and Roger breathing hard over my shoulders, while Walter watched frowningly. Inside, in many swirling letters, Sir Hilary Cavendish sent me thanks for finding the gold and jewelled casket and sending it to him at court via Master Beckley.

"Did Master Beckley mention me in his letter?" I wondered out loud.

"I imagine he did not, but Sir Hilary is a shrewd man," Sir Anthony said dryly. "He can add two and two, and he knows the sum total is four. I will not ask how you found the casket. However I *will* write and tell Sir Hilary what his man, Master Tolbert, has been up to in this part of the world. I dare say he and his henchman will not linger hereabouts, for fear of retribution, but 'tis well if Sir Hilary rebukes him too." He scowled fiercely. "The rogue deserves to be clapped in irons for this day's work!" He looked down at the Mother Abbess' letter which was open before him on the table and grunted, "I hope you find the abbey books. I suppose 'tis why you are going to the abbey ruins."

"Aye, sir," Roger said. "Now the land belongs to my father, we can search for the books at our leisure."

"Very well," Sir Anthony said. He stood up and took me by surprise by wrapping me in a hug as kind as any the Mother Abbess had given me. Gruffly he said, "Thanks be to Our Lord you are safe."

We ate supper together, and I followed Roger out of the great hall when he left. In the porch he pulled his red cap onto his head and grinned, then bowed and said, "Sleep well, Mistress Clare. You will come to no harm now, you know."

Shyly I said, "I want to thank you for rescuing me today. I will not forget it."

"'Tis nothing," Roger said sturdily. "I am more sorry than I can say that you have suffered but ..." He smiled. "I am also more glad than I can say that I was able to rescue you, sweeting!"

For a moment that was both gratifying and startling, I thought he meant to kiss me, as he had under the kissing bough on Twelfth Night. But he did not. He grinned again and bowed his best bow, then went into night singing Walter Ducklington's song: "Who shall have my lady fair, when the leaves are green? Who but I should win my lady fair, when the leaves are green?"

I ached all over but took a long time to sleep that night. *Roger called me sweetheart and Grandfather loves me. I do not belong at Bampton Manor the way I belonged at Kirklington Abbey, but maybe I cannot have everything. And I would rather be loved ... as I am here ... by my family.* I smiled in the darkness. *And my friends.*

After all the excitement with Master Tolbert and the old chapel, the ride to Kirklington Abbey was blessedly uneventful. My favourite purse, my Christmastide gift from Mary Rose, hung heavily at the end of my girdle with the Mother Abbess' rosary tucked safely inside in case it was needed to help find the abbey books. Although my heart was beating hard with excitement at the thought of finding the abbey books, I dreaded seeing the convent in ruins, so I was grateful for the comfort of the rosary: the reminder of the Mother Abbess and of Our Lord and His Blessed Mother.

Towards the end of the journey, Roger and Geoffrey rode on

ahead with Frances trotting valiantly after them on his fat pony. I rode at a sedate pace with Katy, Bess and Mary. Dame Sybil and Lady Drayton's gentlewoman kept us company so everything was proper.

Suddenly the gatehouse came into view. I slowed Meadowsweet and took a shuddery breath. Bess glanced at me sympathetically and we rode on slowly. Geoffrey helped me and Bess off our horses and we went, sadly and silently, to the convent graveyard where we placed a tiny bouquet of rosemary for remembrance on the rough grave of Sister Veronica.

"She was like a grandmother to me, God rest her soul," Bess said. She crossed herself. "She knew I did not want to be a nun and she never scolded me, she just loved me."

"I am sorry she is dead," I said, "but I am glad she did not live to see … this." I glanced at the ruins. "May she rest in peace."

Soberly we left the graveyard and joined the others among the ruins. The refectory and the dormitory over it were sound and so were the Mother Abbess' cosy living quarters. Some tiles were missing from the roofs, the window glass was smashed and the doors were ripped from the hinges, but the rooms were protected from the worst of the elements. The roofs had been ripped off the cloisters, but the walls and walkways remained and there was a lingering sense of peace, although birds were huddled under a corner of roofing above the spot where I had worked at my desk.

We picked our way between the fallen masonry and the greenery that was already springing up between the stones. The scriptorium and the library, the tiles missing from the roof and the rooms exposed to the weather, were empty. Bare shelves and cupboard doors hanging on bent hinges greeted me. There were no books, only a litter of shattered glass and broken earthenware, scattered among chunks of fallen masonry. The scriptorium no longer smelt of parchment, ink and paint, and the library no longer smelt of leather.

Numbly I picked my way through the mess. A familiar shape caught my eyes, and I bent and picked a battered spoon out of the rubble. The pewter was dull, but the spoon was recognisable. It was a maidenhead spoon with a tiny figure of Our Lady, in an old-fashioned headdress from a hundred years ago, at the end of the handle. At one side of the spoon was a worn edge where it had, for more years than anyone could remember, rubbed against a mixing bowl while mixing paints. It was my favourite and I had used it more times than I could remember. I rubbed the pewter clean with my skirt and slipped the spoon into my girdle.

It started to rain – a spring shower which created a watery rainbow – and I huddled with the others in a sheltered corner feeling as cheerless as the weather as I held the hood of my cloak over my head and watched the drops of water fall one by one from the edge of the wool.

Quietly, peering out into the rain, Roger said, "The chapter house is sound, and beautiful too! It will be the new library – the home for any books my father and I find and rescue from other religious houses. They will be treasured by my family." He turned towards the ruins of the abbey church. "My father is going to build a chapel from the stone of that consecrated place."

I smiled as I thought of the relic of Our Lady's robe, carefully hidden in the church, ready to find a new home in the chapel.

"Are the books are in the ruins of the church?" asked Geoffrey. "Did not the Mother Abbess say they were in the care of St Kyneburgh?"

"We saw no sign of leather bindings or parchment pages in the ruins," Roger said. "And the church was dedicated to Our Lady the Virgin Mary not St Kyneburgh."

The boys argued the point, and I dreamily remembered the church as it used to be. In my mind's eye I saw the flickering flames of the candles and the bowed heads of the nuns. Suddenly I started.

"What is it?" Roger asked, peaking his eyebrows. He grinned. "Have you seen a ghost?"

Shortly I said, "I do not believe in ghosts."

A memory tugged at my heart. The church was dedicated to Our Lady, but the nuns honoured other saints too: St Clare of Assisi, St Sidwell from Devonshire and St Kyneburgh.

Quietly I said, "I had an idea, but perhaps it is of no great matter."

"Is it an idea about the abbey books?" Roger asked. "If so then 'tis of great matter! The Mother Abbess asked you to find and keep them. Can I help?"

I glanced at the others, then smiled at Roger and slipped away from the group who were sheltering from the rain. The rain was damping but not soaking. Quickly, holding up my long skirts which were already wet and clinging, I made my way through the ruins and the rubble to what was left of the church. I paused, breathless and tearful, on the edge of the destruction. The church was a heap of ruins, and I was too shocked by the piles of stones and litter of glass – tiny shards of coloured glass which must have fallen from the rose window like rain in my bad dreams – to cry.

"I am sorry you have to see it thus," Roger panted, joining me with a giant leap over a fallen block of stone. He whipped his bright red cap off his head and stuffed it through his belt. "What are you looking for?"

Simply – wondering how I could ever think *bright red for laughter* again – I said, "There was an image of St Kyneburgh in the church." I closed my eyes and remembered the church as it had been. I raised a hand and pointed in what I thought was the right direction. "Over there … behind a pillar."

"You stay here," Roger said. He climbed through the ruins and reported. "There was a pillar here." He climbed further and asked, "Was the image hereabouts?"

"I think so," I said. "Can you see anything?"

Awkwardly Roger said, "Only a lot of stone … some glass … some broken floor tiles."

I sank down on a ragged bit of wall and let my body droop under the weight of misery I felt. The abbey books were not here and there were no clues around the image of St Kyneburgh. I felt sickened by the brokenness all around me. *What is the point of looking for the books? Nothing will ever be the same again and the books cannot help.* Drearily I wished I was at home.

"Cheer up," Roger said. He sat down beside me and put his arm round me, engulfing me in the smell of wet wool and honest sweat. "I swear we shall find the books sooner or later."

"Aye," I said wearily. "I do not much mind if we do or not. 'Tis nice to know the Mother Abbess wanted me to have the books, but I shall be happy enough without them." I pushed my wet hair out of my face and gave Roger an anguished glance. "I wish I had not come and seen the ruins." Tears trickled down my cheeks and mingled with the rain. "'Tis too sad."

Roger looked sorry, and his silent sympathy was a tiny comfort.

"I am glad Sister Veronica did not see this." I sat a little straighter. "She died the night before the abbey was suppressed." I smiled. "She was a local girl and loved St Kyneburgh. 'Twas said among the nuns that Sister Veronica was born a great number of years ago – when the nobles fought for power – in a ruined tower, near the old chapel in the woods, to a knight and a milk maid. The chapel was dedicated to St Kyneburgh, and so Sister Veronica loved the saint and became a nun in her honour."

Idly Roger asked, "The old chapel in the woods where I rescued you?"

"Aye."

"I did not realise it was dedicated to St Kyneburgh."

"Many people do not know," I said. "'Tis on Farmer Mattocks' land. He is a yeoman, and I think the milk maid, Sister Veronica's mother, worked …"

"Clare!" Roger yelled. He jumped to his feet and pulled me up beside him. "What did you say?"

I blinked. "Pray what did I say when?"

"Just now," Roger said. He gave me an exuberant hug. "Good girl!"

"But what did I say?" I asked again, laughing breathlessly.

Triumphantly Roger said, "You said the old chapel in the woods is dedicated to St Kyneburgh *and* 'tis on Farmer Mattocks' land."

"Aye," I said. "What of it?"

"Do you not remember what the Mother Abbess said?" Roger asked. "*St Kyneburgh* will guard the abbey books. *The farmer* knows her rosary. Do you have her rosary with you now?" I blinked and nodded as Roger grabbed my hand and exclaimed, "Come!"

Everyone wanted to help find the abbey books, and we rode away from Kirklington Abbey together. Roger led the way, with Frances and I at his heels. Farmer Mattocks was crossing his farmyard when they arrived. He looked a little surprised but doffed his hat.

"Well met!" Roger cried. "May we have speech with you?"

Roger jumped off his horse and reached up to help me down as I slipped from Meadowsweet. Eagerly he helped me across the muddy, rutted farmyard. He threw me a questioning glance, and I nodded a little breathlessly.

Quietly Roger told the farmer, "Mistress Clare was a novice at

Kirklington Abbey before it was suppressed. The Mother Abbess gave her a letter and bequeathed her the abbey books." The farmer's strong, square jaw twitched, but he said nothing. Politely Roger said, "We think the abbey books may be in the old chapel on your land."

"The old chapel is empty," Farmer Mattocks said uncompromisingly. "You can have a look if you like, but you'll see for yourself that it's empty."

I shivered because I had seen enough of the old chapel for now.

"No one goes there," Farmer Mattocks said, "not even a chantry priest these days." He doffed his hat again. "Good day to you, young master and merry mistress."

"Kind sir," I said, fumbling with my purse at the end of my girdle. "Pray wait. Do you … is there any chance you know this rosary?"

I held the Mother Abbess' rosary out in one hand. The silver links and pearl beads dripped through my fingers and seemed all the more beautiful against the mud of the farmyard and the shabby ricks of straw surrounding the ancient barn.

At first the farmer said nothing, then he took off his cap and held it against his chest. He nodded at me and said, "I beg your pardon for being ungentle, good mistress – and I beg your pardon too, young master. I may have spoken hastily, but I was told to guard the secret well and a man can't be too careful these days." He smiled. "I have three wooden crates of books in my barn. Are you wanting to see the books?" A flicker of anxiety crossed his face. "Are you wanting to take them away?" He touched his forelock. "I beg your pardon for speaking out of turn, but the Mother Abbess thought 'twould be best if you didn't take the books until the times were safer for holy things."

Heartily Roger said, "I believe Mistress Clare thinks so too."

"I do," I said, "but I would like to know they are safe."

Farmer Mattocks led the way into the barn. Roger and I followed, and the others crowded in behind. Together we watched as Farmer Mattocks burrowed through a pile of straw and revealed the rough top of a wooden box. He prized the lid off, and I strained my eyes to see the books through the dimness of the barn. Geoffrey helped me through the straw, and I knelt beside the box with Bess and Frances. Gently I felt inside. My fingers found straw and canvas. Within the canvas I could feel the smoothness of leather and the ridges and furrows, like a ploughed field, of the embroidery and jewels that decorated the cover of a book.

*The great Gospels and the great Psalter.* Tears welled up in my eyes as I remembered the names of the books like a poem: *Book of Hours, Gospels, Psalter, De Doctrina Christiana, The City of God, Confessions, Summa Theologica, Adagia, A Playne and Godly Exposition or Declaration of the Commune Crede, Advice to Anchoresses.* And then I giggled because there were other, less holy, books too.

"Happy?" Farmer Mattocks grunted.

"Aye, very happy," I said. "Thank you with all my heart for keeping the books here until …" I remembered the words of the Mother Abbess: "Until the world is safe for the books."

The box was closed and buried again in the depths of the straw, then Farmer Mattocks led the way out of the barn. I stood in the farmyard, looking at the rosary in my hand, feeling as if the books, hidden here in the care of St Kyneburgh and Farmer Mattocks, were part of a strange dream.

"And St Kyneburgh can be found all over the farm," Farmer Mattocks laughed. "There's the old chapel in the woods, an image of her carved into the beam above the barn door and her name etched into one of the stones around the well." He shrugged his shoulders. "Did you not know this is St Kyneburgh's Farm?"

Geoffrey and Roger exchanged embarrassed glances.

Roger said, "Everyone I know calls it Mattocks' Farm."

"I knew it was called St Kyneburgh's Farm," Geoffrey said unexpectedly. He grinned apologetically. "I fear I never thought of this place and the abbey books together."

"'Tis of no matter," I said. I smiled shyly at the farmer. "Will St Kyneburgh continue to guard the books or will it be too much trouble?"

"It won't be too much trouble unless one of you gossips about this and it reaches the ears of the authorities," the farmer said bluntly. "I won't gossip because I don't want to be punished for hiding the books, and I don't want to see the books burned or left for rubbish on my dung heap. I said I'd keep them because the Mother Abbess was one of the best ladies I knew! They'll be safe enough here, and you can take them when the world is safe for them." He crossed himself. "I pray Our Lord it may be soon."

I crossed myself and whispered, "Amen."

And then we rode out of the farmyard with cries of thanks.

"Are you sorry not to have the books now?" Geoffrey asked.

"Nay," I said. "I am content to wait. 'Tis enough to know the books are safe from the king's men … and Master Tolbert too." I thought of the Mother Abbess' rosary in my purse, of the gift of illuminating, of the greater gift of seeing the world a certain way, seeing beauty everywhere, living to the full with courage, kindness and hope. I smiled with my heart in my eyes and said, "*Truly* I am content."

Roger rode alongside and said, "The books mean more to you than anyone. Have no fear that my father will take them for Kirklington Abbey. They shall be your dowry as the Mother Abbess said. They shall be yours, your husband's on your wedding day and your children's and grandchildren's in the years to come."

I hugged his promise to my heart as we rode, cold and wet, towards Bampton. My heart felt suddenly desolate and the talk of my dowry – which I knew must be small, since my marriage portion had been given to the convent when I was a little girl – made me think of Sir Anthony and his plans for my marriage. *Who is the unknown man who is to be my husband?* I looked at Geoffrey and Bess who, for a little while, were riding side by side accidentally-on-purpose. *Will I be as happy as Bess?*

"What are you thinking of so seriously?" Geoffrey asked, as Katy and Mary joined Bess.

I blushed and shook my head. Instead of answering his question, I asked, "Has Grandfather spoken to Sir Philip Drayton about you and Bess yet?"

Geoffrey flushed and said, "Sir Philip Drayton is thinking upon the matter." He stirred restlessly in his saddle and admitted, "I wish he would let me know his mind."

Wistfully I said, "But Bess smiles upon you."

Geoffrey only sighed and laughed and asked, "And what of you?"

"What do you mean?"

"I am surprised Grandfather has not found a husband for you yet."

I frowned and shook my head. *Why is everyone talking about dowries and husbands?* Crossly I said, "I am happy as I am."

"Are you indeed?" Roger joined us and asked the question curiously as Geoffrey joined Bess again. "Yet you went to court."

"Only because Grandfather bade me do so. I came home as soon as I could. I belong here," I said. *Perhaps I belong here in the country without belonging especially to Kirklington Abbey or Bampton Manor.* Simply I said, "I am happier here because I am myself here." I looked through my wet and stringy hair at the soggy landscape dotted with sheep and new spring lambs and laughed. "Truly!"

"Well," Roger said cordially, "'Tis good to hear, I must say, Mistress Clare."

"I am glad it pleases you," I said huffily.

A heartbeat later I glanced up to find Roger looking at me with a funny little smile dancing in his eyes. Suddenly I knew without a doubt that I was very fond of Roger. But my grandfather was going to choose a husband for me and he was, surely, unlikely to choose a wool merchant's apprentice from Bampton. *Yet I would like to marry a friend. How can I be fond of a stranger as I am fond of Roger? He is my true friend.* I blushed even though the thought was secret.

Merrily, to hide my feelings, I called, "The last one to the oak tree is a sheep!"

I urged my horse forward and so did the boys. We raced along the lane in a breathless, laughing bunch with the drumming of the horses' hooves ringing in our ears. Geoffrey reached the tree first. I raced past the oak, pulled Meadowsweet up, then went back to the join the others under the spreading branches of the tree. I met Roger there.

With a self-conscious smile he said, "By your leave, Mistress Clare, it seems I am a sheep!"

Next day I was painting and refusing to think of convents or ruins or husbands when Sir Anthony walked into the great hall with a handful of papers in his hand.

He grunted a greeting and announced, "Lettice is happy at last."

"Sir?" I paused in my work. "How is my cousin?"

"Well enough," Sir Anthony said. He stood with his back to the fire. "The rabbits I sent Lord Crewe, by way of sweetening, seem to have done the trick. His wife, the duchess, has taken Lettice into her household as one of her maids of honour."

I frowned and asked, "Lettice is a maid of honour to one of the queen's ladies in waiting?"

"Aye," said Sir Anthony.

"I thought she wanted to be a maid of honour to the queen."

"She did … and does still, I suppose," Sir Anthony said. "My granddaughter is not important enough for that now, but perchance the queen will see Lettice serving the duchess and notice her by inviting her to join the royal household as one of her maids of honour."

"Oh." I returned to painting.

"Lettice is sixteen now – old enough to serve the queen," Sir Anthony mused. "Mayhap my granddaughter will serve the queen as a lady in waiting rather than a maid of honour. She is betrothed."

I looked up in interest.

"Lord Woodhurst is the man," Sir Anthony continued. "He is a baron of ancient and noble lineage, and an honourable man besides. The connection is exceptionally good for the Bampton family – better, indeed, than I dared hope for." He sighed. "Thomas and Maud are coming home and bringing Lettice with them for a visit before she enters Lady Crewe's household. Lord Woodhurst will come, too, for the betrothal. We must spare no trouble in impressing him."

Mildly I said, "Lettice will be happy if she is to be a real court lady."

"Let us hope so," Sir Anthony said. "Thank God I do not need to impress anyone on Geoffrey's account or your account."

Pertly I said, "Nay, indeed sir, I am merely a country cousin."

"'Tis nothing to be ashamed of," snapped Sir Anthony. He referred to another piece of paper. "Master Chastleton has agreed to take Frances as his apprentice. 'Tis an excellent arrangement for Frances. He will learn much from Master Chastleton and his fellow apprentices – Roger Chastleton and Peter Atkins." He smiled and stroked his beard. "I am glad I thought of this arrangement."

I frowned and paused, my paintbrush poised over my parchment, sure I had thought of the arrangement. *Or did Geoffrey? Or was it Frances's own suggestion?* I shrugged my shoulders and decided it did not matter. Sir Anthony was contented and Frances was to be happy. *I am glad and I shall tell Roger so.* He arrived, a little later, with Walter Ducklington.

I was making marchpaine from almonds, sugar and eggs in the kitchen. Under Edie's watchful gaze, I kneaded the sticky paste in a bowl and wondered what to make. *Flowers mayhap?* I smiled at the boys, as they hovered in the kitchen doorway, while I cleaned marchpaine off my fingers with a damp cloth.

"Get along with you," Edie urged. She was in an extra good mood that day. "Take some October apples."

I tossed a green apple – *green for courage* – to each of the boys and took one for myself and one for Meadowsweet. Together we walked towards the stables. Roger looked like a subdued daddy-long-legs but Walter seemed in the best of spirits.

Happily, enjoying the warmth of the spring sunshine on my face,

I asked Roger, "Do you know Frances is to be apprentice to your father?"

"So I hear." Roger grinned. "We shall be fellow apprentices. 'Tis an excellent notion. Frances is a good boy, and my father is not a harsh master." He whistled a little tune as we entered the stable yard. Idly he said, "I daresay he will live with us at Kirklington Abbey someday."

"Truly?" I asked. My voice sounded a long way away. Achingly I remembered the sheltering birds in my corner of the ruined cloisters, the broken glass from the rose window, the stained and battered maidenhead spoon I had tucked into my coffer now. I gulped down the feelings of sadness and anger I had felt among the ruins and said, "I hope you will be happy."

"I am sure we will," Roger said cheerfully.

Walter glanced at me, gave Roger a dig in the ribs and said shortly, "We didn't come to talk about that."

"No?" I smoothed the silky hair on Meadowsweet's nose and held the apple in the flat of my hand. The horse's lips tickled my skin as she gobbled the apple in three crunchy bites. I kept stroking and glanced at the boys. "What, pray, did you come to talk about?"

The boys looked at each other, and Walter blurted, "'Tis a great secret but I want to tell you about your family."

"My family?" I blinked at the boys over Meadowsweet's nose. "What about my family?"

"Not your mother's family," Roger clarified.

"Your dad's family," Walter said. His words tumbled over each other with excitement: “Your dad died last summer, but the rest of your family …”

“My father died last summer?” I echoed. “But … how do you know? Who was he? And *why* did he have to die before I came home?” The last words were rung from my heart. My mother had died when I was a baby and I had never known her. *But I almost knew my father.* I did not want to cry and was appalled to realise I was sobbing.

“I …” I thrust my last apple at Meadowsweet and pushed past the boys. Brokenly I gasped, “I pray pardon.”

With a smothered sob, I dived into the stables and scrambled up the ladder into the hay loft. The air, full of the sweet scent of the hay, was comforting, but the pain that threatened to tear my heart in half was a shock. Blindly I felt my way across the floor of the loft to sink into a pile of hay. *Why did my father have to die before I came home?* Sobs shook my body as all the anxiety and insecurity of the last months stormed my heart. *I want to live to the full but how can I live a life that is so different, so strange, from everything I expected?* Suddenly I heard steps on the ladder into the loft. I stiffened and tried to stifle my sobs and hold my breath. I felt the floorboards creak and heard the hay rustle as someone arrived in the loft.

“Clare?” It was Walter’s voice. His voice was calm and coaxing, as if he was speaking to a shy and startled animal on the farm. “I know you’re here. Please don’t be unhappy alone. Where are you?”

I took a deep, shuddery breath and sneezed as I inhaled a particle of dust.

"Oh … there you are!" Walter crawled across the loft to my side, engulfing me in the smell of fresh air, ploughed earth, honest sweat and a whiff of the cow byre. "Master Roger – and me too – we're sore distressed about making you cry."

"I am sorry," I sobbed. "But why did my father have to die? Why was I not at home sooner? Where are the nuns now? And why …" I felt my face contort and buried it in my hands as another sob was torn from my heart. "*Why* did the king decree the suppression of Kirklington Abbey when the nuns were good and kind?"

"I don't know," Walter said. His voice was thick with emotion. "It makes no sense. The changes of this time are beyond what anyone can imagine or begin to understand and many are suffering."

I sobbed, and Walter cleared his throat.

"Everything is changing and I feel confused and *lost*," I said.

"Lost?" Walter echoed blankly.

"I do not know where I belong now."

"Oh." Walter paused as if he was feeling his way with his words. "You belong here."

"I suppose so," I said. "Aye. For now. But not really, not forever, not like I thought I belonged at Kirklington Abbey."

Walter suddenly leaned close and pressed his lips close to my ear. I was startled but I trusted him and did not shrink away.

"Clare?" In a voice of barely-suppressed excitement Walter whispered, "Can you keep a secret about your dad?"

With my heart beating hard and fast, I stuttered, "Y-y-yes." my voice sounded loud even to my own ears. I lowered my voice and whispered, "Yes."

Walter hesitated. I could feel him swelling at my side with breath and the importance of the secret. Then, hoarsely, he asked, "What would you say if you discovered your dad wed again after he lost your mother to the grave and had another family before he, too, died?"

I stared at Walter in dumbfounded silence. Slowly I said, "I do not rightly know."

By staring hard through the gloom at Walter, I could see the outline of his head, his hair sticking up and his ears sticking out. I could sense that his gaze was earnest and intense.

It was my turn to take a deep breath. I let it out as gently as a whisper and asked, "Tell me truly, by Our Lord and His Blessed Mother, is this so?"

Walter's head nodded up and down.

Bewildered I asked, "Who was he and *who* are my brothers and sisters?"

Slowly, his words heavy with excitement, Walter said, "His name was Walter Ducklington. He and your mother were reformers before it was fashionable and 'tis why your mother chose to wed a yeoman rather than a gentleman. Your brothers and sisters are Walter and Mary Rose and John Henry and Rich and Aggie. You are Clare

Ducklington."

"*You*?" I was startled out of my shock. "You are my brother? Mary Rose is my sister? And Aggie too?"

"I'm your half-brother," Walter said modestly. "That's not quite the same as a full-brother."

"But almost the same," I countered.

I grabbed his hand and held on hard. I wanted to check he was real and was afraid he might disappear. He felt real and was not going anywhere, and I bubbled with delight.

"I always wanted a brother!" I exclaimed. "And a sister! I love Mary Rose more than Lettice already. How long have you known?" I thought of Mary Rose's secret-keeping look and demanded, "Does Mary Rose know too?"

"We all know at home," Walter said simply. "My dad … *our* dad … loved your mother very much and spoke of her with affection and respect all his days. After she died, he waited a month's mind, out of respect for your mother, then he married my mam." He squeezed my hand. "He hoped, if he was married again, he could raise you … but that was not to be."

"I was sent to Kirklington Abbey," I said slowly.

"Aye." Walter sighed. "Sir Anthony didn't want you to be a reformer, and he and our dad didn't want you to be argued over by your two families. 'Twas the only thing they agreed about. Our dad never forgot your mother, and my mam bade us honour your mother's memory. Our dad never forgot you either, and he and my mam prayed for you every day. It was our dad's last hope that you would be blessed and happy in life and know Jesus Christ."

"I do," I whispered. I was silent for a heartbeat. My world had changed again. Now there was a grandfather, an uncle, three cousins *and* brothers and sisters with red hair. *And they all love me in their own ways.* I smiled through my tears.

"Are you pleased?" Walter asked.

"I *am* pleased." I spoke unhesitatingly and laughed happily. "Yes, Walter, *yes*!"

He laughed too.

But then, gently, I said, "Your … our … father died of the sweating sickness before harvest time?"

"Aye." Walter's voice was subdued.

"God rest his soul," I said. I crossed myself and whispered, "If I had come home before harvest time, I might have seen my father."

"You'll see him in heaven," Walter said. His voice was thick. He squeezed my hand and repeated, "He never forgot you."

"And I will never forget him," I said. "I will remember him and my mother all my life."

For a moment we sat in silence and thought about our father together.

"Walter?" There was another step on the ladder and a voice called, "Did you find her?"

"Aye," Walter called back. He cleared his throat. "I've got her safely here." He squeezed my hand, then let go and waved his hand over his head. "We're here."

Roger's voice called, "Mistress Clare?" He sounded shy. "May I join you?"

"Aye," I said in a small voice. I watched a shadowy form like a daddy-long-legs scramble into the loft. Shyly I said, "We are over here … in this corner."

Roger crawled across the floor and sat with us, then he said, "I pray pardon for making you cry."

"You did not make me cry," I said quickly. "'Twas … everything. The ruins and the books and feeling alone then not knowing what Grandfather is planning for me then my father and … *everything*!"

Roger blinked. "Everything indeed," he said. His eyebrows peaked. "I am sorry, nonetheless, for anything I said which added to, er, *everything*." Anxiously, without giving me time to speak, he asked, "Have you recovered your balance now?"

"My balance?" I gazed at him through the gloom. "What, pray, do you mean?"

"Your balance in this strange new world of ours."

I pondered his question. My heart ached with memories of the past and mingled hopes and fears for the future. A shadow of desolation touched my heart.

Apologetically, as if I was confessing a sin, I said, "Everything is changing."

"Yes … true enough or so it seems." Roger reached out and took my hand. Quietly he said, "Some things are not changing: Our Lord, the love of our families and friends, the seasons." He paused and added, "I cannot think of aught else at present but there may be some other things that are not changing too."

"Not King Henry or Master Thomas Cromwell or anyone else can change those things," Walter confirmed.

"Jesus Christ does not change," I echoed softly. "He has proved the same in the cloister and the world, from Michaelmas to Christmastide to Candlemas." I thought of the convent and the nuns, and the bustle and happiness of my new life. I thought of the world freezing into winter then melting into spring. "The love of family and friends does not change. The seasons do not change." The words seemed to fall and rustle into the dust and chaff and odds and ends of hay between my fingertips and the floor of the loft. "Everything else may change … but they remain the same. Most of all, *He* remains the same, Our Lord today and forever."

"Try to remember that when you feel as if *everything* is changing," Roger advised. "I was not supposed to be a nun …" I giggled, and he paused. With dignity he continued, "I was not supposed to be a nun, but sometimes *I* feel as if everything is changing. When I do, I think of these things, then I find my balance again."

"Aye," Walter said. "That's good advice, that is, Clare."

Meekly I said, "I shall try to remember."

Spontaneously, as if he was suddenly thinking of something else and not sure what to say next, Roger whistled a little tune. Abruptly he dropped my hand. Through the gloom I saw him stick his thumbs through his bright red leather belt – *bright red for laughter, after all* – and smile.

"Aye?" I prompted.

Roger laughed sheepishly and said, "I am sorry you are worried about your grandfather and his plans for you. I am not in Sir Anthony's confidence, but there are one or two little things I know and I think … that is, I *hope* … I can say you need not worry over much about his plans. I … er … very much hope you'll find them tolerable."

"Mistress Clare!" It was Edie's voice, muffled but sure. "Mistress Clare! Where are you, my lamb?"

"Do you think so indeed?" I asked Roger quickly.

"On my honour," Roger said. "I *hope* you will find your grandfather's plans tolerable."

"And so do I," Walter said. He laughed. "Yes, I do indeed! I think I'm more sure than Master Roger."

"My thanks." I breathed a sigh of relief and said, "If you both think so then I dare say I have nothing to fear." Edie's voice called again, and I scrambled to my feet. Over my shoulder I asked, "What do you think, Roger? I have gained a dowry and a lot of brothers and sisters almost all together. Please tell him the secret, Walter, for 'tis the happiest of secrets." I glanced back and forth between the boys and said, "You both knew!"

They nodded.

"Everyone knew but me?"

"Not *everyone*," Roger said.

"And you know now," Walter said. "'Tis better not to talk of it. Keep it a secret in your heart."

"Very well." I laughed and sighed and said, "I must go and find

Edie now!"

Edie was standing in the middle of the stable yard when I emerged from the loft. She dropped a curtsy and kissed my cheek. She looked flushed and excited.

Amusedly, in spite of my lingering tearfulness, I smiled and asked, "Whatever is the matter, Edie?"

"Sir Anthony wants you, Mistress Clare, to tell you that ..." Edie smiled and folded her lips together as if she wanted to stop any more words from escaping. "Go to him in his chamber. Nay! Stay! You look as if you've been sitting in the hayfield at harvest!"

Edie started picking bits of chaff off my bodice and skirt. I smiled to myself as I smoothed my hair and saw it catch the sun: blazing red and gold and every colour in between. Edie stood back, and I shook the last of the dust from my skirts, then hurried to my grandfather's chamber, almost falling over Mistress Eglentyne on the way. The cat seemed to be practising catching mice on the landing. She was mewing at a mouse hole and pouncing on a tattered kerchief that must have fallen out of a bundle of washing.

Sir Anthony was sitting by the window, looking out over the knot garden, when I entered his chamber. He grunted a welcome. I curtsied and waited.

Finally my grandfather said, "I have found you a husband at last,

Clare."

I gasped with surprise. I opened my mouth, but discovered I had nothing to say, so closed it again. *What if some stranger from court – perhaps Sir Endymion Morton! – has sought my hand and Grandfather has favoured his suit? But Roger and Walter said I would like Grandfather's plans.* Demurely I dropped a curtsy and waited again.

Broodingly Sir Anthony said, "I have always had a mind to connect my family with the Chastleton family, but Lettice was too ambitious to be satisfied with Roger, which was a pity."

I thought of my daddy-long-legs friend, and my heart bounded with hope, but my grandfather's meaning was unclear. I clasped my hands behind my back and waited.

"Mayhap Lettice would have been satisfied with Roger, since he is to inherit Kirklington Abbey and the manor from his father someday, but she is pleased with her court gallant," Sir Anthony mused. "However I still desire a connection with the Chastleton family, and I have you on my hands now." He gave me a smile which was almost fond and took the sting out of the words. "Master Chastleton, meanwhile, has sought your hand in marriage for his son, Roger."

*Roger!*

"I have warned him that your dower portion is small, but he declares himself satisfied. 'Tis no great match for you, but I have given him my consent and 'tis all arranged."

I thought I might faint with a heady combination of surprise, relief and joy. *I am going to marry Roger!* I gasped and sighed both at once and choked as a result. I caught my breath but knew I was blushing and giddy with delight.

"Well?" Sir Anthony demanded. "What does all this blushing and fluttering mean?"

"Nothing, sir, only that I …" I took a deep breath and asked, "You say, sir, I am to wed Roger Chastleton?"

"Aye." Sir Anthony frowned. "I hope you are not thinking of objecting, wench, because I can save you the trouble of doing so by informing you that I have taken a decision and given a promise, and I will not change the arrangement now!"

"Oh, nay, sir!" I said quickly.

Sir Anthony's gaze and his voice softened. "Roger is a good boy, my girl, so I am confident he will be a good husband – and a good father in time."

"I just wished to be perfectly sure," I said. "Roger is a good …" Tears sprang uninvited and unwelcome into my eyes. *But I am not sad. I am glad!* Simply I said, "He is a good friend." I met my grandfather's gaze. "I thank you for your kindness in making an arrangement so certain to make me happy." I caught a glimmer of emotion in his eyes and smiled. "I will beg to be excused now, sir, if I may."

"To be sure," Sir Anthony said gruffly. "I believe Roger is about the place somewhere. He will doubtless wish to speak to you himself, and I will not make a parade of introducing you to each other when you are acquainted already. There is the settlement to sign and he must give you a ring, but that can wait for a few days. Be off with you and tell him that he has my leave to make as many pretty speeches as he likes." Almost to himself he said, "This is a union I have long wanted to witness."

I dropped another curtsy, then I went to him and kissed his cheek. "Thank you, Grandfather, with all my heart." And then, without waiting to see how he responded, I slipped out of his chamber.

Outside the closed door, I pressed my hands to my cheeks and smiled from deep down inside, feeling as if I might explode with happiness.

Ecstatically I whispered, "Oh, Sweet Jesus, thank You more than I can say for … everything! Grandfather and Roger and all my life to come!" I laughed because I could not help it. "Thank You for my life in the world!"

I ran down the stairs and through the kitchen towards the stable.

"Walter!" I called. "Walter! I have such news!"

Flying along, not looking where I was going, I ran into Geoffrey who was coming from the opposite direction. We were both knocked breathless by the impact and staggered backwards.

"I beg your pardon!" I gasped.

"I was seeking you," Geoffrey grumbled in gasps, "and this is what I get for my trouble!"

"Why were you seeking me?"

Geoffrey grinned. "I dare say you would like to know!" He puffed and panted, then stood up straight. His eyes were shining. Simply he said, "Grandfather and Sir Philip Drayton have finally arranged for me to marry Bess. The long wait is over. We are definitely to be betrothed!" He laughed. "And, when I asked her if that was agreeable to her, she said yes!"

"Of course she said yes!" I hugged him hard and said, "Oh, Geoffrey, I am glad! *So* glad! You will be very happy!"

"Yes," he said. "I think I will. I pray I will make Bess happy too. I wish my honoured parents and my dear sister Catherine, God rest their souls, were here to witness all this happiness, but … heigh ho. I am to marry Bess! And I am to spend a year in London, reading the law at Grey's Inn or one of the other Inns of Court, before learning how to work the manor." Gently he removed my arms from around his neck but kept hold of my hands. "I am content."

I smiled at my cousin in a daze of happiness for myself and Bess.

Very kindly Geoffrey prompted, "So, Clare, what of you?" Without waiting for me to answer, he said, "I feel as if you are my sister, and you must know you will always have a home here with me and mine if you wish it."

Airily I said, "Oh, do not trouble yourself about me, for *I* am going to marry Roger Chastleton."

"Oh." Geoffrey blinked. He frowned. "Remember our honoured grandfather said he was not going to let you choose your own husband, Clare, so do not set your heart upon it. I would not wish you to get your heart broke."

"I promise I will not!" I laughed and hugged him again quickly because I was so happy I had to hug someone. "'Tis Grandfather who told me that I am to marry Roger. I suppose we are to be betrothed like you and Bess." I beamed. "My marriage portion is *very* small, but since we know where the abbey books are and can get them at any time, whenever we choose, I am not a bride with no dowry at all."

"As if Roger would care!" Geoffrey exclaimed. "I have long thought that 'tis you – your own self, not your dowry, I mean – Roger wants. And to be sure Grandfather is going to give you as much of a dowry as he can. I am right glad, Clare, more glad than I can say!"

"And so am I," I said seriously. "But thank you for saying I always have a home here with you and Bess, Geoffrey, 'tis truly generous!"

"I see you will not be wanting my home when you can have a home of your own," Geoffrey teased. "But you will always be welcome in my home nonetheless."

"And you in mine," I said cordially.

"Have you asked Roger about that?" Geoffrey asked with a grin.

"Not yet, but I will," I said. "I dare say he will not mind anyway."

"Where is he, by the by?"

"I do not know," I admitted. "We were talking earlier, but Edie sent me to Grandfather, then I ran into you."

"Literally," Geoffrey said dryly. "Be off with you, then, Clare.

Go and find Roger and be happy. And then you had better start working to fill your dower chest."

"I will," I promised. "Have you seen Walter?"

"Walter Ducklington?" Geoffrey looked surprised. "He is in the stable yard, but why … ?"

I did not wait but ran towards the stable yard – with Mistress Eglentyne mewing and dodging my steps – being careful to look where I was going this time.

Walter was sitting on the mounting block, eating a wrinkled apple from last autumn and singing between bites, "Who shall have my lady fair, when the leaves are green? Who but I should win my lady fair, when the leaves are green?"

I smiled and waved as I ran towards him, then I saw Roger perched beside my brother and I stopped in a flutter of embarrassment. Walter laughed, and Roger flushed to the roots of his hair but grinned bravely.

Accusingly I said, "Did you *both* know?"

"Know what?" Walter asked innocently.

"He knew," Roger said, digging Walter in the ribs. "I think everyone knew about this too, except you, Clare."

"And Geoffrey," I said. "I met him just now. He is going to marry Bess Drayton. We are *all* getting married!"

"Are we?" Roger's peaked eyebrows were asking an anxious question. Almost shyly he asked, "And are you … glad?"

I blushed but went forward with my hands out. Roger jumped up, looking like a friendly, sweet-natured daddy-long-legs. He took my hands in his with a little smile meant for me and me alone.

Again he asked, "Are you glad, sweetheart?"

"Aye." I looked down at my little hands clasped in his big ones. My hands were streaked and spotted with blue lapis lazuli paint – *blue for hope* – but Roger did not seem to mind. I laughed up at him and said, "Oh, yes, I am *very* glad indeed!"

"I hoped you would be," Roger sighed with relief and hugged me exuberantly.

"So we are all to be one family!" Walter cried. He jumped up and tossed his apple core into a nearby flowerbed. "Nothing could please me more!" He hugged me and punched Roger lightly on the shoulder. "I shall dance with a glad heart at your wedding!" Laughingly he said, "I shall take myself off now but see you both anon. Roger, you have my permission to kiss her, now you are to be betrothed!"

"What does he mean?" I asked curiously.

"Oh … *that*!" Roger flushed and raised his peaked eyebrows at a comical angle. "Somehow or other he heard how I kissed you under the kissing bough on Twelfth Night. I fear he did not approve. I knew you and Walter were sister and brother … and he knew I knew. He told me while you were at court that he thought you and I ought to get married."

"I told him to speak to his father about seeking your hand in marriage," Walter volunteered.

"Which I did," Roger said. "And then my father spoke to Sir Anthony. But …" Roger grinned. "Walter knew I liked you, so he said I was not to kiss you again until everything was settled."

Slightly mystified, I asked, "Were you going to?"

"Only if we happened to stand under the kissing bough at Christmastide again. Although I thought of it, when we said goodbye, that day I rescued you from the old chapel. And, of course, I meant to kiss you when everything was settled." Roger laughed mischievously and kissed me fleetingly. "And now it is!"

I blushed more than ever and dizzily thought what a happy thing marrying Roger was going to be.

"That's right." Walter nodded and grinned. "I heard your grandfather had arranged the match, so I came to tell you about our dad. I couldn't wait another day!"

"I am glad you did not!" I said.

Walter and I – *my brother and I!* – exchanged a smile, and he sauntered away singing, "The bravest man that best love can, shall win my lady fair. He shall marry my lady, when the leaves are green."

Roger tugged me over to the mounting block and we sat side by side, holding hands, smiling at each other shyly.

Earnestly Roger asked one last time, "Are you *truly* glad?"

"*Very*!" I said. "For *this* I can say, with all my heart, thank You, Lord God and Heavenly Father, through Jesus Christ Our Lord!"

Roger's eyebrows were two exclamation marks of happiness now. I reached up and pressed a sweet kiss on his cheek. Giddily I added, "'Tis just as well I am glad because Grandfather has informed me that he will not consent to any objections on my part!"

"I do not think he will consent to any objections on my part either!" Roger said. "'Twould cost me all my goods and chattels and my honour – and my father's besides – not to marry you now. I have not the strength to fight his right! Especially because I think I quite like the idea of marrying you!"

I blushed and laughed and thought of Geoffrey and Bess in the bare rose garden. *Now I know how happy Bess felt that day!*

"But I fear me you have experienced more change between Michaelmas and Candlemas than most of us experience in a lifetime and this … 'tis another change," Roger said. Hopefully he added, "Mayhap 'twill be a happy change."

Comfortably I said, "Tell me!"

"Well … we cannot get married for a few years – I am still an apprentice, after all – but you will be Mistress Chastleton some fine day," Roger said. "You will come and live with me at Kirklington Abbey when our home is built and …"

"At Kirklington Abbey?" I echoed. "Will we live there?"

"Aye," Roger said. He frowned anxiously. "Will you mind, Clare?"

I gulped, but shook my head and smiled. *I will go home – back to Kirklington Abbey, where I belong – when I marry Roger.* I thought of my daddy-long-legs husband pouring over his account books in the great hall that would surely be built, of the abbey books safe and sound in what had been the chapter house and was to be the library, of babies with red hair laughing and tumbling as they played in the cloisters. *I will have to get up in the middle of the night for babies instead of prayers!* I knew it was a life I could live fully – with all my heart, in the world, for Christ – as full of beauty as any illuminated manuscript I could offer the world.

"We will have lots of sheep," Roger said. "I will still be a wool merchant. We will have dogs too."

"And babies."

"Of course."

I considered the matter and said, "I think 'tis just as well we cannot get married at once."

"Why?" Roger blinked.

"I have to fill my dower chest," I said. "Every girl has a dower chest of things she has spun and woven and sewn for her future home. I have my mother's dower chest now but, of course, I did not fill it, because I thought I was going to be a nun. I keep my painting things inside but 'tis otherwise rather empty." I blushed. "I have nothing but a cushion, and I fear I have not finished embroidering it yet."

"I do not care," Roger said decidedly.

"I do," I said just as decidedly. *I must take my dower chest full of real treasure home to Kirklington Abbey.* Vaguely I thought of coverlets and cushions. "I have the abbey books – but they are not a lot of good in Farmer Mattocks' barn. Geoffrey says Grandfather will give me as much of a dowry as he can, but I do not think it will be a big one because he already paid the convent when I was a little girl, so he says my marriage portion is small." My heart was suddenly anxious. "I do not want to bring you *nothing* when we are wed."

"You will bring yourself," Roger said seriously. "You are Clare. I care not whether you are Clare Bampton or Clare Ducklington now, as long as you are Clare Chastleton someday. I want your own self, not your dower chest. 'Tis you that matters most."

I leaned against him, feeling perfectly content and very much at home, as we sat side by side. *I will do my best to be a notable housewife but I think Roger will love me even if I never bake and spin as well as Edie and Mary Rose.* Suddenly I squeezed his hands and said, "I have just thought that I *will* bring you something else besides!"

"What, pray?"

"Everything I learned in the scriptorium … and a half-illuminated manuscript … and all my paints." I smiled at him from under my eyelashes. "I will bring you lapis lazuli."

"For hope," Roger said.

"Aye," I said. "Lapis lazuli for hope. 'Twill be my true dowry."

*There is a history in all men's lives.*
William Shakespeare

Dear Reader,

I hope you enjoyed reading *Lapis Lazuli for Hope*.

Years ago, when I read about the English Reformation and the Dissolution of the Monasteries, I wondered what it would be like for a young girl caught up in the drama of these events. Clare's story grew out of these wonderings. Clare and her family and friends are fictional but I hope they could have lived, and I hope her courage, kindness and hope inspire you in your everyday life.

What sort of story might you write about a girl (or a boy!) in Clare's situation?

May you always live with hope!
Ella Wren

## Glossary

**A Month's Mind:** When someone lost a spouse, it was considered decent to wait "a month's mind" before getting married again. Men and women who were widowed often needed a husband or wife to provide for them and their children so got married again for very practical reasons. It was not considered disrespectful or hasty, as long as they waited "a month's mind" first.

**Anne Boleyn:** Henry VIII's second queen. She lived from 1501 to 1536 and was called "the queen of a thousand days". She was an English girl and a Maid of Honour to Catherine of Aragon. To this day, some consider her a brazen flirt who caused trouble and unrest in England. Others consider her an innocent victim of political and religious machinations in a ruthless era. And some consider her a Protestant heroine and martyr. It was because he wanted to marry Anne Boleyn, but the Pope wouldn't annul his marriage to Catherine of Aragon, that Henry VIII broke the religious bonds between England and the Catholic Church and declared himself the Supreme Head of the Church of England in 1531. In 1533 Anne Boleyn bore The Lady Elizabeth who became Elizabeth I. In 1536 Anne Boleyn was executed on charges of adultery and treason.

**Betrothal:** Similar to engagement but more binding. The higher up the social scale a person was, the more likely it was that their parents or guardians would choose their spouse, but except for nobles, who had dynasties in mind, most people chose the children of colleagues, friends or neighbours for their children. People tended not to marry for love – but for more practical reasons – but partnership, friendship and love in marriage were considered desirable and normal. At a betrothal the couple joined hands and the man gave the woman a ring. The betrothal was sealed with a kiss and a signature.

**Book of Hours:** A popular book of prayers from Medieval times to the English Reformation era. The book included Psalms and prayers. The book reflected the set times of prayer in religious houses so that Christians "in the world" could follow the devotional pattern of important and meaningful prayers, in their private lives, without becoming monks or nuns.

**English Reformation:** Between the 1520s and the 1550s, under four monarchs, England was transformed from "a Catholic country" to "a Protestant country". Henry VIII broke the religious bonds between England and the Catholic Church in 1531. His motives were personal and political rather than religious. However other people in England were committed to reforming the church and the Protestant Church emerged from the protests and reforms – and martyrdoms – of Christians who wanted an alternative to the Catholic Church.

**Dissolution of the Monasteries:** The closing of monasteries and convents in in England between 1536 and 1541. Initially the intention was to close the smaller religious houses and give their wealth to the king. Very rich, idle or corrupt houses were closed too. Eventually all the religious houses were closed for various reasons. Their wealth was given to the king who sold much of their land to make more money. There were over 10,000 monks and nuns in England. Those who resisted the dissolution – or suppression – of their communities were treated badly and sometimes killed. Some monks and nuns went to Europe and joined other religious houses there. Others returned to their families and communities. Many fell into poverty.

**Nan Bullen:** Another name for Anne Boleyn.

**Catherine of Aragon:** Henry VIII's first queen. She lived from 1485 to 1536. She was a Spanish princess who married Prince Arthur, Henry VIII's elder brother, when they were teenagers. He died before he became king, and she later married Henry VIII. He adored her and got special permission from the Pope to marry his brother's widow. She bore her husband a number of children but only The Lady Mary (who became Mary I) survived infancy. Eventually Henry VIII decided he had sinned in marrying his brother's widow and this was why God had not given him any sons to inherit the English crown when he died. Catherine of Aragon resisted the annulment of their marriage and insisted she was lawfully married to the king – who it seems she still loved – until the day she died.

**Henry VIII:** One of the most famous and intriguing Kings of England. He lived from 1491 to 1547 and reigned from 1509 to 1547. At the beginning of his reign, he was energetic and handsome, but by the end of his reign, he was ill and obese. He is remembered for having six wives and for declaring himself the Supreme Head of the Church of England in 1531. In 1521 he wrote a book denouncing Martin Luther and it seems the king remained personally faithful to the teachings of the Catholic Church until he died. Some people argue, therefore, that he never intended to start the English Reformation. After his death his son Edward VI championed Protestantism, his daughter Mary I tried to turn England back to Catholicism and his daughter Elizabeth I stabilised Protestantism as the state religion. As a man Henry VIII seems to have been charming and educated – deeply cultured and sincerely religious according to his understanding – but selfish and ruthless.

**Illumination:** The art of illuminating hand-written religious books. For many centuries monks and nuns copied and illuminated books in monasteries and convents. Later scribes illuminated books in workshops. By the 1530s, many religious books were printed in Europe, some of which were illustrated by the printing press and some of which were illuminated by hand. Some people, however, preferred to buy more expensive hand-written religious books illuminated by trained monks or nuns. Paints were made by hand from natural ingredients and painted onto parchment with quills and brushes. Gold leaf was added to highlight the pictures. Illuminations were often of biblical scenes or saints surrounded by flowers.

**Jane Seymour:** Henry VIII's third queen. She lived from 1508 to 1537. She was an English girl and a Maid of Honour to Anne Boleyn. Henry VIII married her less than a month after Anne Boleyn was executed. She bore her husband a son – Prince Edward who later became Edward VI – but died soon afterwards.

**Martin Luther:** Sometimes called "the Father of Reformation". He lived in Germany from 1483 to 1546. He became a monk but renounced his vows when he became convinced that they were unnecessary. He later married a nun who had left her convent and renounced her vows too. He was dismayed by the corruption of the Catholic Church and eager to reform it. It is said that in 1517 he nailed his famous "Ninety-Five Thesis" onto a church door in Wittenburg. The emergence of the Protestant Church was a result of reform and counter-reform within the Catholic Church, and the protests of Christians who wanted an alternative form of Christianity. He taught and wrote multiple books and pamphlets to spread his ideas about salvation by grace alone.

**Thomas Cromwell:** A lawyer and statesman during the English Reformation. He lived between 1485 and 1540 and served Henry VIII from 1531 until his death. He was known as the King's Secretary from 1534. He is remembered for overseeing the Dissolution of the Monasteries as well as thinking of ways for Henry VIII to annul his marriage to Catherine of Aragon and deal with the problems presented by Anne Boleyn. He was executed on charges of treason, and Henry VIII very quickly regretted his death and the loss of both his administrative skills and personal loyalty.

Made in the USA
Coppell, TX
06 October 2020